MADISON MICHAEL

Beholden

A BEGUILING BACHELORS ROMANCE

BOOK TWO

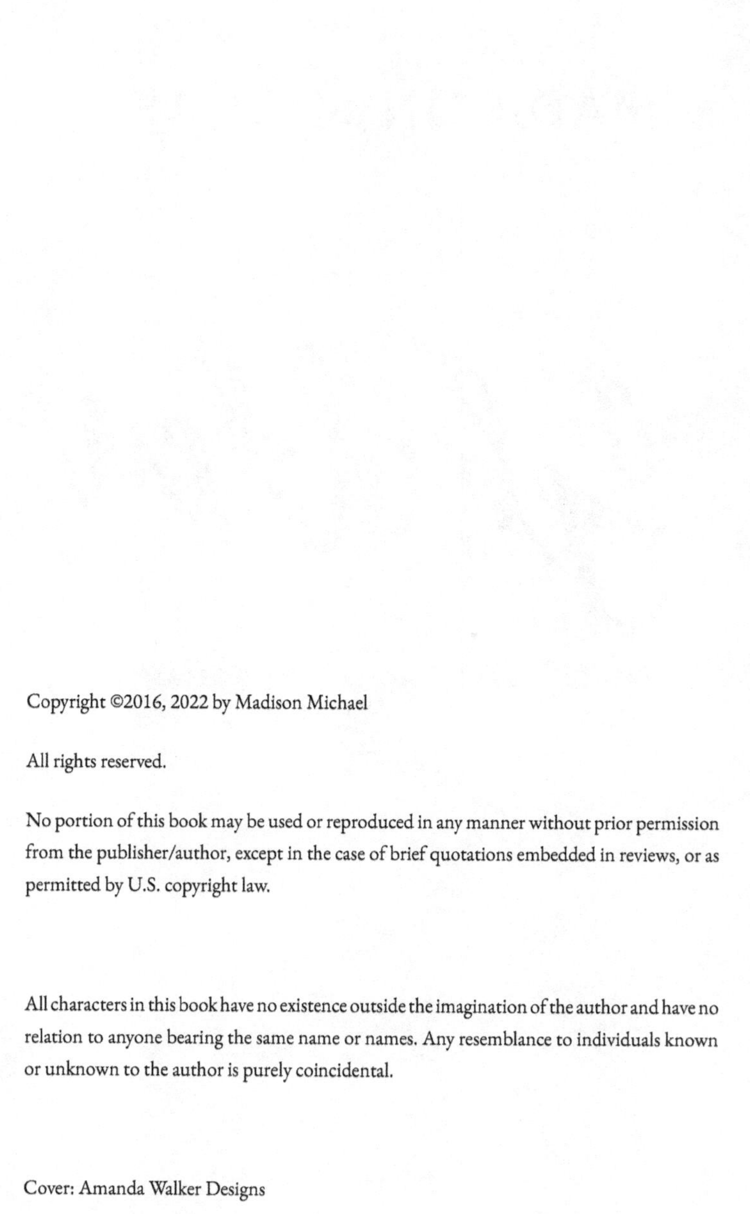

Contents

For my unbelievable friends and family who jumped on the Madison
Michael bandwagon and gave it life.
And to my mom, who taught me to love books.

"If you *will* thank me," he replied, "let it be for yourself alone. That the wish of giving happiness to you might add force to the other inducements which me on, I shall not attempt to deny. But your family owe me nothing. Much as I respect them, I believe I thought only of you."

Pride and Prejudice by Jane Austen

PROLOGUE

S loane was floating on air. The evening had been a perfect success. She had been a perfect success.

Of course.

Everyone declared she was the most beautiful woman in the room, and even if she was the modest type - which she wasn't - she knew it was true. Oh, there were some pretty girls at the Howe Museum gala, some beautiful women, but none of them had her striking features—that alabaster skin, those lustrous sapphire eyes, the lush, kissable lips and that thick curtain of dark hair. She was just pulling the pins out of her hair now, shaking the heavy locks from a tight chignon that had been giving her a headache for the last two hours.

Wyatt Howe IV, her soon-to-be fiancé and chair of the evening's event, had been devastatingly handsome in his custom tuxedo. They had been a cover-model couple—a power couple—stunning, smart, successful, sought-after. They were leaders in that intimate club of Chicago's most elite, the movers and shakers who dictated everything that happened in Chicago society. Anyone who was anyone had stopped by to say hello, to be photographed or, at a minimum, to be seen with them.

Sloane slipped off her Jimmy Choos and reached her elegant arms behind her head to slide down the zipper of her Ellie Saab gown. The pale pink confection would have to go to the cleaners now. She kicked it off with frustration and left it piled on the floor like something she picked up last week at a garage sale, not the $8,000 designer showpiece she had ordered months ago. It would never be the same, she pouted. Not that she was planning to wear it again. Sloane Huyler wouldn't be caught dead in the same dress twice—it just wasn't done.

Still, that stupid server had dropped a salad right down the back of her dress. What an incompetent. Sloane had pretended to laugh it off in front of the guests, acted as if it was nothing. She knew better than to embarrass Wyatt by making a scene in public. Her public persona would never draw that kind of negative attention. There was not a chance in hell she had been laughing. Once they were alone, Sloane told Wyatt to demand the catering company fire the incompetent, redheaded klutz immediately. The stupid cow was probably already looking for another job.

Boo hoo.

Now, after a few hours to reconsider, Sloane conceded that the server was probably quite capable. In fact, the service had been excellent before the salad disaster. Sloane suspected that the server wasn't paying attention. It was likely Wyatt distracted her. He had that effect on women. After all, he was considered Chicago's most eligible bachelor, and he was undeniably scrumptious eye-candy. Who was she kidding? The man was a serious hottie.

Then again, maybe she was staring at me. I looked damn good tonight. Either way, now she was out on her ass. Even if it was a singular slipup, getting fired would teach her not to covet that which she could never have.

Although she demanded that he do it, Sloane was a bit disappointed when Wyatt went to speak to the caterers at the end of the night, abandoning her. She graciously rode home alone in the limousine and let him conclude the evening, but she knew she had just been played.

Wyatt was up to something, had his eye on someone. Sloane was sure of it, although she couldn't put her finger on who the woman might be.

After years of on again, off again dating, she had learned to agree to Wyatt's every request. She was there when he wanted her, didn't whine when he wasn't available, asked for little, offered much and turned a blind eye when he sowed some wild oats. She made sure she was the perfect girlfriend, so he would realize that she would be the perfect wife. After the years she had invested in catching him, Sloane made sure he had nothing to complain about. She wouldn't give him any excuse to walk away. Ever.

She had played hostess at his fundraising event perfectly, charming people into opening their wallets wider while helping him promote his real estate business and his philanthropic goals. If things had gone her way, she would have ended the night with him pumping with adrenaline, pumping hard into her to unleash the force of it or proposing marriage. She would have been happy either way.

Wyatt was a little unpredictable though, no matter how ready and willing she was. So here she was, alone again, when he should have been warming her bed. He did quite a good job of it, she had to admit, and so it sincerely disappointed her not to have him with her. She didn't actually miss Wyatt, but she missed the sex. She wanted to seal the deal already and get the big ring.

Other than that, life was just about perfect.

Sloane had a job she loved as an executive in her father's consulting firm. She had parents she sincerely enjoyed spending time with who were still living in the gorgeous lakefront home in which she had grown up. She filled her weekends with family visits, tennis games, and events at the country club, hobnobbing with family friends.

Sloane had anything and everything that money could buy. In addition, she was well educated, well connected and well heeled. She had the right friends, although she had to admit they were few and superficial, lived in the right neighborhood, volunteered with the right organizations and committees, dined at the right restaurants, had the best seats at the right plays and concerts and any day now, she would be engaged to the right man.

Wyatt was CTO of a huge real estate conglomerate. His father owned it currently, but it would all be his someday soon. He was gorgeous and hunky. She liked him; she liked most of his friends and all of his family. He was brilliant, if a tad geeky, talented with a hockey stick and with his other stick as well. Sloane considered their sex life adequate. Wyatt could be a lot of fun in bed, but the passion just wasn't there. She recognized that occasionally they were just going through the motions.

Still, he was witty and even better connected than she was, so she could overlook anything that wasn't perfect, including his slightly straying eye and unwillingness to commit — so far. He was old money, with all the cache and manners that construed. Their families were friendly and everyone anticipated soon they would marry. It was expected and although Wyatt had not yet presented her with the nine-carat ring she had been eyeing, he also didn't refute their future together when anyone alluded to it. She could wait. After all, being his wife would open the few remaining doors where she desired entrée.

At 29, Sloane knew that she would have to worry about tying him down in the next few years, but she was in no hurry. He may be a catch, but he didn't make her heart race. She could look at him dispassionately and patiently. The prize was worth it. Sloane understood she would be the envy of everyone once she married him, making her half of the most prominent couple in Chicago.

Scrubbing off her professionally applied makeup and running a brush through her lush mane of hair, Sloane slid into the short La Perla nightgown she'd left out earlier. It was barely there, just a whisper of material designed to arouse Wyatt. She thought about grabbing a tee shirt instead, but the nightgown felt so decadent against her skin that she wore it just to indulge herself.

Glimpsing herself in the full-length mirror as she moved to slide between the sheets, Sloane knew she looked stunning and seductive enough to bring any man — even Wyatt—to his knees. She liked the image of him there before her, on his knees, making her feel incredible. She would go to bed slightly—not unbearably—dissatisfied. Sloane was too tired to take care of things herself.

Wyatt should only see what he is missing. I would have him eating out of my hand, or better yet, eating out of my....

Sloane's last thoughts as she fell into an undisturbed slumber were how lucky she was. She would marry Wyatt sooner, rather than later, and then she would have attained her every heart's desire. She would have a handsome, sexy and dutiful husband, a challenging career, the children she had always longed for, influence, prestige and tons of money. T would go to the Alps and Aspen for the skiing, Saint Bart's for warmth in winter, Milan and Paris for the fashion shows.

Within a year, she prophesied, she would have everything she dreamed of—the perfect life she deserved.

CHAPTER ONE

"For our last piece of business," the president of the Children's Hospital board began quietly and seriously, "the board has determined that having Sloane Huyler head the benefit committee is no longer in the best interest of the hospital or the event. I am sorry, Sloane, but we request you step down and let Allyson chair the event from now on." Her face burning with shame, Sloane made eye contact briefly with each board member present, some of whom returned the look, many of whom refused to meet her steely blue gaze. It didn't matter. They had defeated her. In fact, she expected this humiliation to come at last month's meeting, or any of the prior meetings since August. It surprised her it hadn't happened months ago. She supposed she had run out of any remaining goodwill with the headlines earlier this month.

"Of course, I want to do whatever is best for the hospital and the benefit," Sloane choked out reluctantly. She thought of the sick children, of little Chloe was so cheerful when she visited the cancer ward but who needed a bone marrow transplant at only five. Every cent mattered.

Sloane wondered if they were ousting her from the entire benefit committee or just the chair position, but she refused to give these blueblood wannabes the satisfaction of asking. She had busted her butt for this benefit already, so screw them if they wanted anymoreno more of her hard work.

"Sloane, of course we value your expertise and dedication, and appreciate the work you have already completed."

What? Did he read my mind?

"You are very welcome on the committee," the board president was quick to offer. "We welcome your continued help and input—we simply can't have your name at the top of the committee."

"Please accept my resignation as chair for this year's benefit, effective immediately." Sloane spoke in a strong, sure voice, holding her back straight despite the proverbial knife they had just thrust into it. "While I am, of course, willing to help in any way I can, I find I can no longer fulfill the responsibilities of chair. I will follow up with an email resignation letter confirming this as well."

These people will not break me, damn it. I am Sloane Huyler. I used to eat people like this for breakfast. How dare they turn their backs on me now? They are all just nasty hypocrites.

They seconded the motion to replace her and voted upon quickly. That last, unsavory piece of business completed, the meeting adjourned. The board members who would normally have stayed around chatting with Sloane, suggesting they go grab a drink or dinner, instead were slinking from the room, avoiding contact with her at all costs. Sloane had considered these people her friends. Tonight, she'd learned otherwise.

Grabbing her Celine bag from the back of the chair, preparing to leave the room, Allyson Riley, the new chair of "her" benefit stopped Sloane.

"I expect you to send me all your notes, Sloane," she stated without emotion. "Also, I have already assigned you to work with the hotel on setup, catering, and flowers. I will provide oversight and handle fundraising from now on."

"Sure, Al, I understand. Just send me your notes and we can swap roles. You'll do well as cChair, I'm sure."

As if that few sentences had not cost her dearly, Sloane offered a crisp nod to her replacement and exited the room. None of the anger and resentment simmering just below the surface showed on her flawless face.

One more minute with her and I might have put a fist through her perfect little nose job!

Sloane had seen this coming, but that didn't soften the blow. It was just the next disaster in the nightmare that her life had become. For six months, she could not step out her door without another shoe dropping.

Really, is there anything left to go wrong? How on earth can it get any worse?

Sloane was tough. She always had been. For 30 years, she had lived a privileged life, assured by her parents that she deserved every minute. She was whiplash smart, cover-model beautiful, came from a wealthy family and she was about to marry into an even wealthier one. Her future was bright. Nothing could stop her from attaining her heart's desire. Then, suddenly, all that had changed and for the last six months, nothing had gone right.

And isn't that the understatement of the century?

First, they accused her father of doing a shady business transaction, stealing secrets from a client and selling them to the Chinese government. He needed to launder payments, they claimed, so he tried to do it through the company of her soon-to-be-fiancé. When Wyatt discovered the scheme, Sloane's father planned to keep it hush-hush by blackmailing Wyatt's father, then sealing the deal by forcing the long overdue marriage of their children.

How did that all turn out? First, Wyatt called off the engagement, but she was tough. Sloane survived that indignity by telling people she did the jilting. Everyone knew she never loved him, so she pulled that one off pretty well.

The other problems were not so easily resolved. Although it was impossible for Sloane to believe her father could take a step out of place, the Feds arrested him. Sloane thought he would be back home quickly, completely absolved of all wrongdoing. Instead, he was indicted, rapidly tried and just this month he pleaded guilty to theft, illegal transactions with a foreign government and money laundering. Her father was going to serve up to eighteen years in federal prison.

Sloane was sure he would appeal, convinced of his innocence despite evidence to the contrary. This was her father, for God's sake. Instead, the most important person in her life cut a deal for a shorter sentence and blew up the world as she knew it.

Since then, like the fall of dominoes, Sloane had suffered a barrage of events from which she could not recover. Huyler Industries was bleeding clients and money. The business was failing, and she was wracking her brains for a way to keep it afloat. The family fortune, such as it had been, was gone, used to pay taxes and penalties and the exorbitant fees of fancy lawyers. Now her mother would sacrifice her parents' beautiful lakeside home, too.

She couldn't look for help from any of her influential and privileged friends and colleagues because they had all deserted her. Sent overseas to finishing school as a teen, she'd lost contact with most of her high school friends. And perhaps she was a bit too snobbish to develop lasting relationships, but Sloane didn't truly understand until now what it was to be friendless.

She had lost her money, her reputation, and her influence. With nothing to offer, she was a pariah. The city officials, the movers-and-shakers with whom she'd had great working relationships, were the first to desert her. Soon after, all her contacts at banks and investment firms wouldn't return her calls. Other businesspeople, her fellow Northwestern graduates, the group that helped each other out, stopped helping. Finally, she lost her so-called friends. That was the bitterest pill to swallow.

Until now.

She had just publicly lost the chair of the benefit committee. She had been chairing the benefit for the last four years. With her name and connections, badly needed donations flooded into the Children's hospital. She could charm everyone she knew into putting up items for the silent auction besides her accomplishments in gaining large corporate sponsorship. She had a reputation for an enormous turnout, exciting and entertaining events and the ability to raise close to one million dollars year after year.

Even Sloane recognized a pariah could not get the business leaders of Chicago to open their deep pockets. A pariah could not even get them to take her calls. The board was correct in assuming that her name on the top of the committee list was more problematic than useful. For Sloane, the benefit was the last star to which she hitched her wagon. Losing it was especially painful.

Sloane had seen the faces around the room tonight, too. The board was most likely gloating. It didn't surprise her. She was too fortunate before. People were spiteful, and they took pleasure in watching the mighty fall. Like schadenfreude, those around her were experiencing the joy that came from watching her lose it all.

Besides, I was a bitch. Face it; they knew I was looking down my perfect nose at them, because I was. Well, they are enjoying the show now, Sloane. Each one of them is getting the last laugh and you are getting the comeuppance you deserve.

It was a juicy story, after all, with all the elements of a good crime movie—Chicago-style. There was international crime, unethical practices and a perennial Chicago favorite—payola. Her father had expanded their business into China by engaging in illegal practices. And of course, there was the felling of the high and mighty.

The fancy lawyers had bargained eighteen years down to six, which her father had just started serving at the Federal Correctional Institution in Littleton, Colorado. Sloane's mother, Marianne, was trying to make ends meet on a drastically smaller income and it left Sloane to hold together the company responsible for supplying that income. Not a simple task when her father had destroyed the reputation of Huyler Industries and with it any earning power.

It remained a hot gossip item for months, the news ugly, but accurate. A get rich quick scheme by a man everyone believed to be worth millions. Why risk it? It turned out he was broke. Who knew? Sloane thought they were partners and family, but her idol had hidden everything from her until he needed her to make the match of the century to keep them whole. They dragged the Huyler name through the mud every night on the news, every day in the papers.

It didn't take long before Sloane couldn't show her face in public. Huyler Industries lost every client not bound by an ironclad contract. Her mother checked herself into a 'facility' after three months of cameras and scrutiny, just to get away. It was a nice place too, on the beach in the south of France, with fabulous spa services and plastic surgeons. Her mother came home looking refreshed, rested and lovelier than ever, just in time to stand behind her husband when he pleaded guilty.

That had left Sloane holding down the fort, trying to piece together what was left of the business and the family fortune. With her father in jail for another six years, everything sat squarely on Sloane's capable shoulders. At the moment, she was sinking under the weight. Publicly, she could not separate her activities from those of her father. If he was guilty, she was guilty by association. No one trusted anyone named Huyler anymore. Sloane never understood why her father took the deal. Six years was a long time for an innocent man, hell one day was a long time, and a successful appeal would have cleared his name. Even now, Sloane refused to believe ill of her father, or if she did, she denied it. If she had been his little princess, he had been a God in her eyes.

Sloane had braced herself for losing the business, the bad press, and the painful process of discharging workers who had been with HI from its conception. She withstood the bad news about the family finances and even faced the need to sell their beautiful lakefront home, doing it all with her typical chilly demeanor. She had mastered the cool 'I don't give a damn' look when she met prying eyes. Sloane remained poised when people slighted her, when she saw them talking behind her back. But, it took its toll.

Despite what most people believed, Sloane was human.

When she failed to receive an invitation to the social event of the season, Wyatt's wedding, Sloane had chalked it up to her failed relationship with Wyatt Lyons Howe IV. She could hardly expect his new bride to extend an invitation to Wyatt's ex-fiancé.

Still, the wedding was splashed over every newspaper and magazine; even "Entertainment Tonight" and "Extra" had picked up the story. A Cinderella romance with a fairy tale ending for a poor artist and a real estate mogul did not happen every day. When the artist became a major success in the same year, it made the national news.

Over 750 people had attended the August wedding, according to the press. Sloane was not one of them. She had hoped to gain entrée as someone's 'plus one', but try as she might, she couldn't cajole anyone into inviting her when the charges against her father came to light the same month.

She had no expectation of attending the ceremony held in a converted Gilman, Illinois barn, knowing only close friends and family were invited. She had to admit, though, when she saw the photos of the converted space covered in white flowers and twinkling lights, that she felt a small romantic pull and a bit of jealousy. Not that she would ever admit it.

However, when they excluded her from the big reception at the Howe Museum, she felt shunned. It should have been her wedding. Those thoughts consumed her in the days before and after the summer event. Sloane was supposed to marry the handsome Wyatt. She had chased him relentlessly, then waited patiently for her prize, only to have Keeli steal it. Such a thing did not happen to Sloane Egan Huyler.

It became harder to maintain that cool façade since they were a stunning couple, and Keeli made a beautiful bride. Sloane studied the photos of the wedding in every magazine and newspaper. The papers had zoomed in on the gorgeous tiara that Keeli designed to hold her veil. Orders for the now-famous tiara were flooding the workroom of Keeli Larsen Designs, and other jewelers were rushing to copy it.

So here Sloane stood, on a cold, dark, February night, outside the meeting room of the hospital, the only person in society to have missed the wedding: jilted, broke, friendless, and the daughter of a notorious jailbird. Now, to add insult to injury, she wasn't even the chair for the Children's Hospital Benefit.

Hell, she could not even find a date for the benefit. Chill, you still have months to figure that one out.

Lifting the collar of her heavy coat and dropping her chin in case anyone from the meeting was still loitering in the building, Sloane took her signature long-legged stride toward the exit of the hospital, holding back the tears that were blurring her blue eyes, praying she could get to her car before they fell.

"Oof, excuse me," a deep voice offered. Sloane lifted her eyes to see who she had just plowed into, whose large, warm hands remained wrapped around her upper arms, steadying her as she wobbled in her Prada stilettos. "Steady there."

"Randall," Sloane was relieved when she looked up and recognized the man she had almost knocked over was Randall Parker III and not some stranger. "I wasn't looking where I was going."

"Sloane," Randall acknowledged Wyatt's ex with a nod of his head and a bit of a chill in his voice. "In a bit of a rush?"

"A bit." Sloane was clearly trying to make a getaway. She had bumped into him rather forcefully. Rather than release her immediately, he continued his hold on her arms.

She just wanted him to let her go so she could make it out the door before she turned into a blubbering mess in the middle of the hospital lobby.

"Everything ok? Are you ok?" Randall's voice softened with concern. He still held her, but they both knew she was solidly on her feet. He was studying her face too closely, and Sloane was squirming under the scrutiny. "Is everything alright?" he prodded gently, clearly seeing everything she was trying so hard to hide.

Without waiting for an answer, Randall removed his hand and, taking one of Sloane's, he led her to a wooden bench conveniently placed against the wall, encouraging her to sit down.

"I can see that you are upset. Is someone ill? What are you doing here?" He seemed genuinely concerned, but his soft voice and kind demeanor didn't fool Sloane. All of Wyatt's friends had been giving her the cold shoulder since Wyatt dumped her, and Randall was no exception.

Sloane knew him too well. Everything with Randall was about picking up a woman, about the conquest. She remembered, as she looked in his handsome face, that he—like his friends—was a player. This was probably just his strategy to segue into a hookup, despite his previous aversion to her. Randall was such a ladies' man that a few times during her engagement, he had hit on her after a few too many drinks. He chased anything in a skirt, so she knew that his sweet ways now were nothing personal.

"Oh no, everyone is fine, Randall, and I really need to get going." The good news about running into Randall was that she just wanted to get away from him now, and so she had forgotten that she felt like crying. "I was just here for a board meeting. Second Monday of the month," she offered, as if that explained everything. She moved to get up again, but his hand was holding hers in her lap and he was not letting her move.

"What about you? Are you visiting someone?" She could at least be polite.

"'My cousin's son took a spill at a basketball game last month and broke his arm. I drove them over to the doctors as the cast comes off today."

"That was very nice of you." She looked longingly toward the exit.

How much more of this chitchat is required before this oaf lets go of my hand?

"Sloane, what's going on? You look like you just lost your best friend. Where is that feisty woman I know?"

"C'mon Randall, you aren't that naïve." Sloane's usual caustic impatience had returned, and Randall smiled despite himself. "You know perfectly well what is going on, unless you have been out of Chicago for the last year. My world is falling apart, and you know it. Everyone is blaming me for the accusations against my father. I did nothing wrong, but I am the one left to pick up the pieces."

"You did nothing wrong?" Sloane can hear the incredulity in Randall's tone. "You might get away with that with other people, but this is me, Sloane, and I am not falling for your usual crap. Go bat those baby blues at someone who will buy that garbage you are selling. You have never been completely innocent of anything and we both know it."

"Screw you, Randall." Sloane jerked her hand out of Randall's and rose to her feet. He was up like a shot, grabbing her arm. She fell hard against his chest. His arms wrapped around her automatically and he left them there.

It felt surprisingly good.

"Sloane, seriously, something happened tonight, didn't it? Something to upset you all over again?" His expressive eyes were looking at her softly, but with concern, not pity.

I must really be a mess if Randall is being this nice to me. Stiff upper lip, girl.

"What do you care? Just let go of me, Randall." She twisted as if to break from the embrace, but not forcefully.

"I know you Sloane. You can play tough girl all you want with these other people," using his head he nodded toward the few people still loitering in the large space, "but I think you're about to cry. And frankly, I'm not sure I believed you were even capable of tears; so, I thought I would stick around to watch."

"I got kicked off the benefit," she whined in a low voice. "Nothing worth crying over, so show's over. Let me go."

"They kicked you off the benefit committee? But you are the chair. You have been working on this for months." Randall seemed shocked by Sloane's news. "Can they even do that?"

"They can and they have. They don't want my tainted name on the invitations. Bad for business, I guess. I get to collaborate with the hotel caterers and that's it. Allyson Riley is in charge."

"Well, she's good," Randall acknowledged, while Sloane flashed him a malevolent look. "But it was pretty unfair to you," he quickly backpedaled.

"Pretty unfair? Pretty unfair?" Sloane's voice rose in indignation. "It was unforgiveable."

"But Sloane, face facts. You have to understand that people around town might think twice before handing you money right now. You may not be the one charged with wrongdoing, but the suspicion is there."

"Thanks for reminding me, asshole."

"Just calling it like I see it," Randall had finally moved back from her, giving her breathing room that had been strangely lacking. "You can survive this Sloane, all of this. You are a tough broad. One of the toughest I know."

"Randall, no one calls a woman a 'broad' anymore. It's not PC," Sloane tossed back, feeling like herself again.

"Well, no one calls me an asshole either," Randall lobbed back at Sloane quickly. "Besides, I meant 'tough broad' as a compliment."

"Oh, well then, of course, my sincerest thanks," Sloane answered, her tone anything but sincere.

"You are hopeless, Sloane. Months have passed since your father's arrest. You need to stop feeling sorry for yourself and move on. It's been months since your father's arrest. It will be years before he gets out. In the meantime, make a life for yourself. You are yesterday's news. Act like it. Show these snobs that you are made of sterner stuff."

"But what if I'm not?" Sloane surprised herself and Randall with the insecure and hurt-laced question.

"Who is this mealy mouthed woman? Seriously, I have seen you cut a person to shreds with a look. Get your act together already and start walking on people again."

"Hey wait a minute. I don't walk on people." Sloane was indignant, but her voice had regained some strength and power at last.

"Do not bullshit a bullshitter, Sloane. You've made a career out of walking on people, including my best friend. You would have married him for his name and money. Shit, you even tried to get his girlfriend fired. You are unscrupulous, but at least you are superb at it."

Damn Randall, for kicking me when I'm down, and for being right. I would have married Wyatt for his money, and when Keeli spilled salad on me, I tried to have her fired even though she seemed sincerely sorry. Was my dress more important than her job? I could be the one waiting tables if things don't improve.

"What the hell? Stop impugning my character." Sloane was standing taller, indignant at being so accurately sized up.

"Just calling it like I see it," Randall said again.

"Stop saying that!" Sloane said in irritation.

Randall was moving away from the bench and walking toward a woman and child coming from the elevators.

"Gotta go," he lobbed over his shoulder without a backward glance. Sloane stood there, fuming.

Even if he was right about me, who the hell is he to talk? Just a stupid, womanizing oaf. No one ever had the nerve to say to my face what I know they said behind my back. Not even Wyatt.

Sloane started moving toward the exit, her tears completely forgotten. She felt like her old self—imperious, elitist and entitled to anything she wanted, if just a tiny bit humbled. She tried not to think too hard about the fact that Randall had set her back on course, kept her from embarrassing herself. She tried not to think about the fact that she couldn't decide whether to punch him or kiss him.

For an oaf, his hands felt fantastic on her, strong and large and manly. Too bad he was so damn good looking. And smart. And successful. Yeah, and mouth-wateringly sexy.

Sloane realized with distress that if a woman could pin him down, Randall was a catch. In fact, he was the type of man she'd wanted to marry since she was a little girl. Highly accomplished and educated, Randall was strong willed and physically powerful. He was already running his family's investment firm. He worked hard and played hard, and he traveled in the right circles, but was no snob. To cap it off, he was disarmingly attractive. Shaking off the idea of Randall as a catch, Sloane remembered Randall was still a womanizer.

Oh, and a drunk, too. Walk away, Sloane. He parties too hard, likes his booze and his women way too much.

Sloane stood there for one more moment, remembering the feel of his arms around her, the way her hand had felt small with his big fingers wrapped around hers. She remembered the look in his eyes when he was concerned and the pleasure of bantering with him without having the upper hand. She liked the time together, brief as it was. He had made her stand taller and prouder. He had made her heart beat a bit faster, too.

Nope, not happening. She'd learned her lesson with Wyatt and needed someone she could count on to stand fast, especially now. Sloane could never be sure of him and besides, Randall knew what a manipulator she could be. She would never get the upper hand.

Suddenly chilled by the cold wind blowing through her coat, Sloane moved quickly toward her car. She wasn't feeling sorry for herself anymore.

CHAPTER TWO

She caught of glimpse of him from the corner of her eye, heard his voice and knew he had spotted her, despite being engaged in conversation and the crowds filling the large space. Sloane couldn't sneak past him, but she tried, quickening her pace and looking the other way. "Gentlemen, will you excuse me for a moment, please?" Randall requested of his business associates as he rose from the table and hastened across the lobby of the Palmer House.

"Sloane?" he called when he was just a few feet away.

Sloane turned on her heel and acted surprised to find herself face to face with Randall Parker again so soon. It had just been over a week since she had run into him—literally—at the hospital.

"Randall, what are you doing here?" she asked, a bit of an accusation in her voice.

"Down girl. I am not stalking you. I am having drinks with some business associates in town for meetings." He motioned toward three men openly watching the two of them converse. "What are you doing here? Following me?"

Sloane ignored his arrogant grin and sent his colleagues a coquettish wave instead.

Keep him on his toes. Wait, what are you doing? Why do you care if Randall is on his toes? He is a Neanderthal.

"I am meeting with the catering team for the hospital benefit." Remembering the last time she had seen him, when she confessed to losing her top-dog position on the committee, Sloane added, "with just months to go, I have so many details to nail down. I am heading upstairs to meet with the staff and to taste some potential menus."

There, that made it sound like I am still important, right?

"Hey, that could be fun. I'll join you."

"I don't remember inviting you," Sloane said in a withering voice that Randall completely ignored. Traversing the lobby in a few paces, he said good night to his associates and caught up with Sloane as she rode the escalator to the mezzanine without waiting for him.

Pretending Randall was not moving toward her with that long-legged stride, Sloane looked about the lobby as if seeing it for the first time. She was ignoring Randall as best she could—not a simple task when his broad shoulders filled much of her line of vision. She had to labor to look at anything but him, although she couldn't miss the way he checked her out from head to toe.

Before he filled her view, Sloane admired the lobby of the Palmer House. It was still magnificent, even after all these years. Built in 1873, or rather rebuilt, after falling victim to the famous Chicago Fire, the lobby was impressive. Under its painted ceilings, and gargoyles and cupids at the mezzanine level, was the grand staircase, huge candelabras and sofas full of people having afternoon tea or cocktails. There were dozens of muffled conversations taking place under the oversized chandeliers filling the room with abundant light. They drowned out the sounds of background music played by a quartet. Sloane never ceased to be awed by the massive space, unlike any other in the city.

"So, what are we eating?" Randall's question cut into her thoughts as his face blocked her view.

"I am eating appetizers, entrees and desserts," Sloane responded chillingly.

"Lighten up, ice queen, what's a little company gonna' hurt?"

"Ice queen?" Sloane had never heard that before, although she acknowledged it was fitting. Before she could get a response from Randall, a young man in a navy suit approached her, hand outstretched in welcome.

"Ms. Huyler, so nice to see you again," Kenny Wallace attempted to greet Sloane warmly. She barely acknowledged the caterer, offering a cursory handshake. "Kenneth Wallace, Hilton catering."

"Randall Parker, nice to meet you," Randall took the proffered hand in a brief shake before sliding his arm around Sloane's waist like he was staking his territory. Ignoring the evil look she flashed him, he tightened the hold when she tried to twist away. "I am assisting Ms. Huyler with the tasting today."

"Yes, yes, of course." Kenny buzzed around the two of them like a busy bee, chatting about the room size, the set-up requirements and every minor detail for their consideration. His voice sounded miles away from Sloane. She couldn't concentrate on anything beyond the feel of the large, warm, masculine arm hot against her waist. That thought quickly evaporated when Randall pulled her tighter to his side. Then she could think of nothing but the feeling of incredible security and rugged power overwhelming her senses.

What the hell is wrong with me? It may feel good, but it's still Randall. What am I, desperate? Not enough to be manhandled.

"Get your mitts off of me, you ass," she whispered when they were out of Kenny's earshot, pushing at his chest.

Sloane had known Randall for years, introduced when he and Wyatt mentored her MBA class. Randall was also a graduate of Kellogg, along with Wyatt's other close friends, Tyler and Alex. All were elite

Lake Forest boys, all hockey players, all players period, at least until Wyatt had succumbed to marriage without even a whimper of resistance.

They were devastatingly good looking and desirable too. Even Randall, known for his smart mouth and lack of refinement, was a catch for any lucky woman. Of course, his behavior was all an act. No one could grow up amidst Lake Forest society, attend Duke and Northwestern Universities and run a highly successful and stodgy firm without knowing how to conduct oneself. His rough ways were all for effect, and Sloane knew it. That didn't make them any less irritating.

If he is so annoying, why is something as simple as his arm around me such a turn on? I cannot let him see the way he affects me. I would rather die. It couldn't be that Randall Parker affects me like this. It's that it has been months since Wyatt left and I haven't been with anyone since. I would be like this with an ape after so long. Oh yeah, Randall is an ape.

"As you can see, we have laid out several place-setting and napkin options, consistent with your color palette. Just let us know which you prefer. Meanwhile, I will inform the chef that we are ready to begin."

Once he was out of earshot, Sloane turned on Randall.

"Why are you still here?"

"Just being helpful. With so many decisions to make, I presumed you would benefit from my mouth."

Something about the way Randall said that told Sloane he wasn't talking about menu tastings. She felt perspiration form between her small breasts and pool in her bra. Nervously crossing and uncrossing her legs, she willed the sexual thoughts—and this infuriating man—to go away.

"What do you think Sloane?" he drawled, leaning closer so she could feel his warm breath upon her face. "Think you might enjoy my mouth?"

"You are a complete pig," she responded, primly pressing her lips and her legs tighter together, unwilling to concede an inch to the infuriating man.

Sloane stopped fidgeting as a pair of servers placed beautiful china in front of the two of them in perfect unison. The service and presentation were flawless and for a brief time, Sloane could think about something other than her budding and unwelcome desire for the handsome, broad-shouldered specimen sitting beside her.

The platter contained four tastes, each beautifully presented on small plates of differing china patterns. There were small bites on two dishes and two delicate cups, containing a small measure of soup, on the others. Mr. Wallace stepped forward and began describing the offerings with unabashed pride.

"First, we have our salad with brie and baby pear poached in saffron served with a lovely champagne dressing. Next," as he pointed carefully, "is a fresh cantaloupe wrapped in prosciutto and served with tomatoes, Parmesan and seasonal greens. These are popular summer choices, or, perhaps you prefer one of our soups. Today we are offering our lobster bisque—always a favorite, but a slight extra charge —and a delightful asparagus and pea soup. Enjoy."

With that, he stepped away, out of hearing distance, but close enough should he need to be summoned. They left Sloane and Randall to sample the inviting appetizer options and discuss them privately. Sloane resigned herself to tasting the dishes with Randall and watched his face as he tried each choice. Surprisingly, she found herself interested in his opinion.

"Well, I would eliminate the bisque right off the bat," he said almost before swallowing it. She thought the flavors were heavenly and was reluctant to discard it too quickly. "I think people will find it heavy for a summer evening and it's a benefit, so you want to raise money, not spend it." Randall was forthright in voicing his opinion, which Sloane appreciated, recognizing that he was taking this responsibility seriously. Frankly, she thought he was right about the bisque, too. His logic was excellent.

"I see your point," Sloane conceded begrudgingly. Then, after a small spoonful added, "I think this other soup won't appeal to everyone either."

Randall agreed. They savored the non-soup options, discussing the complex flavors and presentation. They argued the merits of each dish before agreeing that either would be a wonderful selection. As soon as he saw they were done, Mr. Wallace motioned to the servers, who swept away the plates efficiently and quickly deposited the entrees.

"We have excellent wine pairings for all the dishes, of course, so you could have a lovely Sauvignon Blanc with the appetizer, say, followed by a Chardonnay or Pinot Noir with the entrée. We can bring out samples, of course. Perhaps one white and one red?"

"Sure, bring them, please," Randall answered quickly, giving Sloane a wicked smile. He was never one to turn down a drink.

"Do not get drunk, or so help me. I will never forgive you," Sloane threatened.

"Promise," Randall responded, crossing his heart like a small boy and flashing Sloane a roguish grin.

When did he get so damn good looking? Stop, stop, stop! The man is crude and disgusting.

If Sloane was completely honest with herself, she had to admit that right now he was excellent company. He approached the tasting thoughtfully and was being both helpful and fun. It was better to have a second opinion when choosing the meal, and Randall was turning out to be an excellent partner for the project. They were comparing grouper with mango salsa, chicken with Brie and tarragon, and a steak that only Randall was sampling since they'd covered it with exotic mushrooms.

"I loathe and detest mushrooms," Sloane explained. First Randall ate all the steak on his dish, then swapped plates and polished off hers. In fact, she barely took a bite of each offering, while he assured both plates were empty when they returned to the kitchen.

"You hardly ate anything," he observed. "No wonder you are so skinny."

"I am not skinny, thank you very much." The remark clearly offended Sloane. "I am appropriately thin."

"Hah! That's a joke," Randall chided. "You are bones, Sloane. Beautiful bones, but still just bones."

Sloane felt a rare blush move up to her cheeks. She wanted to ask Randall if he really thought she was beautiful, but she knew it would sound like she was fishing. She was dying to fish though. She who had been showered with attention had not had a man pay her a compliment in forever.

"Thanks, I think," she mumbled instead.

Randall sat back in the velvet dining chair, wine glass in hand, replete with rich food. He surveyed the room slowly before his eyes came to lite on Sloane again. She had been going for elegant and sophisticated in her long sleeved, high-necked beige dress paired with classic heels and bag. The dress skimmed her delicate curves, her eyes popped against the bland background, a deep Caribbean blue. Did Randall see all that? Did he admire her?

"This will be a nice space for the benefit. You chose well. You did choose this space, right? While you were still chair?" She nodded and he continued before she could provide more of an answer. "I was actually kind of amazed that you were chairing the event and managing a full-time job, especially with everything that was going on with your dad."

"I could have managed it all if they had just let me," Sloane responded, hurt still clear in her voice almost a full week after the repugnant board meeting.

"Yeah, but isn't this actually easier? I imagine work is hell right now, trying to hold on to clients, reassure them and get the work done without your partner."

Sloane picked her head up in a haughty move that she had made her signature. Using one small hand to push her thick mane of dark hair over her shoulder, she prepared to launch into her rehearsed speech about the health of the business, about her superb skill in running it, and how everything was just fine.

She had given the speech almost daily to someone or other. Now it rolled off her tongue easily, if insincerely. She had said these words to her clients. Most left anyway. She had said them to the press, but they still led the news with the worst of her father's offenses and dragged down the family name. She had said them to her so-called friends; those she thought would stand by her through thick and thin. They had been the first to give her platitudes and disappear.

She was thinking all of this as she prepared to put on a brave face and launch into her routine yet again. Then she looked into Randall's eyes. He saw through the façade, eyeing her openly, trustingly. It was the look she had hoped to see from friends, but that had been sadly missing from all around her. Sloane crumpled under it.

"C'mon, let's be honest. My business stinks. My clients are running for the hills. This benefit was about all I had left to keep me busy and sane. And it was my last chance to feel connected to anyone."

That felt remarkably liberating. I should have just told the truth a long time ago.

"Do you want to talk about it? I am happy to listen and help if I can. I hope you know that Sloane." Randall rested his bear-paw hand on her thigh, letting her know he was there for her.

The touch was electric for Sloane. The heat of his hand, bare skin on nearly bare skin, sent warmth through her whole being. Sloane felt power in those long fingers lightly caressing her leg, and a sensuous connection. Tenuous as it was, Sloane wanted the feeling to last. She could think of nothing now but the weight of Randall's hand on her leg, inching toward the edge of her stocking, moving along her body, doing amazing things to her.

He asked you a question, or something. No, he offered compassion. Wonderful, welcome compassion.

Trying to regain her composure and clear her mind of its sexual meanderings, Sloane nodded rather than reply. After a silent moment, she was about to answer, but the servers arrived with their dessert selections. They placed four tempting confections of chocolate or berries and flakey pastries before them on the table. Sloane thought they looked too beautiful to eat, but Randall dug into each with gusto. He left his hand on her thigh, unconsciously, although Sloane was conscious of nothing else.

"Where do you put all that food?" Sloane was curious, but also needed to keep the conversation going, keep her mind off Randall's fingers skimming her thigh.

"Dunno," Randall replied around a mouthful of flourless chocolate cake with a delicate raspberry coulis. "Hockey maybe?" he continued once he had swallowed.

He pushed her plate of sweets closer to the edge of the table in front of Sloane, encouraging her to taste the delights. She took a dainty bite of each then reluctantly placed her fork on the plate. Sloane loved sweets, but years of hearing her mother say "you can never be too thin or too rich" had taught her to be content with only a bite. She took a last, longing look at the four choices before pushing the plate away from her.

"Go with the chocolate mousse thing," Randall suggested offhandedly.

"I was thinking the berries and meringue made the prettiest option."

"You don't eat it cause it's pretty, you eat it cause it tastes good. Go with the chocolate," Randall countered, giving her leg a gentle squeeze as he slid his hand higher on her thigh. "Everyone likes chocolate, sinful, milky chocolate." His voice was a low rumble, warm and inviting.

Is he talking about the dessert, or did we just change topics? And when did it get so damn hot in here?

Bowing to his suggestion, Sloane signaled to Kenny, who returned to the table, clipboard in hand. Sloane gave Kenny the menu choices, selected the place setting and the wine pairings and thanked him for his hard work. After being reassured that he would email everything in the final contract later that day, they prepared to leave.

Randall removed his hand from Sloane's leg, sliding the hem of her dress up her thigh as he stood to pull back her chair. He waited, an expectant look on his face, until she reached for her purse and stood. He immediately wrapped his arm around her waist possessively.

Sloane knew she should make him move it, but she enjoyed the solid feel of him beside her.

"My pleasure, Ms. Huyler. Mr. Parker, so nice to meet you." Kenny shook hands with them both and thanked them profusely. The Children's Hospital Benefit was a good-sized event for the hotel, and Kenny was treating Sloane and Randall as the important clients they were.

Watching Randall say his goodbyes to the caterer, it struck Sloane how different they were in appearance. Randall stood a good four inches above the caterer and had at least 30 pounds on him, all muscle. Randall was broader through the shoulders and chest. He stood now, confident and clearly in control. He'd forced his way in to the tasting uninvited, yet it was obvious to Sloane that, as far as Kenny was concerned, Randall was running the show.

Did I defer to Randall? Did I lose my authority here? How did this happen? Did Randall actually take control? I don't think he did. He simply has that air of authority, the confidence that made Kenny think he was in charge. Hell, for a while, I thought he was in charge. And I liked it.

"Well, Kenny," Sloane regained the upper hand one last time. "I will be in touch to review everything one last time the week of the event. I expect the final headcount numbers will be available a month ahead of time. And I will get the contract soon?"

"Yes, Ms. Huyler, you will have it later today," Kenny reiterated patiently.

Feeling back in charge, Sloane straightened her shoulders, catching Randall looking at her. His knowing smile unnerved her. It also turned her on.

This man knows all my problems. He knows just what a controlling bitch I can be, but right now, I swear he is looking at me like I am naked. What the hell?

"So, where you are you heading now?" Randall broke into Sloane's thoughts. "Maybe we could grab a drink?"

"I should really go back, and get some work done..." Sloane hesitated. He was turning his boyish charm on her. It was working too. The feel of his hand on her leg and his arm around her waist fresh in her mind, she realized she wanted to be with him. "I have time for one drink, I guess. Nothing major. I already had that wine with the tasting."

"That? That was nothing." He flashed her a wide grin. "So, do you want to stay here and find a couch in the lobby, or head somewhere else?"

"Let's head out."

"We could head to Chicago Athletic Club, or the Rittergut Wine Bar has a marvellous view of the river, and it would be quieter."

"I vote for quieter," Sloane responded, appreciating options at both ends of the scale. CAC was the hottest spot in town, with gorgeous views of Millennium and Grant Park. The Rittergut was new and quieter, and more romantic, with its riverside location.

Randall helped her into her coat, throwing his arm over her shoulders to steer her toward the exit. Their long legs easily fell into a matched step, walking the few blocks to the riverfront locale. Fortunate to get a table with a view, Randall helped Sloane into her chair before seating himself across from her. She turned to enjoy the view and lifted the dark mane of hair off her neck where it caught between her back and the chair. The gesture was practical, but also consciously sensuous.

"This is perfect. I am so glad you suggested it." She flashed Randall her megawatt smile. "It was just what I needed."

"If I read things right, it seems like you haven't been having much fun this winter."

"Longer," she confided. "Since the first news of the arrest hit the papers. What can I say? My father pleaded guilty. Now everyone believes he was greedy and stupid. He will pay the price, I will pay the price, and everyone working for our company will pay the price too. All my advertising and PR expertise cannot save me now."

"You know, I have an MBA from Kellogg, one of the best business schools in the country, and plenty of top-notch experience," she continued. "I have used every iota of business skill I learned in school or on the job to stay afloat. Still, I know that our few remaining clients will leave as soon as their contracts expire."

Randall leaned forward in the chair, paying careful attention and taking her delicate hand in his large one, telegraphing his support through the slight gesture.

"I have already accepted the resignations of all the key executives, and by Easter, I fear I will lay off over 1,000 employees. I know most people believe I have no heart. Wouldn't it surprise them to hear I am broken-hearted about closing the business, about layoffs, about selling our gorgeous house in Glencoe?"

"I really am sorry, Sloane. I know that this is awful for you, for your mom and for the business. How can I help?" Randall's turquoise eyes were kind as he stared into Sloane's icy blue ones. He reached for her other hand across the table, taking her delicate fingers and wrapping them in his larger ones.

"You could start by ordering me a glass of Cabernet," she suggested, lightening the mood. Motioning to the server, Randall selected a bottle of expensive Cabernet Sauvignon from the extensive menu. The server approved heartily of the selection, seeing a large tip in his future, and disappeared.

"A bottle?" Sloane questioned Randall now. "I thought we were taking it easy."

"We can handle it," he reassured her. "Besides, I am trying to get you drunk so I can take advantage of you." Randall lifted his eyebrows, Groucho Marx style, and leered at Sloane, squeezing her fingers in his. She laughed it off.

"Not likely," she replied as the server returned with the wine and went through the ritual of showing the bottle to Randall and opening it with fanfare. Sloane slid her fingers from his grip.

Actually, he was more than a little tempting. After all, Randall had that enticing rugged virility barely veiled under his polished veneer. And, damn it, it has been way too long. I know we could have a good time. He has that incredible body. I love watching him talk with those enormous hands and I can just imagine those long fingers touching me all over. Oh, and let's not forget that mouth, Sloane. Those dimples may get most of the attention, but that mouth is luscious. Imagine the things he can do to you with that mouth.

Sloane shook her head, clearing it.

What the hell are you thinking, Sloane!? The man is a big lug who drinks too much. He has no filter on that crude mouth of his and pushes his way in where he is unwanted. And he's one of Wyatt's best friends. OMG, I cannot do it with one of Wyatt's friends. I just know they will compare notes.

Randall had poured the ruby liquid and was waiting for Sloane to raise her glass. He was watching the play of emotions over her face, and she feared she was giving away too much of what she was thinking. She quickly raised her glass to his, schooling her features.

"To old and new friends," he toasted cryptically, lifting the glass to his mouth. She watched him take a deep drink, swallowing over half the glass as his Adams-apple moved along his throat. "Mm, nice."

He was stroking her arm repeatedly, and rubbing her thigh with his under the table. His intentions were more than obvious. Sloane was debating with herself as she lifted the large glass to her mouth.

"To friends." Sipping from the glass as the fragrant wine assailed her senses, she had to agree that he had selected an excellent Cabernet, the flavor complex and fruity. She took a larger sip and savored the flavors in her mouth. "Randall, this is delicious. How do you know so much about wine?" She turned the bottle so that she could read the label. "Miner." She had never heard of it, but she would look for their wines in the future.

"I invest in a couple of vineyards. Well, the firm invests in a few and I invest in a few more. I like to get out to Napa and Sonoma now and then to do some hands-on work. This isn't one of mine, but I discovered it on a recent trip, and I liked it." He was grinning like a fool and Sloane realized she was watching a combination of male pride and too much alcohol.

"What did you have to drink before you came to the tasting with me?"

"What do you care?" Randall was instantly defensive, leaning back in his chair, his legs suddenly pulled away from hers.

"I don't," Sloane tried to deflect his annoyance. "I was just curious about who you were with at the Palmer House."

"Just some investment buddies. We had one drink together. Then I saw you in that little dress, and those long legs beckoned to me. There is nothing like watching a good-looking woman in a short skirt head up an escalator."

Sloane was being presented with those devastating dimples of Randall's that she responded to, but simultaneously, his increasingly crude behavior was leaving her cold. He'd polished off a glass of wine already, and he was obviously feeling the effect.

"Lighten up, Sloane. I was paying you a compliment. We were having a good time. I was thinking maybe we could have a better one." Again, those dimples beckoned to her and a lock of his thick brown hair falling across his forehead made her itch to push it back into place. She felt his thighs rub against hers suggestively.

"Randall, you are not getting lucky with me tonight, no matter what you were hoping. So, what do you say we just keep things friendly, finish our wine and go our separate ways?" Now that Sloane had decided how she wanted to handle things with Randall, she was cool and detached again.

"Oh Sloane, why do you always have to be so cold and controlling? Cut loose for a change. You were always so prim and proper with Wyatt, but I figured you were hot as hell in bed. The cold ones always are."

"That's it." Sloane put her glass down decisively and rose from her chair in one fluid motion. "You have offended me in every way possible. I'm out of here."

Grabbing her coat and bag from the chair, she regained her composure slightly. "Thank you for the wine," she said through gritted teeth, "and take care."

Sloane walked away without a backward glance, head high, and stride normal. She would not let him see how much he had disappointed and angered her.

Sloane walked a few blocks before she even realized she was heading toward home, not back to the office as she had intended. She was replaying the afternoon in her head, the pleasure of the tasting, the compliments, the banter and the delicious sexual undertones. Randall had been funny, clever, intelligent and all man. She had desired him. Her body had responded to those little touches, to his smiles. Her blood was only cooling now.

She had finally walked away when she realized she needed more than a quick romp with a sexy man. She needed a friend, a shoulder to lean on right now, someone she could count on. Maybe Randall could have been that man, but after a few drinks, he lost all his chart. The nice Randall lured her in, but the drunk Randall disappointed.

Of course, it didn't help that his insults hit the mark. Sloane owned his insults. She was cold and controlling, but she had only relied on herself for months, wrapping herself in aloof for protection.

Sloane walked another block, her shoes pinching her toes. Looking for a taxi, shlooked for a taxi, raising her arm like a seasoned city dweller. The cab pulled to the curb sharply and Sloane slid into the heated comfort, gave the address of her condo and sat back for the short ride, allowing her mind to wander.

Who am I kidding? When I was engaged to Wyatt things were no better. I knew that he didn't love me, but I refused to let go, wanting his wealth and cache. So, what kind of woman am I anyway? Why would anyone be nice to be, want me, and love me?

Sitting a little taller, throwing her shoulders back and lifting her chin as the taxi crawled through the Michigan Avenue traffic, Sloane gave herself a mental shake. She would head back to work and try to find the money to stay open a few more months. She would focus on work because that was where she was in control and at her best. Introspection was not helpful right now. She leaned forward and gave the driver her office address instead.

Screw Randall. She would get it together and move on.

CHAPTER THREE

It was a sunny afternoon with strong breezes coming off the lake almost a month later. At least the worst of winter seemed to be behind them. Sloane had to hold down the bottom of her skirt as she crossed the Michigan Avenue Bridge, heading to meet Regan Howe and her brother Ethan for lunch. It was strange to be lunching with Wyatt's siblings, but she was out of options. Moving quickly toward "Sixteen", Sloane was rehearsing what she would say to the two real estate experts. She wanted to find a balance between asking for their help and getting them to offer her assistance before she asked. Sloane could not come off sounding desperate no matter what, but she even needed them to pick up the check at the elegant and expensive restaurant. There was a time she could have paid for a high-end business lunch, but not anymore.

Sloane was relieved that Wyatt was no longer at the helm of Lyons Howe Real Estate. It would have been so awkward doing business with him now that he was married to Keeli. She felt awful that her father had tried to blackmail him into marrying her. She was embarrassed when he didn't care enough to want the marriage, and then her father's illegal dealings had almost ruined LHRE too. It was unforgiveable, but she hoped someday she and Wyatt would move past it. They had been good friends once upon a time. Luckily, unlike so many others, Wyatt's sisters had never blamed Sloane, and the three had remained close friends.

That Regan was at the helm of LHRE almost left Sloane bursting with pride. It was gratifying for Sloane to see deserving, talented women rise in the corporate world and she was just plain happy for her friend. Waving to Regan and Ethan across the open space, Sloane took a brief second to appreciate the soaring ceiling and million-dollar views. When her eyes rested on Regan, she saw a new confidence in her friend.

Running the show always makes a woman more beautiful.

Sloane had taken extra care with her appearance today, and she knew she looked her best. Since the trial, she had lost a few pounds off her already thin frame, but that couldn't be helped. It just made her look even taller than her already lanky 5'8". Her dark hair swung behind her to the middle of her back, shining and thick, perfectly even on the ends. Her exquisite, oval face was a touch pale, but that accentuated the dark slash of her eyebrows and the icy blue of her large, expressive eyes. Sloane made sure of it.

Since this was an important meeting, Sloane had chosen the one new outfit she had invested in this year. Having checked her coat, she moved across the dining room in the elegant, coral Carolina Herrera sheath dress that hugged her slender curves. She felt confident in it and knew it was flattering when she saw a few heads turn. With her low Prada kitten-heels and a deep shade of coral on her upturned lips, she looked like a young Audrey Hepburn—tall, beautiful, confident and successful. Exactly the look she'd been going for.

"I am so sorry I am late," Sloane joined them, kissing the air beside both of Regan's cheeks in the French style before sitting down, squeezing Ethan's hand and accepting a menu from the attentive wait staff.

"You are right on time," Regan reassured her. "And you look fantastic."

Agreeing to order right away, the three perused the menu of the Michelin-starred restaurant before settling on salmon for the women, beef for Ethan. Exotic starters tempted them, but all three settled on an enticing, anything but plain, baby lettuce salad. Ethan suggested a bottle of Chardonnay, selected one, and they sat back to await their meal while making small talk.

It had been months since Sloane had seen either of the Howe siblings, and there was plenty of catching up to do. Avoiding the minefields of Wyatt's wedding and Sloane's father, they settled on updates on their Christmas holidays, travel and quickly segued into their respective jobs. This was perfect for Sloane. The sooner they conducted business, the sooner she could relax and enjoy her lunch.

Ethan finally broached Huyler Industries. "How is your business braving the scandal?" he asked in his forthright way. At 27, Ethan was still learning the business. He had been deep in Wyatt's shadow until last year, when his big brother left to start his own tech company. Now Regan was at the helm and she was mentoring Ethan to be her second in command.

"It's tough. I would be lying if I didn't say so." She needed to walk a fine line today between being a worthwhile investment and being desperate for help. "I haven't been able to attract any new clients."

"And how many of the old ones have jumped ship?"

Sloane cringed at the blunt question, unable to hide her pain. "A few. Quite a few. But we have contracts with many large companies, and most are at least honoring their current contracts."

"And how long do you think that can sustain you?" Regan asked.

"Well, unless I downsize, not long." The Howe siblings nodded in unison, and Sloane plunged forward. "Actually, I wanted to talk to you about that. I was thinking our space down here is very desirable, and very expensive. Maybe we could consider smaller, less expensive office space off the beaten track?"

"We can definitely help you with that, Sloane. We would be delighted to help you relocate to new quarters." Regan made it sound like a lovely choice that Sloane was making, not a last-ditch effort to survive. Regan reassured her that her current office space would fetch a very good price.

As they enjoyed the delicious lunch, the three discussed square footage, amenities and locations. Ethan was remarkably knowledgeable about the world famous downtown "loop," near north and south loop real estate markets. It was not surprising when Sloane considered that LHRE probably owned and managed more than half of it.

By the time the server presented them with the dessert menus, Sloane was feeling much more positive about moving to a smaller, more affordable space. She felt like she had some good options to choose from that would still be in desirable locations. Reputation and saving face were critical to her right now. Her current lease was leaking much needed cash. A quick sublet would put a finger in that dyke.

"Now, one more sensitive issue," she began after longingly considering dessert but rejecting it. "I need to move my mother out of the Glencoe house. It is too big for her to live in alone and too expensive to manage. The taxes alone are an incredible burden now. Can you suggest a residential real estate agent in the suburbs?"

"Oh Sloane, are you sure?" Regan looked almost ready to cry, empathizing with Sloane at the prospect of losing her family home. "Would your father be okay with this?"

"My mother is alone in that house because of my father," Sloane responded bitterly. "He made the deal. He does not get a say anymore. Mom says she wants to get out of the house, and I want to help her.

Can you get me a name?" Sloane took a deep breath, knowing she had raised her voice and become more forceful than necessary. It was not Regan's fault she was in this mess.

"Please, Regan, Ethan, can you help?" Sloane added more quietly.

"Of course, Sloane. Anything you need. Ethan will email you some names."

They sat a few more minutes talking about upcoming theater and black-tie events while Ethan fortunately settled the check.

"Speaking of which," Regan suddenly asked, "How is the Children's Hospital Benefit coming along? It's only two months away, isn't it?"

"Three, actually," Sloane responded. "And we need that extra month. We have the Palmer House all set, the invitations go out soon, but we are still getting in items for the silent auction and they are a critical source of revenue. It is a busy time of year for the benefit circuit."

"We could offer something, couldn't we?" Regan turned to her brother. "There must be a tempting hotel we own where we could offer a romantic weekend. Maybe something out of town, where we could throw in airfare from Chicago? Ethan, make a note to get something over to Sloane this week."

"Actually, can you send it over to Allyson Riley? She has taken over as chairperson."

"Oh no," Regan said, her mouth falling into a deep frown. "I am so sorry Sloane." There it was again, that intolerable look of pity. Regan was about to ask about the change, or say more in that pitying voice, when Sloane interrupted.

"Oh, look at the time. You two have been wonderful, but I have to run. Thank you so much for lunch." Ethan thwarted her escape, suggested they were ready to leave the restaurant, too, and offering to get her coat. Now she would have to walk out with them.

Taking a cleansing breath or two, throwing her coat over her arm, Sloane suppressed her annoyance and went to street level with the pair. Exiting the building onto Wabash Street, Sloane went to make a quick exit when she heard someone calling Regan's name and someone else calling hers.

Walking toward them, looking like a pair of Greek gods, were Tyler Winthrop and Randall Parker III,—two tall, confident, sun-kissed men in custom suits and highly polished Italian shoes. The post-lunch businesspeople and the tourists crowding the sidewalks parted around the men like the Red Sea, as if aware that they were special, designated for greatness. They exuded the confidence that comes from knowing that doors would open for them, that they would rise like cream in their competitive worlds. Even strangers responded to it.

Sloane was mesmerized, watching Randall stride closer. The sun rested on his thick, brown hair, bringing lights of blonde and red out. He'd tamed it today, sweeping it away from his forehead. His eyes were squinting under his heavy brows. Laugh lines radiated from the corners and dimples creased his cheeks as his smile widened upon seeing her. The man was devastating. Even twenty yards away, he was making her heart race and her palms sweat.

When did he begin having this effect on me?

Suppressing an audible sigh, it surprised Sloane to hear one escape from Regan instead. Was there something between Randall and Regan that Sloane was not aware of? Had they come together over the months while she was an outcast from the in-crowd? Sloane turned to see a becoming blush move into Regan's cheeks, alarmed to realize she felt jealous.

Really, what is wrong with me? I was engaged to this man's close friend only months ago and now suddenly I have the hots for Randall? This has to stop now.

When Sloane was engaged to Wyatt Lyons Howe IV, his three childhood friends had annoyed her, constantly surrounding them. Wyatt, Tyler, Randall and Alex had all grown up together and the golden boys had remained inseparable.

Each man was unique. Each was special in his own way. Sure, all were successful, afforded every advantage imaginable. But, where Wyatt was sandy-haired, Randall was dark. Where Randall was solid, Tyler was whipcord lean. Alex was always serious, Randall never was. Tyler was distrusting about business, Wyatt distrusting about life. Wyatt was quiet, while Randall would have a few drinks and be a total buffoon.

The four were thick as thieves, though, no matter what. Like the four Baldwin Brothers—good looking, intriguing and sexy—they were a family in everything from love to business to sports. They had shared each other's best achievements and darkest secrets, helped each other survive fraternity hazing and celebrated "first times." Like brothers, they grew up hanging out at each other's homes.

Before Wyatt married Keeli, no woman had ever come first with any of the four. Even when Wyatt and Sloane were engaged, Sloane knew if asked, Wyatt would choose them over her every time. Watching these two now reminded Sloane that the four friends were possibly the four most eligible bachelors in town until Wyatt had married a small-town girl and thrown Sloane aside.

The dissolution of her engagement and her father's sentencing had culminated in Sloane's ousting from membership in the one per-centers she called friends her whole life. The boys had mostly been absent since then, along with everyone else. Since the first allegations of wrongdoing by the Feds, Sloane had received fewer and fewer, and eventually no lunch invitations. She was dateless and unwelcome at parties. After a while, the party invitations had stopped coming, and she had stopped seeking any except those that supported worthy causes. Even those had to be accepted selectively. She was too embarrassed to attend most events, and even worse, she could no longer afford the high price of tickets and donations. Until recently, she had also assiduously avoided anyone and anything that had to do with Wyatt, except for staying in touch with his sisters Regan and Missy by phone.

Until today.

Here she was on the sidewalk with Wyatt's siblings, watching two of his three best friends and two of Chicago's undeniably sexiest men walking straight toward her. It should have felt awkward, but it didn't. Perhaps enough time had passed, or perhaps although her downfall had given this group a chance to lord laud things over her, none of them had. Last month at the tasting, Randall had actually been rather sweet to her—sort of.

I am not sure what has changed suddenly, but I think things are definitely looking up.

"Well, look at this. Who would have thought we would run into you here?" Tyler was saying as he approached, his hand outstretched toward Ethan. After sharing a firm handshake, Tyler planted a soft kiss on Regan's lips and turned to Sloane. There was clearly some suspicion in his look, but he nodded her way in greeting as Randall spoke.

"So, we meet again," he addressed Sloane, planting a loud kiss on her cheek that surprised his friends.

"We just had a business lunch at Sixteen," Ethan explained, blissfully unaware of the tensions swirling around him. Tyler was looking at Regan as if he could eat her, and Sloane felt her jealously vanish.

I wonder when they fell in love. I wonder if they even know that's what they're feeling. What a merger that will make! It will be interesting to see if Wyatt supports the match, though. He knows Tyler's nasty little secrets after all. He may think Regan is too good for Tyler, and maybe she is.

"Sloane, you're looking well," Tyler finally conceded after seeing how chummy she was with Regan. "How's business?" Sloane couldn't tell if the question was genuine or malicious, so she gave Tyler the benefit of the doubt.

"It's been rocky, of course, but Regan and Ethan have just agreed to help me locate some smaller offices, which will help. And we still have a few loyal customers with iron-clad contracts."

"It will turn around," Tyler offered, "but if you need any legal help, you know you can always call."

"Thanks, Ty, I appreciate that." Sloane knew she had just turned a big corner. An offer of help from Tyler Winthrop meant she was moving back into the inner -circle. Suddenly, things felt promising. Sloane now believed she had support where none had existed for months and the belief allowed her to be more forthright than usual.

"It will take a lot more than a talented lawyer at this point. Our reputation is in the ditch; we are hemorrhaging clients and cash. I'll try downsizing but, I suspect I will have to do an orderly shutdown of the business to salvage enough for my mother to live on. Then I'll take a marketing job anywhere I can and start over."

"Sloane, I really didn't know things were that bad," Tyler responded. They all recognized that the remark was polite if disingenuous.

"You know, I could help." All eyes shifted to Randall's tall, imposing figure at his statement. "I am the one person here who can really make a difference to you right now. I might still get you investors, financing and working capital. If you want it."

The shock on everyone's faces told the complete story. No one believed that Huyler Industries was worth investing in any longer. This group especially knew that Randall's investment business was ultra-conservative and cautious. A business such as HI would be low on their list for consideration.

Sloane had a moment of elation before her normal cynicism came to the fore, along with her famous sharp tongue.

"Not funny, Randall. There is not a chance in hell that Parker, Parker, Harrison and Paine would invest in my dying business and it is unkind of you to tease me that way. I thought you were better than that." If words could cut, Sloane's would have left Randall in shreds. The venom in her voice was almost tangible.

Placing his arm through Sloane's, Randall ignored her anger and replied, "I am dead serious, Sloane. Let's go grab a drink and discuss it." He moved as if to walk away with her, regardless of her desires.

"It's 2:30 in the afternoon Randall. I have to get back to work, and I suspect you do, too." She was surreptitiously pulling against his arm, but Randall held fast.

"This is work, Sloane. And I would think you would be very interested in what I have to say." He raised a quizzical brow and gave her an expectant look, his square jaw set and uncompromising.

"I think you should hear him out," Regan chimed in. "If PPHP can get you funding, you certainly have the smarts to turn things around."

Ethan seconded the words of his sister while Tyler gave Randall a strange, confused look. Some secret message moved between the two. After a hesitation, Tyler added his agreement.

"What have you got to lose, Sloane? I think you should see what Randall can structure for you."

A rare, bewildered look on Sloane's face gave way to resignation.

"Okay, one drink," she conceded to Randall. "I absolutely have to be back in the office in an hour or two."

"No, you don't and we both know it," Randall's low timbre whispered in Sloane's ear so that only she could hear. She could not control her small shiver of response at his warm breath along her neck, and Randall took advantage of the movement by grabbing her coat and wrapping it around her shoulders before placing his arm tight around her waist and pulling her against him.

"That is quite a breeze." His nonchalant observation easily masked her response. He glued himself to her from shoulder to thigh, and she was very aware of every inch of his solid frame pinned against her.

Oh God, what did I just agree to? This man is infuriating. How does he keep manipulating the situation like this?

Regan gave Sloane a farewell hug and a few encouraging words before pairing up with Tyler to walk South. Ethan handed her his card before hailing a taxi in the other direction, leaving Sloane standing alone with Randall on the sidewalk.

"You hate that, don't you?" he asked her cryptically.

"Hate what?" She resisted batting her eyelashes as she looked up into his handsome face.

"Don't act coy with me, Sloane Huyler, I am totally on to you. You hate when I gain the upper hand. You hate giving up even a little control."

"What I hate is that you drink like a fish, and in the middle of the afternoon."

"Why should you give a damn how much I drink or when?" Sloane's criticism obviously annoyed Randall.

"I give a damn because after a few drinks, you turn into a lecherous oaf. Sober, you are charming and good company; drunk, you are a moron. I don't enjoy being around you when you behave like a clod."

"Honey," Randall put his face very close to Sloane's, almost spitting the words at her in anger. "You and I both know that right now you are lucky to be around anybody. So, don't put on your high-and-mighty-airs with me. That bird won't fly."

His words stung and Sloane arched away from him as if he had slapped her. Then she took one deep breath and regained the ice-queen cool for which she was famous.

"Mr. Parker," she said in a low, calm voice, "I would rather be alone than be with you. I would rather have my business fail than take money from you. I would rather that you leave my side and my sight at this very moment."

Then, as if they were not exchanging biting, caustic words, she finished politely, "Thank you for your generous offer to go for a drink, but I must decline."

Sloane turned on her heel, throwing her coat over her arm when the breeze caught it. Head high, shoulders back, she bustled away, oblivious of the direction she was taking, anxious to put as much distance as possible between herself and Randall.

How dare he? Could he have insulted me further? And who the hell is he to call me 'honey'? I may be down, but I'm not out. I am not taking charity from that bastard.

He can rot in hell for all I care.

CHAPTER FOUR

"How dare she?" Randall growled to himself, watching Sloane's back as she almost ran off. "Who is Sloane Huyler to walk away after hurling insults at me? Especially when I was trying to help her?"

Randall stood like a statue, all 6"3" of him, dumbfounded. Pedestrians moved around him, jostling him, mumbling apologies. He just stood there, watching Sloane's slim figure swaying slightly as she walked, her coral dress clinging provocatively to her hips and ass, bright and crisp in a sea of dark business suits and blue jeans.

He could not recall anyone ever speaking to him so rudely. Not even his parents when he misbehaved as a child. In thirty-five years, he could not remember anyone treating him with anything but deference.

Except this woman.

No one had ever accused him of being a drunk. Sure, when he was out with the guys, they might suggest he not order another drink. In addition, perhaps—he wasn't admitting this totally—but perhaps there were a few occasions when he woke up after a night out with a raging hangover, a strange woman and a lapsed memory.

But it was nothing he couldn't control.

Sloane had always been a spiteful cat, even when things were going well. When she and her father were on top of the world running Huyler Industries, she had lorded it over everyone. Even when she was happily engaged to Wyatt, she was still calculating. He could only imagine how sharp her claws must be now that she had nothing left to lose and no one to push around.

Still, he had been incredibly generous today, offering to help her out of an ugly jam. No one else was stepping forward, and for good reason. While Sloane was a marketing genius, great at PR and advertising, it was her father who had been providing the industry expertise and serving at the helm of a company with over 1,000 employees. No one believed Sloane could take the reins and succeed against these odds, not now that the corporate reputation was in tatters.

So why did Randall believe she could do it? He couldn't put his finger on it, but he believed in her enough to offer financial backing, and he knew even as he had said the words out loud, that it would be an extremely tough sell to his partners. PPHP was one of the most conservative investment firms in the city of Chicago, protecting a 50-year legacy and a lot of extremely wealthy clients.

So, he had to ask himself now, finally starting to walk back across the river and in the direction of LaSalle Street and his office. What was it about this woman that made him trust in her when no one else would? Did he believe she could make the business succeed, or did he just want to believe because he hoped to see her back on her feet? Why did he tolerate her caustic tongue and haughty ways?

Why did he want her until he ached with it?

It was not just her perfect face. He had been with beautiful women. Her exotic features, slim body and pale, flawless skin were a magnificent combination. Her dark hair fell thick and straight around her head, catching the light. The dark hair and pale skin made her large ice-blue eyes even more arresting. Add her above average height and she was a crowd-stopper.

And damn if she doesn't know it.

Sloane could bat her eyelashes and flirt with the best of them, often doing it right before she stabbed you in the back. She loved getting her way, loved expensive gifts and loads of attention. She adored being at the center of things, wielding her money, influence and power. Randall could feel how much she was missing all of this. And she was missing her father, his business acumen and their easy camaraderie, not to mention the way the man spoiled her rotten. While she put on a brave face and went on with her life, he could see she was vulnerable and hurting.

Therefore, he had offered to help. It was an act of kindness—an act of charity. But he'd been far from charitable, reminding her she was down on her luck, desperate and needed him. Had he feared her rejection? Was that why she had to understand she needed him?

Yep, he had lost his head. But the woman sent his senses into a tailspin.

He loved holding her body tight against his. She was strong and fragile at the same time. She left him feeling powerful, protective, and aroused. Her waist felt tiny under his fingertips and he thought back to the silk of her skin under his fingertips, the strong muscles in her thigh when they had done the tasting together the previous month.

If her skirt had been two inches shorter, he would not have been responsible for his actions. He could have inched his hand just a bit higher and touched her until she was moaning under his skillful fingers. He would have liked to watch her keep her cool with the servers while he was stroking her to orgasm under the tablecloth.

She's right. I am an oaf. Why would I kick her when she was already down? Especially when I really am trying to help her, when I would love to see her succeed. And when I am so drawn to her? Shit. Drawn to her, my ass. I am hot as hell for the woman.

"I will not apologize, not after what she said to me," Randall vowed, people turning to see who he was speaking to. What options did he have? "Come on, Randall. You can fix this." That's it! I will get my assistant, Amy, to schedule a meeting, all business, and take it from there. Sloane might turn her back on me, but no one says no to Amy.

CHAPTER FIVE

"**M**om, I'm home," Sloane called as she entered through the backdoor of her childhood home. She had driven her Mercedes E400 to Glencoe from her condo in the city for the last time. It was a beautiful, sunny Saturday, perfect for a 45-minute drive in the convertible. She'd sold the car, replaced it with a used Honda. But today, she enjoyed the ride, and the knowledge that the visit would delight her lonely mother. Since the guilty plea three months ago, Sloane was not the only one feeling the chilly rejection of friends and colleagues. The reception her mother, Marianne, had received from the garden club was so awful that her mother had not been back again. Her volunteer work had all but disappeared, as had her previously constant invitations for lunch or tennis.

Sloane was not completely sure what her mother did to stay busy during the week, but she knew Saturdays were particularly bad for Marianne. She had learned to fill her weekdays years ago. Her father was often absent for long days—and nights. Weekends had been family time. In the warm months, they would sit on the patio of their lakefront home or play tennis at the club; then in winter, there was skiing out West, or a city escape for the theater, museums and shopping.

The club had dropped them like a hot potato, so there was no more tennis, even if someone had offered to play with them, which they didn't. Of course, with the money all gone, there were no more days spent shopping. Instead, Sloane spent most weekends inviting her mother to come into the city or she made the drive north. They would sit together, watching TV, talking about current events, and avoiding any touchy personal conversations.

Just last year, Marianne had been planning a huge wedding, a society wedding to top all others. She was busy, stressed, and happy. Some nights of the week, her boisterous husband would come home by 7:00 and they would enjoy a cocktail and conversation followed by a lovely, leisurely dinner prepared with the help of a live-in housekeeper. Now she ate alone, usually in front of the TV or while reading a book, missing her husband's stories of his workday and the housekeeper, and pining for her daughter's lost wedding.

"Mom," Sloane called again, moving through the house to the bottom of the impressive staircase dominating the oversized foyer. "Where are you?"

Her mother's large Mercedes SUV was still in the garage, so Sloane knew her mother could not be far from home. Sloane would have to discuss selling it, but not yet. It was unlikely Marianne had gone out with anyone else, because there was no one else, and she was expecting Sloane.

Sloane was halfway up the stairs when she heard the tap-tap of her mother's shoes coming from the family room at the back of the house. She moved in that direction in time to see her mother come through the door from the sunroom. Her mother, still faintly tanned from her trip abroad, appeared willowy, dressed in wool trousers and a silk blouse. Overdressed for many, this was her normal attire for sitting around the house. Marianne's appearance was always impeccable. Anyone seeing the two women together would recognize them as mother and daughter, although—after her brief vacation—Marianne could pass for an older sister.

"Darling, how wonderful to see you," Marianne Huyler moved toward her in a breeze of Chanel No. 5 and clasped her in a warm hug. "I was just sitting in the sunroom and enjoying the beautiful day. Shall we go back in there?"

"Sure, just let me grab a La Croix," Sloane responded. "Can I get you one?"

Her mother nodded and moved back toward the large sunroom where Sloane soon joined her, padding about in bare feet and balancing a small, lacquered tray that held two flavored waters and two crystal glasses filled with ice. A small bowl of sliced apples was also on the tray, along with two embroidered cocktail napkins.

Sloane filled the glasses, handed one to her mother and tucked her feet under her as she sat in an oversized wicker chair. Sipping her La Croix, her eyes hidden behind dark glasses, Sloane answered questions about her week, about work, and about the upcoming benefit. She did all of this without mentioning she was struggling to keep the doors open at work; she was planning to downsize dramatically, or that she had not been chairperson of the benefit committee for over two months.

Instead, she answered with responses like "I ran into Regan Howe recently. She and Ethan were heading to lunch and invited me to join them. They send their love, of course. It is very exciting; they are developing some new properties. Actually, they have offered us an outstanding opportunity if I will move our offices to their current project early. They need some tenants to attract other lessees and I figure we can help them out."

Her mother would nod at intervals, not asking many questions. It was better for them both if they kept these conversations close to the surface. The conversation was flowing nicely, about clothes, flowers, the weather and a bit about HI. It lulled Sloane into thinking it would be simple to pretend everything was fine. That was, until they got to the benefit. Unfortunately, her mother was suddenly full of questions.

"How are plans for the benefit going? I expect my invitation in the next week or two. The event is only two months away, Sloane."

"Great, Mom. Everything is coming along great. The invitations go out soon. We still have time. The event is still three months away, not two."

"Well, two and a half. And the auction and fundraising? How are the contributions coming?" her mother asked.

"Well, we had so many details to handle with the hotel that I jumped over to take care of that and left the fundraising to Allyson Riley. In fact, I did a fabulous tasting. You will like the menu."

"Allyson Riley? You handed fundraising to Allyson Riley? Not likely. Sloane, what is going on? Allyson was in charge of the venue logistics. You were chairing the event. Now you switched?"

"Mother, it is fine, really." Sloane's tone conveyed her reluctance to discuss it further, so her mother changed the topic briefly, thinking she would return to the subject. When Sloane refused to respond with more than a grunt, her mother finally gave up and moved on to other aspects of the event.

"So, I will like the menu? What did you taste and what did you pick? I have been to so many events at the Palmer House over the years. They always do a beautiful job, but I wonder, is there anything there I haven't eaten?"

Sloane laughed at the truth of her mother's statement and described the tasting.

"... And then we got desserts, four of them. I was struggling to swallow one more bite, but Randall downed those, too."

"Randall? Who is Randall?" Her mother's face lit up like a Christmas tree. "Is Randall on the committee?"

"Lord no. I just ran into him at the hotel, and he manipulated his way into the tasting. Now that I think about it, I am not exactly sure how he did that," Sloane mused.

"Randall?" Her mother would not let go. "Would that be Randall Parker? His mother was such a lovely woman. So sad when she passed away."

"Yes, Mother," Sloane was biting back her impatience now that she could see where her mother was going with her questions. "It was Randall Parker. But while he may have lovely parents, Randall is a buffoon."

"A buffoon? What are you talking about? He is a very handsome man, Duke and Northwestern educated, from a fine family and with a substantial fortune of his own. That is certainly no buffoon."

Damn! Did her mother know the resume of every eligible bachelor?

Sloane felt exactly the way she had as a child when her mother scolded or corrected her. Dropping her head and shoulders in defeat, she conceded Randall was everything her mother said he was.

"He is a splendid catch, Sloane. You could do a lot worse." She was like a dog with a bone.

"Drop this Mom. There is nothing going on between Randall and me. If anything, we hate each other. Besides, he is one of Wyatt's best friends."

There, that should shut her up.

"You know, hate is just the flip side of the coin with love. Powerful feelings are powerful feelings." Marianne was more animated than Sloane had seen her in weeks.

Sloane just rolled her eyes. Her mother would not let this go. A withering glance from Sloane would stop most people in their tracks, but she had learned it from her mother, who was using it on her now. She sat silently and let her mother continue.

"Wyatt does not care about you anymore, Sloane. I know that is harsh, but since you never really loved him, I feel I can say it to you. He is married to that jeweler now and he couldn't care less who you date or who you marry."

Marianne hesitated long enough to make sure she had Sloane's attention.

"Now, that said, Randall would be an excellent date for you to invite to the benefit. You must go with someone, Sloane, and he cared enough to do the menu selection with you. Besides, it is a very good cause, and he can afford to write a very large check."

Sloane smiled and hopped out of her chair to give her mother a swift hug. "I cannot argue with that, now can I?"

"You will think about inviting Randall?"

"Yes, Mother. I will think about inviting Randall."

Pulling back from Sloane's embrace and fixing her already perfect hair, Marianne responded in a tough, no-nonsense manner. "Don't think too long, Sloane. I mean it."

Desperate to change the subject before her mother picked up the phone and called Randall herself, Sloane looked around the garden. It was beautiful, sloping down to a steep drop-off that muted the sound of the waves hitting the beach below. Sloane could just see the top of the wooden staircase that she knew would take her to their private slice of sand and the small boathouse empty of the two sailboats that were there in her youth.

"It really is special here, Mom. I am going to miss it."

"Me too, sweetheart. So much. I came here almost thirty-five years ago as a bride, and I haven't left since. I cannot imagine living in a small apartment somewhere." Marianne's wistful voice and faraway look were heartbreaking for Sloane. Sloane had lived in the house for most of her thirty years. She moved to the city after she finished graduate school five years ago, and she still spent most weekends and sometimes weeks at a time in the Glencoe house.

"I never understood why you and Daddy stayed here so long. Six bedrooms and just the three of us never really made sense to me. I know you never planned a big family. Daddy wanted a son though, didn't he?"

"Oh, honey, you were all the son or daughter your father ever wanted. You played sports with him and went into the family business; you watched the Bears and the Cubs together. Really, why would he ever have wanted a boy?"

She had asked her mother this question almost every year of her life, but Sloane knew in her heart, no matter how many reassurances she received, that her father had wanted a boy. Therefore, when her mother had a series of miscarriages before finally deciding not to try anymore, Sloane made a promise to be the son her father always wanted. Even now, she was only keeping the business open because it carried the Huyler name. It was what Sloane believed a son would have done for his father, so she did it for hers.

"Well, I have some great ideas for places to see, either in the city or out here. Just tell me what you want." Putting lots of enthusiasm in her voice, Sloane helped her mother get excited at the prospect of selling the family home and downsizing dramatically. "You could stay in this area near the club and your friends, or come downtown, closer to me. You know I would love that."

"Sloane, stop pretending. There are no more clubs and there are very few friends. I know the same thing is happening to you. I have faced facts. Even when your father is home again, things will never be the same for us. Just find me a comfortable, affordable, two-bedroom condominium in a safe neighborhood. Somewhere I can walk to a grocery or a restaurant, or for a coffee. Somewhere near a decent yoga studio."

Marianne shifted in her seat, facing Sloane. "You know, dear, I would never have spent all that time in France if I had understood how tight the money was," Marianne continued. "It was selfish of me."

"Oh, Mom, how could you know? How could any of us have known?"

"There were clues. I ignored them." Marianne shook the thought from her head and faced Sloane with a tight smile. "Just find me a nice, affordable place."

They discussed a few possibilities and agreed that something in Sloane's Gold Coast neighborhood would be ideal if it the price was right. Sloane informed her mother that Regan would help find a residential realtor to list the house, which would bring a sizable profit even with the mortgages on it.

"I am sure we can find something lovely," she concluded.

"Then let's soak up this delicious sunshine and enjoy our little enclave for a few more minutes, dear." Her mother gave her a conspiratorial smile. "Because we are spending the rest of today cleaning out the attic and the basement. If we are moving, we have serious work to do."

CHAPTER SIX

Friday night at Gibson's Steak House and it was crowded, as usual. The neighborhood bars and restaurants attract a sizeable crowd. Locals knew the area as 'the Viagra triangle' because visiting businesspeople and neighborhood regulars came to meet and hook up at the numerous trendy hotspots. The number of people, the valets and double-parked cars and the confluence of one-way streets made it a crazy spot any night, but especially on those first warm weekends of Spring. Randall walked over from his River North townhouse, enjoying the warm evening and the people watching. He never tired of looking at the gorgeous girls, frequently exchanging a wishful glance with them, occasionally a phone number. His long strides made quick work of the ten blocks to the restaurant, so he was the first one at the bar at the scheduled meeting time.

Ordering an Oban, neat, he carried it himself from the bar to a table nearby where he had a clear view of the doorway. It was only minutes before Alex arrived, prompt as always. Randall watched his good friend move fluidly across the room, like the consummate athlete he was. He joined Randall at the table and exchanged hearty greetings before ordering a light beer from the server.

"Light beer? Really?" Randall ribbed his friend. "What's with that?"

"I just worked out for a couple hours, so I need to ease into the alcohol tonight," Alex explained.

"What the hell? Didn't I see you in the gym this morning?"

"Yeah, but I am training for the Chicago Marathon. You knew that."

"Buddy, the marathon is not until October. You need to lighten up and have some fun."

Randall's words fell on deaf ears, just as he knew they would. Of the four friends, Alexander James Gaines had always been the most intense. He studied harder than the rest of them and went to Stanford on a track scholarship before joining them at Northwestern for an MBA. He knew how to have fun—they would not be friends with him if he didn't—but he always showed a serious side, an underlying logic and focus that the others lacked.

"How many drinks have you had so far?" Alex asked Randall. When Randall indicated he was just starting his first, Alex quickly reassured him. "I will catch up with you in no time."

The beer arrived, and the two men were about to catch up when Tyler and Wyatt arrived. Backslapping and handshaking interrupted only long enough for Wyatt to signal the server to bring them drinks. The four had been coming to Gibson's for drinks and sometimes dinner for years, originally several times a week, now at least monthly. Women from all over the city knew that the four drank here and they came to try their luck with the highly eligible men. The server nodded her understanding, and the men settled onto the high stools.

Tyler Winthrop had been Randall's first friend in the entire world. Even before kindergarten, the two boys discovered they were neigh-bors and formed a lasting bond. They walked to school together, played sports together, chased girls together. Now Tyler was a success-ful attorney. Shocking them all, he had recently jumped ship from one of Chicago's most prestigious corporate firms where he was a named partner to be top dog in the legal department of Wyatt's new tech company. Even Wyatt was surprised when Tyler accepted his offer. Tyler could be tough, in life and in the law, but if you were on the good side of the lanky lawyer, he could make you laugh until it hurt. He had helped Randall out of more jams growing up than Randall could remember, and never asked for anything in return.

The man he entered with, Wyatt Lyons Howe IV, was now a married man, but he still turned the heads of women when he entered a room. When he was a bachelor, they could count him on to attract the prettiest women. They came in droves and it actually worked out for his friends, who always attracted plenty of women on their own, but also had the option of hitting on the women Wyatt rejected.

He was a golden boy, in looks and in life. Raised to run the prestigious Lyons Howe Real Estate conglomerate, he had walked away from all the prestige it represented to start his own company. Now, just over two years later, he was on the cover of "Fast Start" magazine, touted as the new Mark Zuckerberg or Bill Gates. Last summer, he had married the girl of his dreams, a fiery redhead from a small farm town and watched her dreams come true, too. Keeli Larsen Howe was now one of the most successful and recognized jewelry designers in the country.

Looking at him now, an unwelcome tinge of jealousy. overcame Randall. This was not a common feeling,, although it had been a while since the green monster had reared its ugly head. Randall pushed it back into the recesses of his mind.

It was astonishing to Randall as he watched Wyatt now. The man never even looked at another woman. He was oblivious and disinterested, except if it involved helping his friends find true love. He was a convert and now he was trying to find wives for the rest of them.

Randall was still happy playing the field, thank you very much, but he was enjoying watching Tyler squirm week after week under Wyatt's effort to hook him up with his sister, Regan.

They caught up on the last few weeks over the first round of drinks, making comfortable conversation and fighting off any intrusions from overly zealous women. When the server delivered the second round, Wyatt started teasing Tyler about Regan.

"Seen my sister lately? Have you worked up the nerve to ask her out for anything but a business event or fundraiser? I thought you two did well at the last couple of museum galas, and you danced with her a few times at the wedding, but that was ages ago, Ty. Only a few dates in a year and group dates at that? What are you waiting for?"

"Get off my back, Wyatt. I escorted her to several benefits this winter and you know it. Besides, things are different now."

"Different how?" Wyatt persisted.

"Well, two years ago Regan was a vice president at LHRE, which was intimidating enough, but I was a big shot attorney in a big-ass firm. Now she is the damn CEO of one of Chicago's largest companies. She hangs with the Mayor and his buddies. She testifies before Congress on the post-mortgage crisis housing market and is in high demand on the lecture circuit. I work for you, Bud. We just don't travel in the same circles anymore."

"Are you kidding me?" Wyatt almost shouted. "This is my sister we are talking about. She is not some goddess you put up on a pedestal. If I am not mistaken, you have seen her naked."

"You have, Ty. I was there," Randall offered with a laugh.

"I was four or five years old, guys. Regan was in diapers. I don't think that counts," Tyler sputtered in response.

"Yeah, but there are pictures," Alex could not help himself from pointing out the obvious. The three men laughed, but Tyler looked like he could cry.

"Seriously guys, things are just different. She is polite and all. You know, for a while it seemed like she was warming up to me, but now she is cool again. I know when to take a hint."

"I think it might all be in your head, man," Wyatt offered. "Want me to ask her? I am happy to assist. You two are kind of cute together. She could do worse," he taunted his friend. "Besides," Wyatt looked about the table, "you men need wives. It is time for you all to settle down."

Tyler, seeing an opportunity to get out of the hot seat, jumped at Wyatt's remark.

"Speaking of..." Tyler turned a laser-focused eye on Randall, "I forgot to ask before. What was all that crap with Sloane last month at Sixteen?"

"What crap? Is Sloane causing problems?" Wyatt was quick to assume disaster when he heard Sloane's name. He had narrowly escaped a life married to the woman in a forced wedding. She had been using him for the Howe name and all that it conveyed, and that was something Wyatt found difficult to forgive. He was sorry about her family's current state of affairs, but in a reflective moment, he would admit that, in his opinion, they got what they deserved. It was a lucky escape for him, and he knew it.

"Ty and I just ran into her having lunch with Regan and Ethan three or four weeks ago. She was getting help to move offices—downsizing." Randall described the situation nonchalantly, but Tyler was still staring.

"Well, that makes sense, I guess," Alex offered. "But with her marketing acumen, she would be better off jumping ship and closing the doors. She could get a great job with a big ad agency or as a hotshot exec and any company would be thrilled to have her. Away from her father, she might shine."

Tyler was still staring.

"Knock it off, Tyler," Randall finally said. "It was nothing."

"It didn't look like nothing. You were holding her so tight I thought she would snap in two. Then you offered to shore up her business, which we all know is insane. You know you would have to do that from your personal funds, right? PPHP would never go for it. So just spill. What the hell are you doing?"

"Do you have the hots for Sloane?" Wyatt asked, both insightful and incredulous. "I mean, she is gorgeous and sexy, but she is such a bitch. Trust me, I know."

Randall sat mute. What could he say? He never lied to his friends—never. But he had the hots for Sloane, and he didn't want to admit it. Now that he had heard the words out loud, he knew they were true.

"Ah, quite a telling silence," Alex observed. "How long has this been going on?"

"You know, Randall," Wyatt declared, "You have always wanted whatever girl I had." Before Randall could argue, he continued, "First the girl who sat behind me in fourth grade."

"He's right! I remember that girl. She was cute," Tyler chimed in.

"Guys, that was fourth grade, for God's sake," Randall countered.

"Well, what about that girl freshman year, with the long braids?" Wyatt pressed.

"Amanda," Alex provided, and they all agreed.

"And after Amanda, you went after my prom date, too. Remember? There might have been a cheerleader I missed in between, maybe two." Randall was protesting vehemently, but he knew Wyatt was spot on.

"And so we arrive at Sloane. You were always trying to touch her, dance with her at events, sit next to her at dinners. I never really thought about it until right now, but you did, Randall."

"And remember how pissed you were when Wyatt stepped in after your mother died? He cut you off just days before you were about to try for her," Alex continued.

"Really? You never told me that. You said she was fair game."

"C'mon Wyatt, my mom had just died. I had other things on my mind. What was I supposed to say?"

"You know, Randall, you even hit on Keeli that first night you met her. It pissed me off big time when it happened, but then I realized you were pretty drunk, so I just figured you were being your typical drunk asshole."

Randall was stunned. The guys were right about the women, which was staggering by itself. Then, there was the gut-punch of hearing Wyatt call him a 'typical drunk asshole.' It was alarmingly similar reminiscent of Sloane's recent remark.

"Am I an asshole?" Randall asked. He felt vulnerable, exposed as he'd never felt before. He looked from one face to another. These men would tell him the absolute truth, but Randall was afraid to hear it.

"Randall, we are just teasing you. If you are interested in Sloane, knowing her history and the way she can behave, have at it. You know her, so there should be no unwelcome surprises. I wouldn't touch her with a ten-foot pole, if I were you, but if she's what you want—" Wyatt stopped in mid-sentence, as if a light had come on in his head. "Actually, you might be perfect for each other. You may be the one person in the world who won't take shit from her."

"Wyatt's right, Rand. Go for it. You are welcome to her with our blessings." Tyler got a wicked gleam in his eye. "Wyatt will happily be the best man at your wedding."

"Whoa, Ty. Maybe they should date a bit before you marry them off," Alex suggested.

The men were teasing, but Randall had a stunned and serious look on his face that finally registered with them. "You ok?" Alex realized that while the three of them were laughing and joking, Randall had sat looking stricken.

"Seriously, am I an asshole?" Randall asked again.

"No, dude, we love you," Tyler reassured. "Well, unless you get smashed. Then you actually can be an asshole. And being the guy who has to get you home more often than not, I get to say so."

Randall let the information sink in. "So, I drink too much," he stated finally.

"Not most of the time, but sometimes."

"Yeah, occasionally."

"You have been known to, sure."

The three replies came instantly, and for the first time, Randall realized he had a problem.

"You know, Sloane told me the same thing, but I thought she was just being—you know—Sloane. Starting right now, I am going to watch how much I imbibe, and you guys are going to help me. Got it?"

Tyler was about to say something flippant, but the intense look on Randall's face stopped him. The three men looked at each other, not sure how to answer.

"You're my best friends. I can count on your support, right?"

All three nodded their agreement. Randall relaxed finally, smiling and continuing, "besides, if I date Sloane, she will nag me every time I have a drink."

"So, you're going to go for it with her?" Wyatt asked what all three were wondering.

"Well...that is a whole other problem." Randall looked into the three faces of his oldest and closest friends. This was the most vulnerable he had been with them in years, and now, after saying he was a drunk, he was about to admit he was a snob, too.

"She is pretty unwelcome everywhere now. They made her resign as chair for the Children's Hospital benefit. Her business is failing publicly. I have run into her a few times in the last couple months and—unless she was with your sister, Wyatt—she is always alone. I don't think anyone wants to be seen with her. And sometimes she looks like she's about to cry."

"Sloane?" three incredulous voices asked in unison.

"Yeah, Sloane. She isn't the tough broad she used to be. Not sure if that is good or bad, frankly. But I know everyone ostracizes her. I am just not sure how I feel about being connected with her. Her reputation is shot.

"First you dumped her, Wyatt." Wyatt had the grace to look a little embarrassed. It had been a very public breakup. "Then her father went on trial and to prison. The business papers are all about clients leaving HI. I mean, is this a woman it would be good for me to be seen with? There are people who still wonder if she was guilty, too. She is tough as nails to deal with anyway, but with all the extra baggage, she could hurt the sterling PPHP rep we have worked so hard to put out there."

Randall looked around the table, into three thoughtful faces. Each was considering Randall's words and his response to them carefully.

"I think everyone thinks she knew what her father was doing but turned a blind eye. After all, they were so close," Alex finally offered. "So, I have to agree that dating her might hurt you professionally. But PPHP is so reputable, you might not just weather this, you might help give Sloane some cache."

"Alex is right, Randall," Wyatt agreed. "The world knows your firm for its low-risk investing. Your corporate and personal reputations are better than spotless. If people see you with Sloane, they will assume that she must be innocent."

"Hell, who cares?" Tyler surprised them all. "I saw the way you looked at her. She is beautiful, hot and smart and you are interested. I say screw what everyone else thinks. If you want her, Randall, go get her."

CHAPTER SEVEN

"What am I doing here?" Sloane asked herself for the tenth time since leaving home twenty minutes earlier. She was avoiding asking the harder questions, like why her heart was pumping through her chest in anticipation, or why she had skipped the office this morning so that she could spend extra time on her appearance.It had been six weeks since she had said those cutting words to Randall and walked away from him. She had argued with herself to apologize from the moment she uttered the words, but her pride wouldn't let her. She had expected never to see him again, at least not intentionally.

Yet here she was, walking into the University Club for a business lunch with Randall Parker III. At his invitation, no less. Well, to be completely precise, at the invitation of a highly professional assistant named Amy, who had called last week to schedule this meeting. Sloane had considered saying no, but somehow Amy had her agreeing in just minutes.

She had changed clothes at least three times, trying for the right corporate image. She had already worn her go-to coral dress and hated the idea of something black on such a perfect May afternoon. Everything else left to choose from was too severe, too boring, outdated, or just too big.

I really need to stop stressing and start eating again. Maybe after this lunch I will have less to stress about. Please, God, please.

Finally, she settled on her favorite dress from last season—a Max Mara. Sloane knew she looked good in it. The ocean-blue color set her eyes off to perfection and the shirred waist hugged her frame enough to hint at her slim figure, but not so tight as to show her protruding bones. The sleeveless style allowed her to display her perfect pale skin and her toned arms. She added a little light makeup, ran a quick brush through her heavy locks and slid into Jimmy Choo pumps. She had to admit that she looked damn good.

Good, but not so perfect that it appears I tried too hard. Professional, but approachable. Now, behave that way, Sloane. Don't lose your temper and you will do just fine.

Coming in from the bright sunlight, Sloane stood for a moment, removing her oversized sunglasses and allowing her eyes to adjust to the dark, cool, and hushed interior. Even with people coming and going, the exclusive club retained its quiet. Before she could spot him, Randall was by her side, welcoming her politely, if aloofly, and suggesting that they head directly upstairs for lunch.

"I was pleasantly surprised to get your call," Sloane began as they moved toward the ancient elevators, throwing out the first overture as a peace offering.

"I was actually a bit surprised myself," Randall confessed with a shy smile.

"Well, that's honest, at least. Now I know where I stand."

"Do you?" His barely whispered response caused Sloane to look up into Randall's face, really look, for the first time since she had arrived. She felt a shock of electricity move through her, rattling her nerves and heating the blood rocketing through her veins.

"This is a business lunch, right?" she asked, seeing a certain something in his eyes, suddenly on unsure footing.

"Absolutely," Randall replied without hesitation.

Calm down, Sloane. Get it together.

Interrupted by several people from the club, Randall made small talk with other members, always introducing Sloane if she was unknown to them, including her if when people recognized her. He noticed a few raised eyebrows, but no one challenged him on her presence and soon they stuffed themselves like sardines into one of the small elevators for the brief ride up to the Front Grill.

Moving toward a table near the dining-room windows, Randall stopped at practically every table to shake hands and greet people while exchanging promises of calls and meetings. It seemed to Sloane that everyone in the room wanted to talk to him and she said so when as they were seated in a somewhat quiet corner.

"I did not realize what a mover and shaker you are," Sloane observed. "I always assumed your father wielded most of the firm's power. How unfair of me. You are obviously an important person in a room full of important people. I'm impressed."

"You would have been right a few years ago, but my father has taken to spending more time on the slopes and very little in the office. You know he is an avid skier. Once he felt assured that I could manage things, he started disappearing more often. Surprisingly, I seem to have a knack for investing. I haven't ruined the company in his absence."

Sloane instantly got a stricken look on her face and Randall continued quickly, "That was unthinking of me, Sloane. I apologize. It was just a careless remark. Please forgive me."

Randall grasped Sloane's hand as he apologized, obviously concerned that he had hurt her feelings. He had, but Sloane quickly forgot about it, focused entirely on the feel of his large hand wrapped around hers, warm and sure. It was such a small thing, holding her hand, yet Sloane could not remember feeling safer than she did right now. Not since she had been young enough to be held in her father's arms. Her feelings at that moment were anything but daughterly.

She looked down at Randall's hand holding hers and he immediately released her, picking up his menu and taking a sip of water as if he didn't know what to do first.

"So, let's order, you can fill me in on how you are doing, and we can let the crowd thin a bit before we talk shop, alright?"

Sloane nodded. "Sounds like a good plan." The server came quickly to take their drink orders and see if they had questions about the menu.

"Good afternoon, Mr. Parker. May I bring you your usual? Something for the lady?"

"I will have a club soda with lime, Andrew," Randall responded. When Sloane's head popped up in surprise, Randall simply looked at her with a blank face and offered, "Have whatever you like. They have some lovely wines."

"You're not drinking?" Sloane stammered, blushing at the rude remark.

"Not this afternoon, , but feel free if you like."

Everything Sloane considered saying at that moment would have been exceedingly rude, so she just nodded, ordered the same club soda, and went back to her menu. She completelyd missed the cheeky smile that briefly tipped up Randall's lips.

They each ordered the shrimp special and sipped their drinks, struggling for conversation. He asked her about her efforts to find new offices, but nothing was happening yet on that front. She asked him about hockey, but the season was over. He asked about her parents, but things grew awkward again when she began speaking about her mother. After all, Marianne was currently visiting her father for her once-a- month trek to see him in prison. The minimum-security prison was a long trip, she offered as an explanation. It was in Colorado.

"Is he in prison with Rod Blagojevich?" Randall asked, at first joking, then increasingly excited. "Has he met the Governor?"

"You crack me up," Sloane laughed. "In fact, they are in the same prison, but if the ex-governor is sharing any secrets, they are not funneling to me."

That exchange turned out to be the icebreaker they needed. From then on, the conversation flowed easily. They shared their reviews of art shows or movies, plays and concerts. It turned out they enjoyed many of the same shows and music. They discussed a few new restaurants, but Sloane skirted around the fact that she had been nowhere recently. Instead, she raved about the one event she had coming up: a showing of a Shakespearian play in an outdoor theater in a small, charming park in suburban Oak Park. Intrigued, Randall said might look into it too.

"They do two shows a summer. Try to see one or the other," Sloane said with enthusiasm.

"We should plan to do that," Randall responded. The statement unnerved Sloane and from the look on Randall's face, it had caught him by surprise as well.

I am sure it was just a turn of phrase. He wouldn't really be inviting me to join him. It is one thing to invite me to lunch, but an evening of Shakespeare would be too much like a date. Actually, I wonder if he is seeing anyone.

The room had emptied considerably by the time the server cleared their meal and refilled their glasses. It surprised Sloane how quickly the time had passed. She praised the food and the service, politely thanking Randall for lunch.

"It was my pleasure, Sloane. So," Randall began, clearly changing direction. "Let's talk a bit about HI, where you are, what you need and ways that PPHP might assist."

"Where to start..." Sloane began creasing the tablecloth nervously before she stopped herself and placed both hands demurely in her lap. "Things have been rough. At first, we had a mass exodus of both clients and our executive team. That was the hardest. Then things settled down a bit, and we have been limping along ever since."

Randall listened attentively, leaning forward slightly, urging her to continue. "We have about 30 percent of our original client base. Operating income is virtually non-existent, everything we earn goes into keeping us afloat, so of course there are zero profits. I have been able to reduce our expenses by sixty percent, cutting expenditures for marketing, travel, my salary but with revenues so low, we are bleeding badly. Other than that, of course, things are just great," she ended the sad saga with sarcastic bravado.

"That bad? I didn't realize." He wasn't pitying, or solicitous, simply interested. For the first time, Sloane felt completely comfortable discussing her problems.

"If we had stockholders, we would have folded, but we are still a family business. If we didn't have some clients locked into contracts for services, it would be so much worse, Randall. We would have gone under for sure."

"So, what do you hope to achieve? Where do you go from here?"

"Well, I have marketing strategies for repairing our damaged reputation. I feel confident that they would work in the long run, but I am not sure I have enough time. We will lose almost half of our remaining customers this fall when their contracts expire. At the end of the summer, I will have to cut at least 50 percent of the employees. Besides that, I cannot focus on running things and on a strategic marketing campaign like the one we need. I am spread too thin and so is the money."

They discussed merging with another company, but Randall could see that Sloane was reluctant. He floated the idea of bringing in a new CEO, but Sloane balked at that idea as well. After skirting around the issue for another fifteen minutes, Randall finally asked Sloane the real question he had wanted to ask from the beginning.

"Why not just close the doors, Sloane? What are you holding onto at this point?"

"I can't, Randall. I just can't. People are counting on me. My father is counting on me. He will expect to come back to his company. I am the only one who can keep it up and running and waiting for his return. After all, he has been through so much. How can I let him down?"

"Sloane, you need to be more realistic. Your father will be well into his sixties when he returns. The locked-in customers and the fact that your father is absent are all that is keeping the doors open now. If your father returns to running the business, the trust you have with clients goes right out the window. You won't renew existing business and you certainly won't attract new clients."

Sloane knew Randall was right. She had known this was the problem for months, but he was the first person brave enough to just come out and say so.

"Randall, are you telling me that PPHP will invest if I am running things, but not if my father is?"

Randall looked at Sloane with sad eyes. "I am not saying PPHP will invest at all. But I know they won't invest in your father." He watched as Sloane's face fell and her eyes filled with tears. "Jeez, Sloane, I feel like I am kicking a puppy. This is not a simple conversation."

Sloane pushed her shoulders back and sniffed a very unladylike sniffle. "Randall, I am tough, you said so yourself. I need the facts and the odds if I have any chance here, so just lay it out for me. Please."

I hope that sounded believable, cause right now I feel like a kicked puppy. Buck up, Sloane. Do not let this man make you beg. When all else is gone, keep your pride and do not let Daddy down.

"OK your best bet is to close your doors and let me help you structure a severance package to help the employees transition if there is any money. Then between Wyatt, Alex, Tyler, Regan and I, we should be able to help you land a plum executive position somewhere."

"A severance package would make things easier..."

"A good severance package. I work with a great firm that can shop around for a buyer first, spend a few months, and maybe arrange an acquisition before we have to announce anything? That would be a better solution for everyone."

"I would need to discuss it with the remnants of my executive team, of course, and my mother. I need something to be there for her when this is done. And what about my father? He will be so disappointed."

"Sloane, I will help. Anyway I can. But you cannot protect your father. Think of it this way: he didn't protect you."

The words hit Sloane like a shot to the chest, and she visibly folded. He softened the message, but he repeated that this was her father's fault, not hers. The third time he reiterated it, the message finally sank in. Sloane bit back tears. Why had her loving father failed to protect her, her mother, their business? She longed for answers to questions she was afraid to ask. She hadn't spoken to her father since his guilty plea, slowly letting go of her belief in him, in the world as she knew it.

Sloane satd straighter and lifted her eyes to Randall's. Now was not the time for pity. She had to get to work.

"Okay, assume I let the company go. Where do I get operating capital for the months we remain open? I have to fulfill the existing contracts or be in breach. Can you find me a few investors? Maybe there are some investors willing to consider an acquisition so they can make a quick profit, although that is pretty high-risk."

"You think about all of this and let's talk in, say, a week? Does that give you enough time? I can bring in Maria Canovalli, from our acquisitions team. She's excellent and can start making discreet inquiries for a buyer in the meantime."

They left the conversation and the table and agreed to walk down the grand staircase back to the lobby. Once there, Randall offered to walk Sloane to her office, but she declined. Standing on the sidewalk, Sloane didn't know what else to say.

"I'll have my assistant call you to set something up," Randall suggested, taking Sloane's hand lightly in his. "Okay?"

Sloane looked again at her long slim fingers in Randall's large hand and suddenly thought of that car insurance ad. She felt like she was in 'good hands'.

What was it about this man that was so reassuring? And so unnerving.

"Perfect. I will give this a lot of consideration, I promise." Looking up into Randall's face, Sloane was surprised when it descended to hers and Randall gave her a butterfly of a kiss before releasing her mouth and her hand and walking away.

Had he turned around, he would have seen Sloane standing frozen in place. Her fingers were lifted to her mouth, still burning from his soft kiss. Her thoughts were in a jumble as her heart did a major flip-flop.

I have no idea what just happened, but I know this. That man is no buffoon.

CHAPTER EIGHT

It was only three days later when Randall's assistant called Sloane. "Ms. Huyler? This is Amy Rodriguez, Mr. Parker's assistant. I hope I haven't caught you at an inconvenient time?"

"No, this is fine. You want to set up a meeting?"

"Actually no. Would you hold please for Mr. Parker?" Before Sloane could answer, Amy hit the hold button and notified Randall that she had Sloane on the phone. He picked up instantly.

"Sloane? How are you?"

"Good Randall. You?"

"Fine, thanks. Okay, now that we have that over with." Randall laughed.

Down, boy. Relax.

"Are you calling about our next meeting?" Sloane queried. "Because you said you would give me a week. I still need a few more days before I'll be ready to discuss things."

"Well, yes, and no." Randall answered cryptically. The quiet on the line was deafening, but he was struggling to get the words out. "I am calling about our next meeting, but I thought perhaps it could be a bit more casual, like a date, not a meeting."

There, that was not so bad, right?

"I'm not sure I understand, Randall."

Oh damn. Ok, just ask her, dip shit. Man up.

"I am asking you out on a date, Sloane. Not for business. Just for the pleasure of your company. You and me, dinner, a movie maybe?"

"A date? A movie?" Sloane sounded confused, as if Randall were speaking a foreign language.

"Yeah, a date. Why is that so hard for you to grasp?" Randall's annoyance came through loud and clear. "Is it impossible for you to consider a date with me?"

Oh great. She thinks I am a joke. I should never have asked her out. Now she will politely refuse, making me look like a prize idiot.

"Randall, sorry. I wasn't expecting this. When your assistant called, I was in a business mind-set. No offense?"

"No harm, no foul," Randall said, licking his wounds. She still hadn't said yes, and his confidence was waning.

"When?" she asked.

"What?"

"When? When did you have in mind?"

Randall felt like an imbecile. This conversation was not going as planned. He sounded like a pimply high-school freshman asking the homecoming queen for a date. Where was the smooth operator he had evoked when he called? He never had these problems talking to women.

"Saturday night, if that works for you?"

"This Saturday?"

Oh no. She is going to shoot me down. She has called you every name in the book, so what the hell did you expect?

"OK, sure. Saturday is fine."

It took Randall a minute to realize that Sloane had actually accepted his invitation.

"Randall?"

"Perfect. Great," Stop babbling, dummy. "Let's keep it really casual, easy. I can pick you up around six?

"Six? So early?"

"Is that a problem? If that is a problem…"

"No, no, it's fine," Sloane interrupted. "You know where I live, right?"

"Yes, Sloane, I have dropped you off there a few times in my life," Randall r as if she was a child. "See you Saturday at six."

"Thanks Randall."

"No, Sloane, thank you. I am looking forward to it." Randall realized as he hung up the phone that his hands were sweaty and shaking and his heart was pounding.

Uh oh. This woman is becoming way too important. You need to ratchet things back, my man. Ratchet things back.

CHAPTER NINE

The door person at Sloane's condominium buzzed her promptly at 6:00 to inform her that a gentleman was in the lobby. She struggled for a second before announcing that she would be right down. The apartment was spotless, and she could have invited him up, but she was ready to go, so why bother? At least that was what she told herself, avoiding her fear of being alone with Randall, who left her feeling electrified and jittery. Admitting her attraction and deciding she had made the right decision, Sloane picked up her small purse and keys, locked the door and the deadbolt, and pushed the button for the elevator. She checked her appearance in the mirrored doors while waiting for the car. She looked very tall and very thin. So thin that she hoped it was a just distortion in the glass and not the impact of stress. Her hair was lustrous and thick down her back. Her cotton sundress was simple but sophisticated: the halter neckline created the illusion of more cleavage than she had. The shorter length gave her legs that went on forever. The light material was tight around her tiny waist and flared over her hips becomingly. She was wearing comfortable ballet flats and carrying a cardigan in case the air conditioning was too cold. It usually was, especially in movie theaters on these rare hot nights in spring. No one seemed to know how to handle these odd spikes in temperatures.

She emerged into the lobby from the elevator. When he saw her, Randall's face split into a huge grin, his dimples carving deep grooves into his cheeks. His eyes were bright blue under his dark brows and against his faint tan, and he looked like a movie star. Sloane's heart jumped into her throat. His good looks affected her every time she saw him, but it was that grin. He was sincerely happy to see her.

His sunglasses dangled from the neckline of the polo shirt open at Randall's throat. He wore a pair of designer jeans that showed off his muscular thighs and tight butt and well- worn Nikes. Damn, if she thought his suits showed off his body, jeans were even better. It was a toned body made for athletics and sex, Sloane thought, before forcing her eyes back to his face and her thoughts elsewhere.

Randall's square chin was freshly shaven, and his deep brown hair was windblown, falling across his forehead to make him look a little more boyish. His smile was dazzling. Sloane felt her fingers itching to touch him. Thank the lord she hadn't invited him upstairs. They never would have made it out of the apartment.

He crossed the lobby in two strides and gave her a surprising kiss. Surprising because it was unexpected, and because she believed he found it unexpected too, like he surrendered to a sudden need. She felt the kiss sizzle through her entire body, causing it to heat and respond. Sloane leaned into Randall, resting her breasts against his solid muscles and snaking her arms around his waist.

The kiss was quick at first, easy and sweet. But when Randall sensed Sloane's response, he returned his mouth to hers, his lips coaxing and determined. Sloane felt Randall's tongue probe the moist interior of her mouth, his tongue entwined with hers as his breath stole her own. His arms tightened around her, pulling her hard against him so that she felt his powerful body from shoulder to thigh. She felt fragile wrapped in his solid arms and she liked it. She could have stayed there forever, feeling the rush of blood through her veins as heat pooled in her center.

Randall must have felt the same, as he was in no rush to end the kiss, his arms around her, his hands resting lightly on her buttocks. He reluctantly pulled away from her only after they heard voices at the lobby doors.

"Hi," he said shyly. He was adorable. "You look great."

"Hi," she was equally shy. "You look pretty good yourself."

"Ready to go?"

The doorman gave them a leer as he held the door. They laughed about it harmoniously as Randall held the door of his BMW for Sloane to slide in. He placed a quick kiss on her lips, then straightened and closed the door.

I don't know where this came from, but I like it. Oh yeah, I really like it.

Settling his large frame and long legs into the driver's seat, Randall adjusted the rearview mirror imperceptibly and gave her another protracted look, along with a cocky grin.

"I am so glad you said yes." His dimples mesmerized her as his dark eyes lit with merriment.

"Me too. So, you haven't told me where we are going."

"Hope you like sports, cause I have Cubs tickets. Great tickets. Right over the home team dugout. They are playing the Cardinals, so it should be a great game. Arietta is pitching." Randall was into it, and Sloane could tell he was excited to have the tickets and to share the game with her. He sounded very proud of himself until he said anxiously, "You do like baseball, don't you?"

Sloane laughed, toyed with making him squirm, then just blurted out, "I love baseball. How did you know? I'm a die-hard Cubs fan too."

They didn't bother hunting for street parking; it had disappeared hours earlier. Instead, they pulled into a nearby VIP lot, paid the exorbitant fee, and joined the crowds swarming toward the gates. Sloane tied her sweater around the long handles of her bag then moved it cross-body for safety. Randall wrapped a protective arm around her as the crowds grew thicker, but soon they were inside and being shown to outstanding seats, right next to the section for the players' wives.

Randall was joking and chatting with the wives and people all around him, relaxed in a way that Sloane had rarely seen him. Sure, when he was out with the guys or the hockey team, he was like this, but then he got drunk and spoiled it all. She hoped she wouldn't need to drive them home.

"I had no idea you were so social," Sloane observed when they finally took their seats. They had already stopped to purchase hot dogs, peanuts, beer and a program. He was like an overgrown child, enthusiastic and over-stimulated.

"I'm not, but I know most of these people. They are clients or friends of clients. Most of the players are PPHP clients. You'll have time to meet them between innings. That's why we have these great seats. Wait until hockey season. I get killer tickets for hockey."

Randall amazed Sloane. This was not the serious executive she had lunched with days ago, nor the lecherous drunk she had fought off many times when she was with Wyatt. He was just fun, easy-going and excited about the game in a boyish way. He was full of child-like wonder. She liked him this way.

They set up the program so that she could keep score, juggling hotdogs, peanuts and then popcorn. He suggested more food and so they went for a walk to a nearby stand at the top of the fifth inning. They concluded it was a good time for a break. The Cubs were down three runs, so it was hard to watch the Cardinals at bat.

Standing in line waiting for a slice of Giordano's famous stuffed pizza, Randall told Sloane stories of coming to Wrigley Field as a kid. His whole family, including an uncle and a cousin, would often attend a Sunday game. In addition, the four 'Baldwins' had cut school numerous times to watch games. He had her laughing with anecdotes about convincing Alex to cut school.

"He was such a dedicated student," he explained, "that sometimes, instead of us convincing Alex to go to the game, he convinced us to skip the game and attend calculus. We could never figure out how he did that."

Sloane felt young and carefree; she had not laughed this much since her father's arrest. Randall held her hand, smoothed her hair, or gave her a quick peck on the cheek, touching her throughout the night. It felt like the perfect first date.

They ate pepperoni pizza and warm candied cashews, a pretzel and another beer.

"You had me completely fooled," Randall confessed to her at the bottom of the seventh inning. "Based on the way you look, I thought you must not eat, but you can really pack it away. Oh, wait," he stammered, "that didn't come out right. I meant that as a compliment."

"Well, it didn't quite sound like one, but I'll accept it as a compliment all the same. By the way, who said I am done eating?" They both laughed, and then Randall swooped in and kissed her hard, almost bruising her mouth with his enthusiasm. She made a small sound, so he backed away, looked deep into her eyes, and then resumed the kiss more gently.

I could rip his clothes off right here. I never felt like this with Wyatt. This man can kiss! He is unbelievable—strong, sensible, funny and incredibly sexy. He is kind too, and he likes baseball and pizza. And me. And he is not even a little drunk. Holy crap, he might be perfect.

By the top of the ninth, the Cubs were ahead by one and the fans were going wild. The Cubs had brought in relief pitcher Adam Warren. It was three up, three down, and the crowds cheered. Randall hugged Sloane, lifting her off her feet and twirling her carefully in the tight space. Then he kissed her and kissed her again. She kissed him back with enthusiasm.

"Let's get out of here." Randall was already pulling her through the crowds, hurrying toward the exits. In just a few minutes, they were back in the car, out of the parking lot, and surrounded by heavy traffic.

As the car inched forward, they rehashed highlights of the game. Randall fluctuated between stroking her arm and her leg, touching her incessantly, sneaking his hand higher up her thigh a bit at a time. Sloane rested her hand on his heavily muscled thigh, resisting the urge to move it higher too.

Traffic finally opened up, and Randall looked at the clock. It was exactly 10:00.

"I was going to suggest someplace quiet for a drink or maybe some music," he said slowly, drawing out every word. "But I don't want a drink, Sloane. I just want you." He looked over at her, then back at the traffic. She was quiet, knowing he could not gauge her reaction in the shadowed darkness of the BMW.

The silence dragged a minute or more until Sloane finally responded in a throaty voice, "I don't want a drink either, Randall. What if we just go to my place?"

Randall was so still that Sloane wondered if her acquiescence had registered. He drove quietly. She was about to repeat herself when he stopped at a red light. Randall reached across the center console and pulled Sloane toward him, one arm wrapping around her back to hold her in the awkward pose while his tongue plundered her mouth and his teeth nipped at her bottom lip. The kiss lasted until the car behind them started honking and Randall realized the light was green.

Sloane slid back into her seat. He'd bruised her mouth and chafed her chin slightly with his five -o'clock shadow. She felt thoroughly kissed. She felt sensual, heavy-limbed and womanly. Randall's hand was stroking along her thigh where her dress had ridden up. Neither of them attempted to pull it back down. Instead, Randall's hand just followed it up her leg, his hand big enough to cover most of her thigh, his little finger precariously close to the edge of her panties, sliding along her thigh in a tantalizing motion.

Sloane stroked Randall's arm, feeling the muscles move with his slight movements, admiring his powerful forearm. She rubbed up his arm, then returned to his thigh, stroking lightly, feeling the solid muscles bunch and relax as he applied pressure to the gas pedal.

It was intoxicating, in this dark space alone with this hunk of a man. She longed for his finger to stray higher. Her body grew sultry and damp with desire. She wanted to ask Randall to pull over so she could climb into his lap. Sloane was desperate to feel skin against skin, to feel the weight of this enormous man ram her into a mattress or the seat of the car, or the nearest patch of grass, to ride him while looking at his handsome face. Overcome with longing, her skin was hot, her panties wet.

Luckily, they found a parking space near her building without having to circle the block. Walking toward her building arm in arm, Randall stroked her bare shoulders and back. She slid her hand up the back of his un-tucked shirt. They stopped every few steps to kiss, each kiss thick with promise, lasting longer and demanding more. They were too hungry for each other to wait.

Randall ran his hands over the wide expanse of skin left bare by her halter, and she thought she would melt from the feel of his hands on her. He played with the tie, holding the dress up.

"You wouldn't dare," she hissed at him.

"Don't test me," he responded, tugging playfully, but leaving everything intact. "I would take you against the side of this building right now if I wasn't afraid of getting arrested."

"What's a little jail time between friends? After all, it runs in the family," she quipped, astonishing them both when she joked about her father's incarceration.

"I mean it, Sloane," he growled. "Do not tempt me further."

"I mean it too, Randall."

He spun her around and sandwiched her between his body and the rough brick wall of the nearest building, rocking his body hard against hers, his erection large and insistent against her belly. Sloane wrapped one leg around his lower legs, trying to pull him even tighter to her, crushing her breasts into his massive chest. She pushed at him, dropped her leg and throwing all caution to the wind, she groped for the zipper on his pants. He looked astonished, but he didn't stop her, even helping a bit when she fumbled with his belt buckle.

While unfastening Randall's pants, Sloane felt a cool breeze on her legs and realized that the hem of her dress was high on her hip. He had one hand cupping the spot where the back of her thigh curved into her ass, pulling her to him. While he was kissing her until she thought she would gasp for breath, Randall was reaching to divest her of her panties.

Sloane heard footsteps and froze in place.

What the hell were they doing? They were just yards from her condo. In less than five minutes, they would be safely inside.

She pushed him away, pulled her dress down and made sure she had not progressed too far with his trousers. She placed a shaking hand in his and began leading an unresisting Randall toward the lobby of her building. "Two minutes," she whispered to him.

"Not one second more," he retorted, giving her a threatening look that she knew brooked no argument. Reassured that they were decent enough, they left the darkness of the street and stepped into the pool of bright lights under the portico of Sloane's building.

"Randall? Is that you?" The couple turned in surprise toward the sound of a booming male voice. "Randall, it's John Berensen. What are you doing in this part of town?"

Sloane's heart sank in her chest. She felt like she was just doused with ice water. John Berensen was the attorney who had prosecuted her father. From his greeting, Sloane deduced he was also Randall's friend.

"John," Randall released Sloane to give the small, balding man a hearty handshake. "Nice to see you."

"What are you doing over here?" John asked again. Then the open smile on his face faded. He had noticed Sloane. "Oh, hello Sloane." He couldn't have been less enthusiastic if he tried. "I didn't realize you two were acquainted." The attorney didn't bother to hide his disdain, almost completely turning away from Sloane, effectively cutting her off from any further conversation.

"How's your dad doing? Chasing a mountain somewhere?"

"Well, not so much in summer, but he does still ski every chance he gets."

"I would love a chance to catch up with him. Does he know how you are spending your time, and with whom, Randall? He might have something to say about it, you know. This could cause irreparable damage to the firm. You need to think about that. This won't do, my boy. Mark my words."

"I think my father trusts me to choose my own friends," Randall retorted, but he had waited a heartbeat too long to defend himself and John was saying goodnight, giving Sloane one last look as if she was a bug squashed under his shoe.

He walked off into the darkness, leaving Randall and Sloane standing there speechless and uncomfortable.

"Sorry about that," he said.

"Not your fault," she replied graciously, but the hurt was clear in her voice. "That was certainly awkward."

Randall stood for a moment in silence. Sloane watched the emotions play across his face. She understood immediately—after all these months of experience—the exact moment he decided she was more trouble than he was willing to tackle. Wrapping her arms tightly around herself to stave off the stab of pain, she started saying an awkward goodnight.

"Maybe I should just get going," Randall announced at the same moment, his voice a cross between reluctant and resigned.

"Yeah, maybe that would be best. Thanks for the ballgame; I had a great time."

Sloane didn't wait to see if Randall would kiss her goodnight. She spun on her heel and headed into the lobby, moving so quickly that she yanked the door open before the doorman could reach it.

She got into the elevator cursing that slimy toad, John Berensen. Then she cursed Randall for his cowardice, giving up without a fight, and leaving her uncertain of him and sexually frustrated.

She unlocked the door, flipped on the lights, and headed straight for an ice-cold shower.

CHAPTER TEN

Sloane spent all day Sunday in her pajamas berating herself, annoyed with John Berensen for showing up when he did. The man had spoiled what promised to be a remarkable and very satisfying end to her fun night. She was on a total high with Randall before John showed up and ruined it. It might have been awkward to run into anyone, but no one could have been worse than John. The disappointment she felt with Randall was like a toothache - raw, painful and insistent. She had allowed herself to believe in Randall, in the possibilities between them. She could no longer deny her attraction, and it seemed he was feeling the same. Then she remembered this was Randall she was talking about. Randall.

So, she added herself to the list of people she wanted to strangle.

What had she been thinking when she'd accepted a date with Randall Parker? She knew she was negotiating a sensitive business transaction with him, so why on earth would she have jeopardized everything for a night out?

She had been an idiot to risk everything for some fun—especially involving Randall. It was not like he would commit to her, defend and protect her. After all, he watched his best friend dump her. He knew she was lonely and desperate. She would be an easy conquest—and she had been. He was a player, like Wyatt, like all four men had been since their college days.

She had risked everything for that? If she was lucky, she could salvage the business deal; otherwise, she would lose everything. She had laid out scenario after scenario of how things might proceed from here, none of them good. Perhaps he would pretend nothing happened and conduct business as usual. He might do that, but she had been uncharacteristically vulnerable with him, so she was unsure she could pretend that nothing had happened.

Alternately, he could dredge up the completely embarrassing episode on the street, expressing some feeble apology. Or worse, no apology. She couldn't figure out a way for Randall to finesse that one.

Both required her to see him, and Sloane was concerned about that. She couldn't be sure she could keep her hands off him.

He could drop her as a potential client, causing her to die of shame and lose the business opportunity all in one fell swoop. That was the worst possibility because then she had to live not only with humiliation but also with the guilt of costing hundreds of people their livelihood. How could she ever survive that? How could she explain it to her father?

The last scenario was the one for which she hoped, where Randall just handed her business off to an associate at his firm. They would not have to deal directly with each other again and her business opportunities would remain intact.

And if enough time passes before until I am face to face with him again, hopefully, I could keep my hands off him.

She couldn't envision a circumstance where he admitted he had screwed up, then stood up to Sloane's critics and forged a strong, unshakable team with her. It was too much to hope for. It was the one scenario where she was allowed to indulge her fantasies involving Randall.

She seesawed back and forth, livid with herself or incensed with Randall. What kind of man was he, deserting her at the first sign of scandal? He knew the score when he invited her out. He knew about her father and the way society had turned their backs on her entire family. Why ask her out if he couldn't take the heat? At least he could have tried to stand by her to see if they could make it. They were really connecting, laughing, sharing, communicating and the promise of the sex…

Sloane was so confused when she remembered the sex, or the almost sex. They were mauling each other out on the street, in plain sight, like randy teens. She couldn't recollect it without getting aroused all over again. She may have been stupid to trust him, but she was smart to let him touch her. The man knew what he was doing in that department. All that experience with all those women had certainly paid off.

Half of Sloane wished nothing happened. The other half was thoroughly disappointed that they did not finish what they started. She had tossed and turned all night, unsure if it was her hungry body or her angry mind keeping her awake.

Sloane took control of situations. Things happened because she made them happen. She had racked her brain most of the day trying to come up with a way to take command of this situation rather than waiting for Randall's next move. She was a confident chess player, able to see several moves ahead. Not today. Thwarted desire, serious confusion and total exhaustion muddled her brain. Sloane was over-tired, frustrated, angry and stumped about how to deal with all these emotions.

So far, she had found only one solution. She would stay in her pajamas, eat junk food and never leave her apartment again. Thank God the grocery store delivered. Hallmark Channel movies and TCM oldies would be good for a cathartic cry while reassuring her belief in happy endings—even if they only happened on TV. She would let someone else figure out the tough stuff.

She had no friends left, no one to miss her. Sure, her mother would notice if she went into hibernation, but really, who else would care? She still had a responsibility to the workers at HI, but she was botching the job of running the company. The employees would be better off with someone else at the helm.

Sloane wondered what that said about her life. What had she done with thirty years if she had no one who would care if she disappeared? Had she really been that selfish, that focused, and that useless?

Oh, just say it Sloane, have I really been that bitchy?

It was painful to take stock, so Sloane avoided it with TV and a short nap. Around 5:00, she picked her head up off the sofa and poked her nose through the curtains. It must be a nice day because people were walking across the street to a small park. She saw families pushing strollers and couples hand-in-hand and admitted to herself, finally, that she was lonely. She really should take the time to get outside. At least outside, people would surround her.

She missed being part of something bigger, and not just work, but also the hospital benefit, the country club, friendships. She missed being in a couple too, more than she had acknowledged until right now.

Sloane padded to the kitchen in her bare feet and poured herself a glass of Chardonnay. She took a sip, put both the glass and the bottle in the refrigerator, and moved swiftly down the hall to her bedroom. Throwing on a pair of yoga pants, a t-shirt and her running shoes, she pulled her hair up in a messy ponytail and went to brush her teeth.

Did I really wait until now to brush my teeth? Gross!

Grabbing her keys from the front table, she let the door slam behind her, not bothering with all the locks, then went back to grab ear buds and her iPhone.

Tunes are what I need. Fresh air and tunes will clear my head. This is the start of a plan. Sloane Huyler, you are coming up with a plan. You have wallowed long enough.

After about a mile at a fast pace, Sloane felt her head clear. She surveyed her situation and began making mental plans for the rest of the night and for the future. It included small things like cleaning the junk food wrappers off the cocktail table, and big things like ways to change her situation with Randall. She felt back in control as she mentally reviewed her list.

First, a quick clean- up of the living room followed by a much-needed shower. Second, she would take stock of her skills and match them with the jobs in which she was interested. Salary would be a big motivator. Third, she would analyze the costs for her parents to retire comfortably and review their assets. Finally, she would draft a plan to sell first, but if that failed, create a liquidation plan for HI, including a severance package for as many employees as possible, including her.

Sloane had decided running eleven-minute miles and sweating like a pig. She would liquidate Huyler Industries and move on. She realized as her head cleared that she was trying to save a company for her father, a company he had put at risk, not her. Wasn't it his choices and decisions that were closing HI, not hers? If he was innocent, he should have fought to clear his name. And if he was guilty...she couldn't bear to consider that possibility. Either way, it was time to move on and she was ready to tell that to PPHP - to Randall.

This transition was terrifying to Sloane. What if she couldn't find another job? What if no one wanted to hire her or pay her what she was worth? She would take her chances, Sloane decided, because this option afforded Sloane the chance to start over, to start fresh and build a life. She had just determined that a more balanced life, with people who cared, was what she needed most.

She needed to send a professional, appropriate email to Randall, or his designate, outlining her plans and the associated costs. He could take it from there, hopefully helping find someone to acquire HI or suggest an appropriate alternative. She would have no reason to talk to him.

Yep, email. For the time being, that was the best answer for avoiding Randall while still handling her current financial situation.

First things first. After she did all of that, she could reevaluate her life, relationships, and the potential for happiness. Having an action plan helped Sloane feel back in charge, back where she needed to be.

The sun had almost set, and the streetlights were coming on when Sloane let herself back into her apartment, ready to work on her plan. She was dripping in sweat and her Fitbit indicated she had completed a seven-mile loop. She wandered into the living room and dropped onto the huge green sofa, exhausted, to remove her shoes.

I'll just sit here a minute and catch my breath, Sloane told herself, ready to tackle her big plans. She felt a thousand times better.

She stretched out without removing her shoes and was asleep in seconds.

CHAPTER ELEVEN

Almost three weeks had passed since Randall had taken Sloane to the Cubs game. He couldn't stop thinking about her. He picked up the phone almost daily, only to put it down again. What could he say? When he had needed to 'man-up', he had walked away. When she had needed someone to stand with her against the world, he had sided with the world. Randall wracked his brain for a way to reconnect, but each idea seemed lamer than its predecessor. He wanted to apologize, promise he would be there for her the next time, but words were easy and he had a lousy track record. Why would she ever believe him?

He thought of sending a note. Lame. Setting up a business meeting. Lame. Sending a gift or flowers. It worked for Wyatt when he screwed up with Keeli, but Sloane was no Keeli. Perhaps if he sent her a yacht or two. Otherwise, lame.

To make matters worse, in typical Sloane fashion, she had taken the bull by the horns and sent him an email. A cold, professional email with spreadsheets attached and a request that he help her with a severance package for her employees or a buy-out. She notified him she had decided that neither she nor her father would remain at HI. This should facilitate a liquidation or acquisition. She had ended her frosty note by suggesting, "it might be preferable if you delegate further responsibility for these transactions to one of your many capable colleagues. I will look forward to hearing from whomever you select."

This woman knew how to twist a man in knots.

Couldn't she put herself in his shoes? PPHP was about as conservative as a company could be. Squeaky clean, they were the antithesis of the greedy Wall Street traders, except they handled rich clients. Very rich, very private clients. These were people who became clients because they were affluent. Then PPHP made them even wealthier. And they did it all discreetly. Very discreetly.

Huyler Industries and Sloane Huyler personally no longer fit the description of the ideal PPHP client. Not even close. In fact, HI was the client that made more desirable clients run for the nearest exit. Randall had known his offer to assist Sloane would have to come from him personally, not from the company. PPHP might assist an investment banking firm complete a merger or acquisition; there was little risk in putting together a deal and there was potential for someone to earn substantial fees. However, financing a loan or finding investors from the PPHP clientele would not happen. The risk of default was just too high. Any idiot could tell you not to jump on board a sinking ship unless that big Coast Guard boat is approaching fast.

So that night, when John Berensen had hinted that being with Sloane was bad for business, he was not far off the mark. He may have said it because he was a mean, spiteful bastard—which he most assuredly was — but he was still right. Randall's father would not approve of him working with Sloane, let alone dating her.

How ironic that only eighteen months ago, she was the best catch in the city. Beautiful, well-bred and well educated, Sloane had a knack for marketing and advertising that everyone believed was driving up the revenues of HI and their clients. No one suspected her father was doing shady international deals back then. The Huyler name was golden, their reputation spotless. She was the belle of every ball, engaged to Wyatt, with an incredible future ahead of her.

Randall suddenly realized that he was on that elite list, too. He was also a catch. If he had gotten serious with Sloane, she would have pulled off the coup of the century, breaking off with one bachelor prize only to land another.

Instead, Randall had botched his one date with the beauty and ended up in a cold shower. It was certainly not as satisfying as sinking into her willing body and waking up beside her. He could still recall the softness of her lips against his and the warm sweetness of her mouth. He could almost feel that skin, taut over muscle and bone, smooth as silk under his fingertips. She felt like she would break within his arms, so fragile. Until she responded to his advances.

Wow, could she respond! Sloane was a friggin' hellcat.

Lithe and pliable. Sloane had wrapped herself around his body until they were molded together. She was so responsive, so sensual, and, when he thought it was impossible, she had turned him on even more. She was adventurous; he still wondered what might have happened there on the sidewalk. Her hand felt cool and delicate when it had fumbled with his zipper. Just thinking about finishing what they started that night brought back such vivid sensations that he would sit in the office, needing to do multiplication tables to get his erection to subside.

She was funny, sweet and good company, too. They had enjoyed the ballgame together. She knew baseball, and how to snarf down stadium food. Sloane managed to be one of the boys while still being all woman. She was perfect for him if he just overlooked her reputation.

Holy shit. She really is perfect for me. Why hadn't I realized it sooner?

This difficult, spoiled brat with a father in federal prison was everything he had been looking for. Oh, he did not even know he was looking, but he was. He had been waiting, jumping from woman to woman, never settling down, having fun and sowing his wild oats, waiting for a woman to come along to tame him. Never in his wildest dreams would he have believed that Sloane was that woman.

Or perhaps he had been biding his time, waiting for Sloane all along.

There had been that moment when Sloane was in grad school and he was starting out as a mentor. Like all the other guys, her beauty had attracted him, but he had seen a vulnerability and sweetness behind her tough exterior that touched him and made him note her, made him want to understand her, and made him desire her.

His attendance was sporadic for a while early on and she remarked on it. When he explained, just briefly, about his mother being ill, Sloane had been so quick to offer her sympathy and her help. She researched hepatitis, sharing clipped articles, links to research studies, alternative medicines, and support groups. She had cared deeply, and it had made him care about her in return.

In that moment, Wyatt had swooped in to claim her. She had jumped at the opportunity to date his friend, so, of course, Randall had stepped aside without a word. He had looked on from the sidelines, feeling his loss. He observed her as her family pointed out that she had snagged the richest prize in Chicago and Sloane replaced that softness with greed and haughty condescension and eventually cold blackmail. Randall had completely forgotten that she could be charitable, kind, even sweet.

He remembered now.

Sitting behind his staid desk, in his staid office in the staid financial district, Randall realized that this woman could be all business and still be all pleasure. Regan might have those qualities too, but she had never aroused in him anything but brotherly affection. Besides, Tyler would kill him in an instant if he looked twice at Regan.

But Sloane was another story. She aroused anything but brotherly affection. Instead, she turned his brain to mush with longing; he hungered for her until he ached. Sloane could be carefree and fun in the right setting, like at the baseball game, or when she joined the team for a beer after they played hockey. She had a brilliant business mind. She got along with his friends—well, most of them—and they could patch the tension with Wyatt and Keeli up with a little help. Added bonus? Sophisticated, elegant and poised, she would be the perfect hostess or plus one at any event.

The world might not accept Sloane Huyler, but he did. If only she could feel good about herself again. He hated seeing her so miserable, such an outcast in a world that was crucial to her esteem.

That's it! That's it. Why didn't I think of it sooner? All you have to do is fix her reputation, Dip Wad. You can make this happen and go home with the girl.

Randall broke into a lazy smile, his confidence restored. Reaching for the phone, he took the first step toward setting his foolproof plan in motion.

CHAPTER TWELVE

"**I** was surprised to get a lunch invitation from you," Regan admitted to Randall, cradling the phone against her shoulder. She had not seen him in over almost two months, and even then, it happened because she had run into him on the street with Tyler. She was not conducting any business with him or his firm and they rarely socialized except as part of a group. They usually interacted when there was a major event. "But it would be delightful to get together. My assistant said you suggested next Tuesday, but I am not available. How about Monday instead?"

"Monday would be great, Regan. You should know that I am plotting something. I am inviting Tyler to join us and..."

"What are you doing, Randall?" Regan interrupted defensively. "I need you to butt out of my business. Thank you very much."

"It is not about you, Ree," Randall jumped in quickly, before Regan got even more bristly. "I need you to invite Sloane. We had a minor mishap."

Did I really just call that fiasco a minor mishap?

"I want to make a grand gesture to patch things up and you and Tyler are going to be part of the plan. Please, Ree, I need your help to pull this off."

"Are you going to share the plan?" Regan sounded intrigued. "I'm more than a little suspicious when you have a scheme, Randall. You have drawn me into too many scrapes, ending in my being grounded too many times over the years. I know not to jump in blindly."

"Good news, then. You are too old to be grounded anymore. I promise to share before Monday, but let me get Tyler on board first, and you get Sloane to accept lunch. By the way, if she knows I will be there, she will turn you down flat, so you need to make her think she is just meeting you. Okay?"

"Okay," Regan dragged out the word reluctantly. "But no promises on all this until I know more."

"That's fair," Randall conceded. "Talk to you soon." He disconnected the call, feeling better than he had in days.

One down. One to go.

Randall tapped the intercom button on his phone, requesting that Amy get Tyler on the line. Looking out the window with a satisfied grin on his face, he sat back to wait. In only moments, the intercom buzzed.

"Tyler, old buddy, old friend," Randall began jovially.

"What do you need now, Rand?"

"Who says I need anything?"

"Oh please, you can't fool anyone with that tone of voice. Who is she, and what kind of trouble are you in?"

"That is not fair," Randall fired back before hesitating a long moment. "But since you asked, I need a favor with Sloane. But there is something in it for you, too."

"Randall, Sloane is a bitch. Right now, she is persona non grata too. She is a bitch in a ditch. Hah, good one!"

"Ty, seriously, you don't give the woman the credit she deserves. She wasn't fair to Wyatt, I concede, but she is more than one mistake, and I think she and I could have something special. I want to try. Problem is that right now she won't speak to me. But I have a plan."

"It's been almost a month since your last fiasco with her, Randall. If you haven't been able to weasel back into her good graces by now, you are doomed. Either she never speaks to you again or she lets you back into her life but lords it over you—forever. You will be her lap dog, Rand. Do you want that?"

"Let me worry about how controlling she is, Ty. She's got little to control in her life at the moment. Think for at least a minute, how you would behave in her position. I don't think you'd shine to well, Buddy. None of us would. You just help me get her back, please."

"If you are sure this is what you want, then count me in. What do you need?"

"Lunch Monday with you and Regan. Regan will invite Sloane."

"Are you sure this is about Sloane? Are you matchmaking here?"

"You and Regan will have to figure that one out on your own. I have enough problems without wading into your mess. But I figured you would invite her to the Children's Hospital benefit, right?"

"Randall, the benefit is less than two weeks away. I already asked her."

"Right. And I am guessing that Sloane still can't find a date."

"You are a genius, Rand. You ask her to the event, and you become her white knight. It is a great plan, but why do you need me?"

"I need you and Regan so I can get in front of her. Then I need you to discuss going to the benefit together so that I can bring it up with Sloane. I can't just text her for a date."

"So, lunch? I get it, she won't accept your lunch invite, but she will accept Regan's."

"Exactly."

"OK, Monday? I'm in. But I would think about this long and hard, buddy. You should be very careful what you wish for."

CHAPTER THIRTEEN

"Lunch? Monday? That sounds great, Regan. Is it a special occasion?""Nothing special. I haven't seen you in a while. I have an opening in my calendar, so I thought we could catch up on how things are going. Tyler will join us if that is ok? I know you will need a lawyer at some point, and although he is not available, he might know someone. Anyway, how does noon sound?"

"Sure, noon on Monday is fine."

Like I have anywhere else to be. The invite delighted Sloane. Her work had become dull and depressing. She spent too much time working on exit strategies and sulking. Lunch with Regan was always fun, it would be a welcome break, and lunch invitations were almost non-existeant these days. In fact,that Regan and her sister Missy were the only friends she could name, still willing to be seen with her.

"Where shall I meet you?"

"I will come from the office; I imagine Tyler will, too. Can we meet in the loop? I could get us a table at the Union League Club, or we could just pick a quiet restaurant. How about Atwood Grill? I haven't been there in ages, but the food is always good, and the location is perfect for all of us. Will that work for you?"

"Atwood at noon, Regan. Thank you for inviting me. I am looking forward to it."

Since they had last lunched, Sloane had been meeting with Ethan; initially looking at smaller spaces for HI, more recently he was aiding her in the selection of a single office for her alone. He introduced her to Andi Richland, a terrific real estate agent for the Chicago residential market, who was helping her find a new place for her mother. Andi put her in touch with Suzanne Graber, a lovely woman who was from the Glencoe area. She was working with Sloane and Marianne to prep and list the Glencoe house.

Sloane couldn't think of a single reason Regan would invite her to be the third wheel for a lunch with Tyler, but Sloane would benefit from being seen with the CEO of Lyons Howe Real Estate, so she would happily meet Regan for lunch. Besides, she sincerely liked Regan and missed her company. Sloane was sure that from that respect, lunch would be lovely, however, her curiosity was peaked. Sloane hated not knowing what was going on and she sensed Regan might be plotting something. Too bad she had absolutely no one she could call to ask. Speculating would get her nowhere. She was at a dead-end.

Settling back to work, Sloane returned the earlier phone message she had received from an assistant she was unacquainted with at the investment banking firm Randall had recommended.

"Good morning, Paula Kline speaking," the woman answered, sounding crisp and efficient.

"This is Sloane Huyler, returning your call."

"Yes, Ms. Huyler, thank you for getting back to me. I am sorry to bother you, but we need documents from you. Maria Canovalli wanted me to call and let you know to watch for an email list containing specifically what she may need for due diligence. It is a rather expansive list, so you will want to collect these immediately, if possible."

"Great. Thank you for the heads up, Paula. I will take care of it."

"Thank you, Ms. Huyler. Please call our office if you have questions."

When that call ended, Sloane immediately opened her email to find the request for documents already waiting. The list was extensive, but many of the documents would be easy to retrieve from their offices or her father's lawyers. She would go to work on it this week.

With the list carefully stored in her email, and a hard copy printing, Sloane phoned her mother to ask about her father's papers.

"What is this about, Sloane? You don't sound like yourself, dear. You know more about your father's paperwork than I ever will."

"I am fine, Mom, but I need to provide documents for the investment group. It's an awful lot of records and I am not sure why they want them. This seems unnecessary and convoluted to me, but bankers need a lot more information since the Wall Street meltdown." Although she didn't know why they wanted so much data, the reasoning sounded plausible to Sloane.

"Oh, of course, dear. However, all the documents are with the lawyers or still in the office downtown, which you have full access to already. Oh, wait. There are a few things in the file cabinet in the corner of your father's office here. Why don't you come out on Saturday and look?"

"That sounds great, Mom. I will plan to do just that. And I can take a carload of my things back to the city to help you clean out the house."

"Oh sweetheart, that would be really helpful. I would appreciate it so much. Of course, I'm just happy to get to see you. How are you doing? Are you still planning to liquidate the business? I support whatever decision you make, Sloane. You understand that, right?"

"Mom, we can talk about it more on Saturday, but PPHP set me up with a firm that is hoping to find someone to acquire us. We have some patents and copyrights that are interesting to one business, and another likes our remaining client contracts. Of course, our employees are terrific, so either prospect would want to scoop them up. I'm hopeful, but I'm running out of time."

"Well, Randall is excellent at this, even better than his father was. If he thinks he can find you a buyer, he can. Tell him I send my regards when you speak with him next. He's such a lovely young man, Sloane. You should invite him out to the house one last time before we move."

"Mom, don't push, please. I am not even working with Randall; I am working with a woman he recommended named Maria. He had to avoid any conflict. She's a smart, feisty woman. You would really like her. And she knows her stuff."

"What do you mean? Why aren't you working directly with Randall? It is his business. He passed you off to an associate? I will call and have a word with him. I don't care what has been happening in our family. We still deserve a named partner."

"Mom, relax. He didn't hand me off. It turns out PPHP cannot do investment work and handle an acquisition too, so he introduced me to Maria. I am still getting the royal treatment, Mom, without Randall annoying me."

"Now Sloane, you know I am your mother and I love you no matter what. I wouldn't say anything to hurt you, but I am going to say this, and you better listen to me, Sloane Egan Huyler."

Uh, oh. I am in big trouble now. She hasn't talked like this since I broke curfew in high school.

"Are you listening to me, Sloane? I am dead serious now." Marianne waited until Sloane acknowledged she was paying attention.

"Everyone annoys you, Sloane. They always have. It is not them; it is you. I was walking on clouds when I thought you would marry Wyatt Howe. I was afraid you would never get married. You are prickly and controlling. You are a gorgeous girl, Sloane, if I say so myself. Men accept and even appreciate a strong, smart woman. But no one wants one who always has to be right. You look down your pretty nose at everyone, Sloane. Even me, I suspect."

Sloane was trying to hide the tears forming in her throat. "I never looked down my nose at you, Mom, and I resent your implication that I have.

"It's our fault, honey. Your father's and mine. You were an only child, and it was important to us you grow up smart and confident. But we spoiled you, gave you too much when we should have reined you in. You were always a beauty, Sloane, on the outside and the inside, sweetie. But you let no one see your lovely inside. You were too perfect, too demanding, too cold. I thought it was the right thing back then. But now you need to let yourself thaw. You need to change now. Let Randall in, honey."

The words hurt because they were true. Instead of being confident, she had grown overconfident. Until the bottom dropped out. "But I will give some thought to what you said, and we can talk more about it on Saturday." She needed to hang up before she cried.

"Oh, honey, I didn't mean to hurt your feelings. You are a lovely, bright woman. Anyone would be lucky to have you. I blame myself and your father. We gave you everything and let you run the show because we loved you so much."

Sloane desperately wanted the conversation to end, but her mother wouldn't stop. "But circumstances have changed for us, Sloane. Since your father.... well, you know," her mother still could not say the words convicted, guilty or jail. "We cannot have all the things we had before. This is true even in relationships. You may need to lower your expectations, dear. I hate to say it, but it's true."

"You are absolutely right, Mom. But I have lowered them." Her wobbling chin was obvious in her voice. "I have lowered them to no one. I expect no one to be my friend or to date me. No one. I have to go."

Hanging up abruptly, Sloane sank to the nearest chair, only now realizing that she had been pacing a trail in the carpet during the entire conversation. She reached for a tissue and let herself give in to tears for the first time in weeks. She had not cried since that fiasco with Randall.

Oh no, do not go there. Thinking about him will just upset you more. Not a peep from that asshole for a full month. A full month! The least he could have done was send a note of apology. He had been a complete jerk. Just when she could have used a white knight, he turned out to be the dragon.

At least he had recommended Maria. After the icy email she had sent him, she heard from Maria immediately. She'd completed the transition from PHPP PPHP to the investment banking firm without a hitch. Maria was phenomenal, talented, full of great ideas, and just plain fun to work with. Being with her was the closest Sloane had come to being with a friend since her father.... well, you know.

CHAPTER FOURTEEN

Sloane arrived at the office before seven on Monday morning. She hadn't been there in over two weeks, unable to look at the consultants' and administrators' miserable, accusatory faces. She still did plenty of work, but from the privacy of her vintage apartment. The high-ceilinged dining room was roomy, the thick carpets absorbed any unwanted noise, the gorgeous Baker table afforded her plenty of room and the crystal chandelier provided adequate light. She covered the expensive table with a heavy cloth—protecting the polished mahogany - then spread her papers and computer all over it.

If her back hurt from lack of an ergonomic chair, it was a small price to pay for the view that greeted her when she could look up from her tasks and see the green leaves of the crabapple trees outside her floor to ceiling windows. And, added bonus, she was close to the kitchen too. The stress of work had actually caused her to gain a few pounds. She started each day with healthy low-fat yogurt, fruit and a full pot of coffee, but by early afternoon she was elbow-deep in chips or cheese and crackers.

Back in her father's old office, barricading herself in, she sifted through every single piece of paper still in his files. There was nothing important in the few papers she had taken from the house on Saturday, but the bulk of the material was here in these files. Sloane intended to review every line of every page until she identified potential problems that could stop an acquisition. She was no expert, but even she could figure out if the contracts would transfer to a new buyer. Why else would they be asking for them now?

Piled on the desk were folders from the third drawer of a four-high cabinet. The top drawer sat open with papers sticking out haphazardly. The folders from the second drawer were still stacked on the floor, waiting to be returned to their rightful place.

Sloane had established a system: open a folder, review its contents, put aside anything that might be of importance and throw the rest on the floor. Anyone passing the office, had they been able to get past the locked door, would have been astonished. Sloane was methodical to a fault, neat, organized and a more than a little OCD. Not that she had a doctor's diagnosis of Obsessive-Compulsive Disorder. She was just such a control freak that she was always in command of every inch of her environment.

Not today. Today she just wanted to cover as much as possible before she had to meet Regan for lunch. She didn't want to have to return to the office if she could avoid it, so she was plowing through the stacks, oblivious to the mess she was making. Her assistant, Mike, would clean it up later, filing everything back perfectly. Frankly, Sloane thought, Mike would be grateful for something to keep him busy.

At 11:00, Mike buzzed her on the intercom to remind her of the time. Sloane had requested that he do that at 11:00, then every fifteen minutes until she needed to leave. Looking at the surrounding stacks, she realized that there was no way she could finish everything. Disappointed, she calculated her ability to take everything from the fourth drawer home, recognized the futility and dedicated herself to finishing the third drawer before lunch and the other drawer later this afternoon. She had no choice.

Actually, she could have just delivered the requested documents that the investment bankers requested, but Sloane wanted to understand exactly how attractive HI might be. Of course, she could wait for their findings, but then she would not be Sloane.

The good news was that after sifting through hundreds of request documents, she had only pulled about a dozen from the pile that she thought they might find problematic in an acquisition. Unfortunately, almost all of them dealt with transferring their remaining contracts to new owners. Could that deter a potential buyer? There was no way to know yet. A few didn't seem relevant to a buyout at all. In fact, to Sloane, they looked more like something her father's lawyers might have requested, but she added them to the stack as directed.

By 11:45, the buzzing reminders were irritating Sloane. Smoothing her black pants, she grabbed her suit jacket off the back of the chair, picked her bag up from the small table in the corner and left the mess, locking the door behind her. Now that she was planning to come back, she wanted everything just as she left it.

Wandering into the ladies' room, she ran a comb through her already perfect hair, reminding herself to call Aaron at the exclusive Oak Street salon she frequented. She was due for a trim next week and he would fit her in. He was one of the few people who treated her with the same deference he always had.

One of the very few.

She retouched her lipstick. The deep red was strong for early June, more of a winter color, but it was a signature for Sloane. The bright color gave her wan face an element of drama that fit her personality perfectly and caused heads to turn when she entered a room. Straightening the pale blue sleeveless blouse that complemented her eyes, she tossed on the jacket and headed out to meet Regan.

Sloane spent the ten-minute walk speculating on Regan's agenda. Something was up, she was sure of that. She was wound tight as a drum when she pushed open the door. Taking two deep breaths to steady herself, she approached the host. At the mention of the Howe name, he snapped to attention and, with a wonderfully obsequious demeanor, he showed her to a window table facing State Street where Tyler sat.

Tyler jumped from his chair and stood politely, helping Sloane to take her seat and remove her jacket.

Why do men do that? Who cares? I like it. It's especially thoughtful too, since I know that Tyler clearly doesn't like me.

Fortunately, Regan arrived not long after Sloane. Tyler had been polite, but the two had barely made small talk. That changed once Regan arrived. She spoke easily of music, movies, and books before they even looked at the menu, putting Sloane completely at ease.

In fact, Sloane was comfortable enough to stop worrying about the why of lunch and start watching Regan and Tyler interact. On the surface, they were friendly, but there was an element to their banter that resonated with sexual tension. While they were both sociable and thoughtful, they also enjoyed a good argument, and it was obvious to Sloane that they sometimes forgot they weren't alone.

I wonder if they are aware of how much they are revealing their feelings to the rest of us. They have been friends for so long, but I suspect there is a lot more going on here. Maybe I can help it along. Regan has been such a good friend. It would be nice to return the favor.

The trio shared a cheeseboard along with a delicious bottle of Pinot Noir, followed by Michigan Apple salads for the women and a pulled pork sandwich for Tyler. Just as they were placing the order, Tyler looked over Sloane's shoulder and smiled broadly at someone behind her. Sloane didn't turn around when Tyler stood to greet and shake hands with the intruder, but her demeanor changed when she heard him offer the person the fourth place at their table.

"Love to, thanks," she heard the reply and felt the hairs rise on the back of her neck.

No. No. No. No. Walk away, please, just walk away. What excuse can I use so I can leave? Maybe he will go when he realizes it's me. Let him come up with a pretext. Just breathe and this will all be over in a minute. You can survive a minute.

Randall leaned down to give Regan a peck on the cheek, then turned to Sloane and did the same. He was behaving as if nothing had happened between them. Sloane figured he was playing a role for their lunch partners, so she played along, too. She could adopt a cool, friendly demeanor for a minute or two. After all, a month had passed since their disastrous date. If he could fake their friendship, so could she. If she could just get this blush under control, she knew she would be fine.

Breathe. Then he will be gone. Don't stare at him and don't touch him. Whatever you do, no touching. Just remember to breathe.

Randall took the proffered seat and ordered an iced coffee from the passing server. Sloane's heart sank as she realized he was planning to stay. She could feel the heat of him inches from her bare arm and smell his woodsy aftershave. His hair was slightly windswept, with just one thick brown lock falling over his forehead. He looked young, rakish, and very sexy. He had carefully hung his suit jacket over the back of his chair, and she watched, her mouth watering, as he rolled up the sleeves of his fine cotton shirt.

Although Sloane was having trouble concentrating, the conversation between the four of them was surprisingly easy. It appeared Regan really just wanted to catch up, so Sloane tried to relax as best she could under the circumstances and enjoy the rare excursion. She had a brief memory of lunches like this from the past, of dining with many friends or mid-day dates with Wyatt. She allowed nostalgia to creep in momentarily, then pushed it firmly out of her mind.

Regan told stories of stepping up to the helm at LHRE, about the struggle her father had with allowing a woman to run the show. She made them all laugh. Tyler talked about Wyatt's business, bragging about its success without once mentioning Wyatt. Sloane had never noticed before how charming he was when he chose to be. Sloane raved about Maria's skill and the competence of the PPHP office, omitting the fact that she had stopped all her interactions with Randall.

Despite eddies under the surface that could easily have sunk the entire gathering, the four navigated the conversation all the way through the delicious lunch. Somehow, each time the conversation got dicey—about Regan and Tyler's relationship, about the sale of Huyler Industries, about the ostracizing of Sloane—someone would jump in to steer the subject back into safe waters.

Lingering over the last of the wine, the conversation turned to events Regan had attended recently. The men had been to some, but not all, so Sloane never felt left out of the conversation. Soon they were asking about the Children's Hospital Benefit, only two weeks away.

Sloane gave them an update on the progress because Allyson had updated the board at their monthly meeting last week. Sloane encouraged them all to attend. Tickets were only $350 per person, after all. There were still seats left, and it was for a good cause. She tempted them by sharing bits and pieces of information about the band, the menu, and finally, the best of the silent auction items. Several sporting event VIP seats caught Tyler's attention; a spa day appealed to Regan and a day on a private sailing yacht fired Randall's imagination. Regan promised a bidding war for the yacht until Randall offered to share the day. He even agreed she could captain the boat, and they all enjoyed the spirited negotiations over something neither possessed.

"You can bid online, even if you don't come to the dinner, but I hope you will all attend. It would mean a lot to me."

"We could go together?" Tyler proposed to Regan as if he had not invited her months earlier. He allowed Sloane to assume he was responding to her sales pitch. "Then, at least you would have a dancing partner."

"And a good one at that. I would like that," Regan accepted Tyler graciously before turning back to Sloane.

"Who are you going with, Sloane?"

The question sat there, like the proverbial elephant in the room. There was no good way for Sloane to answer. She was wracking her brain for a smooth comeback, a reply that would not sound hurt or vulnerable. She would not play the victim here.

"Me," she heard Randall reply in a confident voice. "I asked her ages ago to be my date, and she honored me by agreeing. What do you say the four of us go together?"

Sloane sat there dumbstruck, and then it was too late to refute Randall's assertion, even if she had wanted to. But she didn't want to. She was relieved, thrilled, and completely dumbfounded. The conversation swirled around Sloane's head while she tried to figure out what had just happened. She couldn't even decide if they had duped or defended her, but she had let too many seconds go by to undo things now.

"Perfect," Regan agreed.

"Should I get us a limo? After all, it is Sloane's big night. We should make a splash," Tyler was offering.

"All taken care of," Randall replied, squeezing Sloane's thigh lightly under the table to prevent her from objecting, then leaving his hand there to burn through her skin while sending chills up her body. "Sloane and I made plans a while back. We will just expand them to the four of us. It will be great. Right, darling?"

Darling? Where does he get off calling me darling, or calling the shots, for that matter? She would show him. She would show him right now.

Sloane stopped herself from saying something mean, something that would make a liar out of Randall in front of their friends. She remembered her mother's tough talk from the prior week and kept her mouth closed for the first time in her memory.

It wasn't easy. A look from Randall told her that he knew she was struggling to hold back a storm of invectives.

Was he laughing at her? How dare he? That was it!

"Actually..." Sloane began.

"Actually, we should go," Randall effortlessly interrupted. "Sloane has an appointment with Maria. I'm just going to walk her back to my office."

Damn him. He just did it again. The lying, scheming, manipulative pig.

As her brain screamed every nasty name she could think of, Sloane allowed Randall to pull back her chair, help her into her jacket, take her arm and say goodbye for them. She was standing outside on the busy street corner with Randall's arms sheltering her from the throng of passing tourists before she could utter a word.

It was like the fresh air freed her. "Why you over-bearing, lying, conniving pig. You slippery, lying, rotten..."

"You said 'lying' twice." Randall was smiling, wrapping his arms tighter around her. He was laughing at her, maneuvering her, and getting away with it.

But he was cute when he smiled like that. Besides—unbelievably—she had a date for the benefit. And she still had two weeks to find someone else. She would too, just to show Randall that he couldn't push her around like this. Still, until then, a bird in the hand...

"Okay, damn you, you win. I will go with you to the benefit because I need a date and you know it. And I will play along with your little game that we planned this all 'ages ago', although I am not sure why you put that out there."

"Oh, that was for you, Sloane, not for me. I thought you might want them to think you were something other than forgotten. But you were, weren't you? Everyone left you behind. I came to your rescue when you needed someone, didn't I? I was happy to do it, don't get me wrong, but you could show some appreciation."

"What are you, a two-year-old needing some kind of reassurance? Yes, I needed a date, but I could have gone without one. So, no, you are not some kind of hero who rescued me. You are still just a manipulating, lying clod."

"You keep telling yourself that, if it is too hard for you to say 'thank you'. We will both know the truth, won't we, Sloane? We will both know that I just saved your cute little ass back there. And you may not be grateful now, but you will be."

She was grateful, but she would rather die than admit it to Randall. She was furious he was so high handed with her, even if he was doing her a favor. Even worse, he dared to walk away, leaving her standing on the corner, still berating him.

Yeah, just who did he think he was?

CHAPTER FIFTEEN

"I saw Sloane Huyler today." Randall plopped down in a comfortable leather chair without an invitation. Maria Canovalli looked up from her work, about to throw him out even if he was an important colleague and a source of clients. He never knocked or asked if she had a minute. He just assumed everyone had time for him. She guessed it came from growing up so privileged. Maria knew nothing of privilege. She had attended the University of Chicago on a full academic scholarship, studying economics, longing for a career in finance. Joining a small exclusive investment banking firm had been a godsend. They had allowed her to work days, and continue at U of C for her MBA in its evening program, even picking up the tab. She felt like part of the family; after seven years on the job, she was on track for partnership any day.

It didn't hurt that she didn't tell Randall off when he was rude or presumptuous. She knew when to hold her tongue and when to speak up—whether she was dealing with senior partners, colleagues or clients. She had not gotten the opportunity to handle key clients just because she knew finance.

"How is she doing? Things have been really rough for her this year. I am not sure how I would handle things if I were in her shoes. I like her. She's brash, and you know I like that in a woman."

"Rough is an understatement. I imagine there are days when she doesn't want to get out of bed. And trust me, less than two years ago, she was the queen bee, and she knew it. A lot of people were happy to see her take this tumble, but she deserves better."

"Well, she has a good head on her shoulders, Randall. She understands exactly what HI is up against in this pursuit of a buyer. They might have stood a chance of a merger if the management team hadn't jumped ship, but without their influence, it will have to be a relatively cheap acquisition. Not ideal, but better than bankruptcy."

"Maria, just inside these four walls, if no buyer appears by Labor Day, or a buyer tries to lowball, let me know and I will pour some cash into Huyler. I will not let Sloane go into bankruptcy."

Maria's eyes grew wide as saucers. There was something going on here that was not in any of the documents or emails that had passed between her and Randall when he referred to HI.

"What do I need to know, Randall?"

"Nothing for now; keep trying to forging forge a deal, but you have an 'in case of emergency' option in your back pocket. Oh, and that stays between us, of course."

"Of course. You got it, sir," Maria responded with a crisp salute and a smile. After a few minutes spent discussing other shared clients, Randall left her to ponder what he had told her. The offer was as out of character for Randall as anything she had ever seen.

Even in the best situation, it would take millions to save Huyler, and if Maria understood that, so did Randall. The PHPP PPHP board would never approve, so Randall had to be implying that he would invest his personal funds.; causing a very healthy dent in his sizable fortune.

If she didn't want Sloane—or her father to be more precise—to take Randall down with her, Maria needed to close a deal with one of the companies she was pursuing. Two were interested, but neither was hurrying. Unfortunately for Sloane and her employees, time was of the essence.

Fifteen minutes later, Maria took a brisk walk down two flights of stairs to the PPHP offices and knocked gently on the doorframe of Randall's corner office. He motioned to the phone, held up one finger, and motioned her to a chair. She interpreted the signal to mean he would be one more minute and stepped in, sliding onto a comfortable, worn leather sofa set against the wall. She picked up a travel magazine from the table in front of her and prepared to wait.

"Perfect. She never knew what hit her, did she? You did great. Yeah, thanks, Ty, and tell Regan she has my undying gratitude too. It should be fun. Expensive, sure, but we still need fun. Gotta go. See you later? The club? Yeah, tomorrow morning. Okay. Bye."

Moving from behind the large desk, Randall joined Maria near the couch, dropping his large frame into an oversized wingback chair and propping his feet comfortably on the coffee table. He could have been waiting for a ball game to start on TV. He looked so relaxed, but Maria knew that the moment she talked shop, she would have his undivided attention.

"I have been thinking," she began slowly, placing the magazine neatly back in the fanned stack, "about Huyler. I could actually use some advice. Maria reviewed the two clients who were considering HI. "Sloane should be able to get a higher price from them."

"I agree," Randall said, leaning forward, returning his feet to the floor to rest his elbows on his knees. Maria recognized the posture. He was fully engaged, his attention focused. "So, what is the issue? Timing? What is standing in the way?"

"I thought reputation, but it's resolved. I think it's Sloane. They need to know she's walking. No senior management from Huyler to interfere with their plans. She would stay for a smooth transition, of course, but then move on."

"That might make a difference. Personally, I think they fear losing the existing contracts. We need to prove that the buyer keeps all the rights and commitments.

"I have Joanie and Seth over at the law firm reviewing the contract terms, but they may need more help to move things fast enough. Get more of your staff and lawyers working on this. I'll give you back Alan. Sound like a plan?"

"Sounds perfect, Randall. Thanks."

When Randall notified Alan they did not need any longer him, he also asked Alan to provide him with a list of all the contracts they were reviewing and the name and phone number for the key decision maker at each company. Randall demanded it by Friday. With no further explanation, Randall told him the list was 'just between the two of us.'

Having taken care of that, Randall went to the Children's Hospital website and got the information about the benefit. Then he placed a call to the head of his HR department asking her to purchase a table for the event on behalf of PPHP if she had not already done so.

"We have two, sir. But you told me to offer the seats to our top annual performers and their clients, so I did."

"Are they going? Find out please, Carly. I need one entirely empty table I plan to fill personally. If you cannot arrange that from the two we already bought, buy a third, please."

"Happy to handle that for you, Randall. It is certainly well within our foundation budget and guidelines. I will take care of it now and get back to you shortly."

Randall checked the markets, happy to discover they had closed 'up' for the day. He handled some issues for the company's most important clients and sent his father an email summarizing a few corporate activities in case he wanted to be bothered with them.

His father was chasing the early snows in South America like a surfer chases waves. He skied almost twelve months a year now. When Randall's mother was still alive, the family spent the winters skiing together, but since her death, the Parker family hobby had become his father's obsession.

Randall missed having any family around him. As an only child, his mother had fussed over him and he had flourished under her love. His father, in contrast, had been a strict disciplinarian with high expectations and no room for excuses. By high school, the demands relaxed, but by then Randall knew they expected him to be a top achiever. Together, his parents had provided the balance a precocious and overly intelligent child needed. Once he was a young adult, they had given him enough rope to hang himself and instead Randall had soared.

He was a young star at the office, taking over his father's responsibility without slowing his stride. That worked out well when his mother became ill and his father lost interest in everything but her. Suzanne had been fighting a hepatitis infection since childhood and each time it reoccurred, she became weaker and weaker until she died.

The two men struggled to connect after that. His father became inconsolable and withdrawn. He started traveling to avoid their empty home. Randall buried himself in work and women. They exchanged emails for almost a year before his father returned to sell the Lake Forest house and move to Aspen permanently.

He kept an office at PPHP but almost never used it. Instead, the men would meet for a week or two of skiing at Lake Tahoe or Aspen each winter with Wyatt, Tyler and Alex tagging along as company and to serve as a much-needed buffer. His father and he had become colleagues and friends. There were long stretches of silence, or email, but they reconnected for the few weeks they were together. The arrangement worked for them.

Randall had learned to be a lone wolf. He kept his own counsel, worked hard and played harder. He dated a revolving door of beautiful women who meant nothing to him, tamped whatever loneliness he felt in a few too many drinks, and played hockey or lifted weights to burn off excess energy and keep fit for his latest lady.

Wyatt, Tyler and Alex were the brothers he'd wished he had. He trusted them with his life, knowing they would give him the shirts off their back,. R would do the same. He hadn't felt this need to protect and care for someone since his mother had died—until Sloane. That hint of vulnerability hiding under her tough exterior touched his heart. The way she lifted her chin, ready for battle, made him want to kiss her senseless. He had never felt this willingness to put someone's needs ahead of his. Suddenly, there was this feisty, high maintenance woman tying him in knots. He was jumping through hoops for her, risking his reputation, and perhaps his fortune. He would do more, too, if he just knew what it would take to make her happy and to win her. Randall longed to see the shadows leave her blue eyes, to see the carefree, confident Sloane he'd had a crush on in grad school. He knew her compassion, and her fire.

Dammit. How the hell do I outmaneuver a woman known for her ability to outmaneuver everyone else?

Randall texted Alex, checking to verify that he would be at the East Bank Club after work. Alexander Gaines had the best head on his shoulders of anyone that Randall knew and his perspective on Sloane, as a girlfriend and as an investment, would give Randall a badly needed second opinion.

Within minutes Randall received the response he'd hoped for and made a plan to meet in the weight room around 7:00 PM. Randall hated working out at night, preferring to lift before his workday began. He knew his buddies felt the same, since they saw each other most mornings in the upscale health club. Had Alex worked out already and agreed to lift again just to spend the time with Randall? If so, he would never confess it, but Randall suspected it and was grateful.

Dragging a bit lately, Randall couldn't motivate himself to make it to East Bank Club by 5:30 AM. He felt the weight of Sloane's problems on his shoulders and the burden was a heavy one to bear. He was not exactly sure when he made her problems his own, but he could not shake his need to solve this mess for her. So, he dragged into work every morning, exhausted from worrying. It needed to stop here so he could get back to his peak performance and be with Sloane because he loved her, not because she needed his help.

He had the gala covered and Alex would help him figure out the rest.

CHAPTER SIXTEEN

"Don't wimp out on me now, Randall. This workout was your idea." "Yeah, stupid me. I forgot what a tough taskmaster you can be,are, Alex. Give me a friggin' break. It is almost 8:00, and I am exhausted."

"And that, my fine fellow, is why you work out before you go to work and not when you are dying to relax. Give me three more reps and we can call it a night."

Randall pushed the heavy weights up from his chest, counting out the three last presses. His chest muscles bulged with the effort, his arms quivered under the strain, but he completed the task. Grabbing the nearby towel, he wiped the sweat dripping from his face, wiped down the bench as he rose from it, and took a deep draught from the water bottle he kept handy.

"Remind me not to invite you to join me here again," he said to Alex in a petulant tone. Both knew he didn't mean it.

"You'll thank me for this moment when you are taking your shirt off for your latest next weekend," Alex responded wisely.

Randall stood a little taller at the allusion to his body. His flat stomach, broad chest, muscular arms and legs were a testament to his hard work in the gym and on the ice. He was proud of the way he stayed in shape. It certainly didn't hurt that women found him a hunk too. Did Sloane? Randall discovered he didn't care about anyone's opinion but hers.

"OK, lazy, meet you at the bar in twenty minutes, so don't get too far ahead of me on drinks," Randall told Alex, still annoyed that he'd worked out alone. He really needed to get out of bed early again. Alex had been in the gym that morning and again at lunch. Since he was in training, he insisted on staying on his regimen, refusing to lift with Randall. Instead, Alex kept his friend company and pushed his limits.

Freshly showered, dark hair still damp, Randall walked to the far end of the bar, catching the eye of several women along the way. He joined Alex, quickly downed a large glass of ice water, and then ordered a Sam Adams. The bartender put the bottle in front of Randall, confirmed that he would run a tab and moved away, leaving the men hidden in a quiet booth at the end of the club's bar.

"So, now will you tell me what this is all about?" Alex began without preamble.

"Whatever do you mean? Did you think I had some ulterior motive for meeting up?"

"No, Randall. I know you have some ulterior motive. What is going on? Is it work or a woman?"

"Well, to tell you the truth, it's both," he admitted sheepishly. "It is a work problem that I acquired because of a woman."

"Randall, are we still discussing Sloane? You have got to let go of this rescue before she takes you down with her. Her business is sinking too fast for you, or anyone, to save it."

Okay, this was the advice I came here for. Alex calls it like it is, and I just need to heed his sound advice.

"I hear you, man. I do. But I can't let this one go. First, Sloane is paying for a crime that she didn't commit and second, she intrigues the hell out of me."

"Okay, first," Alex stressed the word, "she has you by the balls, and second, you are assuming she is not guilty. If we are going to discuss this, let's discuss this honestly. If you were not so hot for her, you would not believe she was innocent. You weren't so sure before you wanted to get in her pants."

Damn, I have no one to blame for his opinion but myself.

"Let's just say, for the sake of argument, that I am hot for Sloane, as you so tactfully put it. And let's also say that this attraction is clouding my judgment...."

"Randall, let me just stop you right there, cause after a couple more drinks you are going to get belligerent. I would rather finish this conversation before we get to that point. You are hot for Sloane. Now you have to determine if it is real, or if it is more the vestige of your competition with Wyatt."

"I have no idea what you are talking about," Randall responded, a bit too forcefully.

"We can skirt this topic all you like, but you compete with Wyatt over everything. For whatever reason, you have always wanted what Wyatt has, from his position on the hockey team to his grades in school, to the class presidency. Frankly, you have been a bit of a sore loser. You made passes at every womaen he dated."

"Not so, Alex. I know to keep my hands off another man's girl, especially Wyatt's. I would never poach on any of you guys."

"Sober you wouldn't. So now, we come back to Sloane. She is just about the only woman you couldn't quite touch. Until her father's fall from grace knocked the lovely ice-queen off her pedestal."

"You think I just want her cause she was Wyatt's? You have this wrong and her wrong. She's a changed woman, Alex. Sweet, vulnerable. And I know she didn't help her father make those deals."

"Doesn't matter what I think, Randall. What matters is what you think, and clearly you think she's worth it."

"Just between us, Alex," Randall hesitated, taking a big gulp of beer before continuing, "I think I might be in love with her."

"Are you shitting me? What on earth is there to fall in love with? This is Sloane Huyler you are talking about. She is cold, calculating, and manipulative. She is a prima donna and a 'class A' bitch. Ask Wyatt."

"True, she was absolutely all of those things. You aren't listening to me, though. She has a heart of gold. She's all soft and gooey inside. Outside, she is stunningly beautiful, smart as a whip, and when she gets bitchy, she also gets pretty damn clever. She likes to control things, I'll concede that, but I might be the man to stay one step ahead of her. I swear, she is adorable—frustrating, confusing and totally adorable. I want to be the one to fight for control with her, Alex."

"Jeez, man. I had no clue," Alex answered after a long pause. "I thought you were just playing with her because she was you could. She never gave you the time of day before."

"I admit, she's more approachable these days, but I like to think she likes me, too. Are you saying she is only tolerating me until she finds someone better? That hurts, Alex, that really hurts."

"Oh crap, that didn't come out the way I meant it. What I meant was that I didn't think she would let any of us get close to her after Wyatt. We are all too tight, you know, and she is too proud."

"She is extremely proud. She's been through a lot and doesn't want anyone to see what it's cost her. Which brings me to my second issue—work. I am trying to find a buyer for her company. She won't go under without a fight. She is too protective of the HI employees. I'm telling you. You need to get to know her. She'll completely change your opinion."

"So, a buyer," Alex pondered. "I think that will not be easy this late in the game. Is anything valuable left?"

"Well, that is just it," Randall explained. "The value is in the major contract holders. If they transfer to a new owner, it could be worth enough, plus there is the customer list, patents and skilled employees. That should be worth something, right?"

"Yeah, you should be able to make a deal with that." Alex agreed. The two scribbled numbers on a napkin for the next ten minutes, correcting each other's assumptions until they agreed on the figures. "The key is those seven contracts," Alex pointed to the names of seven large companies circled on the napkin.

"That's what I think too. I want to reach out to the stakeholders and ensure that they remain with HI because of the pending sale, and be able to while closeing the deal because the stakeholders are staying."

"It's risky playing one against the other, Randall. But you might pull it off."

"Could Maria Canovalli? I handed this one to her, and she's in charge of getting a deal done."

"Yeah, she could. Maria's impressive. She might need a little hand holding, but this may work. You might have to use your influence to sweeten the pot a little on one side or the other."

"I could do that by promising a PPHP contract as part of the deal. That should work, don't you think?"

"Oh yeah, but if PPHP does any of the financing for the deal, they can't suddenly be a customer, and you know that. Besides, even if you could, the board is way too conservative to invest in HI now." Alex was right, as usual.

Okay, I will just strong-arm Wyatt to sign a contract with them instead. I can use my personal funds to back him if the deal goes south. That would work. I know he would agree. He may not like how Sloane treated him, but he still thinks she got a raw deal when her dad went down. And he wouldn't want to see all those people out of work."

"You would throw in some cash? He doesn't need it, you know. And I could invest instead. I am not suggesting you risk your money."

"I want to do this, and I will, if I have to."

"I hear you, and if you need a bigger contract than you feel comfortable with, count me in. I can certainly afford it. But note, I am doing this for you, not for Sloane. I am not convinced about how adorable she is yet."

After giving Alex a sneer for his last remark, Randall—moved by Alex's generosity—thanked him profusely.

"One more thing, Randall." Alex stated reluctantly. "You have got to watch the booze, man. If you want Sloane to take you seriously, toe the line. She will not tolerate a single slipup from you. The first time you lay a hand on another woman, she will throw you out on your ass."

Pushing away the half-full bottle of beer in front of him with a broad grin Randall bragged, "I can do that easy, Alex."

"You better be sure."

"Oh yeah, I'm sure. This woman is worth it."

CHAPTER SEVENTEEN

S loane returned from her spin class exhausted. In the last week, she realized if she didn't go to exercise class; she didn't leave the house. She was having junk food delivered and avoiding the office by calling in with increasingly feeble excuses. Currently, she was 'nursing her aging and ill border collie, Lucy.' Everyone in the office was appropriately sympathetic. Running to and from the vet with a sick dog while facing the prospect of euthanizing your beloved pet must be heartbreaking. They understood how devastated she must be after ten years of devoted companionship. Only one or two intrepid souls had dared to mention that she had never spoken of Lucy before, or any pet—not even a goldfish.

When did I become this sniveling coward?

Sloane knew exactly when she had lost the last vestiges of her pride. It happened only moments after she found herself sandwiched between the implacable body of an incredibly sexy man and an unmovable brick wall. In that moment, she experienced an emotion she had never felt with Wyatt. She felt tenderness and desire, heat and heart.

Once she dropped her guard and allowed Randall in, she allowed herself to feel something she hadn't felt for months and months before that moment. She allowed herself to feel something she feared she w of course, to assure his family would never want for anything. He mentored her in the business, treated her as the son he never had. In turn, she stepped up and delivered. She would never dream of doing less.

She still had the right Gold Coast address, and a gorgeous vintage apartment that she purchased for a fortune three years ago when the building went condo. The three bedrooms had ten-foot ceilings, custom-designed crown moldings and beautiful hardwood floors, two front parlors, both with fireplaces, and an oversized rustic kitchen. Cooling down from her class, Sloane wandered from room to room, touching each piece, wondering how much longer she could afford it.

With the help of the most sought-after decorator, Sloane had created her oasis, and she didn't want to lose it. Standing under the lovely archway between the parlors, she admired how cleverly the floor to ceiling drapes hid the old-fashioned radiators. Flopping onto a green velvet Baker sofa, she kicked off her shoes and considered how happy she had been when she finished styling it.

Everything about the space screamed muted beauty and unlimited budget, from the gorgeous oriental rug to the large wing chair and the rosewood nesting tables. Without a thought, she put her feet up on the tables and admired a wall of etched mirror reflecteing a Gustavian chandelier hanging from the ceiling and beyond it, a modern painting that had been a gift from Wyatt. Something about the painting jarred her into movement.

Sloane used the second parlor as a library, a haven with shelves of books and artifacts from art fairs and her extensive travels. Her designer had done an outstanding job of creating a different feel in this room, yet it flowed easily from the other parlor. Sloane flipped on a lamp and watched the room come alive. She waked past an inviting set of barrel chairs to run her fingers over the antique secretary tucked between the floor-to-ceiling shelves. With the addition of a small wooden library ladder, the space was reminiscent of Henry Higgins's library in "My Fair Lady," and without being aware, Sloane hummed "I could have danced all night," as she headed to the kitchen.

The back of the house was like another world. The dining room was sunny and modern, and the kitchen, butler's pantry and laundry showed no signs of the original vintage. It looked more like a commercial kitchen. She walked past the doors to both bedrooms and two and a half baths and headed for the fridge.

"Good thing I love it here," she mumbled. It really was her dream home, which was fortunate since she hid in it almost 24/7 now. She had sent her report to Allyson and skipped the last hospital board meeting. She phoned into the office daily for conference calls, and she met Maria in an out of the way coffee shop to discuss the acquisition, when Maria insisted they needed to meet face to face. Except for exercise class and her lunch with Regan, Tyler and the infuriating Randall, she had left the house only twice in the last month.

So, she had gone to spin class and then stopped at Starbucks for a skim latte. Sloane walked to and from a small local gym, jogged or did yoga from a DVD, having dropped her costly East Bank Club membership during the trial. She had expected to rejoin the club when they exonerated her father, as they certainly would. She had thought so at the time, and had planned to rub everyone's nose in her renewed position. That was unlikely to happen now that he didn't plan to appeal.

Meanwhile, she went to the spin class just a few blocks from her home, getting bit of fresh air, saving money and basking in anonymity at the facility. None of her old acquaintances would go to a place like that. In the old days, she would never have set foot in the run-down facility. But she'd discovered she liked it, and the women in her class, although she still kept them at arm's length.

Now safely back in hibernation, she grabbed a carton of yogurt from the Subzero and, after knocking all the decorative pillows to the floor, dropped onto her plush sofa, tucking her sock-clad feet under her. There were no phone messages; there never were. She only kept the landline because her mother could remember the easy number and it was more convenient for long conference calls.

Sloane had binge watched Hallmark Channel movies, read a few novels and was running out of ways to entertain herself. She seriously considered making an appointment with a psychologist; she knew she was suffering from depression. Marianne had gone on medication immediately after the arrest and it certainly seemed to help her. But Sloane didn't know a doctor and was too proud to call anyone for a recommendation.

Sloane knew she was depressed because there was just over one week until the Children's Hospital Benefit and she hadn't even bothered with a new dress. She should have done that months ago. Not that she needed one, of course. She had three large closets full of designer clothes that represented several years' salary for the average worker, but she usually bought a new dress for every occasion. There would be photographers there, and it just wouldn't do to be seen in the same dress twice.

Besides, she knew she would have no opportunities to wear any of her formal gowns after next week. There would be no more in-vitations, no more board positions. It had taken a while to absorb, but she finally understood that nothing would improve until things changed for her father. If he didn't appeal, how could things change? And what if he lost his appeal? Sloane knew she doubted her father's innocence deep in her heart, where she pretended it didn't exist,. Why else would he accept a plea deal?. Unless his sentence was overturned, she would exist in this deep-freeze for six long years. Maybe more.The buzzing of her lobby intercom shook from that morose thought. She was curious, but too lethargic to bother answering. Less than a minute passed before it buzzed again. She rose gracefully from the couch, padded to the wall in her little white socks, and hit the button.

"Yes?"

"Ms. Huyler, sorry to bother you. There is a man here to see you. He said he is your financial advisor, Mr. Parker. Shall I send him up?" Even the doorman had that shocked voice, as if he understood no one came or went from her apartment anymore.

Sloane hesitated while her heart rate revved into a rapid, staccato beat. She thought her chest would explode. She was sweaty already, so the sweat that broke out now went unnoticed. Her hair was pulled into a high messy ponytail, she wore no makeup, skintight workout pants and a tiny, cropped t-shirt over a fraying sports bra.

How could she let him up looking like this? How could she let him get away? "Oh, God. Oh, God, what do I do?" she turned circles in a sudden frenzy. "Listen to yourself, Sloane Huyler. Get a grip. Where is that smart, decisive woman you used to be?"

Sloane took a deep breath and stopped fidgeting. "Tell him I am not at home, John."

"Very good, Ms. Huyler."

It was only seconds before the buzzer broke the quiet again, the noise urgently repeated as if someone were lying on the button.

"Yes, John?" Sloane answered with annoyance in her voice. "What it is now?"

"If you are going to say you aren't home, Sloane, make sure I can't hear your voice. Tell the doorman—John is it? Tell John to allow me up. Now, Sloane."

Sloane heard that no-nonsense tone in Randall's voice. It was the tone that said 'I will get my way, so just give in.' It irritated the hell out of her. It also turned her on immensely.

"Send him up, please, John."

Sloane knew she had less than 90 seconds to get her act together. She kicked off her socks, ran to drop the yogurt container and spoon in the kitchen and rinsed her face quickly over the sink, drying it with paper towels. It was all she had time for before she heard an imperious knock at her door.

Taking three deep breaths to steady the heart she feared would explode through her chest, Sloane moved slowly from the back of the deep apartment toward the front door. An impatient Randall was already thumping forcefully. His hand was still in mid-air when she grabbed the heavy crystal knob and yanked it open.

Standing there in an expensive suit that his powerful body to perfection, Randall took her breath away. He'd combed his dark hair back from his chiseled face and grown a close-cropped beard since she had seen him last week. Although she missed seeing his square chin, Sloane had to admit it suited him extremely well, making him look both rugged and polished, and sexy as hell. His eyes looked a deep coffee color in this light, surrounded by long eyelashes any woman would envy. Dark brows slashed above, currently in a deep V caused by Randall's scowl.

"Are you going to leave me standing in the hall?" His accusatory tone was just what Sloane needed to pull herself back together.

She stood mesmerized. Looking in his eyes left her a goner. "Of course, how rude of me. Please come in. As you can see, I was not expecting company." She waved her arm to indicate her attire. "Perhaps a phone call asking to stop by would have been appropriate." Sloane's voice and demeanor dripped with disdain.

There, that should put the insufferable man in his place.

"Oh, cut the crap, Sloane," Randall retorted snidely, walking past her into the living room and plopping down on her sofa like he owned the place. "We both know that if I had called first, you would have told me not to come."

Damn him and his too-sexy-for words face. He was right, of course.

"Well, if you knew that, perhaps you should have respected my wishes and stayed away."

"Are you just going to hold the world at arm's length forever?" Randall's words were cutting, and they hit Sloane in the face. She crossed her arms over her chest, closing herself to him and offering what little protection she could from his barbs. "I think it's time for you to rejoin the living sweetness," he said more gently, coaxing her with his words and the use of the endearment. Sloane bristled for a moment before capitulating. Randall had just signaled that he had the upper hand and he was keeping it. And she'd let him. Truth was she wanted him here, helping her out of her funk, chasing her.

"Well, you're here now, so I guess my hibernation just ended." Sloane uncrossed her arms, flinging them out in supplication. She gave up fighting with him—for now.

Randall surveyed the space, quickly taking in the empty cookie box, potato chip bag, the soda cans, the stack of novels on the coffee table, one laying facedown and open, and the heavy velvet curtains drawn over the windows.

"Do you ever go out anymore?" he finally asked. Without an invitation, he rose from the sofa and began walking through her apartment as if it were his right. He yanked open the curtains, flooding the room with light. She was so astonished she stood there, saying nothing, allowing him to go wherever he chose.

Randall walked into the library, did a quick circle, running his fingers over the bindings of books placed carefully on one long shelf, reading the titles on the other shelves. He turned without a word and moved down the hall, looking through the large open archway to see her computer and papers scattered over the sleek table in the dining room. He walked past the closed bedroom doors, and with barely a glance into the bathrooms, continued down the long hallway to the kitchen.

He opened the refrigerator and freezer simultaneously, surveying their contents—a six-pack of Diet Coke, a carton of Hagen Daz Dark Chocolate and Almond flavored ice cream and three tiny cartons of Yoplait. Randall shut the doors wordlessly and returned to the living room, where Sloane stood frozen, uncertain what to do with this imposing man stealing every inch of air.

She needed to get rid of the insufferable man dominating her space. Damn him, Sloane cursed, needing to be back in control.

"Meet with your approval?" She sniped at him sarcastically, seething at his unwanted invasion.

"Yeah, it's a nice place to live, but a little under-stocked if you are planning to hibernate until winter." He completely ignored her anger, moving about confidently.

Why must he always know just the right snappy reply?

"Screw you, Randall. How I live is none of your damn business."

Now that he had scoped out the environs, he turned his steely gaze to Sloane. She felt a rare blush rise into her cheeks, but she refused to look away. She watched his eyes widen as he scanned her body, lingering momentarily on the skin bared by the short crop top, boring through the sports bra to visualize her tightening nipples. His eyes moved up to her pinking chest, long neck and finally her bare face.

"Jeez, Sloane, even dressed like this, you are fucking stunning." She wasn't sure if he was talking to her or to himself, but he seemed slightly shell-shocked.

"Oh, cut the crap, Randall. I just came back from spin class and we both know I am a mess."

"If you say so. I think perhaps we should remedy that, and also the fact that there is absolutely no food in this house. Get showered and dressed. I am taking you out to lunch."

"Lunch? What are you talking about? Go back to the office, Randall."

"We have business to discuss, and a date to plan for the weekend," Randall told her in a clipped, no-nonsense voice. "I'm hungry. You don't have enough food to feed a gerbil, and I am taking you out. Go, Sloane. Get dressed or in ten minutes I will drag you out of here looking like that."

That was all Sloane needed, since it was obvious Randall meant his threat. He was going to take her out to lunch, and she was eager, scared, and curious. She ran for the shower, recognizing that she was excited about doing something for the first time in two weeks.

She took the fastest shower on record, pulling her hair into a tight bun since she had no time to wash it. She dried off, quickly applied two coats of mascara to her already long lashes and a tinted moisturizer with an SPF in case they sat outside. It would have to do.

She made a mad dash from bath to bedroom, hoping Randall was not looking down the hall, and grabbed the first sundress in her crowded closet. The green striped dress was perfect, cut low like a tank top, fitted tight to the waist and then falling softly above the knees. She actually showed a tiny amount of cleavage in this dress, along with a wide expanse of chest, her back and a fair amount of leg. It was a lot of pale, pale skin. Grabbing a tiny cardigan to cover some of the bareness and a low-heeled Kate Spade sandal, she was ready to face a summer day, Randall, and whatever else was beyond her doors.

Sloane was ready in only twenty minutes, possibly the fastest on record for her, and impressive to Randall. He smiled when he checked his watch. Meanwhile, Randall had been freely wandering in her space. She wondered if he had snooped in her things, what he was thinking, what her condo told him about her.

"Better. You look beautiful."

The compliment pleased her, although she had heard it before. Somehow, coming from Randall, it was more sincere, more meaningful. And more unnerving.

"Where are we going?"

"Well, I thought we could grab something in Water Tower Place or the Bloomingdales building, then find you a dress for Saturday night. You never bothered with a dress, right? Where would you prefer? How about we eat in the lobby at the Peninsula to discuss it?"

"Are you crazy? You are not being seen with me at the Peninsula and you are definitely not taking me dress shopping."

"Oh yeah, I am Sloane. A very exclusive, very expensive dress in which you feel like a million bucks. Today, we celebrate. All week we celebrate. You, me and Maria. This afternoon we shop, tonight we all meet for dinner and we celebrate."

"Oh my God, you did it?" Sloane asked, leaving her mouth hanging open. "You sold the company?" The play of emotions was priceless, based on the indulgent grin from Randall. Sloane went from incredulous to uncertain, then to acknowledging the possibility of the sale. Finally, she cracked a broad smile, feeling hope for the first time in months.

"I did nothing, but Maria is a genius and should have papers for you to sign by dinner." Randall could not keep the pride and exhilaration from his voice. "She did an amazing job for you. I really shouldn't have stolen her thunder, but she was in meetings all day and I just couldn't wait to tell you."

Sloane danced a little jig where she stood until Randall reached to twirl her. Without thinking, as a gesture of thanks, she went to give him a quick peck on the cheek. Instead, she planted a big, noisy kiss on his lips.

Randall responded instantly to both her energy and her affection, changing the tenor of the kiss and quickly infusing it with passion. His arms wrapped around her waist, his large hands cupped her round behind and pulled her taut against his rapidly growing erection. He kissed her back with heat and passion, spinning her around until her feet lifted a good foot off the floor.

"I am so excited. I am so excited," she bubbled, looking into his intelligent eyes, passion momentarily giving way to celebration.

"Well," he responded in a husky voice, placing her back on her feet, again wrapping his hands around her. Resting his large palms on her butt, he drew her against his lower body and his obvious desire. "I seem to be getting excited too."

Randall flashed her a wicked smile, hesitated briefly, then dropped his face down to meet Sloane's, his lips softly cajoling hers into a kiss that deepened and turned hungry. He nipped at her lower lip until she opened her mouth to him, allowing his tongue to explore further. His bear-paw hands seared heat into her skin through the thin dress as he pulled her taut against him.

Their bodies and mouths locked together, his powerful thighs pressed against hers and the strength in his arms capturing her. Her small breasts flattened against his suit coat and she reveled in the scratchy fabric against her bare skin and the power of his solid body.

Like something out of a movie, he lifted her in one fluid movement and traversed the length of the hallway. He juggled her slightly to free up a hand to open the bedroom door, but never released her from the kiss. She shook her head at the first doorway, and pointed across the hall. Randall marched into the room, and although they were alone, he kicked the door shut behind them.

Randall stood Sloane carefully on her feet beside the bed. She had lost a shoe in her dancing stumble and now kicked off the other. She hardly reached Randall's chin without the aid of the high heels and felt small and vulnerable.

Randal released herin order and placed his hands on her bare upper arms to guide her down to the bed. He followed, dropping to one knee, leaving one foot on the floor so he was half standing as he awkwardly yanked off the suit coat and tugged on his tie. He pulled his beautiful dress shirt over his head like a t-shirt and followed her down to the mattress to lay the warm skin of his muscled torso on her small body. His mouth took hers repeatedly in slow, drugging kisses.

Sloane ran her tongue over Randall's entire mouth, tasting coffee and him. He pulled off her little sweater, then ran his hands up and down, along her skin, from hand to shoulder. His fingers were rough, his hand was the size of a bear's, but his touch was gentle and sensuous. He moved his mouth from her lips to her neck, planting little kisses. The abrasive sweetness of his tongue trailed from her mouth to her ear, then down across her exposed collarbone to that hint of cleavage at the top of her dress. Sloane felt sweet desire spiral in her veins and hot moisture in her core, almost lifting her off the bed with want. Randall's powerful body held her firmly in place.

Randall's clothed leg laid heavily between Sloane's slender ones. Her dress had ridden high on her thigh, exposing her long limbs. His left hand was caressing her leg, kneading the muscle lightly as he moved up from her knee to her hipbone in a lazy pattern. The movement was driving her crazy. She thought she would scream, or worse, beg, when finally, he slid his hand across her lace-covered abdomen to the hot, wet core of her.

She sighed at the weight of his huge hand resting upon her as his fingers worked the edge of her panties. He was teasing, not moving too much, but enough to entice her. She moaned softly, trying again to lift her hips to meet his teasing fingers, begging for more. In response, Randall tugged at the lace, pulling it lower while his head returned higher to capture her mouth in a heart-stopping kiss.

Rolling his muscular frame off Sloane, Randall fumbled with his belt, then the button on his trousers. Sloane reached over and her delicate fingers made quick work of the button and zipper before she slid her hand, cool and slender, into his briefs to feel the hot, pulsing length of him. His erection, already thick and straining, leaped to life, searing her hand, inviting her to stroke him more.

He kicked off his pants while she helped roll them down his leg. Clumsy but effective. She was naked and open to him under the skirt of her bunched dress when she felt him move between her thighs. They were both too aroused to bother removing her dress.

Randall fumbled for protection, then pushed the pants onto the floor and out of the way.

"Hurry," she mumbled against his mouth as her hips rose high, in invitation.

Randall clearly needed no more enticement than that. Sloane felt him plunge into her in a single, searing thrust. She gasped at the movement in obvious surprise, and Randall stayed still, seated deep inside her small body.

"Holy shit, you are so tight," he commented between little nipping kisses along her jawline. "Did I hurt you? Are you alright?"

"Mm," Sloane replied with a languorous smile, then with repeated sighs of "Oh, yes," as Randall moved inside her. He pulled his considerable length out until just the tip of him was teasing her, hovering there for a long moment. Then he slid in again, hard and fast or frustratingly slow. He alternated the movements until her body sensed a rhythm and responded to his. She was lifting her hips high, trying to prevent him from withdrawing, working to keep him deep inside her. When she thought she would go mad from the slow teasing penetration, Randall slammed into Sloane hard and fast, leaving her panting and on the edge.

Sloane wrapped her long legs around Randall, holding him securely against her as Randall plunged into her forcefully and rapidly. She was rising to meet him thrust for thrust. Until he halted.

"Noooo," Sloane cried. "Don't stop." Her body reached for his, begging him to resume the slow rub and heat.

"Oh, don't worry, Princess. I am not going anywhere." He took a few deep shuddering breaths and slowed down the pace. She felt his hands stroking her skin from shoulder to hip and sensed his fingers moving between them. He leaned up just enough to get his large hand comfortably against her belly, fingers dipping lower, then lower still, seeking the tiny nub between her lips and finding it with certainty.

"You are very good at this," she teased between gasping breaths.

"Practice," was his cocky response before teasing the small tight bud more, feeling her losing further control of her breath. He observed her face. Could he see the ecstasy move across her face? Sloane had always prided herself on being in charge, even in bed. With Randall, she knew she was losing control, knew he could see it, but she didn't give a damn. The pleasure was breathtaking. Sloane felt an intense orgasm rising inside her, just out of reach.

Just when she would have gone over the edge into welcome oblivion, Randall eased up on his touch. Her eyes flew open, perplexed, her body straining for release.

"Not yet Sloane, not yet. I am in no hurry, not with you. I want us to really experience this. Enjoy every moment, every touch. I want to be here for you. Take care of you.. Let me take wonderful care of you."

Sloane thought she would find it hard to lie back and let this man control their pace and their movements, but it took only a moment of resistance before she gave in. Instantly, realizing her arousal was increasing even more than she imagined possible, she was free to just feel without thought. He removed the hand that had been toying with her and tugged the straps of her dress off her shoulders. Holding both of her hands in his large one, he gently raised them over her head. With her arms raised and straps down, Randall could use his teeth to loosen the front of the dress and pull it below her breasts, baring them first to his eyes, then to his seeking lips.

Randall latched his mouth hungrily around Sloane's breast, tonguing her nipple to a tight pebble and sending a zing of heat rocketing through her body. She pushed against his mouth as his teeth scraped across her nipple. Her lower body responded, lifting in a futile attempt to entice him deeper. He was playing her body like a Stradivarius. Her back arched, reaching for more, pushing her breast against him, filling his mouth, loving the scratch of his beard against her tender skin. Just when she felt she would die from pleasure, he released her, kissing her mouth tenderly. After a long gaze into her eyes, he sank his head and locked his lips around her other nipple.

He nibbled at her skin, at her pebble-hard nipple, as she writhed beneath him, hands still held above her head. She could only twist from side to side, reveling in the blissful torture as her arousal and need grew.

"Want more?" He asked her, grinning like an arrogant fool before moving to kiss her mouth. He sucked her bottom lip, then released it and bit lightly before allowing his tongue to roam freely in her moist mouth. "I want to give you more. I want to give you more than you have ever experienced, more than you can imagine."

Sloane was lost in a fog of passion, unable to think straight or think at all. She wanted him to thrust into her hard and fast and to claim her. She wanted to feel his mouth on her breasts but also feel his tongue along her skin and in her mouth. She was desperate for his fingers to return to playing with her, craving his touch. He was slowly driving her mad—deliciously, excitingly mad. She wanted all of him, everywhere.

Randall moved his mouth again, leaving hers to trail his tongue along her jaw, along her collarbone. All the while, Randall held himself away from her body, barely entering her tight passage, teasing, withdrawing when she tried to pull him deeper. His arms began to shake from holding his weight above her. He shifted his body, gaining more leverage while still pinning her arms with one hand, using the other hand to stimulate her with his magic fingers.

When Sloane thought she could take no more, when she felt ready to burst into a thousand pieces, she recognized Randall was going over the edge too. He began pumping into her repeatedly, his long, slow strokes gaining speed in their joint desperation. Randall found a new rhythm as he lifted and lowered his hips hard and fast, driving into her, demanding her response.

Sloane was taking tiny useless breaths interspersed with "yes, oh yes". He held still, deep inside her, his breathing shallow and labored. sweat shining on his skin. She admired his rock- hard abs and massive chest, watching his body joining with hers in a dance as old as time. Mesmerized by the look and feel of him above her and inside her, Sloane completely lost control, pulsing around the length and girth of him as Randall expanded to fill her even more. Her body continued squeezing around him until he exploded in his own orgasm scant seconds later. They lay panting, joined in the aftermath of their lovemaking, kissing softly, Randall caressing her skin.

Spent, Randall dropped all his weight onto Sloane, crushing her into the mattress in a way she found remarkably satisfying. She was sated, fulfilled in a way she had never been before, in a way she had never previously imagined possible. Randall had dragged things out, almost made her beg for him.

She recognized with a jolt that she would have begged, and welcomed it. He still held her hands above her head, even now keeping the upper hand, although she had stopped resisting long ago.

They lay like that for several minutes, catching their breath, kissing each other slowly and sweetly until Randall finally rolled off her. He kept his hold on her hands, lowering them so she could relax her shoulders but still leaving her unable to run her hands over his tempting body. Sloane wanted to touch him, longed to caress those broad shoulders, wide chest and tight waist. She wanted to feel the ripple of hard muscle under his warm, sweaty skin, and kiss every inch of him. Already she longed for him, need was spiraling through her although she was sated.

He pulled her with him as he rolled, reaching for the zipper holding her dress in place, sliding it down and moving away from her long enough to remove the wrinkled mess. As soon as he'd divested her of the clothes, he embraced Sloane against him again with a sigh.

"Oh, this is so good. I wanted to feel your skin, but I just couldn't take the time to take off your dress. Sorry about the wrinkles," he said, with a brief look of apology in his eyes.

"Mmmm," was her lethargic response. Randall was sensuously tickling her palm, where he again held both her hands. She wriggled them and he released her as if he had forgotten he still held them. She rolled her tired shoulders as he lightly massaged them. Finally, she wrapped both arms around his broad back and slid her hands all over his bunched muscles from shoulder to rounded ass.

"You have a gorgeous body," she told him as she continued to stroke his skin.

Built like Atlas, Randall was all muscle and strength, and Sloane thought of him in those terms suddenly. Randall really had the weight of the world on his shoulders. He held a lot together. When he was tender, kind and serious like now, she could see just how good he was at taking care of people.

Oh yeah, he sure took care of me. When do we do that again?

"What? What is that little smile? Ready to go again?"

"Why," she asked coyly, "too soon for you, old man?"

"Old? Who you calling old?" With that, he pulled her so she was lying on top of him. She could feel the hard length of him, hot and huge against her flat stomach.

"Ooh, maybe not so old," she laughed, sitting up and straddling his narrow hips with her thighs. He quickly grabbed the protection that she rolled into place, just before wrapping her slender fingers around his blatant masculinity and sheathing him in her wet and welcoming body. When he deep inside and stretching her, she sat still for a long moment reveling in the feeling of this gorgeous, hot man filling her completely. Impatient, Randall took hold of her waist and helped lift and lower her on his shaft while she circled her hips to maximize the erotic stimulation.

"Ride 'em, Cowgirl," he said with a smile. "You look very pleased with yourself right now. I know you love to be on top, back in control, calling the shots."

"I promise to make it worth your while, Randall, so just put yourself in my capable hands."

"That does not feel a bit like your hands, but feel free to use them, too." Randall bent his hands behind his head like a man with all the time in the world and locked eyes with Sloane. He searched her face, seeing too much for her comfort. Or maybe not. Sloane was ready to let someone see her at last.

Then Randall closed his eyes, sheer bliss radiating over his features, and let her work her magic for the pleasure of them both.

CHAPTER EIGHTEEN

The pair finally got out of bed about an hour later, but only long enough to go to the bathroom and get something for their parched throats. Glasses in hand, they returned to Sloane's bedroom and climbed under the rumpled coverlet, propping their backs against a surfeit of pillows. "You confound me, Princess," Randall confessed, punching down a couple of pillows before propping them behind him. "To the outside world, you are all prickly and angular, but in here you are all soft and mushy."

"Is that some kind of insult?" The vulnerability in her voice prompted Randall to lean over and give her a sweet, lingering kiss. Coming up for air with a last quick nibble on her lips, he extended his arm, pointing from corner to corner, the sweeping gesture taking in the entire bedroom.

"Not at all. B, but look at this room." The two took a moment to survey the surroundings.

Sloane looked about her. She was reclining against the upholstered headboard that reached halfway up the wall behind her, perfect for reading in bed. The linens were soft and expensive, white with French lace edging. At the foot of the bed, wedged between the footboard and two diminutive mirror-legged stools, were the rest of the bed linens, in a tangle where they had kicked them. They included a lovely summery-white duvet cover edged in elegant blue flowers and a pale blue cashmere throw blanket. The bed skirt was the same crisp white as the duvet with a one-inch blue border skimming the plush white-on-white rug.

Looking beyond the end of the bed, wondering what it was Randall wanted her to see, Sloane's view took in the mirrored dresser and the pale blue side tables topped with delicate Murano glass lamps. There was a large, healthy fiddle leaf fig tree in a giant white vase masking the metal radiator behind it. Blocking the afternoon sun were floor to ceiling curtains that matched the bed skirt. She had a few pictures of her family and a small bud vase on the end tables, and a comfy blue overstuffed chair that was presently hidden by Randall's carelessly tossed clothing.

"What? I don't see any problem. This room is peaceful." Sloane was clearly on the defensive, so Randall hesitated a moment, choosing his words carefully once he continued.

"It is peaceful, Sloane. It is also frilly. I just think people would expect you to live in a steel and glass structure with modern furniture in shades of black," Randall observed. "Instead, you are all powder blues, pillows and antiques. You are a complex woman, Princess."

"I just like what I like, I guess." Sloane looked into his face. Was she afraid he was criticizing? "I like soft things, pretty things. And I like you."

"Good thing you added that last statement," he pronounced, running his hand boldly over her abdomen, then across her hipbones. "Speaking of soft things, we need to eat. There is not a drop of food in your refrigerator and I've worked up an appetite."

"Trust me, if you open the cabinet doors instead of the fridge, there is plenty to eat here. I subsist on potato chips and Oreos. Who needs more?"

"I do. I am a growing man who skipped his lunch—thank you very much,. What do you say we get dressed, pick up Maria, start with happy hour, then dinner, then hopefully lots of celebratory champagne?"

"I hope you are right about the champagne. That would be fantastic." Sloane popped up in the bed, leaned over Randall's solid chest, planting a kiss on his full lips. "Let's grab a shower and you can tell me everything."

"Yes, to the showers," he agreed, as if issuing a command, "but it's Maria's tale to tell, so I have to save the rest of the surprise for her."

"I hate waiting, but if you insist."

Randall jumped from the bed, energy restored despite the sweaty activities of the last hour. Sloane slapped his ass playfully, then scooted out of the bed to avoid retaliation.

Reaching into a hall closet, she grabbed Randall an oversized bath sheet and pointed to the guest bath. Grabbing the towel, he commented on its pale blue color and followed her into her bath. He showed every sign of following her into her shower, so she relented, hanging his towel next to hers on a large hook. She twisted the water handle for the large showerhead hanging over the old-fashioned claw-foot tub, surrounded by a pale-blue floral shower curtain.

Waiting for the water to heat, Sloane gathered her hair away from her face and neck, securing it on top of her head with a large clip. She tested the temperature of the water, nodded her approval, and Randall held her arm chivalrously as she stepped over the high ledge and into the tub. At the last second, he returned her earlier swat to the behind, and they both laughed. Climbing in behind her, Randall filled the large space as he wrapped his arms around her and kissed her passionately, unleashing a hint of their earlier desire.

Sloane reached for the scented bath gel and a pouf. When she lathered her body, Randall took the pouf from her, placed it back on the shower rack, and poured a sizeable amount of the expensive gel into his hands instead. He began running his slippery hands all over her body, first her back, then around the cheeks of her butt, taking his time, rubbing, kneading, and caressing her. Pulling her soapy body to slither against his, her back to his front, he wrapped his hands around her and began stroking her abdomen, then breasts and chest. His hand rose to slide across her, pinning her firmly against him with a large hand. Having her immobilized, he slid a lathered hand between her thighs to stroke her core.

His touch was light at first, then more insistent. He was sliding his powerful body against her slippery back and butt while stroking her center with his large hand. Sloane could not move, only able to feel his hard body sliding against her while his even, slippery fingers drove her to new heights. Randall again had the aces in the delicious power game they were playing, but Sloane was winning as well, feeling sensations she had never allowed herself to feel when she had refused to lose control.

Turning Sloane in his arms, Randall dipped his head to claim her mouth, exploring its moist heat with his probing tongue, while his hand seductively palmed her sensitive flesh. Lulled into a slow burn by his gentle motions, her body felt a fiery shock that escalated her desire instantly as Randall stuck first one, then two long, thick fingers inside of her. He was almost lifting her off her feet with each plunging thrust as he took her hard and fast against the cold tile wall.

Pinned in place, her legs wrapped tight around Randall's hand, Sloane gave in as his fingers drove her to distraction. One of his hands squeezed the globes of her butt in time with the thrusts of his fingers.

Titling back to open a small space between their bodies, he slid his hand around until it was tight to the bud between her thighs. Soon, his fingers were working her with sure, knowing motions and she was straining, her body craving the release just out of reach. Randall's hands were relentless, as were his demanding kisses. With a sharp inhale, she shuddered and lost control, moaning her joy. She catapulted over the edge, electricity flowing through her veins, followed by liquid pleasure.

"Good?" he asked before she could catch her breath, his fingers still working their magic. Her breasts were rubbing against his soapy muscled chest her nipples hard and oversensitive.

"Fabulous," she whispered, exhausted. "But I need a break."

"Sure?" Randall's head swooped to capture her swollen lips in a searing kiss, sucking her tongue into his mouth, as he slowed his touches.. He released her swollen lips after swallowing her increased breaths and moans. "You aren't acting like you need a break," he teased.

"Don't you dare stop nowt," she commanded, eyes wide as saucers.

It amazed Sloane when the most intense orgasm shattered her body. She shouted, her chest heaving, her legs trembling, as she felt Randall stroke slowly inside her. She could feel her whole entire body quiver from the exertion as she sagged into him, completely spent.

Resting her head back against the tile, Sloane strived to catch her breath. The man had proven himself utterly fantastic. Each time she was sure she was incapable of more, he coaxed a response from her, including multiple incredible orgasms. Her quivering legs could barely hold her and his arm around her was supporting most of her weight as he slid his fingers from her body. She felt a poignant loss at the withdrawal, wanting more, although she knew her sore muscles needed at least a brief rest. His right hand was gently soaping her arms and then her legs while he used his left to keep her from sliding in a weary heap to the floor.

When he was sure she was back on her own feet, he grabbed the gel and quickly washed and rinsed himself, water sluicing down his powerful body. She leaned against the wall, forehead resting on the cool tile, breathing becoming less ragged. Randall turned her in his arms, holding her gently, giving her a lingering soft kiss while reaching behind her to turn off the water.

"Thank you, Sloane. That was incredible. You were incredible." His voice was honey and intimate.

Stepping out, he ran the large blue towel quickly over his arms and chest, then wrapped it around his torso. The feminine color just made him look more masculine, and Sloane openly admired the view. He grabbed the second large towel from the hook and wrapped Sloane in it as she stepped from the large tub.

"You are killing me, woman," he bellowed with a proud, he-man grin on his handsome face.

"Me? You think I am killing you? You have that backwards, Neanderthal." Sloane responded. She softened the name-calling with a quick kiss and then laughed.

"I love that sound," he whispered close to her ear. "You need to laugh more. I want to make you laugh all the time."

Sloane's head whipped around to make eye contact. "You want more?"

"Well, not this very second," Randall countered. "But later tonight, sure. Tomorrow, the next day. Next week..."

"Not a one-night stand?" She suddenly appeared little girl shy, hope in her question.

"One-day stand might be more accurate, but no, not that either, Sloane. I want to try you and me, attempt to get it right. You challenge me. You intrigue me. I want to stick around and get to know you, know us. Is that okay with you?"

"Oh yes. That is very okay."

"But this only works if I get food, and soon." Randall announced, shifting the mood immediately as he went to find his clothes. Sloane was following when she glimpsed herself in the steamy mirror. She halted there, spending a few minutes trying to do something about the abrasions on her chin from Randall's new beard.

"Ah, to hell with it," she said aloud, after failing to cover it with a tinted moisturizer. "It's my badge of honor." Laughing to herself, she went to claim Randall, dress up a bit, and head out. Finally, after all this time, there were things to celebrate.

CHAPTER NINETEEN

Since they never made it to the Peninsula for lunch, Randall settled for the drive-thru at the 'rock and roll' McDonald's on LaSalle. He wolfed down two Big Macs in record time. Although he encouraged Sloane to order, he could only convince her to share his large order of French fries. It was no surprise when he reached for a few more and they were already gone. She really did like junk food. Randall was relieved to get a second chance after that disastrous night at the Cubs game. He never apologized for walking away, and she never questioned him about it. It was as if there was a mutual agreement: "the less said, the better." He was here now, and that was all that mattered. Better to show her his commitment, anyway. Words were easy, actions spoke volumes.

Pulling into his reserved space in the PPHP garage, Randall gave Sloane an evaluating look. Her elegant, straight blue dress stopped just above her knees. It had sleeves to just below her elbows and she looked long, lean and sophisticated. She'd tucked her lustrous hair in a neat chignon, but he could still remember it flowing through his fingers like heavy threads of silk. He felt his body stirring again. She looked cool and in control, so different from just a few hours ago.

Don't think about hours ago or you will be unable to walk.

The woman was incredible—responsive, sensuous, willing to lead or follow. Her body was long and lean. With her shiny length of hair, she reminded Randall of a thoroughbred. Her breasts were lovely, her stomach taut and flat, and her legs long and muscular. She could wrap around him like a cobra and he loved sinking deep into her and watching her hold on for the ride.

Stop thinking about it. Consider the acquisition. Think about French fries. Think about anything else.

Feeling his erection subside, Randall inched into the parking space, turned off the car and went around to open Sloane's door. She sat demurely, waiting for him to help her from the car, and he did not disappoint. The etiquette and manners drummed into him as a young boy would pay off with this woman. Randall knew how to treat a woman like a lady, and Sloane was raised to expect it.

He took her hand to help her from the car and didn't let it go until they stepped from the elevator into the hushed offices of PPHP. Then he let go only to move his own to the small of her back, ushering her down the plush-carpeted corridors toward his imposing corner office.

Sloane understood business. She was savvy enough to recognize that this huge corner office was designed to both intimidate and impress. Finance was about trust, the belief that this company understood wealth—how to acquire and protect it. This space perpetuated the image of success of a solid company that could stand the test of time. All of that was intentional. The surroundings were created to lull clients like Sloane into trusting that their money was well cared for, that they were in the most capable of hands. And Randall knew Sloane needed to believe all this was true. Especially today, when so much was riding on his team to make a miracle occur.

Randall could see that, notwithstanding Sloane's comprehension of the use of surroundings, they impressed her all the same. Dark wood paneling covered the walls; a heavy wooden desk dominated the space. An elegant and enormous Turkish rug covered most of the floor, absorbing hushed conversations and footsteps. The art was modern, in neutral tones. Everything looked powerful, curated, and expensive. The views were the best that money could buy.

As they had passed her office, Randall had asked Amy to call upstairs and let Maria know they had arrived. Soon they could see Maria bustling toward them down the hallway, full of excitement. She met Sloane with a hearty, no-nonsense handshake as soon as she moved through the door.

No limp-wristed stuff for these women. Maria instantly conveyed that same sense of assurance and confidence that the offices created. She treated Sloane as if she were her only client, or at least the only one that mattered. Observing these two women bowled Randall over. They were powerhouses, and they knew it. He could actually observe Sloane's transformative return to her former status. It was clear in her stature and her voice—the confident, feisty Sloane was back in full force.

Sweeping the skirt of her no-nonsense navy suit under her, Maria seated herself across from Sloane. Leaning forward, her highlighted, chin-length hair swung forward to hide her face. Maria pushed it back impatiently and began without preamble. "I am so glad you came in. My team and I have made a terrific deal for you today. My assistant will be down shortly with the papers for you to sign. You will be so happy. It is better than we could have ever hoped, Sloane. You will be thrilled."

Maria was almost tripping over her words with enthusiasm. Randall had stepped out as the two women began speaking, but once he was sure they had completed all but the signatures, he returned quickly to sit beside Sloane on the sofa. His presence seemed to remind

Maria of her professionalism, because she took a deep breath before continuing more slowly.

"You have an offer from Steel Frank, a solid offer." Maria was completing a recap of all they had discussed. "The legal team proved that your existing contracts are tight enough that they will transfer to them as part of the acquisition. That, plus the existing copyrights and patents, sealed the deal. They are offering just shy of the full asking price and will retain about 80% of your consultant staff. Of course, there will be redundancies in administrative staff. We can't avoid that. This will hit HI legal, HR and support staff hard and fast, but Steel Frank will provide a one-month severance, which is generous under the circumstances."

"You and your father are out, I am afraid," Randall chimed in now. "But I think you expected that." Sloane nodded her agreement as Amy stepped in with a bottle of Dom Perignon. "Can we toast, or do we need to wait on this?"

"Oh no, pour me a glass please," Sloane flashed Maria a completely relaxed smile, her first in months—out of bed, at least. Maria excused herself, and stepped into the hallway to meet with her assistant, who delivered the final paperwork. Meanwhile, Randall noiselessly popped the cork, pouring with a flourish.

"I dodged a bullet here, didn't I?" Sloane asked, demanding honesty and watching his face to be sure she got it. "I was very lucky Steel Frank believed the contracts were good, and I know it. I saw clauses that would have allowed customers to walk. Steel Frank's due diligence team might have determined that our long-term deals would not be binding after an acquisition."

"They could have, but they didn't."

"No, they didn't. I suspect you and Maria had something to do with that." If Sloane expected Randall to offer information, he disappointed her, saying nothing further. The three spent the next ninety minutes reviewing contract language. Maria indicated the final terms showed no need for government involvement, and it was a cash deal, so there were no contingencies. This would allow the deal to progress quickly, another reason to celebrate. They happily found reason after reason to sip the expensive champagne.

"Except for the three clauses I noted, everything looks fantastic," Sloane said finally. "As soon as the lawyers review everything and straighten out those three nits, I think we are set. I guess now I leave it to my lawyers, their lawyers, and you and your wizard team of bankers, Maria. Randall, thank you so much for bringing in Maria. She was clearly the right woman for the job."

Sloane was beaming from ear to ear, speaking expressively, using her hands for emphasis, licking her lips, her eyes revealing so much of what she was thinking. Randall watched, mesmerized, appreciating every little motion that made her Sloane.

I am whipped. Totally whipped.

Sloane took the last of her copies, tucked them in her bag, and they stood and shook hands. The teams would meet, beginning tomorrow, to complete everything and transfer the badly needed funds. The deal would be done within the week and announced before the Gala.

The three discussed where to celebrate and decided on the Soho House. It was a perfect night for the rooftop bar. Sloane suspected they would know everyone at the West Loop location and either the party would grow with well-wishers as they learned about the deal before it went public, or people would shun them, in which case the party would end before it started.

Maria called her associates LuAnn, Seth, Joanie and Alan, since they had all worked on the deal. Maria included several others who had put a finger on the deal along the way. They were already a party of twenty when they stepped under the stars on a perfect mid-June evening.

There was a large seating area ready for them.

"How did you do that?" she asked Randall as they approached an area already blocked off from the growing crowd.

"Helps to know people in the right places," he smiled cryptically. "I made a few very strategic phone calls."

The group settled around one corner of the fire pit, ready for much later when they might need it to take a chill out of the air. Regan joined them, along with four individuals from her office. They ordered Champagne for all, cocktails for a select few.

Sloane had met three of Regan's companions before. She was delighted to accept the exuberant congratulations from Ethan and Martin, and Sloane knew one woman, Astrid, Regan's general counsel, a smart, funny woman who took her work seriously but knew how to party. Astrid, in typical lawyer fashion, gently reminded everyone to be careful about what they said and to keep their voices down. This deal would not be public for about forty-eight hours more and discretion was still important.

The unknown fourth person was a lovely woman with a short bob of dark hair that was full of coppery highlights, deep brown eyes and a golden tan Sloane envied. She was lean and leggy, reminding Sloane of a greyhound. Although not too tall, she was clearly not a gymnast, so Sloane figured her for a tennis player or maybe a runner. She introduced herself as Charlotte Roche, the LHRE Director of Finance, as of last week. With her thick Boston accent, Sloane had trouble understanding everything she said, but she liked her open smile immediately.

Over the next hour, Alex joined them, saying hello to everyone. He had financed enough deals for him to know most of the people in the group and joined their conversations easily. Wyatt and Keeli arrived a while later. Wyatt plunged in immediately, offering sincere congratulations and an awkward hug while Keeli stayed on the outskirts of the group waiting to assure that she would be welcome.

Randall observed the interaction carefully. Wyatt noted Randall's hand on the small of Sloane's back as soon as he arrived, signaling to all they were together. Sloane followed Randall's every movement, like a flower following the sun. The combination showed everyone that she was with him. Randall made sure Wyatt understood all of that clearly. Alex nodded to Wyatt, confirming the lay of the land. With a big, approving grin, Wyatt nodded to Randall before he politely asked Sloane if she was comfortable with Keeli joining them.

"The more the merrier," Sloane responded, slightly tipsy and full of good will. "I love everyone tonight."

Keeli approached shyly after a sign from Wyatt, offered heartfelt congratulations to Sloane, and quietly suggested they get to know each other better when Sloane had more time.

"Oh honey, I have nothing but time." Sloane gushed. "Call anytime. Really, it might be fun."

Keeli looked surprised by the answer, but pleased. "I will do that, Sloane. I look forward to it."

The large assemblage drank champagne, ordered tons of food and enjoyed the pleasure of each other's company until late into the evening. Men approached the group, hitting on women at the fringe of the party, and a few participants paired off and disappeared. Regan left early, claiming too much work, but her coworkers stayed. Sloane assumed Regan departed because Tyler was a no-show, but said nothing.

The group expanded until around 10:00, then contracted until it was Alex and Charlotte, chatting with their heads close together;

Maria, Ethan and Astrid, talking shop; and a tipsy Sloane, with her head resting on the solid shoulder of a surprisingly sober Randall.

Clustered together around the fire pit, they began a serious discussion about going in search of ice cream. They were comparing the relative merits of Margie's versus Jeni's versus Black Cow and checking their phones to see if any of the three restaurants were open late. Eventually, they just abandoned the whole idea since Sloane was half asleep, propped up by Randall.

"Hey sleepyhead, maybe I should get you to bed?"

"I think you did that already, Neanderthal," she giggled up into Randall's indulgent face.

"Are you drunk, Sloane Huyler?" Randall pretended to be shocked.

"I am barely tipsy, sir. The big question is, why aren't you?"

"I am your errant knight, destined to assure you of a wonderful time and a safe arrival home. It is my job and my pleasure to see to your every need tonight, my lady. I shall pay the check, get the car and tuck you safely into my bed."

With that, Randall gestured an exaggerated bow and signaled for the check. He noticed with pleasure that she had not argued about going home with him, nor had she minded his unceasing attention. She had allowed him to place a hand on her back, around her shoulders, or clasp her hand all night. He had staked his claim, and she was on board with it.

He handed the valet ticket to a passing waiter, tipping him heavily to take it down to the valet, and then said their goodnights. Alex gave Randall a hearty pat on the back and a "way to go, man" before returning to his engrossing conversation with Charlotte.

Once he had Sloane settled in the plush interior of his BMW, Randall leaned over, snapped her seat belt into place and gave her a slow, passionate kiss. She sighed with contentment as he pulled back from her and put the car in gear.

"What a good time," she mumbled. "Everyone was so nice. You did that for me, didn't you? You made everyone accept me again."

"Sloane, you know these people. I cannot make them do anything they don't want to do. They were nice to you because you were nice to them. And because they were genuinely happy for you."

"You believe that if it makes you happy, handsome, but we both know that they were kind to me because I was with you. You worked your hocus-pocus, and I am very grateful."

"Is that what they call it now, hocus-pocus? I always called it hot sex, but what do I know?"

Sloane laughed that tinkling laugh that he relished, rested her head back, closed her eyes and smiled while he drove the short distance to his River North townhouse, where he pulled into his space in the underground garage. When he looked over again, Sloane was sleeping. Too much stress, too much partying and too much sex could do that to a woman.

Wait a minute. Did I just say too much sex? There is no such thing.

As if to prove his point, Randall leaned over and gave Sloane a hungry kiss, tongue probing the warmth of her mouth where the taste of champagne lingered. His hands roamed possessively over her body until they reached the bottom of her dress, which he lifted slowly.

She was wide awake now.

"Stay just like that," he dictated, stepping from the car and coming around to her side. Randall opened her door and swung her legs out of the car, allowing the dress to ride up further, following its hem with the pressure of his warm hands until they found the heat he was seeking. He slid her very damp panties down until they dangled from one foot, then wrapped her long legs around his torso. He was wasting no time.

I love how ready she is for me, all heat and warmth and woman. God, she turns me on!

Tipping carefully to keep from hitting his head, Randall bent over Sloane, reclining her on the large seat and kissing her before she could voice a protest, which he feared she might in the public setting. Instead, she did a quick glance around and nodded her approval. He quickly undid his pants, pushing her hand away when she reached to assist him. He stood over her, hard as a rock and throbbing with need. Pulling her tight against him, he slid into her without preamble, thrusting hard, pulling back, then thrusting until he could go no further. She was so responsive that she turned him on even more until he feared he might not last long enough to pleasure her.

His breath sounded like a freight train;, her moans were anything but quiet. If anyone was in the garage, they were getting at least a reverberating sound show, if not more. He didn't care. He could not get enough of Sloane. Her hands were scrabbling at the edges of the seat, trying to avoid hitting her head on the console while trying to provide the counterthrusts.

"Lift your arms," he demanded as he yanked her dress over her head. Rather than protest, she did his bidding, even helping him with the resistant fabric until she was naked except for her shoes. "Wrap your arms around my neck and hold on tight."

Once Sloane was holding him securely, he shifted from the car, taking her with him, never withdrawing from the heat of her body. He carried her to the front of the car and laid her across the hood, still warm from the engine. She released his neck to lie back on the metal, reaching to grab what she could of the front grill as Randall propelled them both up the sleek surface. His mouth was everywhere—sucking her breasts until her nipples rose in taut peaks, nipping and tonguing them before sucking her entire breast hard into his mouth. When she could take no more of the sensation, he shifted to nuzzle into her neck, his hands hard against the hood of the car, his body moving relentlessly over hers, demanding her body's sensuous response.

Randall stilled, placing his finger against his lips. Between the moans and heavy breathing, he heard heels clicking on the cement. They were not close, but he couldn't discern the distance or direction of the noise. Sloane was still breathing hard, her gasps echoing in the open space, so Randall placed his mouth over hers and kissed her soundly while lying across her body to provide a modicum of modesty. They waited like that until the sound receded, when Randall began again as if nothing had happened. Sloane had a powerful orgasm almost instantly, pulsing insistently around him, crying out in pure pleasure.

No longer able to care about a potential audience, Randall let go with a roar, spilling inside of Sloane until he had nothing left, falling across her body, wasted. He kissed the small shell of her ear, biting it gently before saying so softly it was barely more than a breath, "you drive me wild, woman."

Sloane laughed, a hearty, full-bodied laugh that shook Randall's whole body because of their position.

"I cannot believe we just did that," she repeated, laughing and peppering his face with kisses until she finally stopped, taking his face in her hands and holding him for a long, searing kiss. "That was crazy. We are crazy. That was utterly amazing, Randall. You are amazing."

"We are amazing." Randall looked about him as if suddenly aware of their surroundings. "We are amazing, and you are very naked. Perhaps we should fix that?"

"I am wearing shoes," she corrected him in a saucy voice, showing off her Taryn Rose heels. She remained laying across the hood, kissing him repeatedly, apparently in no hurry to dress.

Randall stood, tucked himself back into his pants, and was immediately immaculate. He had not a hair out of place. He reached in the car for Sloane's dress, turned it right side out, attempted to smooth the wrinkles from it, and handed it to her with an apologetic grin. She slid it over her head, while Randall picked her panties up from the garage floor and shoved them in his pocket.

"A souvenir?"

"Perhaps," he responded evasively, but with an impish lift of one eyebrow.

He removed his suit jacket and wrapped it around her shoulders, leaving his arm around her as they moved in unison toward the elevator. Alone in the car, he pushed her gently to the wall, leaned into her heavily, and kissed her like she was water to a drowning man. He did not relent until they had moved to his door and he had to fumble for his keys.

"I have never seen your place," Sloane mentioned as he opened the door.

"And you won't see much now." He bypassed the light switch and lifted her over his shoulder in a fireman's carry.

Randall moved through his dark townhouse, pretending to gasp for breath when he carried her lithe body up the stairs to the second floor. She laughed at his silliness, enjoying how comfortable they had become with each other. The mood turned serious. As Randall strode down the wide corridor, kicked back a door dramatically and dropped her into the middle of his bed. He quickly removed his clothes, again lifted the dress over her head and heard her kick her shoes to the floor. He was on her in seconds, like a teenager who could not get enough.

"Spread your legs for me, Princess," he told her even as his hands were moving to spread them himself. She felt his shoulders against the back of her knees and protested, butwhen the words died on her lips at the rough feel of his beard on the inside of her thigh. He could feel her pulse under his mouth as any protest died on her lips.

"Randall, wait. A shower…"

"Shh, I don't care. Just lay back."

Randall kissed his way up the inside of one thigh, rough fingers sliding up the other. She felt his hot breath against her curls and his fingers spreading her nether lips. He felt her take in a deep breath and hold it. She was taut with anticipation and desire.

He waited for her exhale, waiting her out and allowing their anticipation to ratchet up further. Finally, he sank his face into the scent of their recent sex and ran his tongue along every sensitive inch of her, tasting her, tasting himself on her, feeling her tremble with desire.

He made his tongue wide to touch as much of her as possible, and then switched it to tight and thin, allowing him to stab inside of her. Going back and forth between long licks and plunging jabs, he soon had her writhing under him, unable to lie still, hips lifting to meet his every move. She had already had five orgasms today and was rapidly approaching her sixth, head swinging wildly from side to side, feet shifting along the covers restlessly, hands fisted in his hair, holding him tight to her body as her need escalated.

He briefly wished he had turned on the hall light. He wanted the illumination to watch her face when she came. She was a sight to behold then, this woman who worked so diligently to maintain control. She was stunning when she lost it. He was as enraptured, knowing he could push her over the edge as he was with the actual feel of it.

And it felt incredible.

Sloane was pulling at his shoulders, trying to encourage him to move up her body and slide deep inside her. She was trying to control the situation to get what she craved. He was tempted, briefly, to give in to her, but he resisted, aware that the more he teased, the more intense her eventual response would be.

In playing this game of cat and mouse, he discovered his forte. He had greater sexual control than she had. He could hold out for an orgasm longer. When Sloane wanted release from her wild desire, she demanded anything and everything that would get her over the edge.

Randall was more patient. Not significantly more, but enough. He could wait her out, push her further and further until she had to let him take the lead. She felt so damn good that it was hard to wait. However, he had learned that if he delayed just a little longer, they would both win.

"Please, Randall, please." She was begging him, pulling at his broad shoulders.

"Please what, Sloane? Tell me what you want, Princess. Tell me what you need. Do you want me to stop?"

"Oh God, no," she pleaded.

"Just let go. Trust me to take care of you. Let me take care of you."

Randall lifted his head long enough to take a slight break, knowing he was driving her crazy. He knew Sloane thought he was about to move up her body, that he was giving in to her desires. He slid his tongue up her inner thigh lightly, teasingly, until he reached her center again where he barely touched her. Sloane moaned.

"That feels incredible. More. Please, more, please." He did it again. Sloane tried to raise her hips, but Randall was stretched across her lower body.

"Please what, Sloane. What do you need?"

"You know what I need, damn you." He could feel her toes clench, her fists tighten in his hair. In response, he lightened the touch of his tongue even more.

"Just tell me what you want." He was relentless. She didn't want to ask. It would mean she had handed over control. He wanted that capitulation as much as he wanted to give her pleasure. Not to break her, never that, but to show her she could trust him. He would happily let her have the upper hand, but from this day forward, she would understand that they were equals, that he could take it back.

At least in this, they would be equals, capable of give and take. It might keep her from trying to push him around or take him for granted. It was the only way they could love each other and trust each other. He felt like this struggle was the only way to teach her she could rely on him to be there for her.

"Fuck me, damn it. Fuck me already," she growled at him.

"Tsk, tsk, what kind of language is that for a proper young lady?" If she could have reached for a lamp, she might have smashed it over his head, and he knew it. He dipped his head one last time to run his tongue over her, sucking her hard nub into his mouth until her hips bucked wildly around him.

Lifting off her in a fluid movement, he propelled into her body in one powerful move, sinking deep into her heat, filling her completely. He felt her tighten and spasm around him instantly, before he even moved. He paused for her orgasm to subside before kissing her deeply, letting her taste her juices on his mouth and thrusting his body into hers. The powerful muscles in his ass bunched and released as he slammed forward repeatedly.

He wanted to last just a minute longer, but he couldn't do it. She excited him too much. Using every ounce of power, Randall continued to rise and fall, sliding along the walls of Sloane's passage, feeling the friction and heat. She was still so tight around him, even after he had filled her repeatedly. She felt perfect.

Sloane had her legs wrapped tightly around Randall, his body pinned her to the bed with his weight, and his arms shook with tension. He bent his head to kiss her mouth, sucking on her lips and tongue, breathing into her mouth and taking her breath in return.

When he felt like his heart would explode, Randall felt Sloane shudder under him with a last, long, low moan of pleasure. He plunged into her and released the last of his pent- up desire before falling upon her like dead weight.

His arms still shaking from the effort of holding himself up for so long, but he realized his trembling was nothing compared to the quivering of Sloane's entire body. She clung to him, slowly regaining the ability to breathe and to think, as the overwhelming rattle of her breath subsided.

Randall lay upon her for a long time before finally moving away and rolling onto his side, bringing Sloane with him, spooning around her. She was fragile, tiny, with his bulk wrapped around her. Her breathing was still labored and harsh.

"Ssh, hush now, love," he said, stroking a sweep of dark hair away from her face. "Sleep, Sloane. I've got you. Just sleep."

He heard her quiet finally. She must be exhausted. Randall knew he was. He allowed himself to close his eyes, never letting go of her, and fell asleep feeling like a king.

CHAPTER TWENTY

Sloane awoke to the smell of coffee. Seeing the shirt Randall had worn last night thrown haphazardly on a bench at the foot of the bed, she threw it over her naked body, intending to find a bathroom and then the source of that delicious aroma. Putting on the enormous shirt—he really was a mountain of a man—and rolling up the sleeves, Sloane took a moment to look about her. The room was enormous, modern and masculine with a king-sized bed flanked by two highly functional nightstands and modern lighting on the wall above them. Persian rugs covered polished dark wood floors, adding reds and blues to the otherwise neutral space. A wall of windows hid behind floor to ceiling plantation shutters, currently closed tight. They were unable to block out the light of a dazzling sun.

Sloane had no idea what time it was. She found a beautifully appointed bathroom, also enormous, with double sinks and an oversized shower, used the facilities and ran her fingers through her hair to untangle any unruly spots. It was unnecessary, just habit, since it hung in a flawless and shiny curtain down her back, as always.

Padding barefoot out the bedroom door, Sloane passed another large bedroom, an enormous and stately office, another modern bath, and two closed doors she assumed were closets. She ran her hand over the dark wood bannister, shining from a recent waxing as she wandered to the lower floor. It was one huge, high ceilinged open space that included kitchen, dining and living rooms. It was all dark woods and white walls with nothing blocking the view from end to end except a gorgeous light fixture over the heavy glass dining table and a modern steel hood hanging above the stove.

She ran her fingers lightly over the wall of cabinets, sleek and shiny white running the length of the room, then moved across the open space to look through an expanse of doors and windows. The two sets of sliding doors opened to an expansive yard. Besides an attached narrow deck, she spied a brick patio at ground level, surrounded by flowering trees and shrubs. At the far end of the open space was an impressive outdoor kitchen and modern teak sofas, tables and chairs. Their modern lines somehow blended flawlessly with the old-fash-ioned brick fireplace and chimney. It looked inviting, a peaceful oasis in the heart of the city. Sloane wondered if perhaps Randall would allow her to sit out there a while before returning home today. It was so beautiful.

Speaking of Randall, Sloane had not heard a sound anywhere on the two floors. She went in search of coffee and Randall, feeling em-barrassed and shy about seeing him in the bright light of the day after the previous 24 hours of decadence.

Finding the coffee pot first with an empty cup in front of it, she poured the brew and took a fortifying sip. On the counter beside a bowl of sugar substitute, she found a note saying "Good morning, Gorgeous. Trust you slept well. Didn't have the heart to wake you, but I miss you already. Call me."

He was gone? It explained the silence at least. Randall had left Sloane alone in his home. ? She glanced at the clock on the stove and quickly understood why. It was almost 10:30. She had slept over ten hours. She never slept this long or this late.

Then again, I have never had seven—OMG seven!—incredible orgasms to wear me out so completely.

Seven. The man was a modern marvel. In the light of day, it mortified her to realize some risks they had taken, the things they had done. He allowed her to explore an untamed, wicked side because she trusted him not to push the envelope too far. Not to take risks that were dangerous or from which they could not escape.

Wow, I really do trust him.

When had she stopped trying to maintain total control and just trusted Randall to take care of her? She wasn't sure exactly when the power had transferred, but she knew she felt safer with him, cherished and cared for. For a strong, capable woman who had never relied on anyone, she couldn't deny that it felt pretty damn good.

Don't let anyone know that, Sloane, or you will never have the upper hand again.

Sloane sipped at the strong coffee as it cooled. The expensive coffeemaker was still on, keeping the coffee at the perfect temperature so that it tasted like warm heaven on her tongue. Wandering the kitchen, Sloane touched the cool marble surfaces lightly as she went past them. Everything was immaculate and sparse. The sun reflected off the bare glass and stone surfaces and brought a warm hue to the dark wood trim.

The neutral palette and bare floors continued into the living space. A very long brown sofa faced two low-slung steel and leather chairs across a large square glass coffee table piled high with biographies, memoirs and best sellers. A spectacular rug covered the large floor, creating a conversation area, and a modern gas fireplace surrounded by black slate created a visual wall with marble running up to the high ceilings. There was no art on the walls; the garden view, the carefully chosen furniture and rugs were all the art needed. The space felt open but not cold and Sloane surmised that any piece in the room, the small sculptures, the rug, the furniture, was worth more than everything in her apartment combined.

Climbing the openwork wooden staircase more appropriate for a conservative New York brownstone than this modern space, Sloane wondered who had designed the townhouse. The combination of traditional and modern worked well together. She wondered who kept it so immaculate. Everything was spotless, with not even a dust moite revealed by the bright morning sun.

She wandered into his office, all dark woods and bookshelves, then the guest room reminiscent of a fine hotel and the well-designed bath in the hallway. She admired his views of the river from the second-floor windows. When Sloane looked up at the ceiling, the exposed wooden beams and pipes reminded her that Randall lived in a converted warehouse. She marveled at the conversion. It was impeccable and suited Randall perfectly. She loved every inch of the space. As different as it was from her upholstered and wallpapered condo, it was still gorgeous, and felt like a home.

The townhouse was massive. The downstairs was wide open, so while she could see it was big, she didn't really feel the size of it. But upstairs, with rooms offering north, south or river views, she could get a sense of how large a space he really owned. To capture views like this, he had to cover an entire city block, an almost unheard-of feat in such an expensive neighborhood.

Sloane was brazen in her inspection, opening drawers and closets shamelessly. Everything was neat, clothes folded perfectly, expensive dress shoes lined up with shoetrees assuring they would retain their shape. Even the desk in his office was neat, the surfaces cleared of papers, minimal knick-knacks, and only in the best of taste. There was a small crystal paperweight that she knew came from Tiffany's and a few framed pictures of his mother. A gorgeous Mont Blanc pen sat in a holder at the top of a large leather blotter. Very conservative. Very banker. It looked and felt remarkably similar to his office downtown.

Where the walls on the lower floor had been bare, the art on the walls upstairs was large and eclectic. She saw Wyatt's influence in some of the modern selections. Wyatt. Why had she wasted so much time with him? Sloane now realized she was much better suited to his friend. Randall understood her better, knew what she needed. He pushed her around in a way that made her feel strangely safe. He knew she was a strong woman, and he treated her like the intelligent and successful woman she was. They felt evenly matched to her, like partners.

But he also knows how to take complete control. He keeps me off guard, on my toes.

Randall could read her like a book, anticipate her petulant and demanding moments and head them off before they started. He enjoyed her wit, but by having Randall a step ahead of her, she found herself witty but not bitchy.

Randall brought out the best in her. When she was with him, Sloane realized she liked herself more. She felt good about her choices, her interactions with people. Instead of competing, she participated. She could be with people without strategizing how to best them or put them down.

Not only was the man too handsome for his own good, smarter than her (she acknowledged begrudgingly) he was also imaginative and wild in bed. That could have been enough for her. It was certainly far more than she had experienced with other men.

On top of everything, she enjoyed spending time with him, liked matching wits, sharing a meal, sharing a bed. She could appreciate problem solving with him, too. She realized she admired him, looked up to him and depended on him when he wasn't drinking.

I have barely seen him take a drink when we've been together. Could I have misjudged him or has he changed?

Sloane heard her cell phone ringing in the other room and ran to answer it. Assuming it was Randall, she didn't bother to check caller id and answered with a chipper "Hi there."

"Well hello yourself, Sloane, it's Sandra Berensen calling from Addison, Fine, and Stark. I hope I haven't caught you at a bad time."

"No, not at all, Sandra. What can I do for you?"

It surprised Sloane to get a call from her father's law firm, especially from Sandra, the daughter of John Berensen, her father's horrible prosecutor. Since the firm had helped negotiate the reduced sentence and depleted the Huyler's savings, she believed she would never hear from these people again.

There should be nothing left to talk about.

"How are you and your family, Sloane?"

"Good, Sandy, if you overlook the fact that my father is in jail and my mother is losing her home. Of course, you must also ignore the total collapse of our family business. Otherwise, we are doing really well."

"I guess I had that coming, Sloane. My apologies. You know the entire team did everything we could to help your father, but the evidence was pretty damning."

Even when she apologized, this bitch said mean things. Sloane paced, needing to relieve herself of a sudden nervous energy. Sloane's radar was at full blast. She never trusted lawyers—her distrust greater now that they'd lost her father's case. Sloane felt better with her claws exposed, but she retracted them to learn why her family suddenly interested Addison, Fine, and Stark.

"Sandy, did you need something?" Sloane tried to hide the disdain slipping into her voice and her obvious urge to get through this call quickly.

"Well, as you know, most of what we need is in the files from your father, but we need your tax returns, personal and corporate, for the years since his indictment. It's just last year and this year. So, if you could get us the copies, we should have everything we need."

"Need? Why would you need anything?" Sloane asked, clearly bewildered.

"It should be obvious, Sloane. We are trying to get ahead of things."

"What things?" Sloane's pacing increased.

"Well, we are trying to prevent your indictment. Head it off at the pass, so to speak," Sandy continued, impatient with Sloane's lack of understanding.

"Me? They are indicting me? What the hell are you talking about?" Sloane stopped mid-stride, her voice rising. Just when she believed she would weather this storm, things looked to be getting worse.

"I thought Mr. Addison already called you about this, Sloane," Sandy responded, annoyed. "We received information last week that the federal government was reopening the investigation. An informant notified us they are looking into you. They believe they have a case against you on charges of conspiring to defraud your clients."

Sloane felt like a dead weight landed on her chest. She dropped onto the bed, her quivering legs no longer able to hold her. After a few labored breaths, she found her voice.

"What? I don't understand! I did nothing wrong here! Yes, I knew my father was negotiating contracts with Chinese companies assisted by the Chinese government, but that was all I knew. And there is nothing illegal in that. I handled marketing and advertising stateside.

There was no way I knew about the client theft and government bribery. I was never involved with any of that."

"Sloane, you need to be careful of what you say, even to me, unless you retain me as your counsel. We just got word of this, so I have little to go on. If there is nothing to find, they will find nothing."

"That is what they said about my father, and he is serving six years. I don't understand. Why would they think I was guilty?"

"Sloane, calm down. It's the association, I imagine. Everyone knows how close you are with your father, so I would speculate that they think he shared information with you. Mind you, that is just speculation." Sloane could hear that Sandy thought she was guilty, too.

Sloane was silent, flustered and unsure of what to say. It was true her father loved sharing the business with her, but the international contracts had been very different. He had investors with whom he worked entirely separated from her.

"So, you will want to engage our firm again if it becomes necessary, Sloane. After all, we are already so familiar with the case."

"Yes," Sloane answered, realizing that Sandy was talking to her still. She was in shock from this revelation. "Yes, I will engage Addison. Fine for sure, when the time comes."

"Remember Sloane, right now it is an investigation. I am sure we can prevent it from going further if you have nothing to hide."

"Is it public knowledge? Will this be in the papers?"

"No Sloane, if they cannot prove anything, it may never be public. We should know in about a month. So, we received most of the documents from PPHPPHPP already, but we need those last few things from you. Do you need me to repeat what you need to send over?"

"PPHP? What are you talking about? How is PPHP involved? I appreciate the call, and the information, Sandy, but now I am more confused than ever."

"Randall Parker hasn't said anything? Damn, I guess he didn't want you to know he was involved. Forget I mentioned it, Sloane. Just get us the docs and we can take it from there."

Sandra avoided answering any further questions, and the two women said their goodbyes. Sloane sat there, numb, like a marble statue, pale and lifeless. She could feel the cold in her fingers and toes, hear her heart beating in panic. She slowly disconnected the call when she realized she was still holding the phone in her hand.

What to do now? This is about to become a much bigger problem. Her father knew what he was up against and still had the money to fight back. Sloane had nothing and no clue. How the hell did she end up here? "What am I going to do?" she muttered, dropping her head into her hands, all energy seeping from her body. "And why the hell is Randall involved?"

This shook Sloane to the core, but at least it wasn't public yet. Sloane lifted her head, squared her shoulders and sighed in relief. She had a brief reprieve, long enough to get through the gala and maybe figure out a thing or two. Smiling an ironic smile, Sloane considered how much had changed in an instant. She was worried about a new dress for the gala when she should have been worrying about an orange jumpsuit.

Might be time to binge watch "Orange is the New Black."

Sloane was still sitting there when she heard a key in the lock and the sound of a heavy footfall moving down the hall toward her.

"Still sleeping?" he hollered as he moved through the rooms until he saw her. "Good morning, sleepyhead. Why didn't you call when you got up?" Randall came over and scooped her into a bear hug of an embrace, kissing her soundly.

Oh God, what about Randall? Sandy said he was involved. What was he hiding from her? She couldn't drag him down with an indictment, not when she cared so much. But, if he knew something and kept it secret, how could she care about him? How could she trust him? After everything, she needed someone she could believe. Was Randall still her person?

Sloane schooled her face, hiding her alarm, her confusion, and her heartbreak.

"I have only been up a few minutes;, I am embarrassed to admit." She was the consummate actress, and Randall behaved as if all was fine.

"Well, I came to make sure you ate something and got home in one piece. But you haven't even showered yet."

"Right, let me do that now." Sloane wriggled out of his embrace and moved toward the bathroom. "Get me a towel, please?"

"Act normal. Act normal," she whispered to herself. "Come on, just act normal until you get home. Figure out what to do and how to ask him about this. Just pretend everything is the same. You can do this."

Randall left the room, returning a moment later with a clean towel—beige, of course.

"I see you like neutral tones," Sloane observed, holding up the towel, keeping the conversation light.

"Sloane," Randall took her hand and pulled her over to the bed, sitting on the edge and pulling her into his lap. "What the hell is going on? Has something happened?"

So much for acting normal. Was the man clairvoyant?

CHAPTER TWENTY-ONE

"Of course not, silly. What could have happened? I haven't even left the house. I just need more coffee to get me going and then I'll get out of your hair. "Randall heard Sloane's words. They were sensible, logical, and a total lie. This woman had been in his arms all night. It turned out that they were both cuddlers—spooners in the calm after their wild storm of a night. He knew her every nuance, how she moved, how she tasted and smelled. He also knew when she was erecting a ten-foot wall around herself, like right now.

After what they had shared, why would she be pulling away? He extended forward to kiss her, and she pulled back to avoid him - well, as much as she could while sitting on his lap. Besides, she had a wild-eyed look, like she had seen a ghost.

He approached her slowly, carefully. She reminded him of a wounded bird, and he did not want to scare her. Randall sat beneath her on the bed, admiring her long legs on full display below the hem of his shirt, and rested his hand on her thigh gently.

He felt her attempt to skitter away before she caught herself and stilled. It was barely a flutter, but he had felt it like a knife to his chest. Could it be that she was no longer interested in him? Randall had thought yesterday was the beginning of something lasting and strong.

He had hoped that she had learned to let him into her heart a little and not just her body. That was what he wanted, despite all the advice to the contrary. She had an undeniable pull on him. He was seriously evaluating building a life with Sloane.

If she could not look him in the eye, though, he needed to rethink things. If she could not trust him enough to tell him what happened, then perhaps they had nothing after all. Oh God, if nothing had occurred, as she asserted, then perhaps she was trying to tell him she just wanted the sex and was not interested in anything more. It would be hard to hear, of course, but better now than later.

"Why don't you grab a quick shower and I will drive you home? If you are in a hurry, we can grab a few things to stock your fridge, but I timed this so we could have a leisurely lunch together."

"Lunch? I can't possibly do lunch," Sloane fairly barked at him, but with panic not anger.

"Look, Sloane," Randall took her hand in his. It was like ice. "I can tell something is wrong. Please talk to me. You can trust me with anything. I care about you, Sloane. I am just trying to help."

"Really, Randall, I don't know what you mean. Everything is fine, just fine. I will go take a quick shower. Yes, I just need to grab a shower. Oh, and do you have an extra toothbrush, perhaps?"

Sloane is babbling. He had never, ever heard Sloane babble. She was too controlled. Whatever this was, it was bad.

"Sure, let me get you a toothbrush. You go shower."

It took a moment for Sloane to react to the words, rise and enter the bathroom. She was holding herself, walking like a robot, as if any sudden movement might cause her to break into a million pieces. Eventually, she got into the shower. Randall could hear water running, so he went in search of a toothbrush in the guest bath.

He returned with a refill of her coffee and a cup for himself as well as the toothbrush. He knocked gently on the bathroom door and pushed it open with his foot. Sloane was standing under the spray, head back, eyes closed, just letting the hot water hit her face and sluice down her body. She looked like a gorgeous nymph to Randall, who responded instantly until he willed his body back under control.

"Sloane, honey, I brought you more coffee."

She lifted her head away from the spray to look over at him. "Great, thanks."

He wiggled the toothbrush in its plastic container, and she smiled. "Thanks for that, too."

She stayed under the powerful spray for another few minutes, stepping from the steamy stall pink from the hot water. He helped wrap the large towel around her and she let him wipe the wet from her back and shoulders that immediately got damp again from her dripping hair. She hadn't washed it or protected it from the moisture. Randall reached for a smaller towel and started rubbing water from the bottoms of the long strands.

He resisted the urge to ask again what was wrong. At least she didn't flinch when he touched her, and she was moving more freely. Still, she refused to make eye contact, and the conversation was clearly one sided as he worked to keep up a steady banter.

"I need to be back in the office before 2:00. What about you? I know you are waiting on signatures from the lawyers over at Steel Frank, but do you have anything else going on today?" She shook her head no, , but offered nothing. "So, we could go have lunch, sit outside somewhere and enjoy Chicago's weather. It's a beautiful day. What do you think?"

No response. "In the mood for anything special?" Another non-response.

Randall wrapped Sloane in the large towel like a mummy, her hair wrapped in a second towel, and scooted her over to the toilet. He dropped the lid and gently pushed her to sit. He squatted down, forcing her to look him straight in the eye.

As soon as she lifted her head, Randall could see the tears pooling in Sloane's sad blue eyes. Within moments, they were spilling over soundlessly.

"Oh baby, what is it? Please tell me. Let me help you," Randall pleaded.

She sat crying in silence for what felt like an hour, but was a few minutes. Finally, she spoke in a tiny voice that he had to lean in to hear.

"Randall, I wish you could help me. I wish anyone could help me, but they can't. I am about to be in big trouble, and the best thing you can do is get as far away from me as you can."

Randall took her elegant hands in his b, holding them lightly but surely. "I am not going anywhere, Sloane."

Then he waited, and waited, and waited, but she offered nothing else. No explanation. Nothing. Randall was unsure how hard to push her for information. He had believed minutes ago that she was going to share her situation with him, but she just sat there with tears streaming down her face. He knew how to handle the strong, willful Sloane, but this fragile Sloane was new to him.

"I should go." Sloane made a move to get up and Randall stood, moving out of her way, then following her back to the bedroom. She divested herself of the towel with her back to him, modestly, pulled on her dress, then looked around for something. Her shoes were on the floor where she had kicked them off last night and eventually, she stopped looking around and put them on.

"Please give me back my underwear," she asked Randall politely, detached. She could have been asking him to hand her a comb, but he knew what it cost her to ask under the current circumstances. She had been acting as if they had not shared a night of incredible intimacy, but this question broke that barrier. Her face was red with embarrassment.

"No."

"No? What do you mean, no? They are mine. Just give them to me. They are not some damn trophy for your conquest, Randall."

"I don't want a trophy, Sloane, and it was not a conquest. It was the start of something very special." He was relieved to hear some fight come back into her voice. She was standing taller, too.

"You tell me what is going on and I might return your panties," he bargained, dropping to the bed and crossing his right foot over his left knee like he had all the time in the world.

"Oh, you might return them? You expect me to tell you my deep dark secret and then you might return them? This is not some damn game, Randall." She had emphasized the word 'might' like she was spoiling for a fight, and Randall egged her on, wanting his old Sloane back.

"Yeah, I might... or I might not." He reached his hand into his pants pocket and her eyes followed his every move.

"Is that them in your pocket? Hand them over, seriously."

"Or what, Sloane. Will you beat me up?" He was daring her like a child's game, but it was working. She was getting furious.

Sloane stepped close to Randall, reaching for the hand still in his pocket, pulling on it to try to dislodge it and take what was hers. She was unprepared when Randall fell back on the bed, taking her with him.

Lying on him, their faces mere centimeters apart, he looked at her; the fight gone out of him. "Just tell me, Sloane. You never have to handle anything alone again. Not while I am still breathing. Do you understand? I know you are tough. I know you are smart. I am not saying you can't handle things. I am saying you have an extra shoulder to lean on— – mine."

"Oh Randall," the tears were coming again, and she dropped her head to his chest. He could feel her shaking with sobs and he let her cry all over his shirt, wrapping his arms around her gently and stroking her back.

"Shh," he repeated until she calmed and lifted her head to look him in the face. He handed her his handkerchief, and she laughed lightly before she used it.

"I didn't believe a man carried these anymore."

"I do."

"I'm going to prison, Randall. That is my problem. I am going to prison. You need to get as far away from me as fast as you can. The indictment will probably come down in a few weeks and before then you will want to make everyone believe we never met. Let me go home Randall, then walk away. Please, for both our sakes, walk away."

CHAPTER TWENTY-TWO

Randall held Sloane close while she repeated most of Sandy's conversation. He did not interrupt, just rubbed her back to keep her calm. She did not mention that Sandy had talked about PPHP and Randall never offered the information, either. "But she said 'maybe' Sloane, and a 'maybe' is not a definite. We have to believe they will find nothing, since there is nothing to find. Then all of this will go away and no one will ever need to know anything about it. You need to stay calm and keep your mouth shut while we close this deal with Steel Frank and dance the night away for a worthy cause. Understand?"

Was this about the Steel Frank deal? Is that why Randall was working with the lawyer - so that his friend's firm would earn its fat fees? Could he hold her like this and just want her money? She found that hard to believe. Maybe Sandy is making the whole thing up about PPHPPHPP's involvement, the spiteful bitch. But how would she know to mention it?

Randall was looking deep into Sloane's tear-filled eyes, demanding her understanding, her promise. She shook her head, but Randall demanded the words.

"Sloane, tell me you understand."

"I do, Randall. I understand. How can you be so calm?"

"I will panic when there is something to panic over. Right now, the only issues on your plate are having lunch with me and sending the lawyers your recent tax returns. Nothing else is looming besides a fun night with friends in forty-eight hours."

"You almost make me believe you." Did I tell him about the tax returns, or did he already know? Shit, I can't remember now.

"You should, you know. I am an extremely capable and smart man."

"Confident too," she teased, the old Sloane emerging again.

"As I should be. I feel like I can slay dragons, woman. You did this, Sloane. Being with you makes me feel like I can conquer the world. And eat a horse, so finish up and let's go."

Randall swatted her round behind as she walked past him.

"Hey there, if you are going to hit that, dress it. Give me back my panties!"

"Nope, I like the idea of having lunch with you, knowing you aren't wearing any. It turns me on."

"You are a crazy man!" Sloane laughed briefly, but she did not ask for the clothing again. Sloane decided she would stop wracking her brain for an hour and just go with the flow.

A few minutes later Randall was driving toward Sloane's apartment, finding a parking space on the street and stopping to give her a hard kiss before going around to open her door. He watched her dress rise slightly as she swung her legs from the car and she blushed bright red.

"I love our little secret," he told her, running the tips of his long fingers softly up her thigh. He watched the sensuous fog start in her eyes and stopped just short of indecent.

"Lunch, Sloane. Let's go get food."

Randall was serious about eating a horse. He had chosen a barbeque restaurant, Chicago Q, and after eating a basket of hushpuppies, he ordered the generous prime brisket plate and devoured it quickly along with cornbread and a mac and cheese side. Meanwhile, Sloane made equally quick work of a lighter salad, discovering that she was hungry as well.

"Do you exist on coffee?" Randall asked when Sloane requested a second refill on her iced coffee.

"Yep, I really do. On anything with caffeine really—Diet Coke, tea, coffee, doesn't matter."

"With the way you exercise, you need to eat more."

"Like you do, he manHe-Man? Where do you put all that food?" She could tease him about the heavy lunch, but she knew for a fact that Randall's body was perfect. Not an ounce of fat marred his masculine beauty.

"I was in the gym while you were sleeping, Sloane, and then I worked for hours. Not to mention the strenuous workout a certain woman gave me yesterday." They shared a knowing smile as he took her hand in his.

"It was really special, Sloane."

"It was." God, I want to trust him so much.

"Now," Randall began as the server came with her coffee and he released her hand to pick up the check, "Let's talk about Saturday. Do you need to be there early?"

"Nope," Sloane answered between sips of coffee. "Everything is all set at the venue. I will go over in the afternoon to check out the flower arrangements, place cards and bar set up. Then I am done."

"Great, I have a limo picking me up at 6:00, Tyler will be with me, and we will swing by for you and then Regan."

"Seriously? I thought you were joking about the limo."

"Oh no. This is going to be a huge night. I have it all planned. We are going to eat like pigs, bid on every auction item, drink too much, and dance until they throw us out."

Although she raised her eyebrows when Randall said something about drinking too much, she told him it sounded perfect.

"I am wearing a tux, of course. Will you have time to buy a new dress? We kind of sacrificed our shopping time yesterday to other activities." Randall had a charming, devilish look in his eyes that made Sloane laugh.

"No new dress this time. I have so many already, and frankly, money is a little tight right now."

"This deal will help with that, Sloane. You can certainly afford a new dress, if you want one."

"To be honest, I have a few vintage dresses I would enjoy resurrecting.' Sloane sounded excited at the prospect.

"OK, if you say so. I am sure you will look beautiful. I will pick you up around 6:30. Can you live a night without me until then?"

"Oh dear, how will I manage?" she taunted him, although she wondered where he would be instead even as she felt relief that she had time to come to terms with all these newfound emotions.

"No joke, Sloane. I am not sure I won't be tearing down your door around 3:00 AM. I just figured we might want to catch up on sleep tonight and, you know, conserve energy for tomorrow." Randall was openly leering at Sloane and running his fingers up the inside of her thigh under the table.

Sloane was relieved to learn Randall didn't have another date, although she was annoyed with herself for the emotion., She needed a girlfriend to talk to, to discuss this budding relationship and her sudden feelings of jealousy and possession. She couldn't talk to Regan or Missy. They were Wyatt's sisters, and while they might be sympathetic, it would be too awkward. And her mom would just push her straight at Randall.

Squirming under the delicious sensations Randall's hand was creating, Sloane wondered if perhaps she couldn't last the night without Randall. He made her laugh, turned her on and kept her dragons at bay, at least for the length of a lunch. She wished she could stay with him tonight, but her pride kept her from suggesting it, from displaying the depths of her feelings. It was that same pride, and distrust, that prevented her from asking about the lawyers.

Pushing his hand away gently, she leaned forward seductively. When his lips were just inches from hers, she spoke in a low, throaty voice.

"Oh, Randall. An entire night?" Randall responded with a gleam in his eyes and a seductive smile on his face. Sloane leaned back. "Yeah," she ended, voice full of sarcasm. "I can manage."

Laughing, he signed the credit slip with an arrogant flourish and drove her home.

CHAPTER TWENTY-THREE

"You look stunning," Randall blurted out unfiltered when Sloane opened the door Saturday evening. She took his breath away. The deep indigo blue gown that skimmed her slim body shimmered with crystals spattered like stars from her knee to the floor. Fabric pooled about her feet, reminiscent of a fashion shoot. The low-cut bodice and back displayed exactly the right amount of creamy skin. His fingers itched to touch her. Sloane wore no jewelry around her neck, allowing the cut of the dress and her elegant figure to draw the eye, but she had a few delicate diamond tennis bracelets about her wrist and small diamond drop earrings hanging from the shells of her ears. The effect was classy, elegant... and damn sexy.

Her hair shimmered, thick and dark, pulled into a low chignon at her neck, a jeweled barrette twinkling against the inky tresses. Randall wanted to unpin it, wrap the locks around his fist, and drag her to bed. He felt like the Neanderthal she had named him. He wanted to dance about the room tonight, showing her off to the world like a God. Everything about her was flawless.

And she's with me.

He had seen Sloane dressed like this many times before, but this time she was his date. She would hold his hand, dance in his arms, and sleep in his bed. He felt like the luckiest man on earth.

"Ready?" She broke his trance as she reached to pick up her evening bag and a light jacket. He followed her out the door, admiring the way the dress molded to her, hugging every delectable inch of her ass.

"You look very elegant, sir." She was flirting, her aquamarine eyes peeking coquettishly from under long lashes. "We will be the best looking couple at the event." No modesty there. She had been told she was beautiful too many times not to know it and he was certainly no slouch, broad shoulders showing off his custom tuxedo like he was a GQ model. The blue of her dress, with her blue eyes and fair skin, was arresting. She would stand out in the sea of tuxedoed men and elegant women garbed in the somber black they so often selected these days.

"Tyler and Regan are waiting in the car. We picked her up first because she was ready and antsy," he explained as they walked to the elevator. Once they were heading down, he took her into his arms and kissed her soundly, holding her tight between himself and the elevator wall, ravaging her moist, minty mouth until the doors opened. When they did, he adjusted his suddenly snug trousers while Sloane used a perfectly manicured finger to neaten the edges of her lipstick. She stepped from the elevator as if nothing had occurred, but Randall could see the sparkle in her eye and the rapid beat of the pulse at her throat. She, too, had been affected.

The limo driver hovered, waiting to open the door of the long, black limo sitting at the curb. As he caught sight of Randall, he jumped up and stepped forward. Randall motioned for Sloane to precede him, then watched with lust in his eyes as she stooped and entered the car. He slid in behind her, settling his large frame close beside her despite the spacious interior. He wrapped her hand in his securely, holding on as if trying to prevent her escape.

"Regan, you look just lovely," Sloane was admiring her friend, who did indeed look elegant in a sleek black dress, although her pretty blonde looks paled next to Sloane's dark beauty. The women talked about dresses, jewels, and shoes for a solid five minutes after Sloane and Tyler exchanged perfunctory greetings.

Randall caught snippets of the women's conversation while speaking with Tyler about potential auction items on which to bid. Tyler had been studying the website for the event and had his eye on tickets for hockey, basketball and, strangely, the women's roller derby. Despite following the conversation with Tyler, he learned that Regan had purchased her dress months ago while Sloane had still been undecided as late as that afternoon.

"I wore this to a Howe Museum event several years ago," she was telling Regan, "but at the time Wyatt and I weren't engaged, so there were few photos of me. I'm hoping no one remembers I have worn this before."

"Are you crazy?" Randall blurted out without thinking. "No one could forget you in that dress."

"Oh no, do you think he's right?" Sloane asked Regan, fear and disappointment clouding her features. She completely missed the blatant compliment.

"That is not at all what he meant, Sloane." Regan reassured her with a smile. "Randall means he could never forget you in that dress. What have you done to the man? He is totally smitten." Randall could have corrected the assumption, but why? It was true.

"He is pretty attentive," Sloane admitted shyly.

"Like it?"

"Love it."

Regan beamed at the news, and Randall turned away to hide his smile. Sometimes eavesdropping was gratifying. "You two are good for each other, you know. You can tone down the party boy in Randall and he can be a caring, reliable man in your life just when you were sure there were none left."

"I don't need a man," Sloane hissed under her breath. Randall's heart stopped. Sloane continued more gently, "But even I can't deny that he is pretty damn cute." Randall sucked in much needed air. For a minute, he thought Sloane was slipping through his fingers. He was all in with her, but maybe she was still hesitant? Tonight, he needed to woo her and win her heart.

The short drive ended swiftly and soon the men were helping the women disembark from the car to join the crowds of gowned women and tuxedoed men moving toward the ballrooms. The four of them turned heads as they made their way through the historic lobby. Randall actually saw one jeans-and-tee-clad tourist position on his phone, snapping their picture.

Our red-carpet moment. Sloane will love it when I tell her.

Taking a delicate shrimp appetizer from a passing server, Sloane voiced her relief that everything looked perfect. The flowers were a variety of sizes and textures but all in creamy whites and greens. The food was being passed efficiently, and the crowds were gratifyingly large. Members of Chicago's elite wandered by, including several people from the Hospital Board. All of them nodded in greeting, but none stopped to talk. Randall took the bull by the horns and began stopping people he knew, which it seemed was everyone. He shook hands, made small talk, and never removed his hand from around Sloane's waist, drawing her into every conversation.

No one is snubbing my girl tonight. Not if I have anything to say about it.

Once the ice broke, Sloane and Randall easily settled into conversations joined by Wyatt and Keeli when they arrived. They greeted Wyatt's parents, who were happy to see Tyler and Randall, and unfailingly polite, if cool, to Sloane. The conversation was superficial, 'how are you' and 'how is your family', 'isn't the room lovely' and so forth. The women admired each other's dresses, or their hair or jewelry.

Soon Wyatt's parents moved on to seek out more of their own friends and Tyler disappeared, returning with their place cards. Sloane hoped they would sit together. She understood it was out of her control since she'd been unable to purchase a table herself. Elegant script, obviously done by a professional calligrapher, graced each card. All of their names said 'Table No. 12'.

"Oh good. We are all together," Sloane said happily. "It will be so much more fun being with friends."

"Of course we are," Tyler said, with a hint of exasperation. "Randall bought the table for us."

Sloane's eyes flew to Randall's face in time to catch his sheepish grin. He had not told her. Tyler had the good grace to mouth a quick "I'm sorry" to Randall. Sloane looked a little shocked, then thrilled. Randall breathed another sigh of relief. Nothing would go wrong tonight, not if he had any say in the matter.

"Let's go check out all the auction items before dinner," Tyler suggested. They all agreed enthusiastically, and the six of them moved as a unit to the long tables set up against the wall strewn with baskets and posters and an odd assortment of goods.

Some items had opening bids in the thousands, some in the tens of thousands. There were trips to Europe, Russia and South Africa, the rental of a house in Tahoe, another in Maui and an apartment on New York's upper east side. The LHRE donation, a flight to San Francisco with two nights in an exclusive hotel, brought a smile to Sloane's face, and she gave Regan's hand a grateful squeeze when she saw it.

"The committee got some great donations," Sloane admitted without rancor. "We should raise a lot of money."

There was a gorgeous piece of jewelry donated by Keeli Larsen Designs, a wide bracelet encrusted in sapphires and diamonds. It was locked in a Plexiglas case, but the women stood over it, admiring it and wanting to try it on. Sloane's mother came over to admire the piece as well, looking lovely in a cream-colored gown. She had arrived on the arm of an old family friend, one of the few who still supported the Huyler family, but Sloane was gratified to see her chatting with quite a few people.

"Having fun?" Sloane asked her mother under her breath.

"Oh yes. Dear, you have outdone yourself. Everything is lovely," Marianne offered before they returned their attention to Keeli.

"Let me see if I can get the case unlocked so we can play with it," Keeli offered.

"Play with it?" Sloane and Regan had both turned to Keeli at her choice of words, and the three giggled together. "You don't play with something that beautiful. At least don't let the person who already bid $18,800 hear you use that kind of language for such an exquisite piece." Sloane pointed to the card, showing several bids.

Wyatt was writing his name on several auction items, the Tahoe house, the Maui house and some sports equipment, where bids were already well over $1,000 and much more. Sloane added her $50 bid to win dinner for two at one of Chicago's new seafood restaurants. Tyler had upped the bids on all the sporting events, and Regan had increased the latest bid on a trip for two to Barcelona and a girls' spa day for up to ten friends.

"What appeals to you?" Randall asked as they walked down the row together. "How about the sailboat? I could do the sailing if you wanted. I know how."

"Mm, that sounds nice," Sloane answered as she walked further down the row. She didn't stop as Randall added his name to the bidding here and there. She didn't expect her friends to be the successful bidder on more than one or two things. It was all in fun, and for a good cause. She wandered the table laughing at their outrageous choices. Randall caught up with her a few paces away, reading about a week at the world-famous Canyon Ranch Spa.

"Does the spa look good? You've been under so much pressure, maybe a relaxing getaway appeals to you?"

"Aren't you perceptive? All the auction items that include a get-away appeal to me right now. Running away from my problems sounds pretty good."

"Trying to run from me?" He leaned in to run a soft trail of kisses on the edge of her hairline and ear, adding in a whisper, "cause I am not letting you get away that easily."

Blushing furiously, Sloane pushed him away and watched as he added his name to bidding for the retreat.

"Are you ashamed to be seen with me, Sloane?" Randall asked, placing his hands over his heart and feigning his hurt feelings with a little-boy pout that was at odds with his tall figure, broad shoulders and the rugged face still covered in a close-cropped beard.

"I would think it would be the opposite, Randall, and you know it."

"Oh Princess, I am the proudest man here. Trust me. You better stop looking at me like that, too, or I'll drag you to a dark corner."

Laughing seductively, Sloane changed the subject to a safer topic. "I have to give kudos where they are due. I am so impressed with the quality of the donations. Allyson did an amazing job. I need to be sure to let her know before we leave. And thank you, Randall, for your generosity. Buying a table tonight was so sweet of you."

"So sweet of you," Tyler mimicked. "What's with you, man? Sloane has you wrapped around her little finger. Not like you to settle for Wyatt's leftovers."

Alex joined them at that moment, saving Randall from responding, or slugging his friend. What kind of friend was Tyler to say that shit, anyway? He knew Tyler hadn't forgiven Sloane for her treatment of Wyatt, but now she was obviously with Randall and needed to stuff it.

Randall relaxed the fists he had formed and reached for a drink from a passing server while Alex introduced them to a statuesque woman with flawless skin and exotic features, who turned out to be a model he had flown in from L.A. for the event. Aimee was very nice, but she seemed to have difficulty finding a comfortable spot among the group of old friends, so she clung close to Alex and suggested that the two of them go find the bar. Randall joined them, using the time to stop fuming.

It seemed like no time before someone subtly herded the guests into the enormous ballroom. Sloane had seen the space late that afternoon and knew it was stunning, but the others oohed and aahed over the décor, the flowers, and even the orchestra, a well-known group Regan announced she really enjoyed.

They found their table with no trouble, neither near the front nor the back, and Keeli slipped her arm around Sloane's waist as they worked their way toward it.

"Last time we were both at one of these, I dropped a salad down your back. Can you believe how much has changed since then? And can you ever forgive me?" A pained look of remorse moved across

Sloane's face. Randall was about to step in and rescue her when Keeli waved him away.

"I don't wait tables anymore and you didn't get me fired, so now we are friends. We are friends, Sloane. You know that, right? You can reach out to me if you need anything. I sense you don't have many people in your corner right now." Randall saw Sloane's pained expression but resisted the urge to intervene. "I would like to be there for you."

"You are being so generous, Keeli. More than I deserve. There is the Wyatt issue, though. I don't think he wants to be in the same room with me if he can help it, and I suspect he would like to keep miles between the two of us."

"Men, what do they know?" Keeli laughed. "You and Wyatt had a business arrangement, nothing more. He can just get over himself. As for me, there's no jealousy here. Well, except for your smarts and that dress," she held Sloane at arm's length to admire the blue gown.

"Are you kidding? You are the stunner tonight," Sloane blurted, leaving Randall beaming with pride. Recently, these two women were arch enemies and Sloane didn't have it in her to compliment another woman. Oh, how far they had both come.

Keeli looked magnificent with her red hair piled high on her head, a few loose curls hanging down in the back. Her simple white dress was the perfect backdrop for a dramatic necklace of gold, diamonds, and rubies the size of marbles. Heads had been turning all night and Wyatt had been stuck to her side like glue. Randall made a mental note to seek his friend and have a man-to-man conversation. If he was going to be with Sloane, and she was going to befriend Keeli, Randall needed to tie up any loose ends.

Randall had stopped listening, trusting Keeli not to hurt Sloane. Sloane's expression shifted from stricken to open and friendly, leaving him wondering what Keeli had said to make Sloane look so relaxed.

Whatever it was, it delighted him that they'd dodged a potential land-mine. When they took their seats, Sloane tried to sit next to Keeli, but the men made sure that they alternated man-woman instead.

The food that Sloane and Randall had selected was impeccably served and to rave reviews. The wine flowed and Sloane voiced some concern as Randall drank more that she thought he should. They had a limo; he reminded her, so she didn't have to worry about anyone driving drunk, and he still had himself well under control.

The music played softly early in the night, giving way to several long, droll speeches and reminders about the auction. Tyler slipped out during dessert to make sure no one outbid him for sports tickets, and Randall tagged along. Everyone else agreed that whatever happened would happen. Randall returned looking a little ruffled and began drinking more heavily than he had earlier in the evening. His friends tried to slow him down, to no avail. Tomorrow, he would remember their efforts and cringe.

When Tyler returned, he invited Regan to dance, then Keeli and then Sloane. Wyatt also danced with the three women, as well as Sloane's mother, and so did Randall. Between dances, Randall caught Sloane watching Tyler and Regan as they moved about the floor, holding each other very close. They made a beautiful couple, but Randall took it in mind that they needed a break. Tyler did not seem happy when an obviously tipsy Randall came to claim the next dance, but he gave up his date for the length of one song. Then, finally, Randall took Sloane in his arms.

In a move Fred Astaire might envy, Randall twirled Sloane onto the dance floor. "You look so beautiful tonight, so serene. I am incredibly proud of you." He dropped kisses on her collarbone, left bare by her low-cut gown, and moved a hand toward the side of her breast.

Twisting in his tight grasp, Sloane pulled away. "Randall, you are drunk. Get yourself under control."

"I'm so sorry, Sloane. It's nerves. I don't know what comes over me."

"Well, you better find out, and soon."

Randall heard the ultimatum. He needed to control his alcohol consumption if he wanted to keep Sloane. And he did.

"My sincere apologies, Princess," Randall mumbled under his breath, holding her as he should and moving her through the rest of the dance. He needed to sober up and quickly. He had planned a romantic evening and was determined not to spoil it.

Randall was an excellent dancer, light on his feet. He apologized again, placing a swift kiss on her lips, before twirling her around the room. The movement, combined with the alcohol, left him a little nauseous, so he slowed down. "You feel amazing," he whispered. "I can't wait to get you out of this dress."

"Shh, people will hear you, Randall." Sloane blushed a pretty pink, but she didn't push him away.

Alex never let go of Aimee the entire night, and they excused themselves early to go back to the hotel room they had reserved upstairs. The men ribbed him about it, but all in good fun. Randall latched on to the idea of leaving early too, eager to get Sloane alone.

"How late do you have to stay?" he queried Sloane a little after 11:00.

"Ah, another advantage of losing my chair position. We can leave whenever we like."

"How are your feet doing?"

"A little sore," she confessed.

"Well, how about you rest them? Let's me make the rounds and do a little business and then, if you are up for it, you and I can share a last dance and sneak away so you can kick off those shoes?"

"Sounds like a plan," Sloane agreed, sinking into a nearby chair. Randall knew her eyes were following him as he strode across the room to chat with a group of men from the world of sports. He was so proud to be her date, so proud of the success she had made of tonight's event, how beautiful she looked, poised and calm in a room full of people waiting for her to slip up. The men were talking games, scores, agents, and contracts within minutes.

When they each ordered another drink, Randall asked for a glass of water. No better time than the present to start on the course he intended to take. The conversation bored him, and he struggled to concentrate, focused on Sloane, on getting out of there and getting her alone.

He spotted her at the bar, her back to him. A young man was chatting her up and the green monster rose in Randall faster than he could have imagined possible. Barely excusing himself, he was across the room in seconds.

Wrapping his arms around her waist, Randall nuzzled into Sloane's neck, nibbling kisses along her cheekbone. "I am so hot for you. What do you say we get out of here?"

"What the hell?" Whirling in his arms, Sloane turned sharply to face him. It wasn't the reception Randall expected. And for good reason.

Oh fuck! The woman in his arms wasn't Sloane. Also, Randall was seconds away from being slapped across the face. He lunged back, almost losing his balance as the room swam around him. Wyatt stepped between him and the seething victim of his error.

"Apologize this instantce," his friend demanded, his face contorted with rage.

"I thought you were someone else," Randall said, putting his hands in front of his face reflexively.

"Clearly." The woman's drawl didn't hide her fury. The young man beside her took her hand and led her away with a backward glance that brimmed with disgust. Randall froze in place, mumbling apologies to those around him who had witnessed his embarrassment. He needed to find Sloane and get out of here before he humiliated them both more than he had already.

"My apologies," he said with a little bow to no one in particular. Wyatt dragged him away, silent. "I need to find Sloane."

"I don't know what you think you need, Randall. But I suggest going home and sobering up."

Randall moved to where he thought he'd left Sloane earlier, but he was disoriented and unable to focus. Between the size of the crowd and a few too many drinks, he had no idea where his date was. He spotted Tyler hustling toward him quickly and went to meet him.

"What the hell have you done?" Tyler began without preamble, exchanging a frustrated glance with Wyatt.

'What's the big deal?" Randall answered, belligerent. "I thought she was Sloane. It was an honest mistake."

Tyler pointed at the woman, looking their way, venom shooting from her eyes. "Does she look anything like Sloane?"

Looking again, Randall saw that there was no way the woman he accosted was Sloane. They weren't the same build, their dresses were different, their hair was different too. It wasn't an honest mistake. It was the behavior of a drunken fool.

"Randall, I love you like a brother, but if you had done to Regan what you just did to that woman, I would deck you right here in the middle of the dance floor. I am tempted to do it, anyway. You are lucky that woman has a date with more tolerance, or better manners, than I have. It's the only reason you are still standing."

"I apologized," Randall argued. "More than once. It was a simple mistake."

"No, it was not," Tyler hissed. "I think it is time we got out of here."

Randall couldn't agree more. "Let me just find Sloane." He looked about for the dark-haired beauty, but she was nowhere, and the movement made the room spin uncomfortably.

"You idiot," Tyler said, taking Randall's arm and leading him toward the exit. "Sloane left already. She stormed out and you'll be damn lucky if she ever speaks to you again."

CHAPTER TWENTY-FOUR

Randall was out of ideas. He had become well known to the florist already but clearly, a fortune in flowers would not soften Sloane's anger. She was still not picking up the phone when he called. Finally, he had cut back the calls, fearing she might report him as a stalker. He still called a few times a day and sent four or five texts, all to no avail. He had sent flowers to the woman he accosted as well, with a note of apology for his shameful behavior, and received a very nice email saying she understood. Not quite forgiveness, but better than he deserved. He was lucky there, and he knew it.

Randall had been a jerk. He knew it even before his head cleared. The evening had been so perfect. He was there with the most desirable woman in the room. She had floated like an angel in that blue dress, somehow both a seductress yet totally above reproach. She was all business in the front, and all bedroom in the back. He could not stop touching her bare skin, skimming his hand down the entire length of her exposed back.

The food was delicious; the company was grand. People were chilly to Sloane at first, but warmed to her as the evening progressed. She was a different woman than they expected, warmer, kinder. He had been bursting with pleasure and pride for her success. The dancing had been a perfect form of foreplay and he could not wait to get her home, watch that dress puddle around her feet, then take her naked body in his bed. He figured they would still be making love at dawn.

But stupid, stupid me, I had to drink too much. Again.

Randall wasn't sure what it was about parties that made him drink too much. He got so uncomfortable. He was amongst friends, mostly, or business associates with whom he felt totally at ease, so that was not it.

He drank with his buddies pretty regularly, but usually stopped before making a complete ass of himself. He had been to plenty of dinner parties in people's homes or professional events where he knew exactly when to call it quits.

There was just something about certain events and parties that made him nervous. A misplaced word, an odd look–it took very little to make him feel out of sorts and not quite good enough. Once that feeling crept over him, he calmed his nerves with one or two extra drinks.

Maybe two or three, but who is counting? Okay, three or four. It was time to own his problem, not underestimate it.

The worst was how inappropriate he got after too much alcohol. His hands went everywhere. He became the man he normally abhorred. He honestly did not know where it came from, especially when he cared so much about Sloane.

So here he was, almost two weeks after the benefit, waiting for Alex to meet him for coffee. No meeting for drinks for this conversation. He had learned one lesson at least. Alex was one of his oldest friends, but he was as jittery waiting for him as he would be waiting for a blind date.

"Hey man, hope you haven't been waiting long?" Alex strode across the almost empty Starbucks, hand outstretched, broad smile cracking his thin face, a lock of his light hair falling roguishly over his forehead. Randall took the hand for a firm handshake and returned the smile, along with a friendly slap on the back.

"Thanks for meeting me, Alex. I appreciate it."

"Sure, of course. But what the hell are we doing at a Starbucks?"

"Alex, am I a drunk?" Randall asked without preamble.

"Wow, let's just dive right in, why don't we?"

Randall had caught Alex off guard, but his friend pivoted quickly, took the seat across from Randall and wiped the grin from his face.

"No, my friend, you are not a drunk. Do you drink every day? Drink until you pass out? Find yourself needing a drink all the time? Need more and more booze to feel a buzz?"

Randall had repeatedly shaken his head no, as Alex asked the rapid-fire questions.

"But the night of the gala?" Randall could not say more. However, Alex immediately knew what he meant. Both Tyler and Wyatt had repeated the story to him, and it was ugly.

"Yeah, you were mighty fucking stupid. You are lucky that some guy didn't punch your lights out, or Wyatt's. I understand he got between you and the poor girl."

Randall dropped his head into his hands in shame. "I couldn't tell if he was there to take the punch for me, or slug me himself. It was the latter, of course."

"What do you think happened, Rand?" Alex sat quietly, waiting for his friend to respond before offering any opinions or advice. This was why Randall called Alex and not Tyler. Tyler would have berated him and blown a gasket before calming down for the more serious, and necessary, conversation. For a lawyer, Tyler could be thoughtless with his words.

"I don't know, man. I really don't know. Sloane was a goddess that night. Everything I wanted, so I don't know why I ever left her side."

"My, my. A goddess? How poetic."

Randall shook a fist at Alex in annoyance, feigning a slug to his jaw.

"Okay, so it wasn't desire for anyone else. We can establish that much."

"I swear it was an honest, if drunk mistake. I never would have done it sober. I thought the woman was Sloane. I can't imagine why. But at that moment—" he let his words trail off. Alex waited patiently for him to continue. "Sloane is more than enough woman for me. I swear."

"Okay, then. We'll come back to that in a minute. When do you get drunk, Randall? Think about the last five or ten times you went on a bender. Can you name them?"

"Well... there was the Hospital benefit obviously, and the wedding. I was really drunk at Wyatt's wedding. I was still hung over the next night. Hmm. The last time we went out after hockey, I got pretty wasted, but we won. I was celebrating. A couple months ago, I double dated with Keeli, Wyatt and that museum curator he fixed me up with. She was hot, but I got drunk that night, made an ass of myself, and she wouldn't go out with me again."

"Seeing a pattern here yet?" Alex was prodding less than gently.

"I get drunk way too often?".

"C'mon man, you are not stupid. You get drunk around Wyatt. You always get drunk around Wyatt. If Wyatt is within 100 yards, Randall, you get drunk."

"That is not true."

"It is completely true, man. I have known it for a long, long time. I told the guys the reason you did so well at Duke was that Wyatt wasn't there. Otherwise, you would have been drunk your whole way through college."

"Well, I was sometimes, but I didn't party as much as I did in grad school."

"Yeah, and you and Wyatt went head- to- head over Sloane right after that. And you lost the woman of your dreams. I'm no shrink, and I am sure there is more going on, but for starters, you, my friend, have a problem with Wyatt, and it's time to come to terms with it and move on."

"You know," Randall started, thinking aloud. "I was fine for weeks, my drinking completely under control. But Tyler said something at the benefit that really pissed me off. I was a goner after that."

"What did he say?"

"It's so rude I really shouldn't repeat it, but he was commenting on my being with Sloane and that I was settling Wyatt's..."

"Never mind," Alex cut him off. "Tyler needs to watch his mouth. But he hit your Wyatt nerve. You are really oversensitive about the man."

"But that makes no sense, Alex. Wyatt and I have been friends since grade school. We all have. We do everything together."

"Yeah, but, sorry to be so blunt here, he does everything just that iota better and I think you have a problem with it. The rest of us have just come to accept it, but Randall, I think since that science test in fifth or sixth grade, you have been in an unhealthy competition with Wyatt."

"Oh, come on. That is nonsense. That was fifth grade - a million years ago, Alex."

"But you remember it, right?"

"Yeah." Randall's shoulders sagged suddenly. "I remember it like it was yesterday. I remember Wyatt boasting to me—it hurt—but I am surprised that you can still recall it."

"And it still hurts," Alex asked, a bit more gently. "Doesn't it?"

Randall could not believe that at thirty-six, with a hugely successful business and accomplishments from his education to athletics to his stature in the community, he and Alex were discussing the results of a year-end science test from fifth grade. Their private Lake Forest school had promoted confidence and creative thinking in children, as well as offering an excellent overall education, but it was competitive. All the way through his school, Randall had found himself right behind Wyatt on every test, in every subject, at every science fair, on every sports field, and with every girl. Wyatt usually excelled, coming in first on almost everything, while Randall was always just one step behind.

In fifth grade, Randall complained about it until his father decided that things needed to change. They worked together on his science projects and on his science homework. They walked in the woods or along the beach discussing the bushes, the bugs, and everything they saw for a big assignment about nature. His father helped him study, then quizzed him for that last exam. After all that preparation, Randall had bragged to everyone in class that this time he would beat Wyatt.

Meanwhile, Wyatt did his usual prep, enough but nothing out of the ordinary. He was smart and very capable, and he knew it. Things just came easily to him. He still studied. He took nothing for granted. His father insisted he do well, really well, and the pressure to bring home A's and A+'s was constant. But for this exam, Wyatt did nothing special.

The test was hard, as Randall remembered it now, challenging and comprehensive. Still, when he left the classroom, he was confident that he had done well. Wyatt had been uncertain about two or three questions, so Randall continued to brag about his imminent success.

Then, that Friday afternoon, they posted the results on the hallway bulletin board. There was Wyatt, just ahead of Randall, as always. Randall remembered the embarrassment and frustration and the uncontrollable jealousy that had welled up in him. Even now, sitting there in the Starbucks all those years later, he felt the humiliation, and he had to breathe through it.

Alex watched the emotions fly across the face of his friend, saw the tightening of his jaw, watched as Randall relived that moment.

"Why was that test so important, anyway?" Alex asked now.

"I don't know, but it was. My father had raised the stakes on me for that one and gotten personally involved. You know, he never treated me the same after I came in second. Second. It wasn'tt like I flunked. Now, thinking back on it, he had lower expectations for me from that moment on. Still high, mind you, but just that bit lower than before. In everything—sports and every school subject. He never helped me again, no science walks, no catch in the yard. Nothing, until I went to work for him. He mentored me the same way when I came to PPHP as he did before that exam. But of course, Wyatt was not a member of the firm, so it was different."

"But you weren't. You were still competing. You have wanted every position Wyatt ever played, in field hockey, soccer, ice hockey, even lacrosse. Randall, you hated lacrosse! You took every course he took. If he volunteered for charity work, you volunteered. for everything he volunteered for. You tried dressing like him, wore your hair like his, ate where he ate, shopped where he shopped, dated everyone he dated, drank when he drank. You have been like a little brother chasing his elusive big brother."

"Jeez, I sound pitiful, don't I?"

"You sound like an only child with a stellar friend who impressed you. Hell, if I am honest, Wyatt impressed us all. The rest of us had families to help us keep a better perspective, I think. I am no psychologist. I don't have the faintest idea why it affected you like this and not me."

"But it did," Randall said softly, below his breath.

"But it did," Alex reiterated. "So, you are jealous and competitive, no biggy. At least you are not an alcoholic." Alex grinned boyishly at his friend. "I think you take it out on women because you compete better with Wyatt when it comes to women. So, Rand, you might clear the air with Wyatt, and maybe your dad too, and get your feet back under you."

"You're right, but I'll have to figure out what to say."

"Yeah, but do it soon, man. Sloane won't be available forever. Thanks to you, she is back in circulation again."

"What?" Randall bellowed in shock. He continued more quietly, trying to be calm. "What do you mean? Is she already seeing someone else?"

"No, sorry. Not what I meant. Just that you have rubbed the tarnish off by going out with her and now she is interesting to the right men again."

"Shit, how the hell am I going to fix that problem? I can't lock her up and keep her away from everyone else. But I will kill anyone who touches her."

"Seems you have a mess on your hands, Rand."

"A mess of my own making," Randall admitted.

"What are you planning?" Alex asked.

But Randall wasn't paying attention anymore. He was just mumbling to himself, "I can't lock her up. Or can I?"

CHAPTER TWENTY-FIVE

First, there were the flowers. Sloane had to admit they were beautiful. The first day it was a large mixed bouquet; the second day it was roses—four-dozen gorgeous, fragrant white roses. She tried refusing them, but when the poor delivery person looked befuddled, she accepted them, running them over to the Children's hospital every day or two. When five dozen roses arrived, the doorman began assessing her when she went to the lobby to pick them up. His curiosity was obvious. What could she say if he asked? She hadn't a clue. The long white boxes and tissue filled the recycling room. The apartment smelled like a hothouse. She started calling an Uber to pick them up and take them to the medical center, her mother's house, Regan's office, Keeli's studio, anywhere she could think of, not able to stand the scent for even one day.

Next came the phone calls, none of which she answered. The first day there had been silence. She guessed he was giving her time to cool off, or perhaps himself a day to sober up. Initially, the phone messages were all the same: 'I was an idiot', 'I am sorry', 'I was drunk'. "My behavior was unforgivable, but I am begging you to forgive me." He was leaving upwards of ten each day. Then, of course, there were the texts too, dozens of them.

She wanted to forgive him. She did. It was simply not in her nature to do so. She was too proud, and it had been too public. He had humiliated her in front of the few people she could still call friends, as well as a room full of people just waiting to judge her harshly. He had embarrassed his friends and offended a perfectly respectable woman.

How could he?

Sloane cried all the way home, thinking of how the night should have ended, wondering why he wanted someone else and not her, wallowing in embarrassment and fury. She raged toward him for his actions, and then she was angry with herself. Having known Randall for nearly ten years, she knew he was a pig when he drank too much, and that he liked to drink too much.

Why had she trusted him to behave, believing that he had changed? After all, Sloane had been the brunt of his drunken behavior more than once while she was engaged to Wyatt, the rude remarks, the hugs she didn't want. Once upon a time, she would have welcomed his hugs and kisses, but not when she was engaged to his friend. Sloane berated herself repeatedly, wondering if she had only been a source of business, a lucrative deal.

Two weeks after the event, Sloane learned it was a great fundraising success. That was one good thing. During the recap event Sloane cheered the results, and the way she people treated her. It appeared she was no longer persona non grata. What a relief that was. She suspected she owed much of it to Randall and the team he had surrounded her with that Saturday night. It was not enough to get her to forgive him, but it softened her heart a tiny bit.

Two weeks and she still mourned the loss of a budding love that she'd believed had a real chance of success. Sloane hadn't left the house except to visit the kids' wards, attend exercise classes or go for a run. She had been in contact with the office, even touched base with a few clients, thanking them for their business, although most preferred not to deal with her directly since her father's trial. She spoke with Maria almost daily. The deal with Steel Franks had progressed, and the final signatures and money transfers were complete. She no longer had an office to go to, nor did she have the energy to follow up with Ethan about office space.

Why bother when she might never get to use it?

So far, there was no word on the streets regarding the potential renewal of the scandal and accusations in the Huyler family. Sloane was just praying that the silence continued. And Sloane was not a woman who prayed.

That awful lawyer, Sandra, had called several times, as recently as yesterday. She needed more documents, correspondence this time—tons of it. Sloane asked what was going on, explained that she really wanted to understand. When she heard the answer, she was sorry she'd asked.

"It's like this Sloane," Sandra began in her brusk, no-nonsense manner. "You know your father bribed the Chinese to do business in China. That was pretty close to treason, considering the secrets he offered, but that was on him. No one is associating you with that at all." She almost sounded disappointed, while Sloane was breathing a sigh of relief. "But he also stole those secrets from Blocker Manufacturing before he sold them to the Chinese. It has come to light that it was you who won the Blocker account for Huyler Industries. You had a personal relationship with Les Blocker."

"We went to grad school together. Les and I are friends," Sloane answered defensively.

"Be that as it may, you brought in the account and you need to consider how that appears. Your relationship with Wyatt Howe IV opened the door for your father to do business with his family. That arrangement gave your father the avenue to launder the income he got from selling secrets of a company you brought into the fold."

"So, what are you saying, Sandy? What am I accused of?" Sloane was furious at the veiled accusations she was hearing and frightened by how guilty they made her sound. "You sound like you think I am guilty. I don't want to be represented by a lawyer who doesn't believe in my innocence. Why are you even involved with this case, anyway?"

"It doesn't matter what I think, Sloane. I will do my best for you, I assure you. The firm put me on this case the second my father retired because I am the best person for the job. I have the right legal background. Do what I ask, please."

"Here is your situation," she continued. "To an outsider, it looks like you set the whole deal up, Sloane, and that your father just executed your strategy. The feds are evaluating whether he was the dupe here, not you. That's why we need the correspondence between you and Blocker, and your private emails with Wyatt. That is what I need to mount your defense."

"This is ridiculous," Sloane muttered into the phone before Sandra extracted her promise to provide the documents to the law firm as soon as possible. Sloane agreed, but then slammed the phone with a satisfying crash.

Of course, she knew she was innocent. However, she also knew that innocence and conviction had nothing to do with each other. There were cable and Netflix programs, and podcasts galore about the guilty going free or the innocent being jailed. She was rightfully nervous. In her limited experience, the U.S. Justice Department did not accuse unless they thought they could convict.

She lost sleep night after night, fearing a knock on the door, and an ugly arrest. Every time she dozed off, she would imagine herself dragged away in handcuffs, waking with a jolt, bathed in sweat, unable to fall back asleep.

Today, rather than brooding about it any longer, Sloane ignored Randall's messages and pulled herself together, dressing with care. She put on a bit of makeup to cover her dark circles and headed north to visit her mother for their usual Saturday ritual, refusing to think about jail one more minute. If only she had Randall to talk her off the ledge.

The drive helped Sloane clear her sleep deprived brain. The traffic was light for Chicago, and Sloane made excellent time getting from her downtown neighborhood to her family's suburban home. Pulling up in front of the manicured green lawn, Sloane had a moment of nostalgia. The "sold" sign in the middle of the grass hurt each time she saw it, but she had a cheerful smile plastered in place by the time she pulled open the side door.

"Mom, where are you?"

"Upstairs, honey. Grab me a coffee please and come on up."

Dropping her purse on the counter, Sloane pulled two porcelain mugs from the cabinet, splashed some organic milk she found on the refrigerator shelf into one and added the freshly brewed coffee for her mother. The other, she left milk free for herself. Juggling the two cups carefully, she made her way through the hallway, where her steps echoed in the space, then up the grand staircase to her parent's large bedroom.

Chaos reigned in the massive room. There were boxes and clothes strewn everywhere–on the floor, on the bed, on every surface. Sloane surveyed the entire space, looking for a safe place to rest the hot liquid before setting the mugs down on a window ledge.

"What on earth happened here?" Sloane asked, placing a quick kiss on her mother's soft cheek. "It looks like a tornado came through."

"Tornado, Marianne," her mother responded proudly. "The realtors promised there would be no people coming through for inspections or anything else today, so I thought I would take advantage of the time to pack up as much as I could of my winter things. I won't need any of them again before the move, so it seemed like a good idea to me."

Looking around the room, seeing it through Sloane's eyes, she laughed. "Believe it or not, there is a method to this madness. Want to help?"

Marianne instructed Sloane on what items went in which boxes and soon the two women were working side by side like a well-oiled machine. As they worked, Marianne filled Sloane in on the status of the house sale. Initially, three families saw the house at least twice. When one couple came back a third time, she realized she'd better pack. They seemed like a lovely couple who would raise teenage sons in the house.

"I feel good knowing they are a family. This is a house meant for a family. And boys too. Your boyfriends always loved playing football in the yard or sailing from our beach. It will be nice to think of someone loving the place like that." Sloane wrapped her arms around her mother, who had reached for a tissue to wipe a tear or two. "I will miss this place."

"Me too, Mom. Me too."

Marianne blew her nose and ordered Sloane back to work. They cleared the room In an hour; the boxes closed and labeled, and they were planning lunch. "In or out?" Marianne asked. "You look so lovely today, although a bit tired." Sloane offered no explanation. "Perhaps we should go into town and have a bite. We could go to Frank and Betsy's and share a cookie or two."

"Mmm, I love the cookies there. OK, let's go out. I can drive."

Sloane roamed about her old room, now empty of all but a few pieces of old furniture. She ran her fingers lovingly over the surfaces, feeling every dent with nostalgia, and waited for her mother to put on makeup and run a comb through her hair. Marianne emerged from her room ten minutes later, looking like a runway model. Despite a few laugh lines, it was obvious where Sloane got her beauty. Tall and dark, like Sloane, her mother had the same piercing blue eyes and lean figure. Sloane had youth on her side, higher cheekbones and a wider, full mouth that made her look exotic where Marianne looked softer. Still, they made a beautiful mother-daughter pair.

Driving the ten minutes to the restaurant, Sloane gave her mom an update on the gala. Sloane focused on the results of the event, rehashing the updates from the meeting earlier that week and easily sidestepping her mother's questions about Randall and her early exit.

"It really was a lovely event. You should be very proud ofn what you accomplished. Of course, you looked beautiful. I was proud when I watched you with your friends."

"Thanks, Mom. We raised a lot of money. Every aspect went well, ticket sales, donations, the auction. I could not have been happier. Well... except if I had been chairman."

"Honey, you know you did a lot of the work that made that event a success. You don't need your name at the top of a program to know in your heart that you made a real difference to those kids and to the hospital."

"Thanks. I needed that."

Betsy greeted them warmly, as the regulars they were, and seated them in a booth near the front where the natural sunlight warmed their seats. Both women ordered salads and ice tea, then sat back to enjoy their time together. Before her mother could grill her about her love life, the sound of Sloane's cell phone ringing interrupted the women.

"Go ahead, dear, you can take it."

"I am sure it's noth... oh, it's Missy. Do you mind, Mom?"

Sloane was already answering as her mother gestured to take the call.

"Sloane, it's Missy. Splendid party last month, I should have called sooner to congratulate you. You should be so proud. I was sorry we didn't get to sit together, but Stephen had to fill his table."

"Thanks, Missy. It was so wonderful to see everyone. And I am grateful that Stephen bought a table. Your husband is a generous man. You looked beautiful."

"Yes, for a woman who is still losing the last of that stubborn baby weight from her last pregnancy. The dress designer was a genius, wasn't she? Anyway, do you have two minutes?"

"Sure, I am just waiting for lunch to be served. I am with my mom. We are at Frank and Betsy's if you want to join us?"

"I wish I could, but with the kids..."

"Of course, maybe next time."

"I don't want to keep you, so let me get right to the point. Wyatt was the winning bidder on a house in Lake Tahoe at the auction. He suggested we use it for a girls' getaway four weeks from now. He will arrange a private jet and we will have the lodge for a full week. It's Keeli, her friend Linda Stuart, you and me. I think you might know Linda already. Regan will come for the weekend if she can get away from the office. Please say you'll join us. It will be fun."

"Oh, Miss, I wish I could. Tahoe this time of year would be peaceful and fantastic, but my mom is getting ready to move and..."

"Go, honey," Marianne interjected into the conversation. "They have FedEx If I need you to sign anything and the realtors are taking good care of me. You could really use a getaway."

She should only know. It may be my last chance before they hand down an indictment. Wow, my last chance. I better take it.

"Ok, Missy. Count me in. Thanks for including me. Isn't it Keeli's place to invite me if Wyatt won the bid?" Sloane couldn't resist voicing her thought. "I don't want to crash anything."

"Yes, it is hers, and you are not crashing. She wanted to be sure you came along and was afraid you would say 'no' if she asked herself."

"Not a chance. This is wonderful. Thank you so much. Thank Keeli. And Wyatt too, I guess."

"Keeli will email you the details when she has them. See you soon. Say hi to your mother for me."

"Will do. Thanks again."

Sloane relayed the message to her mother and told her about the invitation. While she was a bit surprised Keeli would include Wyatt's ex-fiancé, Marianne was happy to see Sloane included in the girls' trip and said so.

"You have been way too reclusive of late, Sloane, and I worry about you. At least you have Randall Parker getting you out and about."

"About Randall, Mom..."

"Sloane Huyler, do not tell me you pushed that young man away!"

"It was justified, Mom, I swear. He was manhandling another woman."

"Was he drunk?"

"Yes, of course. Isn't he always? It doesn't excuse his behavior."

"No, it doesn't, but I heard he thought the woman was you. Have you let him apologize? Heard his side of the story? I am not excusing him, not at all, but Sloane, you need to learn tolerance. Randall may have a drinking problem, but you could help him kick it. I saw the way he looked at you. The man would do anything you asked."

"Except keep his hands to himself," Sloane argued.

"You're right, of course, and nothing justifies manhandling another woman. Nothing. Still, the boy might deserve a second chance, or at least a chance to explain himself. He had a father who abandoned him and a mother who died. He is still struggling to figure out where he belongs."

"He's thirty-six years old, Mother. He should have figured it out by now."

"But he adores you, Sloane, and I know you love him. Find it in your heart to forgive him. He has never been drunk in our home. He gets up and goes to work with no problem and trust me, young woman, no one who drinks to excess has a body like he does."

"Mom," Sloane groaned in embarrassment.

"I may be older, but I am not dead, Sloane. I know a good-looking man when I see one. I know how he feels about you, honey. Since your grad school days, Randall has never stopped watching your every move. I think you want to give him another chance."

"I can't, Mom. It was so humiliating to have him mauling someone when I was right there, in front of everyone I know. They all saw that he wanted her and not me. It was mortifying."

"Or he really thought it was you and it was an honest mistake. I am not taking his side, I swear. I am simply suggesting you hear him out."

And there is more, Mom, that I can never tell you. He was lying to me. For all I know, he may be assisting the Feds to convict me of a crime I did not commit.

Sloane bit her tongue while her mother continued.

"I want to be sure you aren't overreacting, Sloane, like you sometimes do. I would hate for you to lose a man you love, a man who loves you, without at least hearing his apology."

"But Mom..."

"Do not 'but Mom' me, Sloane Huyler. Randall is a good man, and he has been by your side during a tough time. Don't underestimate the strength of character it takes to march you up to Chicago's snobbiest people. He shied away from no one at the fundraiser. He made you the belle of the ball, my dear. He gave you back your cache."

"Yes, but..."

"No buts. This man cares for you, Sloane. He shows it openly, in the way he looks at you, the way he speaks to you, and the way he speaks for you, too. Not that you can't speak for yourself. Believe me, I understand that, but you are too much like your father Sloane. You are quick to judge and slow to forgive. I love you, but think about that. I am not making excuses for his unacceptable behavior, merely suggesting you talk to one another."

"You are too hard on Dad. Don't you mind he is sitting in a jail across the country serving time for a crime he did not commit? I am proud to be too much like my father." Sloane was defiant.

"Sloane, I love you, but it is time for you to take off those blinders you wear to justify your spiteful, uppity behavior." Sloane inhaled as if someone had physically punched her in the stomach. "Yes, uppity and spiteful. I am sorry, but you need someone to talk some sense into you. Your father IS guilty Sloane. He bribed the Chinese. He stole secrets from Les Blocker's company and sold them to the Chinese. And almost took down the Howe family by laundering the money he received through LHRE. And he would have married you off so he could blackmail your new family into the scheme, my dear. So, if I were you, I would stop defending him."

Sloane sat like she had been slapped,; too hurt and surprised even to cry. "But, Mom, you have to be wrong."

"I am not wrong, darling. He confessed it all to me. That man loved to confess. He was like a spoiled child. He would make a misstep, break a vase, have an affair. Then he would confess and say 'I am sorry', and that was supposed to make it alright again."

"He had an affair?" Sloane thought things couldn't possibly get any worse when her mother responded. "Several."

"Oh, Mom, how awful for you."

"And for you too, dear. When I talk about having a good man, believe me, I understand the difference between one who looks good and one who is good. I stood by your father because I loved him and because I cared about appearances. But that didn't make him a good man. And I watched, heartbroken, when he would be there for you, loving and kind, then disappear and ignore you for days. I know he hurt us both, but you always forgave him in a way you never forgaive others."

"But you just described Randall, mom, and told me to let him apologize and forgive him."

"No, I said listen to what he has to say, then decide whether to forgive him. That decision is yours, as it should be."

Sloane was struggling to process all this information about the men she adored, but she knew from watching her mother's expressions that everything she was telling her about the scandal was the truth

"I don't know what to say," Sloane finally admitted, crestfallen, "except It still hurts to hear you say this about Dad, and to have you call me spiteful and uppity."

"Well, Sloane, I love you, but it is the truth."

"Mom, you always say "I love you" just before you criticize me. 'Sloane, I love you but...' Sloane mimicked her mother. "I have been hearing that my whole life."

"I love you, Sloane, more than anything. And dear, I am not criticizing you, ever. I am criticizing your behavior. Never forget that. Remember that when you have children of your own. Speaking of which..."

"Mom, stop pressuring me. Really."

"Has Randall apologized?"

"Oh yeah. He sent flowers, dozens of flowers, hundreds of flowers. And he called and left hundreds of messages."

"And did you listen to any of them?" Sloane shook her head. "Listen to the man, decide to forgive him if it's warranted. Go away with the girls, relax and rejuvenate, and come back to a fresh start."

After the painful revelations today and the horrible accusations yesterday, a fresh start was exactly what Sloane needed. She needed time to process everything and to decide if she could forgive Randall. She didn't think she could stand any more news.

She still didn't know the truth about Randall and his role in the legal proceedings, either.

The server put two large salads in front of the women, allowing the conversation to halt for a few blissful minutes. Marianne began eating with gusto, but Sloane had completely lost her appetite.

Yeah, keep eating, Mom. You can't tell me horror stories and scold me if your mouth is full. And I hate when you scold me—especially when you're right.

CHAPTER TWENTY-SIX

Lake Tahoe was more beautiful than Sloane remembered. The flight had been so simple. Keeli handled everything and Sloane had merely waited for the Lincoln Town Car to show up at her door and whisk her away. Because they had a private jet, she even avoided O'Hare Airport with their crowds, traffic, and long security lines. It was heavenly and Sloane could not prevent herself from thinking for a moment that all this might have been hers. She shook off wallowing in jealousy and got back to laughing with her traveling companions over who had the most luggage. Surely, Keeli was carrying the most baggage, but she had brought sketchpads, precious stones, metals, and soldering equipment, which technically had to be excluded in the comparison.

Once they eliminated Keeli's paraphernalia, she turned out to be a lightweight with only one 24-inch bag of clothes for the entire week. "There is a washer in the place," she said. The women stared at her like she was insane. None of them considered doing laundry while on vacation.

Missy was traveling with a large and a medium suitcase, as well as an oversized tote that she could hardly lift onto her shoulder. "Books," she explained, sending the other women into whoops of laughter.

"Haven't you ever heard of a Kindle?" Keeli asked.

"I just like the feel of an actual book in my hands."

"Yeah, Missy, but do you like the feel of actual books in your luggage?" Linda set them all to laughing again.

"You can bring as many books as you want," Sloane said, "as long as it's you lugging them and not me!"

"I wouldn't be one to talk," Missy fired back at her. It was true. Sloane had brought two medium designer suitcases, one of those old-fashioned hard-sided make-up cases, and a large tote slung over her shoulder.

"I couldn't decide what to bring, so I brought it all," she conceded as they laughed at her.

"But a makeup case?" Linda couldn't resist observing. "Even if we were getting all dolled up, which we aren't, no one carries a makeup case anymore."

"Oh, that." Sloane reached for the case she had carelessly tossed on an empty seat of the jet when she came aboard. "That's for emergencies." She piqued the women's interest with this comment and they were leanving over her when she opened the case. It had a small amount of makeup and sunscreen on the top tray, but when she lifted out the top layer and revealed the larger open compartment, it was full of candy bars.

"Oh my God, I love you," Linda squealed, reaching into the container for a Nestlé's Crunch as Missy removed two Snickers. "You are the perfect traveling companion."

"So much for the baby weight," Missy mumbled between bites of the gooey chocolate and peanuts.

The four women traveled companionably for the four-hour flight, talking, dozing or reading. It turned out that Linda and Sloane were vaguely acquainted, and they all got along beautifully, right from the start. They had dinner plans for the first night and agreed not to plan anything beyond that other than glorious relaxation. They would take in the mountain air, eat some good food, hike, lie by the pool and, maybe, if they were brave enough, try swimming in the cold lake waters.

And they would shop. With their combined wealth, this group of women could improve the economy of the area easily if they chose to, and several wanted to pick up toys or souvenirs, do some early Christmas shopping or just find things for themselves. Shopping was definitely in the plan.

A limo met them at the small airport and soon they were following the road around the bluest lake Sloane had ever seen, in the most picturesque setting she could imagine. It had been years since she had been there. Warm memories of family vacations flooded her before she realized they were all an act then and would never occur again.

They drove past the casino and promised to come back during the week. Linda confessed to being an avid gambler. "In and out of the casino," Keeli had added, a reference to some private joke between the two of them. They spied shops and restaurants that might be interesting and grew increasingly excited as they approached their home for the week. Sloane left her melancholy behind as they drove along the scenic route.

Soon the car turned off the main road and made its way uphill on a winding, secluded road. The only sign of other mountain inhabitants were mailboxes strategically located at a few turn offs. The quiet was overwhelming after leaving the constant noise of a city like Chicago. Sloane lowered the window beside her and caught the faint song of an unseen bird. The trees were thick at the bottom of the road, blocking the views, but they thinned as the car climbed closer to the mountaintop. Before long, Sloane could catch a glimpse between the trees of a large house, and here and there she spied views of sparkling turquoise beyond. She could only imagine what awaited them. She knew Wyatt had spent a lot of money to secure the home for a week, and he had exquisite taste.

Nothing prepared the women for the gorgeous stone and redwood home that stood before them when they finally came to a halt. The building was more modern than most in the area, but it captured a rustic feeling, too. Sharp-angled wooden peaks and enormous expanses of glass reflecting the sun into their eyes topped massive rock walls that seemed to be a part of the landscape. The house was just at the edge of the tree line, and it felt strange to look down at the pines below.

"Wow, would you look at this place?" Keeli said in awe. "I feel like I just stepped onto a movie set or something."

"This is spectacular," Missy echoed, looking at the others to gauge their responses. "Sloane, pick up your chin."

Sloane didn't mind the good-natured chide. She was certainly standing there gaping. The vista was magnificent, and the house was an architectural marvel. She did not know where to look first. Their home for the week had many rooflines and balconies and the marriage of wood, stone, steel and glass looked to her to be an engineering wonder. It appeared to grow from the land it inhabited. She could barely see one corner of a roof way below them; otherwise, they were utterly alone with nature. They were in a paradise that—only a few months ago—Sloane believed she would never experience again.

Keeli removed the keys from her bag and moved toward the door just ahead of their driver, who was weighed down with his first load of luggage. Poor man, he had to make two more trips, but Sloane figured he was well paid and well tipped for the effort. Keeli was still pressing bills into his hand when Sloane walked past her into the house.

Stepping into the shaded interior, Sloane stared past a massive stone hearth at the over 180-degree view of the lake. The sun reflected off the deep blue of the water until it was hard to tell where the lake ended and the sky began.

"I have never seen anything like this," Keeli whispered reverently as she joined Sloane. "I don't think I can ever get used to a view like this. How does someone walk away from all this and rent it to total strangers? I would never, ever leave."

Sloane was thinking the same thing. "If this was mine, I think I would stay here year round. It's so peaceful looking out at all this." It was a cloudless day and Sloane felt her spirits lift, as they had not done in ages. She felt free here. Unencumbered by the troubles awaiting her at home, unconcerned about her loneliness, her problems with the Feds or with Randall.

"This is truly a place for renewal." Missy said. Sloane nodded slowly. "That is exactly what I was thinking."

"I agree," Linda responded from across the enormous room. She was standing in the open kitchen, all redwood and stainless steel. It was a gourmet chef's dream. The open floor plan allowed the four women to be in the same room yet still need to shout across the expanse. Keeli was already standing on one of several decks near the dining area, pointing to an outdoor grill and a table for ten. She told the women that she could see another deck below "with a huge hot tub, just for us."

Sloane could not contain her pleasure as she moved from room to room. There was a gigantic screen in the media room, a billiards room, two offices, and seven bedrooms for them to choose among, each with a stone fireplace. The master suite had a separate loft with a spiral staircase leading up to it, and by mutual consent, that room went to Keeli.

After selecting a large bedroom with a platform bed, windows from floor to ceiling and a modern black metal walled fireplace, Sloane wandered back to the main room and into the kitchen. Normally not much of a cook. The space made her itch to try her hand at a meal or two. There were two Gaggeneau ovens and a 5-burner gas stove, a high-end microwave and a fully stocked wine refrigerator.

Pulling open the Sub-Zero refrigerator, Sloane found it stocked with fresh fruits and vegetables, bowls of whole apples and pears next to containers of cut up pineapple and mango, the blues and reds of berries peeking through the chunks of yellow and orange. It all made her mouth water. There were prepared foods from a gourmet shop in town that looked fantastic, cold cuts, cheeses and containers of lettuce in the crispers and drawers. There was milk, orange juice

and even yogurt in all her favorite flavors. Opening the cabinets, Sloane oohed and aahed at the bone china and Irish leaded crystal.

Who leaves this stuff available to strangers?

The wine selection was outstanding. Sloane expected it to be under lock and key, but it wasn't. There were baskets of breads and rolls, and cabinets filled with canned goods. There was a completely stocked bar against the far wall. She couldn't think of anything she might want that wasn't here, and she wracked her brain trying.

A note sat on the counter that read "Welcome, ladies. Enjoy my home as if it were your own. I have tried to guess what you might like and stocked the kitchen, but call the caretaker, Dana, if you need anything else. Keys are in the cars, but be careful on these roads at night. There is a stack of menus from local restaurants in the kitchen drawer, as well as the number for an excellent chef who will come in at your request. Enjoy!"

Although the note deciphered easily, it was signed with a bold, illegible scrawl. For Sloane, that signature conjured up the image of a strong hand attached to a very handsome man. She tried to imagine what kind of person owned all this. She had wandered into the two offices and it was obvious someone actually worked from here, but there were no personal items to give away anything about the owners. It certainly did not have the feel of a vacation home, and she wondered if someone lived here most of the year, someone who had graciously agreed to be displaced just to help raise money for the Children's Hospital.

Not likely.

She didn't have long to think about all this before Keeli came from her bedroom—or at least somewhere in that vicinity, since Sloane felt as if she needed a map to find her way around. Keeli was waving a piece of stationery in her hand and shouting excitedly.

"Calm down," Sloane said soothingly. "I cannot understand a word you are saying."

Missy came from some other direction, eyes big as saucers from taking the house tour. "What's all the commotion?"

"Wait until you see this," Keeli approached Sloane at the same time Linda and Missy did. "You won't believe it. We have two full pre-paid days at the Ritz-Carlton spa. One for the day after tomorrow, for the four of us, one for later in the week after Regan arrives. Full days, the royal treatment. We have dinner reservations in their dining room too, but the note says to just cancel if we don't want to use them."

"Wow," Missy exclaimed. "You have certainly changed, my brother. He was never this thoughtful or generous before he met you, Keeli."

Sloane confirmed Missy's opinion. "He's never done anything like this in all the years I have known him. I wouldn't have thought it would even hit his radar."

"But that is just it," Keeli was breathless with excitement. "It's not from Wyatt. It is from the people who own this place. See, that signature is right there. Can you believe it?"

Sloane could not believe it and took the vellum card out of Keeli's hand to review it herself. There it was, that mysterious scrawl again. Perhaps their mysterious host would stop by while they were there, and she could thank him or her. Whoever it was, they had sparked her imagination.

Sloane had decided the signature was definitely male. It was a strong, scrawling set of totally illegible letters, similar to a doctor's mark on a prescription.

A signature like that means he is confident, powerful. But perhaps he is as sweet and handsome as Randall. Stop that. You are not thinking of Randall anymore. You promised yourself to let him go.

When Sloane accepted the invitation to join Keeli, Linda and Missy, she had thought long and hard about her mother's words. Randall was still texting several times every day, although the flowers and calls had finally ceased after about two full weeks. She considered sending him an email, just to agree to talk, but by the time she was ready to do it, too many days had passed and it felt awkward and clumsy. What could she say when she was so furious and so confused? Instead, she vowed to put him out of her mind, along with work and legal problems, and just enjoy herself for a solid, uninterrupted week.

Seven blissful days of denial and leisure. Then, I will figure everything out.

Perhaps, Sloane thought wistfully, a mysterious stranger with a generous spirit and exquisite taste in spas, wine and houses will come into my life this week and make all my problems magically disappear.

You can always hope, Sloane.

"This place is amazing. I am going to finish exploring and call Stephen to talk to the kids before it gets too late." Missy outlined her plans.

"I am going to unpack a little and set up my Lake Tahoe Studio while I have the energy and the natural light," Keeli responded. "How 'bout you Sloane?"

"I think I will walk a bit of the grounds and then plop my white body in the sun on that gorgeous deck for a little while."

"Sounds great. Wear sunscreen," Missy replied as she left the room.

"Good for you, Sloane. I just want a nap," Linda said, heading for the nearest sofa and dropping onto it like a stone.

"See you out there in a while," Keeli told Sloane.

Sloane wandered the rest of the house, taking in the amazing architecture and use of organic materials like slate and glacier stone. It was truly magnificent. She ran her hands along the sleek desk in the office and imagined being able to work from a place like this, with a view like that.

Maybe it's time for me to get out of Chicago and start over. Maybe I could find a job that I could do remotely or move to somewhere in sunny California.

Sloane allowed her imagination to wander, knowing she would never move that far from her mother. She found her way back to her room, shook out a few blouses, hung them in the enormous closet, and dug out her hiking boots. She hadn't worn them in years, but they still fit, and she figured if she had carried them all this way, she was damn well going to wear them.

Wandering out the front door, Sloane made her way around the house to what she believed must be the edge of the property, a spot where the trees were thicker and the grass ended. She could hear the movement of birds above and small animals rustling in the pine needles blanketing the ground. Everything had a hushed, otherworldly feeling. She walked down the hill a bit, across the long driveway that wound in her path and up the rocky incline in front of her. After about 30 minutes she was feeling the burn in her calves and in her lungs, so Sloane made her way back to the deck, unlaced the heavy boots and laid down in the afternoon sun, turning her face to the sky. Shutting her eyes, she took three or four deep breaths and felt herself completely relax. In moments, she was asleep.

Sloane was only vaguely aware of Keeli joining her, stretching out on the lounge chair beside her, but she closed her eyes again and dozed a while longer. Afraid she was being rude, although Keeli had certainly said nothing, she eventually pulled herself awake and opened her eyes to find Keeli's nose buried in a book about jewelry.

"Do you never leave your work behind?" Sloane asked good-naturedly.

With a shrug of her shoulders, Keeli replied, "Hazard of loving my job, I guess. My brain is constantly designing new jewelry. You will see. I grab scraps of napkins to sketch wherever I go. I'll try not to embarrass you."

"Oh, believe me, I don't embarrass that easily. After this year, I have grown a very thick skin."

"It's been a rough time for you, I imagine."

"Oh, I did not mean to dredge anything up, Keeli. Really, I'm just fine. Nothing to worry about."

"Sloane, I hoped we could get to know each other better on this trip, really become friends. I don't have many friends. I have Wyatt's sisters, of course, but they are his sisters. I have my friend Clarice, a wonderful artist, and my sister-in-law, Sarah, but she is back in Gilman. Another business woman to be friends with, someone who knows the same people I know, that would be great. It's been fantastic getting to know Linda and imagine we could grow close too, if you let us."

"What would Wyatt think of all this? Are you sure he would approve?"

"First, he doesn't get a say in who I am or am not friends with," Keeli retorted sharply before continuing less hotly, "and actually, it was his idea for me to invite you this week."

"His idea? You have got to be kidding. That makes no sense on so many levels."

"Why would you say that, Sloane? You and Wyatt used to be very close. Neither of you had your hearts broken when he called off the wedding, so why not resume the friendship?"

"Well, for starters, my dad went to jail for a scheme that almost ruined Wyatt's father and his business." Sloane could not hide the bitterness from her reply.

"That was your father, Sloane, not you. Besides, you are paying a high price for it now, from what I can see."

"You know, Keeli. I heard you were a sweet girl from the farms, but I figured a sweet girl from the farms could not land a man like Wyatt. I had you pegged as cunning and clever, someone who set out to win him for his prestige, his family name and his money."

Sloane waited for a response from Keeli, but the redhead just sat calmly, giving Sloane her full attention.

"I had you all wrong, didn't I? You really are exactly what you appear to be. No wonder Wyatt dragged his feet with me. You are exactly what he was waiting for. I was too cynical, too sharp around the edges."

"I don't know about that, Sloane, but I know I love him with my whole heart, and I think he feels the same. I know we're happy. As for your cynicism, you can lose that, you know. You are a brilliant woman who has sold her business and is about to start anew. Seems to me you can be whatever and whoever you want."

"No. It's a delightful fairy tale, but still just a fairy tale. There is no money, so I will have to take a job quickly. There is a scandal following me everywhere I go, and some who think I'm guilty, too."

"Who thinks that? I don't think that," Keeli was quick to offer. "I think you were blindsided, like the rest of us."

"Thanks, I appreciate the vote of confidence." Sloane flashed Keeli a sincere smile and gave her hand a quick squeeze.

"Regan believes in you, and so does Randall, right? They are business geniuses. They read people and opportunities for a living. If they will invest in getting you back on your feet, then I know you have a bright future."

"Okay, Pollyanna. Enough, Tell me about Keeli Larsen Designs for a while. I want to know everything. I am so impressed with how you have built this vast enterprise in just a year. Wyatt must have invested a lot to grow things so fast."

"Actually, I never took a penny of Wyatt's money, although he offered." Keeli laughed at Sloane's astonished face. "Really, a girl has to have her pride, right? I took an investment from Linda, but I have paid her back everything. She helped to get me the push I needed. I owe her a great deal."

"You owe me nothing," Linda Stuart corrected, joining the tail end of the conversation. "It was a pleasure to help launch my talented friend here," she explained to Sloane. "I held a trunk show and threw a few bucks her way. She did the rest."

"That's an understatement if ever I heard one. I have no business sense. You were instrumental in helping me see possibilities. Now I am counting on you to help me grow and expand intelligently. I am in so far over my head."

"Wyatt? Isn't he helping you there?" Linda asked.

"A girl has to have her pride," Keeli and Sloane responded in unison before falling into a fit of laughter.

The three women spent the next hour sharing stories of business successes and failures. Keeli explained she was now heading a business that had grown from non-existent less than two years ago to grossing more than $8 million last year. She expected it to double again this year. Keeli was running two manufacturing sites, employing five interns besides her regular assistant. Her designs were available in every major department store, from Nordstrom to Neiman, and she expected to deliver four distinct collections each year. She was still creating an exclusive collection for one of Chicago's most exclusive boutiques.

"Thank heaven Linda has such a good head for business or I would have sunk under the pressure. It helped that Lyon Tech Solutions was growing even faster. I kept telling myself, if Wyatt could handle it, then so could I. He's been so supportive. I feel so fortunate. Who could have imagined this would be my life? I was lonely and living on Ramen noodles two years ago."

"I am so happy for you. I think if anyone deserves all this joy, it's you. When you talk to Wyatt, please tell him thank you for suggesting I join you this week. It was an inspired idea. I cannot remember being so relaxed and happy. Not in a very long time."

Keeli seemed sincerely pleased by Sloane's admission. The late afternoon sun still warmed them, but Keeli rubbed her arms with a bit of a chill and suggested they move inside. With the sun moving lower in the sky, an evening chill had really set in, unusual for August.

Missy was napping, and Linda went to unpack. Sloane and Keeli slipped into the hot tub to warm up. Sloane had been wise enough to grab a bottle of Rombauer Chardonnay from the fridge and the women sipped the buttery wine, laughed at their luxurious life and talked about nothing until almost 6:00 p.m.

Missy came to find them, jealous to have missed the hot tub and whining about how she was hungry. They had not taken the difference in the time zones into account when they had made their 7:30 dinner reservations. By mutual agreement, they rushed to get cleaned up and headed to Soule Domain on the chance they could get seated earlier at the popular location.

Missy offered to drive when they were ready to head out, since she had missed the afternoon wine tasting. Moving toward the garage, chatting away, all four stopped in mid-sentence when they opened the garage doors. Sitting in the two-car garage were a very practical Jeep Cherokee and a far less practical but elegantly sleek, midnight blue Jaguar.

"Jag?" Missy asked with a conspiratorial grin.

"Do you think we should?" Keeli asked, swinging her view from Missy to Sloane to Linda and back again.

"I definitely think we should," Linda replied, moving toward the passenger door without hesitation.

The car was quiet and smooth on the roads, handling the curves and twists as if d for them. Too soon, they were out of the car and entering the restaurant.

"I feel like a princess," Keeli whispered as they were seated early, just as they had hoped.

"You are a princess," Sloane replied.

"Yeah, but you know what I mean. We don't live like this at home, you know?"

"You could if you wanted to, Kee. Wyatt would give you the world if you wanted it." Missy was right, of course, but the wonderful thing about Keeli was that she would never ask for much.

"Besides," Sloane surprised them all by saying, "if you had this every day, it wouldn't be special now." Perhaps the spoiled and demanding Sloane was learning a few lessons. Her hard edges seemed to be softening, after all.

They dined on shrimp, scallops and duck all prepared perfectly, then they were too full to do justice to the one decadent chocolate dessert they ordered to share. Besides, they were all so tired. By the end of the meal, the four were dead on their feet.

Missy drove very carefully back to the house, joking that she should have put out breadcrumbs to find her way back. The roads were dark, as the note had promised, and winding, but after only one wrong turn the women were safely inside for the night, gas fireplaces blazing to keep their toes toasty as they fell asleep.

CHAPTER TWENTY-SEVEN

Randall had been see-sawing between Huyler Industries' clients and lawyers the entire week. He felt like his head would explode. Besides managing Sloane's life, he was still trying to keep his own afloat, so here he was at 1:00 in the morning trying to get through portfolio evaluations for his own clients. He knew he looked like hell, and why wouldn't he? He had been averaging about five hours of sleep each night, eating crap if he was eating at all, and the stress of not knowing what was going to happen was driving him crazy. Not to mention his fear that Sloane might find out how involved he was with everything. Perhaps that was making him craziest of all.

When he overheard the original conversation about Sloane at that lawyer's cocktail party, he knew he should stay out of it. It was casually mentioned. It was not his fault that the incompetent, indiscreet legal team was not guarding their conversation more carefully. After that, it had been easy to alert Addison's firm and get them involved again.

Sandra Berenson's involvement didn't thrill him, either. He never imagined that Addison, Fine, and Stark would engage her for Sloane's case. When the original case was tried, she'd needed a Chinese firewall since Sandra's father was the prosecutor. He knew she was the best on legal espionage issues, and, with her father retired, there were no longer any conflicts. Still, Randall assumed Sandra would recuse herself. No such luck. He couldn't explain why, but he just didn't trust Sandra. She was the shark lawyer that spawned all those jokes. She liked to talk too much. He had discussed it with Addison directly, and now he was trying to trust the man's decisions.

Randall believed he'd covered all his bases before he had Amy ask Sloane to pull documents for due diligence, but then Sandra, the blabbermouth, almost ruined everything by calling Sloane directly. What the hell happened to discretion? Of course, lack of discretion was why they had a jump on all of this.

Rubbing his massive hands over his tired eyes, Randall decided he had done everything he could for today. Or for yesterday, to be more exact. He'd used his influence and called in all his favors to make the customers who had threatened to leave HI sign on with Steel Frank and each had a signed renewal option now as well. It was his promise that had sealed the deal with Steel Frank and he now closed that book at last.

Sloane and her mother would be comfortable. The negotiations had gone well. Maria had been a force to be reckoned with, leading the investment banker team to get a more than fair price for the company. Her mother could stay in the Glencoe house if she hadn't moved already, but the important thing was she could choose. Once he was completely certain of all the details, he called to let her know the good news. They had held an interesting conversation once they strayed off the topic.

"Did Sloane get in touch with you?" Marianne had asked him out of nowhere.

"No, I have not spoken to her since the benefit. Maria Canovalli was working on this deal, so she would not have needed to contact me."

"I wasn't talking about work, Randall. After my last conversation with her, I thought she might finally talk to you about the night of the benefit. I thought she was ready to listen."

Marianne was laying it on a bit too thick. Randall knew Sloane told her mother exactly why she'd shut him out. He blushed to realize her mother knew about his behavior. Good thing it was a phone call and not Facetime.

"No, we didn't speak."

"Well, she is out-of-town now, in Lake Tahoe with friends, so I hope she calls when she returns," Marianne said before ending the call with her gratitude.

Of course, Sloane placated her mother by saying she would call him. It had been weeks, and she never called. He knew Sloane well. She would never forgive him for the insult. Proud and too easy to anger, Sloane was slow to forgive. She would never believe he mistook another woman for her. It was farfetched, a feeble excuse even for a drunk three sheets to the wind.

Besides, now that she was a woman whom eligible men wanted to date, she wouldn't waste her time with him. Many considered him a catch, but not her. She would believe she outclassed him and aim higher. She had before and she would again. He had missed his chance.

Yet here he was, working with Addison's entire firm to prevent the Feds from indicting her. He had done everything he could to get the price of her company pumped up. Damn, he had even assured the women invited her to that damn girls' week in Tahoe. Wyatt had not been easy to convince.

That, too, had been an interesting conversation. After speaking with Alex over coffee, Randall had done some serious soul searching, and had a brief conversation with his dad about that science test long ago. His father hadn't even remembered it until Randall reminded him.

"How can you not remember, Dad? You helped me study. We went for nature walks. I told everyone I would come in first, but of course, Wyatt did. After that, you stopped helping me. You gave up on me."

"Gave up on you? Son, I have never once in my life given up on you. You have made me the proudest of fathers every single day since the day you were born. Why on earth would you think I gave up on you?"

"Well, you stopped helping me with my homework, or playing catch or anything. It was as if I wasn't worth the effort or something." Randall felt all the hurt again that he had felt as a fifth grader.

"Oh, Randall. You should have said something sooner. It was actually your mother's doing, as I recall. She made me promise not to put so much pressure on you. That was why I backed off. Not because I didn't believe in you. But you know how your mother was, Son. She would have had my hide if I disobeyed her."

The two men laughed at the truth behind that statement and Randall was relieved to learn he had misunderstood all those years ago. Having cleared the air with his father, Randall felt stronger about discussing things with Wyatt. He knew he was better prepared for the emotions that he would experience around the incident, too.

After convincing Wyatt to have Keeli or Missy invite Sloane to Lake Tahoe, he suggested they meet for a drink, just the two of them. Wyatt accepted, and they met after work the next day.

Randall began by falling on his sword again about his mistreatment of the woman at the benefit.

"You had one too many, my friend, but you really stuck your foot in it this time. Randall explained he sent flowers the day after the benefit and apologized profusely, and that the woman had been kind, if cool.

"It was better than I deserved."

"These things happen to you too often, Randall, although this was certainly the worst."

"Yes, they do. That is my whole point, the reason I wanted to get together. My destructive behavior happens every time I drink too much, and it happens to your date, or your ex-girlfriend, or your fiancé. I only get stinking drunk around you, Wyatt."

Wyatt's brows shot up in surprise. "Is that really true, Rand? I do know you seem to be drunk a lot when I am with you." Wyatt gave the flippant response, unaware of how important this was to Randall.

"Yeah, it is true. Alex helped me see it."

"Well, Alex never lies, so it must be true. Are you saying I drive you to drink? I thought we were friends." Wyatt continued to keep things light, lightly punching Wyatt's arm.

"We are friends, Wyatt. Of course, we are friends. But since fifth grade, we have also been adversaries, and that is why I drink."

"No, bro. I have never considered you an adversary. Only a friend. Always. You have been a good and true friend, Randall. I always knew you had my back. Why would you think differently?" Wyatt finally took things seriously, leaning forward on his elbows and looking Randall in the eye.

Randall related the story of the science exam, of the misunderstanding he had about his father's change in behavior. "And that made me want to beat you at anything, hell, at everything, from that moment on. I just had to come in ahead of you on something."

"I had no clue, Randall. Over the years, you have beaten me a million times. You are smart and strong, a force to be reckoned with on the ice, on the tennis court."

"Actually, Wyatt, I have never beaten you. Not once. Not in all these years."

Wyatt was stunned. Randall watched the play of emotions revealed on his friend's face as Wyatt remembered game after game, test after test, and girl after girl.

"I never meant to do that to you, Randall. I would never purposely beat you. You know that, right? I just did my thing."

"You just did your thing, better than me, hell better than anyone. I rolled with it until Sloane. Between my mother's death and losing her to you—" Randall ran a shaky hand through his hair. This was painful for him to admit, but he was ready to let it go, face his problems, and fix them. "It's cool now, Wyatt. Really. But I needed to clear the air with you. I need to stop competing with you so I can move forward."

"Consider it very clear, Randall. I am here for you, always. Jeez, I even agreed to send Sloane away with my wife for you. I hope they don't kill each other."

Laughing, Randall replied, "Oh, I think they will come home as the greatest of friends, Wyatt. I really do."

"Well, in that case, you must know something I don't."

"I do, Wyatt. I know the real Sloane." Wyatt raised a quizzical brow, but Randall changed the subject. They talked about work and sports until eventually Randall excused himself to return to the office.

Randall had cleared the air with Wyatt, and he would know before the end of the week if they had avoided a judgment against Sloane. Today, he had fulfilled his last obligations to Steel Frank. Like ticking off a list, Randall was putting all his ducks in a row. He had not heard fireworks from Tahoe, although he wished he had heard from Sloane. He missed her.

However, that was another problem.

CHAPTER TWENTY-EIGHT

Sloane was just leaving for a long walk with the girls, then some time at the casino, when her cell phone rang. She intended to ignore it and reached to turn it off when she recognized the number of Addison, Fine, and Stark. "Go ahead without me and I will catch up in a few minutes," she told the women, waving them off, turning back to the privacy of her room. She shut the door behind her, although she knew the women would be on their way down the mountain already.

"This is Sloane," she answered crisply.

"Sloane, it's Sandra Berensen from Addison, Fine. Do you have a few minutes to talk?"

"Actually, I only have a very few, Sandy. I am supposed to be on my way to an appointment." This time the excuse was actually true, but Sloane would have made one up to get rid of this viper.

"Well then, I won't keep you long. I wanted to keep you apprised on activities here at the law firm. I thought you would want an update."

"Yes, I would like to know what progress you have made." Sloane was icy and formal. She wanted the update, but hated that her legal issues were intruding on the beauty of Tahoe. Sandy knew she was unwelcome and sounded less assured when she continued.

"After working closely with outside sources, the Justice Department is looking at releasing your father and dropping all charges against him."

"That would be fantastic, Sandra."

"With these sources, and the documents provided to our firm by you and PPHP, of course, the government believes they have the additional evidence to indict you instead. They believe you masterminded this operation, identified and attracted the client through your connections. Finally, you assisted in the money laundering by providing a relationship with Wyatt Howe that would assure everyone at LHRE cooperated in your clever scheme. I, of course, must recuse myself from the case again now that they linked it to the case my father prosecuted. Mr. Addison will follow up with you directly."Sandra stopped to take a breath, continuing in a voice dripping with venom. "I confess, I always thought you were involved, Sloane. I will watch the trial from the sidelines, wishing I had listened to my father and become a prosecutor instead. It's a shame really, I would have really enjoyed taking you down. Good luck to you Sloane. You're going to need it."

Sloane was sitting with her cellphone still held to her ear, dumbfounded. The line was dead, but she was paralyzed with shock, both at the accusations and the nasty wishes of her supposed counsel. Sandra hated her, wished her serious harm.

Think, Sloane, think. You know you are not guilty, but it looks like even your lawyers think you are. I had forgotten for a moment how many people hate me. They want me to be guilty. And you can save Father. How can I not take the fall for him after all he has done for me? It would be so much better for Mom, too. Oh God, what do I do now?

Sitting there for thirty minutes, Sloane's head was no clearer. She needed help. She needed a new contact at the law firm, or a new law firm altogether. Yes, a new law firm. She scanned her contacts list until she found the number she was seeking, then dialed it with shaking hands.

"Hello?"

"Tyler, it's Sloane. I am so sorry to bother you, but I could really use a friend and a lawyer right now."

"Sloane, this is a surprise. Don't worry about it. I am certainly a lawyer, and I try to be a friend. What's up? I thought you were in Tahoe with the girls. Regan is on her way there tomorrow."

Sloane explained the whole situation and answered the dozens of questions Tyler peppered her with along the way, interrupting to get details, clarification, names, dates and times.

"I can't help you, Sloane, but I think I know someone who can. Let me reach out to Jonathan Chen. He helped get the Howes out of the relationship with your dad, and he is a brilliant international lawyer. Hopefully, he has the resources to tackle this."

"Tyler, whatever help you can give me would be fantastic. I just don't know where to turn. I am so scared."

"Don't be scared, Sloane. We have your back, Randall and I. We will make this go away."

"Randall? What does Randall have to do with this?"

After a long pause, Tyler replied, "Well, uh, I know Randall cares about you. He has been helping you on the business side. Yeah, that was all I meant." Tyler had never sounded less truthful, but Sloane could get nothing more from him except a promise to contact Jonathan on her behalf and get back to her.

"Go enjoy Tahoe, Sloane. Worrying won't help, but some fresh air will."

"Thanks, Tyler, for the help and the advice. I really appreciate it."

Sitting there after disconnecting the call, Sloane looked at her watch and realized an hour had passed. She dried her tears, washed her face to hide the evidence and, throwing her shoulders back, she was ready and waiting to join the women on their casino trip.

After all, her whole life was a gamble now. Why not try to cash in on it a bit?

CHAPTER TWENTY NINE

"It really is a tremendous change for her," Sloane overheard as she moved toward the kitchen the next morning. "But she had to know it was coming. Randall would have warned her, right?" "You know what, Keeli? I agree. Randall really saved her ass up until now, and this has been hanging over her head for months, if not longer," Missy added. Sloane froze in place, hidden by the large beams, eavesdropping shamelessly. The coffee she thought she would die without would just have to wait.

"What happened? I mean with Randall?" Linda queried.

"Well, you know her father went to jail, right? Guilty as sin, really shameful. No one would ever have guessed, either. He was always so charming. Poor Marianne Huyler, you couldn't meet a nicer woman." Sloane smiled at Keeli's kind words about her mother. "It never made sense to the people who knew him."

"Anyway, after the indictment, Sloane wasn't welcome anywhere, the business was tanking, and their life was basically over. They were broke and shunned everywhere. And no one cared; people figured she deserved it."

"Except Randall," Missy picked up the story. "He determined to rescue Sloane. Long story short, he invested in HI through Wyatt, invested tons. Wyatt was against it, but nooo, Randall would not let my brother dissuade him."

"Right," Keeli continued, the story gaining steam. "First, he got a contract from Wyatt—well, from Howe Tech Solutions. Randall used his own money to pay for it, of course. Wyatt would not have given them a penny."

"A lot of of his own money, so it would be a big contract." Missy said, relishing her contribution and emphasizing the words 'a lot.'

"Yes, like half a million dollars," Keeli continued as Linda grew wide eyed. It was as if they were telling her a ghost story around the campfire, voices low, building to the really scary parts.. "Then he called all the current clients and told them HI was secure enough that Howe Tech had just signed a big contract with them. That got those CEOs rethinking HI at least for long enough to broker the acquisition deal. With his help, the bankers found a buyer, and he's so shrewd he helped get Steel Frank to pay far more money than they mhave otherwise. Maria Canovalli could not have done it without Randall's efforts in the background. Not in time."

"Oh, I read about that in Crain's Business News. Nice for every-one," Linda acknowledged. "Sloane makes a bundle on the sale, and Randall makes a bundle for his buddies over at the investment bank."

"True," Missy conceded, "but Randall went further. He dated Sloane, despite her reputation as the biggest bitch in town, despite her father's situation." Missy leaned into her tale as the others listened, rapt. Sloane hugged the wall tighter, pained by the joy the women seemed to have in telling her woes. Were they her friends? "Poor Sloane, she never realized what a womanizer her father was. No surprise he went through all his money. I think he was keeping, like five or six, different mistresses in high style. But I never imagined he would do something illegal. Anyway, Randall stood by her despite all of that. He stood by her, well, at least until he took that new info to the lawyers."

"Yeah," Keeli picked up the story again. "Going to the lawyers and getting ahead of the feds was brilliant. Of course, now Randall has to decide what to do if they indict her. If it comes out that she was the mastermind of her father's whole money laundering deal, I don't see how he can stick around."

"I hear the paperwork is pretty damning. No one expected that," Linda commented.

Sloane couldn't listen to another word. Her knees were wobbly, and she was afraid she would drop to the floor in a heap.

They knew everything. Worse, they thought she was guilty. Mortified, mortified, she made her way back to her room as quietly as possible, climbed into the bed she had just made, and rolled to face the wall.

She was never coming out. Never.

When the girls came looking for her a few minutes later, she pretended to be sleeping. Later, she claimed a headache. She avoided them until Regan arrived.

Sloane heard the women welcome Regan, heard the mumble of voices while Regan took a tour. She heard voices lift now and then. The house was impressive, even for Regan.

It was less than fifteen minutes later when Regan strode into Sloane's room without knocking, yanked back the covers and grabbed her hand, dragging her from the bed.

"Oh, no you don't," Regan announced powerfully. "You are not hiding in here like some scared rabbit. So, you are in trouble. Guess what? We know all about it. Soon everyone will know, so get it together and push through it."Sloane stood before her friend, speechless. "I want to see that tough bitch attitude you are so famous for, and I want to see it right now." Regan stamped her foot for emphasis and Sloane jumped in surprise. "You are getting your sorry ass out of that bed and going out to dinner. We are not going without you."

Sloane stood before her friend, shoulders slumped, head down, defeated. Tears pooled in her eyes.

"Please go away," she pleaded. "They hate me."

"Ten minutes, Sloane. I mean it." Regan stormed from the room, Sloane's tears and pleas completely ignored. Knowing she couldn't fight Regan, Sloane slowly changed from her rumpled clothes, washed up and walked like a zombie to the living room where the women waited.

It may as well be a firing squad.

"Sloane, you could have talked to us," Missy said, walking to where Sloane stood, pulling her further into the room. "We're your friends."

They were just the words Sloane needed—fighting words. Sloane stood tall and braced for a good fight. "Friends, ha! I heard you talking earlier, about me, about Randall setting me up, after all. You all think I am guilty. I heard you."

"We are your friends. We are here to help you, if we can." Missy repeated. "None of us think you are guilty. Not at all." The others nodded their head in agreement.

"You talk about it behind my back and are nice to my face. How can I trust any of you?" Sloane came out slugging.

Regan walked over to Sloane and wrapped her arm around Sloane's shoulders. "No one here believes you are guilty, Sloane. I don't know what you think you overheard, but if we were talking about the situation, it's only because we have been waiting for you to tell us yourself. We have been racking our brains, trying to come up with ways to help you."

The breath went out of Sloane and Missy spoke again. "I don't know what you heard, Sloane, but none of us think you are guilty. I will admit, we think you look guilty. However, you well know, those are not the same things. Regan told us that Tyler is working on getting you in to see Jonathan. By the way, she says you will love him. And then we will see what happens."

"We are here for you, Sloane, really," Keeli seconded the sisters' comments. "Let's go to dinner and talk about how we might help."

"Really, you really want to help?" Sloane couldn't believe her good fortune. These strong, successful women were not turning on her. "I can't believe how lucky I am to have each of you. So fortunate."

Grabbing jackets and purses, the women made their way out the door. Sloane was near the back with Regan when she took her arm to hold her back for a moment.

"Thank you, Regan. You showed up just when I needed you most."

"I was coming anyway, but after I spoke with Tyler, I knew what I was walking into. Fight this, Sloane. You cannot concede defeat now."

"I will fight it. I swear I will. Just keep that snake, Randall Parker, as far from me as possible. I will kill the bastard if I see him. I swear I will."

CHAPTER THIRTY

"Look at me, after five days with Keeli I am all 'please' and 'thank you'. I think maybe it even feels good."Sloane was sitting in the luxurious spa lounge mumbling to herself and recovering from 60 minutes of intense yoga, followed by one of the best massages she had ever had. Wrapped in fluffy terrycloth robes, the women met in the lounge for a lovely luncheon.

Surrounded by her friends, the women who had buoyed her up non-stop for the last two days, she was thanking them yet again for their support, ideas, and for inviting her to join them in Tahoe. The women filled the lounge, having it all to themselves as they sipped either cucumber water or white wine.

"This spa day has been incredible," Missy said. "How will I ever return to the mundane life of wife and mother?"

"Oh, puh-lease," Regan challenged her sister, "you live for mothering."

"Too true, but I could seriously get used to this. I love our mystery hosts for providing us with such a wonderful vacation."

"To our mystery hosts," the women toasted.

"I wonder who he/she/they are anyway," Linda mused.

"I wonder too," Sloane said. "I could allow them to arrange my life indefinitely. Gourmet food, award-winning wines, a five- star spa and an architectural masterpiece in an unbelievable location. These people have impeccable taste."

"I checked with Wyatt and he swore he didn't arrange any of the groceries, wines or events. He also swears that he never saw all these additional items listed in the Lake Tahoe auction item."

Keeli told them she embarrassed Wyatt. When he discovered someone else thought of it and not him, he grew uncomfortable even discussing it. That left the women wondering about their enigmatic benefactor, but it had also allowed them to speculate wildly, which they did over lunch. Then they got back to Sloane's issues.

Sloane raised her glass, looked at each woman and toasted. "First, let's celebrate the five of us—powerful, loving women who have had the unbelievable pleasure of a week in a relaxing and luxurious location."

The four women quickly agreed with Sloane's assessment and drank from their glasses.

"Second, staying positive, we are celebrating the sale of Huyler Industries to Steel Frank. To Maria Canovalli, another strong, wonderful woman."

"Here, here" and "congratulations" flowed around the table as they emptied their glasses further.

"Third..."

"Wow, there's more?" Keeli interrupted.

"Third," Sloane went on as if Keeli had not spoken, "I am celebrating the fact that Jonathan Chen and partners have agreed to take my case and they believe we have a very good chance." The chatter at the table was instantaneous, as the women peppered Sloane with questions about her case. All agreed she was innocent, but that she had still had a long way to go.

"To Sloane and her freedom." Regan raised her glass, while the others echoed the statement.

"A little premature, Regan," Sloane admitted sadly. "Although I guess we can toast to my glorious unemployment. I really am free in that regard."

There was a moment of silence as each met the eyes of the others before ascertaining if this was good or bad news. When they saw the open smile on Sloane and her relaxed posture, they toasted at last. "To your freedom!"

Their spa lunches took the next hour. The salads, chicken dishes and salmon plates were passed from person to person until everyone had a bite of everything.

"How can they make food that looks and tastes this incredible but has a measly 350 calories?" Missy wondered. "If I had this chef cooking for me every day, I would have never struggled with this stupid baby weight."

"But you look beautiful now, Missy, struggle or not."

"You do," Regan agreed. "You are certainly back to your pre-baby weight, maybe even less?" Missy accepted the compliments and confessed that she was thinner than before she became pregnant.

"Speaking of pregnant," Regan went on, "how is Stephen doing with the kids? Or should I ask how he is doing with Father and Mother?"

"Oh, he should definitely have stories to tell, but he is so patient with them."

"The kids or your parents?" Sloane asked.

They all laughed as Keeli and Regan both answered for Missy, "the parents."

"Seriously, Mother is in heaven having those kids for a full week. Olivia has never been dressed better and Cole has never stayed clean longer, according to Steven."

Missy got a little homesick as she talked more about her children, especially their newest baby, Reynold, who was still just a toddler. "Good thing we head home soon. I could not be away from them too much longer," she confessed. "Much as I love you guys."

Keeli talked about the pressure she was getting from the Howes, who were eager for more grandchildren. "Well, how do you think I feel?" Regan countered. "I get the 'when are you getting married speech' almost daily now.

"When are you getting married?" Sloane asked with a deadpan expression, causing them to burst out laughing.

"Not you, too," Regan asked when she regained her breath. "Better find me the guy before you plan the wedding."

Four sets of eyes bored into Regan looking at her like she was insane. "What are you talking about?" Keeli finally asked. "You have had the guy for years."

"Keeli is right," Sloane agreed. "You and Tyler are obviously a couple. What are you waiting for?"

Trying to defend her sister-in-law and deflect the question, Keeli challenged Sloane. "Well, what about you and Randall? Have you reconciled?"

The look of pain that crossed Sloane's face changed the mood instantly.

"I am sure this was all a misunderstanding?" Missy said. "You two seemed so happy at the benefit. You looked perfect together, and we had such a great time."

Sloane and Regan exchanged looks before Sloane answered. "There was just too much other stuff going on in our lives, I guess. We couldn't make things work after all. But Regan, it was you we were discussing, not me."

By unspoken agreement, no one probed further, and Sloane sat back in her chair, visibly relieved.

"You and Tyler have been circling each other for nearly two years," Keeli offered.

"Oh, way longer, Keeli. You just didn't see them before you met Wyatt. They have been playing cat and mouse their whole lives."

"Come on, we are childhood friends, you know that. He's like a brother to me." Regan didn't look her friends in the eye as she told the bald-faced lie.

"Oh no, you two definitely do not look at each other like siblings," Sloane charged. "There is something going on there, so just spill already."

After a bit of harassing and chiding, Regan finally admitted to having feelings for Tyler.

"I have liked him a long time, but in the last year and half or so I have really noticed him, you know? He is so honest and smart. I like that about him. He doesn't take my shit, ever. And he is so friggin' hot."

Laughing, they all agreed with Regan's assessment. "So, what is the holdup, Regan?" Missy finally asked. "Mother really wants to plan another wedding."

"Him, damn it. He is the holdup. He takes me to benefits, places where we will both be anyway, when one of us needs a 'plus one'. Otherwise, he is polite and aloof. It drives me insane."

"Why don't you ask him out? Make the first move? It's not like you're shy," Sloane suggested. Missy and Keeli jumped on the idea and they finished lunch, laughing and joking over ways to approach Tyler for a first date. Linda chimed in, but, not knowing the couple, she kept quieter than usual. Besides, she had seemed preoccupied during much of their lunch.

Walking back toward the locker room, Keeli spoke to Sloane under her breath. "I think you should talk to Randall, Sloane. I really think there is more going on here than you think."

"There is more going on, Keeli. He is trying to send me to prison. Not exactly the act of a loving boyfriend," Sloane sniped, closing the subject to further discussion.

The women went their respective ways for the rest of the day, getting facials, wraps or massages all afternoon. They met again later, Regan finding Sloane collapsed onto a chaise drinking a glass of strawberry infused water. Regan accepted a drink from the therapist who had escorted her to the lounge. Sloane was cradling the glass of cool, crisp liquid, eyes closed, her face glowing and pink.

"Sloane?" Regan whispered, in case she was asleep.

"Hmm," Sloane replied drowsily.

"I'm sorry. You were sleeping."

"No, I am awake. Just too relaxed to open my eyes."

"This is heaven, isn't it?"

"I confess, I have seriously considered just staying here. I am not sure I could live in Tahoe year-round, but I could spend huge amounts of time here. When I am here, I feel so different. If I have the chance to choose, of course."

"You wouldn't really move though, right?"

"No, of course not. I can't just up and move and besides, I want to be near my mom. And, except in the dead of winter, Chicago is a great city."

"And your friends are all there," Regan offered with a squeeze to Sloane's limp hand.

"Speaking of," Regan continued hesitantly. "I am just asking as a friend, mind you..."

Sloane opened her eyes now and looked straight at Regan. Something was bothering her, or she would have just said what was on her mind. Regan was usually direct.

"Yes, Regan. Just spit it out."

"What about a job, Sloane? We toasted your freedom, but what are you going to do about work? I will help where I can, of course, but I have no opening for you. I wish I did."

"You are so sweet, Regan, but I am not looking yet. I have a little money after this sale; it will buy me a couple months to recover. And I have this 'thing' hanging over my head that may resolve everything. If I can shake it, I will make a plan, maybe reach out to an executive recruiter then. I know I will have to overcome my name, believe me. I would start a business if I had the funding. Market some product or service, hire a great staff and run the show. It will be hard being under someone else's thumb after calling the shots for so long, but I will figure it out. I am really not worried about employment yet. I have enormous issues to resolve first."

"Okay," Regan responded. "If you are not worried, I will leave it alone." Sloane could see that even though Regan said she would leave it alone, the wheels were turning in her brain.

Sloane was content to let Regan worry about it, at least for now. She had much bigger problems than a job and knew it. But knowing Regan, Sloane figured her friend would have an idea or two before the month was out. Hopefully, so would Jonathan Chen.

There was a minor commotion in the doorway as Linda, Missy and Keeli joined them in the quiet lounge, all dropping onto a sofa near the fireplace, looking like they could hardly walk.

"Good massage?" Regan queried with a laugh.

"The best," Keeli responded. "Not that I have a lot to compare it with."

"I could get another massage tomorrow and the day after and the day after that too," Missy dreamed aloud before confessing," "I hate the idea of going home, although I cannot wait to see my kids."

"Me too. I have to help my mom clean out the house and move. She cannot decide on a new place either, so we will go back to house hunting too," Sloane offered, not discussing other things waiting for her back home.

"I have work waiting too, but this week has been fantastic. I got so much done."

"I know," Sloane responded to Keeli. "The latest designs and those earrings you made the other day are incredible. Your pieces are amazing. You have so much talent."

"Why thank you Sloane, that means a lot to me, coming from someone with such exquisite taste."

"You are always so sweet, Keeli."

"Not always. You should see me when I am bookkeeping. I do nothing but curse."

Sloane laughed at the image of easy-going Keeli cursing, fist raised.

"That is when you see the real redhead come out in me."

"You hate the business side of your job, don't you, Keeli?" Regan pried.

"Yes, absolutely. It has, without a doubt, been the worst part of being so successful. It takes up too much of my creative time."

"Really?" Regan dragged out the word. "Why don't you hire a manager? Someone who can run your operation while you create."

"Wyatt and I have discussed that, too. He wants me to incorporate and hire a President, elect a board. He says now that I am this big, I really need to. But, you know how it is Regan. You need just the right people by your side."

"Yes, you do, Keeli, yes you do." Regan dragged out the words enigmatically.

Linda smiled a small Cheshire smile. "I have nothing pressing to go back to except—of course — my continued meddling in the lives of my friends." She made them all laugh, but she and Regan exchanged a sudden look. Had the others seen it, they would have known instantly that something was up, but they chatted away in ignorance. Linda excused herself, and Regan jumped up, suddenly energized, and followed her into the locker room.

When the two emerged ten minutes later, Regan sat beside Keeli on one side. Linda sat beside her on the other side and mumbled in her ear. Regan looked across at the other women, then whispered as well. Missy watched in confusion. Sloane was laying back, eyes closed.

The two women continued whispering quietly with Keeli, who tried to read their faces to understand. Regan caught Keeli's eye and then nodded her head toward Sloane. Keeli looked at Sloane, baffled, then back at Regan, who just stared back, her blue eyes meeting Keeli's green with an urgent message that Keeli was not receiving.

Suddenly, Keeli's entire face lit up with understanding and she looked over at Sloane like she was seeing her for the first time.

"You know, Regan," she said, as if their earlier conversation had never ended, "I believe you are completely correct. With the right person at the helm, I could easily turn over operations to a new President. She could handle hiring the executive team and work with the board. She could handle everything. But where, oh where, would I find someone able to do all that? And where could I find someone who could do all that and still be someone I could get along with? It would certainly take a rare person."

All eyes were on Sloane.

CHAPTER THIRTY-ONE

The women were sitting in the bar sipping Diet Cokes and planning their busy afternoon. "You should call the poor man and put him out of his misery," Keeli told Sloane.

"Well, boss, aren't you being authoritative now?" Sloane teased in return.

"I agree with Keeli, Sloane, it's obvious you like the guy, maybe love the guy. Why are both of you in total misery? It's been over three months. Call the man."

"Clarice, you have never even met Randall. How can you already be taking his side against me? And I might forgive some of the meddling, but he tried to have me arrested. He would have watched me go to prison. He believes I am guilty."

The three women were sitting over lunch around the corner from Keeli's large West Loop studio space. With Sloane's help, Keeli had located and leased the light open space and Clarice had quickly sublet some of it from Keeli for her own studio. Having her best friend and fellow artist nearby had made the chaos of moving well worth it.

The move in date was set for October first, only days away, so the three friends were taking a rare moment of relaxation. They seldom got the chance to actually go out for lunch. Usually, all three grabbed whatever they could and gobbled it, hunched over drafting boards and desks.

"I have been dying to try this place," Clarice said now about "Little Goat."

"Obviously, the trick is to come for lunch here because you can't get near a dinner reservation here or across the street. I have yet to make it to "The Girl and the Goat.""

"Mmm, who cares?" Sloane added, savoring a bite of her patty melt. "The food here is so good."

"Where the hell do you put all that food, girl?" Clarice asked Sloane. "I have this giant booty and I don't pack away half of what you devour."

"Remember, she runs."

"Ah, that explains everything," Clarice conceded defeat. "No way you could get me to go for a run. I would rather have my fat ass any day."

"I run to deal with the anxiety, Clarice. You have no anxiety, well, a lot less."

"You will have a lot less soon, Sloane, I am sure of it."

"If you say so, Pollyanna. If you say so."

Sloane had been working for Keeli Larsen Designs for over a month. Her official title was President. Keeli was CEO. They had incorporated and half of the Board was in place, an impressive membership representing the top department stores, classic Fortune 500 companies, even the head of one of Chicago's most prestigious old banks. Alex Gaines would be a Bboard member, bringing his investment and consulting expertise. Wyatt had suggested Tyler as well. Instead, they had brought in legal expertise via a partner from their outside counsel, just to keep any conflicts at work away from the Howe home life. Regan had agreed to join the board, though, so there was a strong Howe representation. Having her join had helped attract several of the other big names.

Sloane was slammed. She helped her mother find a new condo and pack her belongings for the move or for storage. Her mother was transitioning well, already having joined a book club that met in her new Gold Coast neighborhood, as well as a yoga studio.

Meanwhile, at work, Sloane was busy interviewing candidates to head their HR department. The sooner she filled that slot, the sooner Sloane would finish doing all the interviewing, so it was her top priority. She secured office and studio space here in the West Loop and expanded manufacturing space further south. Sloane loved working with Keeli and frankly, she was having fun again.

"Ladies, I am too busy to make time for Randall or any other man right now, even if I wanted to. Which I certainly do not."

"I think the lady doth protest too much," Keeli quoted Macbeth with an impish light in her eyes.

"Shakespeare? Was that Shakespeare?" Clarice hooted. "So, all that reading did pay off. I am suitably impressed, my friend."

Keeli blushed, but she was thrilled that Clarice recognized all the hard work Keeli had done to extend her education beyond community college. When the two sat beside each other at summer art fairs, before their big successes, Keeli would retreat to a shady corner, reading the classics to 'better her mind'. Secretly, she was very proud of herself, but for Clarice to notice was especially rewarding.

"I am not protesting, just stating facts," Sloane defended. "You both know how hectic it is with work and now with the moves, yours and my mom's. I have my hands full."

"Yeah, but if you call him Sloane, you could have your hands full of something much more interesting," Clarice taunted. "Way, way more interesting."

The women laughed, but Sloane admitted to herself that she missed the feel of Randall's hard body, missed his sensuous kisses and slightly risky, hard-driving sex. Sloane missed how he made her laugh and how cherished he made her feel. She had believed they had a future, but she couldn't reach out after all this time. She couldn't swallow her pride and he had finally given up trying to contact her, too.

He tried to have me arrested for god's sake, after driving up the price of my business so he could get his school chums a bigger fee. He was drunk and pawing another woman. Why should I forgive him? Why should I believe anything he says or does? No, I am better off this way.

"Ladies, I am done with this conversation. I am not calling him and he has stopped calling me. It's over. Let Randall Parker III go break some other woman's heart."

"You sure? Cause I heard he started dating someone else, if you want to know the truth," Keeli admitted. "I assume he would prefer you, but Wyatt said he was bringing some woman he knew in grad school to that fundraiser for diabetes next weekend. I wouldn't have said anything normally, but if you really don't care, I figured you should know before you run into them together."

"Oh, yeah, thanks, Keeli. I am glad to know he moved on. And I appreciate the heads up." Sloane pasted a smile on her face, but it was tight and forced, and they all knew it.

The snake. He is seeing someone else already. No wonder he stopped calling. Hmmm, Sloane. Make this work to your advantage. Show him up.

Clarice and Keeli were discussing the layout of the studio. Sloane appeared to be listening, but her mind was hard at work. She was back to her old ways — taking back the upper hand.

CHAPTER THIRTY-TWO

I t took Sloane three phone calls to line up a date for the diabetes event. She was actually excited to be going, and not only because she wanted to one-up Randall. The event was known for its clowns, magicians, silly toys and giveaways. It would be a fun night for a change.Her date was a partner in one of the city's premier law firms, a budding politician with a good chance of winning his primary, and an extremely good-looking man. He had been seen with Sloane on and off when she was waiting for Wyatt to propose. There had always been an understanding between the two that neither was looking for anything serious. She could count on Edward to be an attentive escort who would make Randall superbly jealous. Edward was a catch, and he liked to touch Sloane. At least he had liked to when they dated before. She figured that would drive Randall crazy.

She had called her mother's realtor, who had mentioned Edward in passing one afternoon. She was great at fishing and quickly found out he wasn't seeing anyone seriously. Next, a call to a mutual friend where she casually dropped that she had this great new job but no man in her life. Juxtaposing that with two additional questions, "Have you seen Edward lately?" and "Are you attending the diabetes benefit?" got the right wheels turning. A day later, her friend had placed the phone call to Edward and Sloane had a date.

Nice to know you haven't lost your ability to manipulate. Yep, you still got it, Ggirl.

Edward was picking her up in a few hours, and Sloane was pulling out all the stops. She had her hair professionally blown out until it shone like silk, a thick fall down to the middle of her back. The eye makeup was smokier around the eye than usual, a little redder on the lip, courtesy of wiz with makeup at her favorite salon. She looked exotic, almost Asian with that dark slash of eyebrow and pale skin. She was slathered in fragrant body lotion with the scent wafting around her subtly.

Thank god, her mother would not attend tonight. Her dress was not her usual classic, elegant Sloane style. Instead, she wore red and showed an unusual amount of skin. The Narciso Rodriguez dress had a low bodice that revealed the tops of her small, creamy breasts, discreetly hinting at more. Spaghetti straps crossed her back, the only things keeping the low front and much lower back from falling off her body. The back dipped almost to the top of her buttocks. What there was of the dress clung like a second skin, opening just enough for her to walk and dance.

Sloane almost reconsidered, small butterflies in her belly right before she opened the door. One misplaced little finger could send the dress tumbling around her ankles. It was not improper, not by a long shot. Sloane had seen more revealing dresses when she went to Neiman Marcus. It was just that she would be substantially barer than she had ever been at an event like this, or any event. She was making a statement and second-guessing herself at the same time.

Get a grip, Sloane. You want him to notice you, right? Yeah, but he won't be the only one to notice. Stop! Answer the door and stop arguing with yourself.

Sloane knew she had chosen well when Edward's eyes almost popped out of his head. "You look amazing," he gushed. Was she giving her date the wrong impression? That was certainly not her intention. Sloane felt lucky they made it out the door. She could immediately see that she would have to be vigilant with Edward's wandering hands. She gave him a quick kiss on the cheek, backing away before he could claim more.

It was a typical autumn night and Sloane wore a lightweight coat she would need when they arrived at windy Navy Pier. Edward gave the car to the valet, took her coat, and they entered the enormous room. It took less than ten seconds for Edward to work the crowd. She shook hands and made small talk easily. This was her old element, after all, and it felt good to be back.

People were polite. It was still not public knowledge that she was under investigation and Jonathan assured her it would stay that way. She waved to people she knew, stopped to make introductions or be introduced to potential big-money donors for Edward. No one ignored her.

Oh yes. It felt very good to be back.

While Edward got caught up in a legislative conversation, Sloane slipped away to greet Allyson Riley, receiving a warm reception. She was fully engaged in their conversation, so she was surprised when she felt a massive hand rest on the bare skin of her back.

Her heart rat-at-tatting in her chest, Sloane turned slowly. Initially disappointed to find Wyatt standing with Keeli, she enjoyed seeing the couple. They exchanged air kisses and made small talk before Sloane asked where the usual crowd was, pulling Edward into the conversation simultaneously.

Stop asking about him. Get yourself together. You do not care about Randall.

Keeli pointed across the open space and there was Randall, clearly visible, a mere thirty yards away, standing inches taller than everyone around him. He took her breath away. He always wore a tuxedo better than any man she knew. His shoulders were broad, his waist narrow. He had his arm casually draped around the shoulders of a petite woman with lush brown hair streaked with highlights. She was lifting her pixie face to look into Randall's and even from this distance, Sloane could tell she was hanging on his every word.

"Come say hi to everyone," Keeli suggested now, taking her arm.

"Sure, go ahead," Wyatt suggested. "I actually have a few things to talk to Edward about."

No, No. No. This would ruin the plan. I cannot have Randall see me without Edward.

"We'll wait," she told the men, slipping her arm through Edward's and leaning into him slightly. "No rush. We have all night."

Sloane tuned out the conversation and surveyed the room carefully. Whoever organized this event had done a stellar job. There was a large crowd, a remarkable number of silent auction items and entertainers working the crowds, keeping things festive and loud.

"Are you listening, Sloane?" Keeli asked, touching her free arm lightly.

"I'm sorry, I couldn't hear you above all the noise," Sloane lied smoothly.

"I just suggested you walk with me to get another drink," Keeli suggested, leaning closer to Sloane's ear to be heard and shaking her empty wineglass.

"Sure, of course," Sloane responded distractedly. Keeli told her husband where to find them and they had hardly moved away before the two men were deep in conversation.

"You look fantastic, Sloane. If this dress doesn't do the trick, I don't know what will."

"I don't know what you are talking about, Keeli. But thanks."

"Sure, Sloane. I'll play along if you want me to pretend this isn't all about Randall. But you would do a more believable job if you stopped staring at him."

Sloane's eyes swung to Keeli's in alarm. "Am I that obvious?"

"Just forgive the poor bastard. Wyatt says he hasn't had a single drink since the night of the Children's' Hospital benefit, that the legal stuff is just a misunderstanding. And he loves you, Sloane."

"Do you really think so? Has he said anything?" Sloane heard the hope in the pitch of her voice, giving her away.

"Do you hear us?" Keeli was laughing. "We sound like school girls. Will you pass him a note and ask him if he likes me?"

Sloane laughed, her first sincere emotion of the night. At that exact moment, she felt another enormous hand on her back, sending tingles to her fingers and toes.

How could I have mistaken Wyatt's hand for Randall's? These long, elegant fingers get a reaction from me every time.

Schooling her features, ignoring the feel of her blood coursing through her body, Sloane turned to face Randall.

"Mr. Parker, how lovely to see you," she said formally.

"Ms. Huyler, you are looking exquisite this evening, as always," he responded in kind. "I understand congratulations are in order. Keeli tells me you have joined her company as President. A brilliant solution for you both."

With that, Randall leaned in to give Keeli a chaste kiss on the cheek. He did not do the same for Sloane and she felt bereft. If he cared about her, he hid it well. He was behaving like a stranger, or a nodding acquaintance. Nothing more.

"Come say hello to everyone," he suggested to them. Sloane wondered if he addressed the statement to her or Keeli. She was unable to tell.

"Sure," Keeli responded for them both, taking Sloane's hand.

"But, Edward…"

"He's fine. He's with Wyatt. They know where to find us." Keeli pulled Sloane's arm gently and moved her toward the small circle of friends chatting together.

"Look who I found," Randall announced to no one in particular.

They quickly were absorbed into their regular crowd. Regan and Tyler, Alex and Charlotte Roche—he's with Charlotte?—Missy and Stephen were all present.

"May I present Alyssa Moore? Alyssa, this is Sloane, an old family friend."

An old family friend? Why that sniveling, dirt-eating, slime bag, how dare he?

"How nice to meet you, Alyssa," Sloane extended her long hand to shake Alyssa's. "And what a beautiful dress you are wearing. Is that de la Renta?"

"You have a good eye, Sloane. Isn't it beautiful?" Alyssa did a half-pirouette, showing off the dress. The two women chatted comfortably about clothes and the event. Sloane quickly learned that Alyssa had indeed gone to school with Randall, but at Duke, not Northwestern. They went way back, Alyssa stressed, before explaining that she had recently moved to Chicago for her work. She was a reporter and Sloane peppered her with questions about the assignments, reassured that her own situation was not on the reporter's radar. Sloane asked how she liked the city. Had she been here yet or there?

Take that, you pig! I can stay perfectly cool and aloof. I can charm the pants off this little girlfriend of yours.

Sloane learned that Alyssa had seen little of the city yet. Perhaps because Randall had not been showing it to her? With all the aplomb she could muster, she turned to Randall.

"Alyssa tells me she hasn't even been to a sporting event here. Not hockey, not the Bulls. Randall, you are falling down on the job. Take the poor girl to see the sights."

The conversation had no time to digress into a fistfight since Wyatt and Edward joined them at that moment, deflecting the sparks poised to fly. Edward placed his hand on the bare skin of Sloane's lower back and suggested they find their table for dinner.

"Too bad Sloane didn't turn around," Keeli whispered to Regan as the couple moved away. "She would have loved seeing the steam coming from Randall's ears." The two women laughed, catching Tyler's attention.

"What are you two plotting?"

"Us? Whatever could you mean?" Regan simpered, batting her eyelashes. She looked totally guilty.

"Oh no, Regan, you do not fool me. After all these years, I know when you are scheming, and you two are definitely scheming. I suggest you stay out of this. They will figure it out if they are supposed to."

"Come on, Ty. We all know they belong together. A year ago, I would have said let the bitch rot in hell, but it turns out Sloane is funny, sassy and, under all that armor, sweet. I want her to be happy." Keeli nodded in agreement, and Tyler knew he was defeated.

Looking from one woman to the other, he said, "I need to meet this Sloane, cause I haven't seen that woman yet."

"What are you guys whispering about?" Randall asked.

"Just work stuff," Keeli answered quickly. The three stood watching Randall, who was staring longingly at Sloane as she glided away with another man's hand caressing her bare skin.

Alyssa came to take his arm and, when he didn't move of his own volition, dragged him to go in search of their table.

CHAPTER
THIRTY-THREE

Randall was barely holding it together. If he saw the slimy politician touch Sloane's perfect skin one more time, he would not be responsible for his actions. For the last hour, he had been reminding himself to unclench both his jaw and his fists. He was completely unaware of anything that was being said around the table. He had no idea what he was eating. *This is just plain torture. The woman is torturing me.*

As servers poured coffee, the magicians and clowns circulated the room, and the band played dance tunes. Wyatt immediately asked Keeli to dance, and they slipped away. Randall sat drinking the rich brew and brooding.

"This is surprisingly good coffee for such a big event," Alyssa commented.

"Mmm," Randall responded, watching Sloane take the dance floor in Edward's arms.

The man was running his hands up and down her body, and for the first time since she'd walked out on him, Randall understood—really understood—how he had made her feel. He wanted to kill Edward and feared that five more minutes might be all he needed before he someone arrested him for murder.

"Mmm." Randall responded again to something Alyssa said before she took his arm and shook it.

"What? What did I do?"

"I just told you I was planning to strip naked and jump off the building."

"Ha, very funny. What did you really say? I admit it. I wasn't listening."

"I said I was planning to strip naked and jump off the building. Seriously, that is what I said. Just give up Randall and go get her."

"Her? What her? I don't know what you mean."

"Randall," Alyssa explained to him as if he were dense, "I am an investigative reporter, remember? If I can't figure out that you are at least lusting after Sloane Huyler and are more likely deeply in love with her, they should fire my ass."

"That obvious?" Randall asked, dejected.

"If it makes you feel any better," Alyssa offered, "she might have it even worse for you."

Randall sat up like a puppy being offered a treat. "Really? You really think so?"

"I know so. Go get her, tiger. I will catch a ride home."

Randall planted a huge kiss on Alyssa's mouth. "You were always the best friend a guy could have. I'll call you soon."

Without another thought for Alyssa, Randall was out of his chair and striding across the dance floor. It was so easy to spot Sloane, despite the crowd. Between her height and that red dress, or what there was of it, he couldn't miss her. Nor could he stop staring at her. She was a vision tonight - more beautiful than he ever remembered.

Maybe absence really makes the heart grow fonder.

He moved toward her like metal to a magnet. In seconds, he was standing behind Edward, tapping him on the shoulder. Randall could see the interruption startled the man. They were standing eye-to-eye, similar in height, although Randall was definitely broader in the shoulders and chest.

"May I cut in?" he asked instead of throwing a much-desired uppercut to the chin.

"Uhh," Randall watched as Edward battled with himself. The proper thing was to be polite, but he clearly preferred to keep Sloane in his arms. Randall couldn't blame him, even felt sorry for the guy. He could put himself in Edward's shoes. If it were him dancing with Sloane, he wouldn't stop. In fact, once he had hold of Sloane, he was not letting go. Edward was done for the night.

"Sure, of course," Edward finally stumbled over his words, realizing he had hesitated a moment or two longer than was polite.

"Thanks, Eddie," Randall said, slapping him on the back like they were old friends having a beer together. "You're a stand-up guy. Have a good night."

Leaving Edward annoyed by the nickname and wondering what that last statement might mean, Randall twirled Sloane into the crowd and away from her date. He was holding her too close, too tight. He knew it, but he couldn't let up. Her skin felt like satin under his fingers, her body molded to his perfectly. He leaned into her. She smelled of an expensive floral fragrance that touched a chord in his memory.

"Randall, what are you doing?" Sloane asked, indignant when Randall began planting tiny kisses along her hairline and skimming his hand dangerously low on her back.

"Making up for lost time."

"You are holding me too tightly. I can't breathe."

"I am holding you perfectly, and if you can't breathe, you and I both know why."

He twirled her several times, forcing her to cling to him, using it as an excuse to run his hands even lower down her body and pull her closer still.

"Seriously, Randall, let me go," she pushed at his chest ineffectively.

"You can do better than that, Sloane. If you wanted me to let you go, you would say so. You would demand it. And you would push a lot harder." He was baiting her;, they both knew it.

"I am just trying to avoid a scene."

"Feeble excuse. Just relax and enjoy the ride, Sloane. I'm driving for a while. Let yourself go, please. Just let go."

It surprised Randall when she did just that. She relaxed in his arms and they danced in silence until the music ended. When she tried to step away, he took her hand and pulled her toward the door.

"Randall, my date. Alyssa. You can't simply drag me out of the room. Stop. You need to stop."

"I don't give a damn about your date, Sloane," he said, but he stopped in the doorway, pulling her off to the side out of harm's way. "Please trust me, Sloane, even if I don't fully deserve it. I would like, with your permission, to take you out of this whole place. and bring you to my home. When we get there, I would very much like to remove that gorgeous little dress that you have been using to tease me all night."' Randall's words excited Sloane, as did his presence. She licked her lips, and Randall restrained from kissing her senseless. "Then, Ms. Huyler, I plan to make love to you until the sun comes up. Maybe longer. Got it?"

"Uh huh," she responded, dazed by his authoritarian voice. Randall looked at her face and knew the exact moment she figured out that arguing—even if she wanted to—was futile. "Wait! My coat."

Randall removed his tuxedo jacket and wrapped it around Sloane's bare shoulders. "Leave it. I'll buy you a new one."

He thrust a ticket into the valet's hand along with a $50 bill. "It's an emergency. Hurry please." His ploy worked. They were in the BMW in less than five minutes, the heat on and seat warmers toasting the back of Sloane's legs.

Randall drove like a man possessed until the first stoplight. Coming to a complete stop, he threw the car into park and tugged Sloane's slight frame across the center console to kiss her thoroughly. When cars started honking, he released her reluctantly. She sat back, stunned. Her face was already pink from his beard and her lips were bruised from his kiss. She looked perfect.

And the night was just beginning.

"You're very quiet," he said as he maneuvered through traffic.

"I don't know what to say. I have never been hauled from a black-tie event by a Neanderthal before." She flashed him a beautiful, bewildered smile in the passing glow of the streetlights, removing any sting from her words.

"Well then, I guess you better get used to it, because this Neanderthal has absolutely no intention of letting you go."

"Promise?" Was she being coy?

"Oh, honey, do I ever."

Randall ran his hand up her arm, reaching under the jacket wrapped about her shoulders. Her skin was chilly, but he did not suggest she put her arms through the jacket. He loved the feel of her skin. After driving another few blocks, he took her hand, kissed the back of it and then her palm.

"Put the jacket on, Sloane. You'll be warmer," he finally suggested.

"I'm fine," she shook her head. "Just get me home."

Randall was happy to oblige. He pulled into the parking garage and screeched to a halt in his parking space. Planting a quick, firm kiss on her lips, he said, "let's go" and jumped from the car. Sloane needed an extra minute to manage the long dress, but he was swiftly by her side, almost dragging her to the elevator.

He punched the button repeatedly, anxiously. She laughed at his impatience. The doors opened, and he stepped back, allowing her to precede him, whisking his jacket from her shoulders as she passed and pushing her up against the cool wall.

"Cold," she noted with a slight shock.

"I'll fix that."

He sandwiched her between the wall and his rock- solid body, grinding his lower body against hers, leaving her in no doubt of his desire. His long hands moved down, tugging at her dress and lifting it, followed by the strong stroking of his hand, higher and higher up her leg. Sadly, or luckily, it was just one flight from the underground garage to the townhouse's main floor entry. Still, Sloane's dress was almost around her waist and his fingers were firmly nestled between her legs.

"Warmer now?" Taking her mouth, he didn't wait for an answer.

Randall loved the little sounds coming from her throat, turning him on. She had been groping at the front of his pants - ineffectual movements for getting his clothes off, but very efficient if she wanted him to explode. In keeping with her Neanderthal comment, he removed his hand from her panties and lifted her over his shoulder, her head hanging down his back, her pale legs completely exposed.

He placed his hand on her butt to hold her in place, but then started rubbing the soft curves, loving the feel of her, sliding the little sliver of her thong panties lower each time he circled. Randall kicked open the door, banging it into the opposite wall.

"Randall, put me down."

"In a minute, Sloane."

Randall's long legs quickly covered the distance to the living room, where he placed her on her feet next to the sofa. He slid one finger under the tiny strap of her dress where it rested on her right shoulder, repeated it with his other pinky on her left shoulder.

"I have been waiting to do this since you walked into the benefit tonight." Lifting his fingers slightly, barely skimming them across her shoulders, the dress lifted from her body and dropped in a pool by her feet. She stood before him in a strapless bra and a tiny scrap of red material half on and half off her behind.

With one hand, Randall undid the bra easily, while with the other he slid the panties the rest of the way down her legs. He told her to step out of them and lie back on the sofa.

Thank god, for once her life, Sloane did as she was told.

"Randall, wait, we should talk. We need to talk," Sloane suggested, trying to slow things down.

"Now?" His voice rose three octaves. "There will be plenty of time for talk later. Right now, I think I might die if I am not inside you. I promise we will both feel better in less than one minute. Please, no talking." Randall should have known better. He was in love with a strong-willed woman, and if she wanted to talk, they would talk. Yanking his tie loose, ripping at the studs on the front of his tuxedo shirt, he pulled it from his shoulders and wrapped it around Sloane's naked body. "Fine," he grumbled. "Let's talk."

"This changes nothing," he heard her say in a voice so tiny he thought he imagined it.

"It changes everything, Sloane. It changes everything. I love you and I am never letting you go. No more drinking. I joined a group to help me if I get weak again. I am there for you. Haven't I proved that to you with my actions—standing by you, helping you sell the business?

"But you tried to have me arrested," Sloane stated, shocking Randall into forgetting his lust. "You used me. You conned me. Moreover, you humiliated me, Randall. How am I ever supposed to trust you?"

"But I—"

"You hurt me, Randall. You hurt me badly. Even worse, you embarrassed me. I was already struggling to hold my head high, and you knocked my knees out from under me." Randall could not remember Sloane allowing herself to be so honest and vulnerable before.

"I did, and I am so sorry. You deserved better."

"I did. Completely. Although I must admit, you certainly know how to grovel." He dipped his chin, looking up with a little boy smirk, pretending to be humble. "OK, that's cute, but seriously, here is the primary reason I am determined not to forgive you."

"Sloane, whether or not you like it, you have been forgiving me for the last hour."

"Cute, but stop interrupting me. The main reason I didn't return your calls, Randall, is that you and I both know it is just a matter of time before you do it again. You will go to some party, some bar, you will tie one on and fondle some babe. You came on to me when I was with Wyatt. You did it to a stranger at the gala, for god's sake. What on earth is wrong with you?"

"That was a mistake," he rushed to say. "I thought she was you."

"Are you crazy?"

"No, but I was drunk. And stupid. Please, sit back and listen because I swear, Sloane, I am a changed man."

Randall told Sloane about his conversation with Alex, about realizing he only got drunk around Wyatt, about tracing his issue with Wyatt all the way back to the fifth grade, about his unconscious jealousy and constant need to compete and about how it was all tied up with his feelings about his relationship with his father. Sloane sat silent, listening attentively and stroking Randall's arm with her soft fingertips.

"I spoke to my father after this had all sunk in, asked him about losing his love, his attention, his faith in me. It had been extremely painful for me, especially at that age. What a revelation, Sloane. It was never about that. My mother had told him to back off and stop pressuring me. Too funny. She saw how crushed I was not coming in first on that stupid exam, so she told my father to ease up his demands on me."

"Oh Randall. They both loved you very much. Your father may be a vagabond now, but he still adores you. I know because he turned his precious business over to you completely. How much more faith could he display?"

"You're right, but you know how it is. I just couldn't see the forest for the trees. I was, what, ten years old? Amazing how much baggage we carry and for so damn long."

"But you and your dad are good now?"

"All good. Oh, and I had a humiliating talk with Wyatt. I confessed everything, apologized for years of stupid competition and jealousy, and of course for my inappropriate behavior over all those years with you—and others."

"That must have been a tough conversation."

"It was, but not as bad as I had feared. Wyatt was not even aware of the problem. Well, he knew I got sloppy drunk, of course. Actually, he knew I wanted to date anyone he wanted to date, but he was completely oblivious to the rest."

"So, you are with me because I was with Wyatt? Is that what you are saying?"

"No, you idiot, I am with you because I love you."

Sloane stared at Randall in confusion, her eyes like enormous sapphires, her mouth a small 'O'.

"Yeah," he looked away, embarrassed. "I said it. You may be infuriating, tough and hardheaded, but you are also strong and smart and lovely. I am totally in love with you Sloane, and I have been for quite a while."

"Wow," Sloane finally answered, drawing Randall's eyes back to her face, "You love me? But you tried to send me to prison? That is certainly not an act of love."

"I swear, I never tried to send you to prison. I worked my tail off keeping you out."

"This is so surreal, and certainly not how I would have predicted the evening would end when Edward picked me up earlier."

The pair started laughing hard, tears streaming down Sloane's face, Randall holding his stomach until they caught their breath.

"That is your response? I tell you I love you and that is your only response?"

"Well, it's me, remember. What did you expect?" She went off into peals of laughter again, until Randall wrapped his arms around her, slid his shirt from her body and rolled them down to the floor. Then began the serious work of kissing her senseless.

Several minutes later, Sloane pushed at Randall's hard shoulders. Once she had put enough distance between them for her to look him directly in the eyes, she started talking.

"I love you too, Randall. You are controlling and domineering, but you are my Neanderthal man and I love you." She craned her neck to kiss him lightly on the tip of his nose before continuing, "But you are not off the hook, you know. I still want answers. So, what do we do now?"

"I have a few ideas. Do you want those answers now?"

"They can wait," Sloane replied, batting her lashes.

That was all it took for Randall to yank his tux off, strewing clothes everywhere, until he stood before Sloane as naked as she was. Pulling her gently onto the sofa, he positioned himself between her spread legs, wrapped his long fingers around the inside of each thigh, and slid her closer toward him. Sloane slipped lower on the leather sofa. Her hips rose as he sank deep into her body, a sigh of satisfaction escaping his lips.

Randall had his hand under Sloane, lifting her against him to savor the feeling of her tight around him, setting a hard-driving pace. Sloane put her hands hard against the sofa cushion to get the traction she needed to rock her hips hard against Randall, meeting him thrust for thrust.

"God, you feel so good, so hot and tight," Randall told her before bending over her face and demanding her mouth with a scorching kiss. He circled Sloane's tongue and sucked it into his mouth, bruising her lips with the power of his kiss, scratching her chin against his beard, claiming every inch of her.

Randall felt Sloane responding like a flower opening to him and he slowed down to enjoy himself longer, to please her longer. She groaned when he held still and tried to slide herself against him when he refused to move. Surprising her, he wrapped her legs tight around his ass, told her to hold on, and lifted her from the couch. Once he had repositioned her so she was lying flat along the length of the sofa, he came down on the full length of her, sinking deep, gasping for breath as he felt her shatter around him. He loved the feel of her letting go, her body squeezing him, pulsing around his shaft while she shivered and shuddered her release. The look of ecstasy on her face was magnificent.

"Oh my god, Randall, that was incredible," she told him when she regained her breath.

"Again, my beauty, do it again," he requested, rolling her off the sofa, barely missing the coffee table. He positioned her so that she straddled his lean hips and began gliding her up and down despite her feeble protests that she wanted to rest.

"Later, sweetheart," he promised, covering her face in kisses, nipping at her mouth, teasing her into a state of heightened desire again. "You can rest later. I have missed you ttoo damn much."

"Me too," Sloane confessed, taking up the rhythm greedily, rising and falling, lifting herself until she was teasing both of them, sliding back down the length of him, increasing the friction and the heated sensations along every nerve ending. He thought he would die from pleasure and was barely holding on to his control when she began pounding feverishly, grinding her hips in small circles, trying to get closer. He flipped her over onto the thick rug and, retaking command, plunged into her deep and fast, crushing Sloane into the floor.

Rather than complain, Sloane came hard, shouting loudly until she drove Randall over the edge, and he joined her in release. She slowed, caught her breath, and strained up to kiss him. She covered his face and neck in kisses, sucking lightly in places so that a small aftershock moved through his lower body.

After several minutes, Sloane stilled, rolled, and rested her head on Randall's massive chest, laying quiet.

"I promise, Sloane, we will fix everything, talk about everything. If it takes a lifetime together, you will learn that I am behind you, there for you, always. Not now though. I need to feel you again now. I need you again, Sloane."

"Already?"

"You have that effect on me," he offered apologetically before sliding his hard length inside her again. She was wet and ready for him, too. "Aaah," he said in pleasure," "and I seem to have that effect on you, too."

Kissing her tenderly, Randall took his sweet time with Sloane and with his own pleasure, stroking in and out slowly, stopping to tease them both, then starting again. He nibbled on her neck, then on one breast, biting softly at her nipple, drawing it into his mouth until it was hard, and she was whimpering her desire.

"Too much?" She shook her head no, so he moved to the other nipple, repeating the process while moving his hips with more purpose. He felt her tightening around him, saw her clench her fists, listened as her breath hitched. "Wait for me, baby. Wait."

Randall watched Sloane struggle to delay her orgasm, and slowed his movements further, helping her catch a breath but teasing her horribly as well. He loved the way she responded to his every move, his every thrust, and his every touch. He could barely hold on and soon he shouted," Now! Come now!"

As if she could orgasm on command, Sloane did exactly as Randall had ordered, clenching hard around his heat, rocking hard against his body, kissing him like she would swallow him whole.

They calmed each other with small kisses and gentle touches and finally sat up, backs to the sofa, touching from shoulder to hip. Her hand was making lazy circles on his muscular thigh, while his fingers trailed from one nipple to the other of their own volition.

"I cannot believe I just walked out and left Edward at Navy Pier," Sloane finally said, breaking the silence. Except that she was naked, and her lipstick had been kissed away long ago, replaced with a chafed rosy glow. She looked as perfect as when she began the evening five hours earlier.

"I think I made it pretty clear to him he was not getting his hands on you again."

"Oh yes, my Neanderthal man. Where did that come from, by the way?"

"Desperation," Randall chuckled before placing a slow, tantalizing kiss on Sloane's lips. "Why didn't you return my calls, Sloane?"

"I was angry and hurt. I still need to understand every detail."

"And you shall, my love, every blasted detail. Should I make a pot of coffee?" he was sincere, although it was the last thing he wanted to do tonight.

"I guess it can wait until tomorrow," Sloane said in a low, seductive voice. "So, what do we do now?"

"I imagine I can think of something," he responded, waggling his eyebrows with a leer.

"Again?"

"Oh yeah, definitely, again."

"Can we at least move to the bed where it's softer?"

"Well, only if you insist, my love. Otherwise, you can just be on top."

CHAPTER THIRTY-FOUR

Sloane was thrilled to be having lunch with Maria. She hoped they could become friends. Now that they completed all the acquisition work, she wanted to develop a genuine relationship with the smart, tough woman. She was getting much better at being a friend, but with her recent track record, she had been reluctant to push too hard with anyone. She was learning a lot from Keeli about patience, and winning with honey instead of vinegar. It was amazing how nice people were. Once once. he was nice to them. Sloane jumped from a taxi and strode quickly across the plaza in front of the Wrigley Building. She wove her way through the crowds, down the breezy sidewalk and across the plastic enclosed patio of the Purple Pig. In summer, the outdoor space would have been teeming with people, but today it was empty and cold. She was momentarily nostalgic for the warmth of summer, but she let it go, pulled open the heavy door to the warm restaurant and scanned the bustling interior.

Maria waved from a table against the wall, and by the time Sloane joined her, she was standing. The two women hugged tightly, sincerely delighted to spend time with each other.

"You look fantastic," Maria commented as Sloane divested herself of her camel wool coat and Hermes scarf, before taking the seat across the small table from Maria.

"Amazing what less stress can do for a woman, isn't it?" Sloane teased.

"No kidding. What a history of flux since we met. You have sold a company, dodged a major legal bullet—I promise not many people know that—gotten a plum new job, and taken a fabulous vacation."

"Let's not leave out the fact that I have gotten my mother out of that immense house in Glencoe and into a great two-bedroom on Pearson. She is so content. She loves walking everywhere, and of course, the shopping in the neighborhood is outrageous. It helps that she has some money again. Thanks to you."

"I will take the credit, but I really shouldn't."

"She really will do well down here, instead of isolated up in the suburbs. It's been the best thing to happen to her in a while, and she really deserves a break."

"So did you, Sloane. I am so delighted things worked out so well."

"Me too. I am so relieved."

They buried their heads in the menus for several minutes, before they ordered a combination of small plates that tempted them both—meats, cheeses, salads and smears, as they were called—and a couple glasses of a deep ruby wine from Montepulciano.

Waiting for the food and wine, Sloane rehashed the legal results. Jonathan had been a marvel, digging through documents that the government said incriminated her, then finding companion documents to exonerate her. It had taken months, and before they were done, they had deposed people she cared about, including Wyatt, Randall, even her mother. Sloane had chosen not to be present for the depositions, fearful of what people she loved might bring to light.

She and Randall were still a fledgling couple, and she didn't want to hear anything to destroy their fragile trust. He had offered to have 'the conversation' dozens of times, but as much as she thought she wanted it, she had put it off.

Sipping wine, the two women caught up on each other's work and got to know each other better. Comparing the University of Chicago to Northwestern, they had a friendly competition. Maria was actively involved with her alumni association, convincing Sloane that she should do more for Kellogg, now that she was on her feet again.

"I love your jewelry, by the way. It is so unusual and original."

"Perk of the job," Sloane responded. "I spend a lot of my paycheck in the studio, I admit, but sometimes I just borrow a piece or two. This is one of my favorites." Sloane held out her arm, pushing back the sleeve of her sweater to display the bracelet by Keeli Larsen. The entwined white and yellow gold was delicate, appropriate for Sloane's slender wrists, with a smattering of sapphires dotting the metal. It was a stunning piece of jewelry.

"It's gorgeous," Maria breathed.

"You should come by the studio and pick something out. Keeli could design something special for you, too. She is amazing."

The women talked for several minutes about the irony of Sloane working for Keeli, nibbling on the delicious tidbits that comprised their meal. "If Wyatt had not bought that silent auction item, none of this would ever have happened. It must have been fate."

"Fate?" Maria asked dumbstruck. "What in god's name are you talking about?"

Sloane looked stunned and confused, realizing that suddenly Maria was more than a little angry.

"Well, you know," Sloane continued more cautiously, "if I hadn't gotten to know Keeli better when we were in Tahoe, she never would have offered me a job. I guess I should give Linda Stuart or Regan Howe credit for seeing it would be a good match."

"Are you really this stupid, or are you just baiting me?" Maria confronted Sloane, her voice sharp.

"What? Did I say something to offend you, Maria? I think I must be missing something here."

"I'll say," Maria spat. "You owe all of this, every bit of it, to Randall Parker. He went out on so many limbs for you. Everyone advised him not to, but nooooo," she dragged out the word for effect, "he had to invest his own money, call in every favor. I can't believe that you give everyone but him the credit for your current success. You just about owe him your life." Maria sat back against the leather banquette as if spent from her small tirade.

"Sorry, I did not mean to get so emotional, but the Parkers have been so damn good to me over the years and I owe them and PPHP for a lot. Randall helped me get my job. He threw business my way and so much more. I don't like to see him unappreciated. Again, I am sorry. You are, of course, entitled to your own opinion."

Sloane sat immobilized. After a moment of bewilderment, she chose her words carefully. "Maria, I think perhaps we are talking about different things. There is certainly some confusion here. I don't know what you think Randall did or didn't do. Of course, I heard what he did for the acquisition, although I give most of the credit to you for pulling off a brilliant feat." Sloane sent Maria a beaming smile. "But Randall had nothing to do with me landing a new job."

"Okay, never mind," Maria responded, her voice cutting. She was silent, before rethinking things and continuing. "Do you really not know that Randall arranged all of this? Has he still kept you in the dark about his role?"

"His role in what?" Sloane asked, exasperated, and uncomfortably nervous about what might be coming.

"Well, let's start with the obvious—your company acquisition. He called every last one of the HI clients to get them to agree to stay the course through the acquisition and become Steel Frank customers. When it wasn't moving fast enough, he had Wyatt open a contract with HI—which Randall funded to the tune of over a million dollars, risking his own fortune to save your ass."

"A million dollars," Sloane responded in disbelief. "I heard it was half of that."

"I saw the paperwork, Sloane, I would know. An infusion of over one million, of course, made the current clients feel more secure, so they agreed to stay. Poof, the acquisition goes through quickly and at a very good price."

"A sizeable chunk of which was paid to your firm. I know your businesses are cozy-cozy, so let's not make it sound like he was completely altruistic. I know you send business his way and he sends business yours."

"You stupid girl. He made us waive our fees to HI and only take expenses, so you and your mother would have a bigger share. He covered the fees to us. Did he tell you nothing?"

"We haven't had the talk," Sloane admitted. "I was afraid. Still, how could I not know any of this? Why would he keep it secret? Hell, why would he do it at all? And why didn't you tell me this before? Why didn't he?"

"Good questions. I said nothing because I figured he would tell you. But that is just the tip of the iceberg," Maria went on. Now that the floodgates were open, she was relentless in her need to share what she knew. That she was beating on Sloane was obviously secondary.

Sloane was nonplussed, and visibly upset. "I don't understand."

"That makes two of us, Sloane. Let me keep going, it just gets better and better. Your benefit, he arranged lunch that day with Tyler and Regan, told them to bring up the benefit so you could save your precious pride when he asked you to go. He knew you didn't have a date."

"But..."

"Wait. Wyatt didn't buy any damn vacation at the silent auction either. Randall arranged for the house, made sure it was set, then strong armed Wyatt and Keeli into getting you there. She would never have invited you otherwise. I overheard that conversation. It was a doozy. Wyatt wanted you no closer than, say, fifty miles from Keeli. He had to be sweet-talked for a good hour before he let that one happen."

Sloane sat speechless, the color coming and going from her pale face, tears shimmering in her azure eyes, threatening to spill over.

"Is there more? I can't believe there is more," she asked in a barely audible voice laced with embarrassment.

"Oh yeah, Sloane, the pièce de la resistancerésistance. Randall was at a business dinner and overheard lawyers say that they thought the case against Huyler Industries might not be over. He eavesdropped shamelessly to get that information, called your father's attorneys to see if they could prevent the charges against you. Then, to top off everything, he paid the damn legal fees, both at Addison, Fine, and with Jonathan. I am sure those weren't cheap."

"I paid Jonathan, Maria. I paid him."

"A pittance, Sloane. Randall paid the rest."

By now, the tears were streaming down Sloane's face. She made no effort to check them or wipe them away. Maria, done with her tirade, suddenly realized what she had done and slapped a hand across her spiteful mouth.

"I am sorry Sloane. I don't know why I told you all that. It was unkind and unfair."

"But it was all true, too. Right?"

"Yes," Maria murmured in response. "I just got angry that you did not give Randall credit when he did so damn much for you. I should have kept my mouth shut."

"No, Maria. Despite appearances, I am really glad you told me. I needed to know. Randall offered to tell me, but I was a coward."

That is the understatement of the year.

The outcome had been great. She couldn't deny it, but Sloane sat there feeling like a fool. She was so unlikeable that Randall had bribed someone to take her on vacation. Her business was so awful that he had to shore it up before Maria could find a buyer. He lied to her at every turn, manipulated her, deciding what was best, as if she were a child, an idiot or both.

She thought what she overheard in Tahoe had been humiliating, but it had barely scratched the surface. Randall had been manipulating her life for almost a year. Her friends all knew, Maria knew. Randall had let everyone in on his little secret but her.

How could he do that and still say he loves me?

"Let me get the check," Maria offered, as Sloane wiped her eyes with her napkin, the rest of her food untouched. "Sloane, I am really sorry."

"Don't be, Maria. I really am glad you told me. It was the work of a loyal friend. You were just honest. I hope I can count on you to be honest with me, always." Sloane waited several seconds before she asked in a tiny, vulnerable voice, "Did he arrange for my job?"

"No, you got that all on your own. You deserved it. And I hear you are doing an outstanding job."

"Thanks, I am certainly trying. That is a tremendous relief. I wouldn't know how to face Keeli otherwise. I'd be so ashamed. I am so ashamed."

I would have needed to resign too.

"Oh no, Sloane. Please don't say that."

"Well, look, Randall obviously thought I couldn't fix my own problems. Worse, he thought he couldn't even tell me what they were. He should never have gone behind my back like this. Never. He must think I am the stupidest woman alive."

"He must love you, Sloane. He must love you very much."

CHAPTER THIRTY-FIVE

Not again. This was the fourth time in two weeks that Randall had tried to get together with Sloane, and it was the fourth time she had been unavailable. The weeknights he had understood. Keeli Larsen Designs was opening a second location this weekend and the packing, the moving, the dealing with suppliers for tables, machinery. He was aware of the effort that took. Then there was the night she held her first board meeting, such as it was. She still needed to fill four slots on the board, but they had bylaws now and were moving forward.The weekends were harder to accept. A day with her mother made sense, but why did Sloane need to stay overnight? Marianne had transitioned beautifully to the new condo and was making friends already. Needing to spend the night with her mom sounded like an excuse to him.

Until two weeks ago, he and Sloane had been inseparable, and he had been ecstatically happy. He even had clothes hanging in her closet already, and she had quite a few things in his. They slept together most nights—if you called that sleeping—and took turns moving between her vintage apartment and his modern townhouse. But that arrangement had stopped suddenly two weeks ago.

Sloane was tired. She was coming down with a cold. She would get home too late or she had to get up too early. She was full of reasons, none of them good. After two weeks, Randall was sure something was up, but he had no idea what changed for her. He certainly felt the same. He loved this mysterious and difficult woman.

If something was on her mind, he figured she would talk to him. Maybe not.

It had been over three months since they had declared their love for one another. They had made it through the stress of the Christmas holidays. Randall had presented Sloane with the beautiful antique desk she had admired in a store window. He had it delivered to her new office, so that it was there when she walked in on Christmas Eve. He had loved her over-the-top response, especially when she thanked him later, in bed.

Randall discovered she liked to cook, bake, and decorate for the holidays. She went all out, including a trip to church and lots of family events. She bought him ski clothes, expensive, elegant ski clothes, which he wore when he met his father for a week last month to celebrate a late holiday with him.

Had something happened while he was away? He and his father had spent a fabulous week of skiing a lot, working a little, laughing and talking and then even more skiing. The time had flown by. He had spoken with Sloane every day, since she had been too busy to come on the trip west. He thought they were doing well when he returned. Within days of the trip, though, she had changed.

They had fallen into a routine together. He kissed her goodbye and left her sleeping most days, braving the cold to get to the gym early. On most nights, they met for dinner around 7:00 or 7:30, usually dining out or carrying in. Some nights he would have hockey practice, she would watch, then they would join his teammates for a beer—only one—come home and cuddle. On nights home, Randall would disappear behind a computer screen for an hour or two after dinner, she would do the same, or read or watch TV and by 11:00 PM or so they were wrapped in each other's arms, making love or making small talk, or both.

That had all stopped two weeks ago, and he was sick of sleeping in that big, cold bed alone. It was time to beard the lion in her den and find out what the hell was going on. He started with Marianne. No, she told him; she did not know of a problem, but she was expecting Sloane for dinner later that night and could ask her then.

"How much later? Do you mind if I wait for her at your house?" Marianne wanted nothing more than to see Sloane settled with Randall, so, of course, she said yes. With the trap set, Randall settled in to count down the hours and, if he could concentrate, finish some work.

Promptly at 6:30 he was at Marianne's door, so when Sloane let herself in at 6:45, Randall was lounging on the sofa, chatting comfortably with her mother.

"What..." she sputtered, clearly caught off guard. She threw her mother a "how could you" glance but got a completely innocent look in response.

"I think you have been avoiding me, and it needs to stop." Randall took Sloane's coat, hanging it up as if he lived there, handing her a drink and pointing to the sofa. Marianne disappeared into the kitchen with a warning that dinner was in 30 minutes.

Randall saw immediately that Sloane was spoiling for a fight. He just had to get her to speak, and he suspected he would get an earful. What did he expect when he fell in love with a hellcat? She flopped down in the corner of the large sofa, clearly exasperated and positioning herself so that he would sit in the other corner. Instead, Randall dropped his large frame right next to Sloane, taking her hand in his.

"Princess, you are going to have to learn to talk to me when you are upset," he started. It was as far as he got.

"Don't princess me, and don't you dare speak to me about talking. Like you share everything, you hypocrite! You lied to me, you went behind my back, you took over my life, you told me nothing and now you sit there, Mr. Holier than Thou, and tell me to let you know what's on my mind!" Sloane's voice was shrill and furious.

In fact, Sloane was fuming. Randall had unleashed a maelstrom.

"What? What did I do?" he asked in innocent confusion, although a suspicion that she had learned the truth lurked in his eyes.

"What? What did I do?" she mimicked in a singsong voice. He sat up, dropped her hand and turned to her, clearly angry now too.

"Now I have your attention, I see," she continued spitefully. "Let's talk," she spit the words at him.

"I have offered to talk repeatedly, so let's have it."

"First, did you or did you not interfere with the acquisition of HI after I specifically asked you to butt out? I told you I didn't want to work with you. I was working with Maria. But nooooooo," she complained, "You had to go calling my clients, strong-arming Wyatt, risking your money."

"But Sloane, PPHP is my company. I get to run it as I see fit. And what I do with my money is my business too. I made it my mission to get you the best deal possible, and, thanks to Maria and her team, that is just what happened. Damn it. They got you an excellent price. Why are you so angry?"

"If you were just making good financial decisions, why did you pay their fees? Why didn't you discuss it with me? How could you just be so high-handed?" she attacked, hands moving up and down in front of her in a universal gesture of confusion and utter frustration.

"You weren't speaking to me," Randall answered simply, thinking that resolved the issue. Boy, was he wrong.

"That's the whole point. You were supposed to stay out of it." They were going in circles, Sloane shouting in annoyance. "Your answer might make sense, but so does mine. If you were going to be involved behind the scenes, someone should have told me."

"Maybe you are right…"

"Maybe? Maybe?" She was hollering. "There is no maybe about it."

"Would you have let me be involved, if you knew?"

"Shit," the steam went out of Sloane. "Not a chance. Okay, maybe I see your point. But what about Tahoe? You organized Tahoe and begged your friends to take me away. What was that all about?"

"Who told you that?" Randall was immediately defensive.

"Does it matter? It's true, right?"

"Yes, but you were having a meltdown over everything and dying to get away. And I wanted you far away from other men," he admitted sheepishly, thinking that it would soften her. "Besides, you had heard about the legal mess—you were never supposed to know about that…"

"That's another thing," she jumped in, not the least bit softened.

"One thing at a time. You needed to get away, and I had the means to make it happen. I needed to buy myself some time to win you back. I knew you were furious at me—rightly so. I couldn't just suggest you take a little vacation on my dime. Instead, I conjured an auction win that made it all work. Besides, you had a great time, you landed an unbelievable job, and it all turned out great."

"Randall, you are completely missing the point. You didn't consult with me; you didn't trust me to make my own decisions. You didn't even think well enough of me to tell me about it. How do we move forward if you think so little of me?"

"Oh Sloane, I think you are brilliant. I think you could out-ma-neuver me any day of the week. But you were too close to things. Your emotions were getting the best of you. I was just trying to help you because I cared. I care. I love you."

He could see Sloane softening, but she was still resisting the urge to see his side of things. "You acted like a typical, high-handed man. You left me out of things and made me feel stupid when I finally found out. It may have been well intentioned, Randall, but it was cruel."

"You know I believe in you, Sloane. You know I do. What if I promise to never, ever do it again?" he asked with a boyish grin, crossing his finger in an x over his heart.

"Well," she smiled, "if you pinky swear too, and let me reimburse you for my legal fees," she kept him from arguing, "Uh uh, that is non-negotiable."

"Jeez, you know everything, huh? Okay," he took her hand and wrapped his little finger around hers, "I swear. And we can work out a payment plan for the fees. Perhaps I could take it out in trade?" He said the last while sliding one hand under her skirt, leaving her in no doubt of what kind of trade he had in mind.

"Dinner." Marianne called from the doorway. Randall swiftly returned his hand to his own lap. "I thought I heard a truce brewing. Is it safe to allow the two of you around knives?"

"It's all good, Mom. Let me come help you." Sloane got up to help put dinner on the table, Randall following behind. Soon, the three sat down to a companionable dinner.

Crisis averted. Lesson learned. Randall knew it could have gone much worse for him.

"I am so glad to see you two happy again. I was concerned for a while that you might not patch things up. You need to involve Sloane in your decisions, Randall. Otherwise, you will have a very unhappy girlfriend. That's it. That is all I am going to say about the topic." The two were staring at her, wondering what she knew. "What? It's a small condo and your voices carried," she explained, unashamed for eavesdropping.

"I was just trying to help, you understand. Trying to help Sloane be happy again, so she could be happy with me."

"Well, Sloane, you can't argue with that."

"Mom, whose side are you on?"

"Both of yours. I mean really, if you think about it, even the perfect hero, Mr. Darcy, went behind Elizabeth's back to marry Lydia off to Mr. Wickham. The entire Bennett family was beholden to him. He saved their reputations and their place in society. All completely in secret, while she thought he was lost to her forever. Seems to me that if it was okay for Fitzwilliam Darcy, it must be okay for Randall Parker."

Sloane howled at the comparison and barely managed to speak. She was laughing too hard. "Well, who am I to argue with Jane Austen?

"Exactly," Marianne confirmed.

"Oh good," Randall chuckled, "Thank God for the classics. I am redeemed."

CHAPTER THIRTY-SIX

On a bitter cold night in early March, when Sloane was dozing in front of the fireplace in her apartment, Randall looked up from the work he was doing and asked her if things were stable enough at the office to get away for a few days. She responded that with a few days' notice, she could pull it off. "What do you have in mind?"***

"I wanted to introduce you to my father and get in a few days out west. Sound good? I will have Amy make the plans for next Thursday?"

"OK. Where again?"

"We will fly into Reno."

"Oh Randall, Reno. I don't really like Reno. It's all built up with casinos. I thought your dad was in Colorado or Montana, somewhere with some open air."

"He is, Hon, we have to drive a little way from Reno. C'mon. It would mean a lot to me."

"Okay. It's just a few days. I am sure it will be fine." She sounded less than enthusiastic.

The following week, the couple disembarked from their first-class flight into the Nevada sunshine. Sloane enjoyed the cold, brisk air and the realization that it was two hours earlier here. She was also happy that they would arrive at Randall's father's home while it was still light.

If they were lucky. Holy shit, there are chains on those tires!

"Where are we going? Why do we need chains on the tires? Isn't four-wheel drive enough?" Sloane was climbing into the seat of a large rental Jeep that looked to her like it would drive through concrete.

"Not far, but the last few miles are off the main road. Besides, the law mandates chains at this time of year."

Randall knew the routes well, and they quickly left the neon casino lights, strip malls and congestion of Reno behind, traveling on open roads with beautiful views of mountains all around.

"This is stunning," Sloane conceded. "It reminds me a bit of Tahoe."

"Well," Randall explained, "Tahoe is actually pretty close. I can see that you don't know your geography very well."

"I guess not. I didn't realize they were that close. Reno and Tahoe certainly feel like worlds apart. Hey, maybe we can drive into Tahoe and wander along the lake? I can show you the house we rented, if I can find it again. Oh yeah, forgive me, that would be the house you rented."

Randall flashed her a grin and then a look of relief. "It is so great that we can joke about that stuff now."

"Now. It wasn't funny at the time, but I think we both learned some valuable lessons."

"I know I did," Randall admitted. After a few minutes of silence, Randall continued. "Anyway, we will do some skiing and hanging out with my father, but I think we should be able to get into Tahoe at some point. Maybe go out to dinner there tomorrow night? That should work. I am not sure about getting my father off the slopes to join us. He is a fanatic."

They spent the next half hour of driving discussing Randall's father, Randall, Jr., who went by his middle name, James. At one point, there had been three Randalls, so nicknames had become critical.

"Were you ever a Randy?" Sloane asked now. "I cannot picture you a Randy at all."

"Rand, never Randy."

"Rand." Sloane repeated. "I can live with that."

Looking around her, Sloane let her mouth drop open. Randall grinned from ear to ear upon seeing her expression.

"Okay, don't get mad. I might have done a little organizing without discussing it with you," Randall pleaded.

"You got us the same house as last time? I love this house. What about your father? Does this mean we won't see your father?"

"Oh no, he'll be here, just as I promised."

"Oh, this is just perfect," Sloane beamed with pleasure as they pulled up in front of the now familiar stone and redwood mansion. Randall tapped the horn twice and a young man came out to help unload the car.

"Dana, this is Sloane. I don't believe you two met last time she was here. Sloane, this is the caretaker for the property, Dana."

The two shook hands and then, wordlessly, the men started unloading the luggage.

"Is my father here?" Randall asked as they walked up the front walkway.

"He's been back from the slopes for about an hour. He was trying to be showered and dressed before you arrived."

"Welcome home," came a booming shout from a room or two away. "Welcome, welcome." A tall, fit man with a head full of silver and black streaked hair came into view. The resemblance between them was obvious, although Randall was broader through the chest and thighs where his father was leaner. James was red faced from a day in the winter sun, but Randall would match that shortly. Together, they were a devastatingly handsome pair.

"Come on in," James grabbed his son in a bear hug before releasing him and giving Sloane a less rib-breaking squeeze. "You must be Sloane. My, my, you really are a beauty. Randall didn't do you justice."

Taking her small carry-on, James led the way, with Dana following behind, saving Sloane from the need to respond to his compliment. They dropped the luggage in the master bedroom Keeli had occupied previously.

"Pleased?" Randall whispered.

"Totally."

"Hungry? Let's get a drink and watch the sunset," James suggested, following them into the room with the last of the bags.

"How long have you been here?" Sloane asked as they all moved to the kitchen, curious when she noticed how much James had made himself at home. He was doing a stellar job acting as their host, putting out a tray of cheeses, a basket of crackers and bread and opening a bottle of wine.

"Let's see… about a month, I guess, maybe longer. I will stay as long as the snow is good," he explained.

"My father has the luxury of moving around the world to find the best skiing," Randall offered.

"Which I can do because I left my ultra-capable son in charge back at the office."

That comment led to about 15 minutes of shoptalk until James finally looked at Sloane with a sheepish grin, just like Randall's. "But we are being rude to Sloane. Please forgive us." It was obvious where Randall got his smooth-talking ways, too. His father proved to be a charmer.

"So, dinner tonight," James was saying, "I thought we could just throw steaks on the grill here. I can get Dana to whip up a salad...."

"Oh, let me,," Sloane offered. "I loved cooking in this kitchen the last time I was here. Perhaps one of you will put the steaks on the outdoor grill, and I will handle the rest."

"I will brave the cold for you." Randall made it sound like he was offering to slay a dragon, and they all laughed and fell into easy conversation, which segued into dinner. The men sat on barstools at the kitchen counter while Sloane made a salad and a rice pilaf and Randall disappeared briefly to grill the steaks perfectly.

"Something about the air here just makes me hungrier," Sloane said, slightly embarrassed to realize how much food she had consumed as she pushed back from the dinner table later.

"Wait until we get you on the slopes tomorrow, then you can really work up an appetite," James promised. Randall warned James about augmenting Sloane's appetite, but James was skeptical. He would have to see for himself, he said.

"Oh, believe me, Dad. You will be amazed."

They made a plan for the next day. Since Sloane had not skied in several years, Randall would trade off between the black diamond runs with his father and time on the less challenging trails with Sloane until she got the hang of things again. Then they would reassemble in time to go out for dinner in town. It all sounded perfect to Sloane, who told the men that she was 'all in', reiterating how much she loved being in Tahoe and in this house.

"Randall, you need to bring Sloane here more often. Bring work. Stay longer," he commanded.

"Oh, I wish you could. I kept imagining myself living here for months at a time, the last time I was here. There are those big offices with great work space and magnificent views. I just feel better breathing the air up here. It makes me happy."

"Well then, we will just come more frequently." Randall seemed to enjoy indulging her, and she told him she would hold him to that promise. "Go ahead. I mean what I say."

"Okay. Just like that it's done?" she asked, but he nodded yes.

"I plan you give you the world, Sloane, if I can."

She was still laughing at the idea when she and Randall said goodnight and headed to their room. As tempting as the fancy bath was, Sloane took a quick shower, her hair piled high on her head, dried off and jumped under the covers while Randall was still fiddling with the gas fireplace, trying to get just the right amount of heat.

"Hurry," Sloane whined, "it's cold and lonely in here."

"Your wish is my command."

Five minutes later, the two snuggled close under the thick down comforter, soft light coming from the fireplace. Randall smelled of soap and the outdoors. Sloane ran her hands over the muscles of his biceps repeatedly, as if mesmerized.

"Where's your head?" Randall asked, pulling a barrette from her hair that she had forgotten to remove earlier.

"Right here, with you. I am so happy. Everything in my life is absolutely perfect. I have a job I loved. My mom is settled and, if not happy, at least content. My father is surviving, which is all he deserves, frankly. I have new and wonderful friends." Her eyes softened as her voice grew husky. "I have you, Randall, the love of my life. I could never have predicted we could be this happy."

"No kidding," he said, dropping small kisses on Sloane's lips. "We used to fight like cats and dogs and look at us now. Once you understood I was the boss..."

"Oh, you..." Sloane slugged Randall's arm playfully. "You really are a Neanderthal man."

"And you, my love, are wonderfully controlling, but it works for us, doesn't it? Trading power seems to be our modus operandi."

"Mm hm." Sloane responded sleepily. "Thank you for bringing me here."

"Oh no, my girl, you are not falling asleep on me," Randall slid his hand down from Sloane's cheek to her clavicle, moving lower until he cupped her breast and the nipple hardened under his hand. "I am just getting started," he added as he dropped his mouth to her nipple, sucking hard, sending a zing of sensation straight to her core so that she arched off the bed.

She ran her hands over his back, pulling his mouth harder to her, her long legs wrapping around him, kissing the top of his head. Randall lifted his head, and she pulled on his body, encouraging his mouth down to hers for a searing kiss. He was on her and in her in only moments, sinking deep into her moist, waiting body. He pushed in deeper and Sloane sighed with contentment, using her legs to kick off the heavy blanket.

They made love slowly, Randall sliding from her almost all the way, and then slipping back in tiny movements until he could sink no further, an action that built up the intensity for them both. Sloane gripped his ass, trying to speed him up, but he set a pace designed to make things last longer, to increase their pleasure. Rising on his elbows, he looked into her stunning face, her blue eyes grey in the low lights.

"I want to be like this with you forever."

"We have to get out of bed once in a while," she teased.

"Seriously, I want to spend my life with you, Sloane. I want to make slow, tortuous love to you until you scream. I want to have babies with you, solve problems with you, and explore the world with you. I want to grow old with you. I am deeply in love with you, Sloane, and happier than any man deserves to be because you love me too."

"Randall, do you understand what you are saying? It's the beauty of these settings, and the sex, of course. I am difficult. Oh!" Sloane was interrupted from her words by the feel of Randall's hand between her legs, reaching and finding that tiny nub of flesh that would drive her insane. She was panting in seconds, unable to talk.

"There, kiss me. Until you can just say yes, this is a much better use of your mouth." He claimed her mouth fiercely, running his tongue into its warm depths, sucking her tongue into his mouth. When he came up for air, they were both panting. He was holding himself perfectly still, just playing with that small inch between Sloane's legs. She was writhing under him, her body begging for something just beyond her reach.

"Marry me, Sloane. Marry me."

Sloane was hanging on to Randall, hands sinking into his muscled arms, back arched, reaching for release. Randall continued to tease her, playing with the small bud, sliding slowly in and out, then quickly, softly, then with power. Finally, Sloane was wracked by a powerful orgasm. "Oh god, yes!"

"Was that for the orgasm or the proposal?" Randall asked when she was coming down from her high.

"Can you do that again?" Sloane asked slyly. "Cause if you can, it was to the proposal. I want that again, years and years and years of that. Oh, and of course, years and years with you."

She lifted her head from the pillow, seeking his mouth, sealing her promise to him with a searing kiss.

Randall began moving his hips hard and fast, quickly taking them both over the edge to oblivion, binding them body and soul to one another.

"Alright, that will do," Sloane said several minutes later when their two hearts stopped pounding like freight trains. "You have proven that you can do it again, so I will honor my commitment," she teased him, nipping at his mouth as he rolled his heavy body and laid beside her, pulling her tight against his side.

"Well, it's not like I don't know what I am getting myself into, you demanding wench," Randall laughed. "I can see that life with you will be a series of tough negotiations."

"Is that so? If I marry you, I intend to win these negotiations. I warn you."

"If? Oh no, Sloane. You said yes. No backing out now."

"But you didn't get on one knee…"

"What if I were to sweeten my offer to make up for the no-knee proposal?" Randall probed. He lay perfectly still, poised for her response.

Sloane leaned up on one elbow, curious. "It was already a pretty good offer, but I am listening."

"You, Sloane Huyler, will be my wife. You will set a wedding date no more than six months in the future—the sooner the better." Randall put his fingers over her lips when Sloane protested that six months wouldn't be enough. "You will continue to share my bed and my life. We will be a team, a fabulous power couple. We will make each other deliriously happy."

"Hmmm," she pretended to consider his 'contract.' "I see a problem here. Do I tell our grandchildren you proposed while we were having sex? How will that sound?"

"Well, I see your concern. What to do? What to do?" he chuckled. "I see that I have created this problem for you and that we must renegotiate this contract further. So, if you like my sweetener, you will overlook this minor problem with the grandchildren?"

"What are you offering, Mr. Parker? You better make it good."

"Good, huh?" Randall pretended to think for a long minute, looking about the room for an idea to strike him. "How about the house?"

"The house?"

"Yes, how about if I throw this house into the deal?"

Sloane sat up sharply, elbowing Randall in the process and distracting him with the sight of her body. His hands instinctively reached for her nipples. Sloane swatted them away.

"Seriously, Randall, this is no joke. Can you buy this house? Can you even afford it?"

"No. I doubt it, to be perfectly honest. It isn't for sale and even if it was, it would be prohibitively expensive, even for me."

Sloane's face fell, and she idly ran her fingers over Randall's chest, her disappointment evident.

"That was cruel, Randall. You shouldn't have teased me with the possibility of this house knowing how much I love it."

"But..." he dragged out the word, "six years ago it was for sale and I could afford it then."

"What? What are you saying, Randall Parker? Is this ours?" Sloane was bouncing on the bed until Randall feared she might break it.

"Not ours, Sloane. Mine. But... were you to agree to my contract, I would add this house to the previously mentioned marriage contract. Do we have a deal?"

Sloane reached out as if to shake Randall's hand. "I guess I can find a story to tell the grandchildren," she said. "I think I just bested you, Mr. Parker, but you have yourself a deal."

Laughing, Randall pulled her back into his arms, correcting her. "No, my love. I believe I just made the best deal in my life. I get you."

DEAR READER,

I hope you enjoyed *Beholden*. These characters were two of my favorite to write in this entire series. Who doesn't love a reformed hero, or a lovely lass who learns her lesson?

I hope you will take a moment to leave a review of *Beholden*, before you continue the series with *Bedeviled,* a suspenseful novel about the logical Alex and mysterious Charlotte, LHRE's newest employee. You might remember meeting her briefly at Sloane's celebration party. *Bedeviled* has murder and intrigue at the heart of the romance, and some fans have told me it is their favorite of the series. I look forward to hearing what you think. Read on for a brief introduction to *Bedeviled.*

Learn more about *Bedeviled,* and all my novels on my website ww w,madisonmichael.net/books. I love hearing from my readers, so stay in touch!

Happy reading, and thank you.

THE BEGUILING BACHELOR SERIES

Four men of wealth and privilege considered Chicago's most eligible bachelors. Four friends since childhood.

Blessed with all things — education, success, position, money and good looks, everything should be perfect, but it's not. Instead of flying high, family obligations, secrets and lies weigh these men down. Women, jealousy and youthful mistakes hound them.

What they each need is a fresh start — with the right woman.

And that is just what they're going to get.

Bedazzled : Wyatt and Keeli begin the ups and downs of this Cinderella story with an unlikely occurrence in an elevator.She is a starving artist; he is one of Chicago's most powerful men. They both want to make it on their own terms until those terms come between them. Can they find their way back to one another when they are bedazzled?

Beholden: Randall and Sloane have known each other since school, when she was his best friend's girlfriend, then fiancé. Now she's free, and she needs him to rescue her from an impossible situation. Can he overcome his jealously? Can she take aid from him when it's offered? Will they find love if they are beholden?

Bedeviled: Alex and Charlotte want each other, but they want to guard their secrets more — secrets that could keep them apart, ruin their families, cost them everything. When their past comes calling, it throws the couple together. Now, they must bare their souls in the name of love, or remain bedeviled.

Besotted: Tyler and Regan have danced circles around one another since childhood, their attraction undeniable. He's stayed away, danger threatening his every action. But when a distinct threat lurks—a man who might steal Regan away —it's time for Tyler to put up or shut up. Will he protect his love or pursue her, because Tyler is besotted.

Find the entire *Beguiling Bachelor* series at www.madisonmichae l.net/books

Bedeviled Chapter One

Charlotte was hiding something.

Alex could feel it in his bones. Since they had met in June, she had been elusive and mysterious - even cryptic sometimes. If she wasn't so damn alluring he would have walked away by now. He had never waited around for a woman in his life. They had flocked around him like pigeons. Not Charlotte.

He had vacillated between wanting her and wanting to get away from her, but wanting her always won. He had wondered if she was keeping some deep, dark secret or if it was a suddenly overactive imagination, but today, once she had 'the accident', he was sure. She was definitely hiding something.

Their morning had started much like any other. Their run had been companionable, ending near the beach where they watched the last tinge of pink leave the sky over Lake Michigan.

"Good time today," Alex praised, shaking off his constant, simmering desire for her long enough to stop staring at her. He checked his stopwatch as they toweled off and gulped from their water bottles. Sitting on a low stone wall, the beach behind them, Lincoln Park and the Chicago skyline before them, they shared the sunrise of a crystal clear morning and the healthy exhaustion that followed their workouts. "We have to go longer tomorrow."

"I know," Charlotte had responded, annoyed. "I hate early mornings. Yeah, yeah," she headed him off before he gave her a lecture, "I know we have to do it, and once I am running I'll be fine, but until then just let me complain. Not all of us can just talk ourselves into ignoring pain and exhaustion."

Alex listened to her non-stop loathing of that early morning alarm. It was a routine by now, repeated out of habit.

"I'm tired," she would complain. "It's those stupid nightmares I have. They wake me up and then I can't get back to sleep."

"Talk to me about them, Maybe that would help," he offered as he had countless times before.

"It's nothing, really."

But he knew it was something. Another piece of the puzzle that was Charlotte. "You have them all the time, Charlotte. It's not nothing."

"Just drop it," she sighed and so he did, reminding her instead that if she wanted to train with him, she would have to get up early. She complained, but she always showed up and she always ran hard.

Their training was shorter runs interspersed with long runs requiring the 5:30 a.m. start that she so vociferously complained about. She hated those long run days but with only six weeks to go until the Chicago Marathon, they were pushing each other hard.

Pushing each other's buttons, too.

"How long will you be around this time?" she queried, breaking into his thoughts of her, of her funny habits and quirks that he had come to know, of her body so temptingly close to his. He could smell the light floral scent of her soap or shampoo mingled with the smell of perspiration. The combination aroused him, as always.

What had she just asked him? Concentrate, you dolt.

"I head to California week after next. You?"

"I need to be in Boston next week, so it looks like our schedules won't overlap – for a change. What keeps taking you to L.A. anyway? This must be your second or third trip this month. You were gone all that time over the summer, too."

So the verbal dance began.

"Just business. The usual," Alex gave her his standard answer.

"Whatever that means," came Charlotte's sarcastic response.

"Well, what's with all your trips to Boston?" he turned the tables on her.

"Harvard stuff," her response was too quick and equally vague.

"Whatever that means," Alex mimicked in a sing-song voice. He dropped the subject though.

I can't push her if I don't want her hounding me, damn it all.

Alex clammed up. He could share little of his life with this woman unless he was prepared for her to notice discrepancies, pick up on his little mistakes. Even after decades of cover up, he worried about letting something slip. He didn't have to stay on his toes as much with the vapid L.A. models he usually dated.

Alex tamped down his curiosity, resisted pursuing further questions on the subject and allowed her to do the same. Instead, he let their conversation returned to the mundane while they caught their breath.

"I wanted to ask you for more advice on structuring the financing for my deal in St. Louis. I could really use your logical approach on this one."

"I'm happy to help, Charlotte, but you know you can do it on your own. You always can."

So, we will stick with finance. I shouldn't get in to trouble with this topic, but of course, neither will she.

"But this is my biggest deal yet. I think I covered everything but I would feel better with a second set of eyes on it, especially yours. Maybe I could come by after work today or tomorrow?"

"Sure, I am happy to help. Not today though, I have too much going on. Tomorrow?"

"We could do lunch. I'll buy," she offered, persistent.

"Okay, that works," Alex readily agreed.

Lunch keeps things casual so that maybe we can talk about you for a change, Charlotte.

Alex knew that Charlotte didn't need the help she was requesting. She might lack the confidence in her new job, but she was brilliant. Too brilliant. She was certainly smart enough to fool most of the world with very little effort if she wanted to. Alex recognized that if she had secrets, she was far too clever to be found out easily. They had been running together every day for almost four months, at least when they were both in town. Add the fact that they usually followed their runs with coffee and all that togetherness meant a lot of talk time.

They had covered a lot of territory in their conversations, speaking easily on a variety of subjects. She was extremely well educated, from a blueblood Boston background. Surprisingly, she was not well traveled. She had never even been to California, so she was always asking him about L.A. or his school years in Palo Alto. She was well read and quick witted. They discussed books, theater and politics.

Of course, they conversed on financial topics too, from what it was like for him to run an entire bank to dissecting her new position as Director of Finance at Lyons Howe Real Estate. Her ability to crunch numbers in her head and see the long-term impact of them staggered him, but of course it was that ability that had earned her the new job and brought her to Chicago.

She was easy to talk to, warm and interesting. And interested in him. Too interested. She asked way too many piercing questions. He had learned to deflect the conversation back to her by asking her about settling in Chicago. Charlotte talked about the challenges of living in a new city, finding her way around, using public transportation – which had surprised him too. He expected her to have a driver, or at least take taxis. But she was more down to earth than that. She was openly excited to explore her new home. They talked about how they spent their time and their careers.

They didn't share anything intimate. They certainly didn't share the truth.

Both were focused and ambitious and that emerged in their debates. Clear about their futures, they could describe their career goals and what steps they would take to achieve them. But any discussion of either's personal life was always a bit sketchy with the details murky. The conversation always returned to safe topics.

"So, how are the wedding plans coming?" Charlotte asked, as by tacit agreement they headed in the direction of the nearest Starbucks.

"I am so glad to be leaving town. There are too many parties. I am sick of them. Aubrey is thrilled to see everyone and I think she is enjoying the attention. My parents' house is overflowing with gifts," Alex laughed. "God only knows where Aubrey will put everything, and there are still two months until the wedding."

"How about your brother?" Alex asked, keeping the conversation in safe and innocuous territory. "He should be graduating soon, shouldn't he? Those gifts must be coming in by now too. Kitchen stuff, I would imagine? Has he shared any new recipes with you this week?"

Charlotte's brother was graduating from the Culinary Institute of America in the winter. It was one of the few things he knew about her family. He also knew there was another, older brother that had graduated from Harvard. He had no idea what he did. Besides 'business'.

"And how is the rest of your family?"

"No new recipes this week sadly. But, did I tell you? Don is starting to receive job offers already. I am so excited for him. The Culinary Institute is the Harvard of cooking schools, so I shouldn't be surprised."

"Speaking of Harvard, didn't your parents have a problem with your brother choosing to be a chef? I would imagine they wanted him to follow in your footsteps. How do they feel about a chef in the family after you and Jake both got Harvard MBA's?" Alex presented the question innocently enough but he noticed the instant Charlotte stiffened up, and that she tried to hide it.

"Of course they don't mind, they love us and just want us to be happy. It's like you feel about Aubrey, protective and full of brotherly love. It's how I am sure your parents feel about you, although you have certainly exceeded everyone's expectations, haven't you?" Charlotte changed the subject, as she always did when he asked about her family.

Oh yes, she is hiding something and I am tired of waiting for her to come clean. Either she trusts me or she doesn't.

Today's chat had been open and easy when discussing ways to improve the economy but when they switched to her family, she shut him down. When they discussed plans for the Chicago Marathon next month she was fully engaged, but when they attempted to schedule their next several training runs, Alex watched Charlotte become vague – again.

He was amazed that he noticed since it was difficult concentrating with her so near. He was caught up in the feel of a lightly grazed arm, the sight of her fit body in her running clothes, the way she periodically pushed her hair behind her ear.

Despite their relaxed banter, Alex was acutely aware of her every move, her every breath, so he recognized the moment she 'went fuzzy' on him, as he liked to call it. That was when Charlotte, decisive and articulate, suddenly forgot things, confused things or failed to mention things. It was a complete shift in her speaking style, full of the lengthy pauses she needed to create a good story or remember the previous lies so she didn't contradict them. An unintelligent woman would have made more mistakes. Not Charlotte; she was anything but stupid.

Keeping his mind on the topic always took all of Alex's effort anyway. When Charlotte sat hip-to-hip with him as she had today, he felt the heat of her skin, saw the long length of thigh exposed in front of him, heard her heavy post-run breathing until he was in sensory overload. She smelled so good, not stinky and sweaty like he must. She smelled classy and expensive with all those clean, floral scents. She smelled like a woman he could trust.

More like a woman I want to trust.

Thinking back, Alex recognized that she had been hiding something all along. When he wasn't lost in a sensual fog, he was able to zero in on where the conversations lagged, when she got testy with his probing or tried to change the subject. It had something to do with her life in Boston before she moved to Chicago and it was something that had been going on for a while. She was practiced at her excuses by the time she used them on him. She was making too many trips back East for 'Harvard stuff.' She had met Regan Howe through this same 'Harvard stuff' yet Regan went back to her alma mater only once or twice a year, if that.

Oh yeah, Charlotte is definitely up to something and I intend to find out what. I have been patient long enough.

Sitting waiting now for Charlotte to arrive at Starbucks, Alex promised himself that he would get to the bottom of this or walk away.

Since she had declined his offer of a ride, Alex currently sat at a shady outside table enjoying the last of summer, waiting for her to walk over and speculating on her possible secrets. He was planning his subtle interrogation during the few minutes Charlotte would need to make her way across the park,

Stubborn. She should have just accepted the ride.

"You driving over or walking?" she had asked him, once they caught their breath.

"I have the car if you want a ride?" When she hesitated, he tried tempting her. "I have the new car."

Alex was the proud owner of a brand new Mercedes AMG. The sleek, luxury sports car suited him despite most people's image of him as logical, conservative and staid. The need for speed was actually deep in his blood. "You will love it, tight on the curves, fast and quiet. She purrs," he had bragged.

Charlotte hesitated on his last remark and Alex had been sure she would accept. "The new car, huh?" she sounded intrigued. "I am excited to see it at last, Alex. You have certainly been talking about it long enough."

"I need to walk off this tight hamstring, so I'll have to pass this time," she had replied reluctantly. "Meet you there in ten." Of course, Charlotte had been Charlotte, and that included being unpredictable.

Charlotte, leaving Alex standing there, had taken off across the park without a backward glance. Alex stood dumbfounded a moment, watching her slow jog-walk toward the trail across the grassy lawns of Lincoln Park. She was heading directly toward their usual post-run Starbucks and if he didn't get moving, she would be there first.

Still he stood, willing her to look back and flash him that smile that changed her whole face. She didn't, of course, and Alex was left standing there, admiring her lithe figure and the smooth bunch and release of her muscles in those tiny running shorts as she moved into the distance. Reminding himself to close his gaping mouth, Alex jogged to the parking lot, trading an extra moment of admiring a beautiful woman for a few short moments admiring his beautiful new car.

Arriving at the coffee shop several minutes before Charlotte, Alex was forced to cool his heels. He spent the time piecing together anything he could think of to uncover Charlotte's deep, dark, secret. Admittedly, he needed the ten-minute head start away from her to give his overheated blood a little cooling time too. He kept envisioning the two of them in that sweet ride, sitting close with their sweat-slicked bodies. The image had intensified the jolts of electricity already coursing through his veins from running beside her scantily clothed body.

Too bad she turned me down. One of these days we will be in tight quarters, all alone, and I will make my move. I have resisted too long already.

Since the mention of her tight hamstring, all Alex could think about was massaging her leg, and moving up from there. Did the woman not understand what she was doing to him? After all, he was a healthy red-blooded man. How long was he supposed to watch her round little ass wiggle in front of him, or the glide of muscles in those incredible legs - or OMG - her breasts bob up and down in those little running tops. The woman was killing him. He wanted her so badly he could taste it.

He chided himself to stop thinking of her that way, as he always did when he lusted after her. He would catch himself wanting her and repress the overwhelming sexual response that had plagued him since the beginning. She was so much more than just beautiful and sexy.

She was a brilliant woman, funny, witty, complex and delightful. She considered him a running partner, and a friend...

...but that body, oh, that body. Stop it!

Alex determined to stay focused on what she might be trying to cover up and got his desire under control. He reviewed the signs - when she changed topics or failed to make eye contact. He carefully dissected her words while he waited for her to arrive. He knew she was being intentionally elusive. Alex resolved again that today would be the day he found out what she was concealing, beginning as soon as she arrived.

Speaking of arriving, Charlotte should have shown up long before now. She would have, unless something had happened. How long had he been sitting, pondering? How much time had passed?

Heart racing like a freight train, Alex ran into the park. Unsure why, he was terrified of what he might find.

Find your next book boyfriend and continue Bedeviled at www.madisonmichael.net/books

Crazy to Wed—An All's Crazy in Love Prequel

Six Months in the Future - Gabriella

"What do you mean, the wedding's off?" I'm sure the guests heard my mother's shriek. Nearly one hundred of them had gathered for our rehearsal dinner. "You better be joking."

Tears streaked my professionally applied makeup. I know it upset Mom. Hell, I was beside myself, but she didn't make this easier for me. I couldn't keep the annoyance from my voice. "Do I look as if I'm laughing?"

"What the hell." Hell was blasphemy for my mother, but I reduced her to swearing as the truth registered. She became blissfully speechless for once. Sadly, her silence was short-lived. "What did you do, Gabriella?" she asked, pointing an accusing finger at me. Her teeth clenched, and her chin wobbled as tears formed in her eyes.

So typical of my mother, always jumping to the conclusion that made me look my worst.

"Why do you assume it's my fault?" How many times had I said those words to her? At least anger had replaced my misery for a minute.

I flopped into an oversized upholstered chair in the ornate powder room, wondering how long I could hide out and how I face the
remaining rehearsal dinner guests. Thank god it was late, and half
departed earlier.

Do I tell say the wedding is cancelled? Do I let everyone show up
tomorrow and find out for themselves?

Less than an hour ago, I looked forward to the happiest day of my
life, laughing as Rob and Rachel, the best man and maid-of-honor,
toasted our marriage. Now we had no future, and I sat crying my eyes
out in a run-down public bathroom, my world in tatters. I watched
dispassionately as tears stained the raw silk bodice of my gorgeous
Rachel Lowell original dress.

"Was it your fault?" Mom asked, lowering her voice and handing
me a box of cheap tissues. My nose chafed. But who cared?

"No, Mother, this time it wasn't. All I did was give him his gift."

Chapter One – Gabriella

The Four-Season Rule

"Is six weeks too soon to plan a wedding?"

Strolling the streets of Georgetown with my seven best friends, I should have been sightseeing, window shopping, or choosing where to get lunch. I wasn't doing any of those. Nor was I appreciating this rare time together with the Crazy Eights. No. Not me. I was thinking about Brad. I thought of him morning, noon, and night. I needed to shake him off so that I could stop grinning like a hyena and enjoy my besties, but so far, nothing worked.

Images of Brad flashed into my consciousness, moments when he made me laugh so hard, I snorted, or brought me flowers, or sang to me. He wouldn't make it as a front-man for a band, but he was pretty good. And he got to me with this head-tilting, eye-locking thing he did, pouring his soul into love songs until I melted.

I couldn't ignore Brad's talented hands, either. Whether he was strumming the guitar, tinkering under the hood of a car, pounding the keyboard of a computer, or especially caressing my body. Very skilled. I jiggled my head to clear the visions before Rachel caught my dreamy expression and harassed me. Like a sister, we were mind-melded, except she had a dirtier mind.

"Not if you're a professional wedding planner, which you are not. But if you met a guy six weeks ago and think it's time to drag him to the altar, then it's definitely too soon. Besides, Gabriella, has he proposed?" Rachel snapped me back into the moment with her pointed question. "Aren't you getting ahead of yourself here, not to mention breaking your famous four-season rule?"

Rachel had a point. I was looking at wedding dresses, but I didn't have a groom—at least not yet. Brad and I hardly knew each other.

I scowled at the redhead, wanting this conversation to go differently. I was off-the-rails in love and needed my sister-from-another-mother to be on board with me. Instead, she offered a hard dose of reality.

"When I introduced you two, I said you were perfect for each other, and I meant it." Rachel looked away from me, stopping in front of the display window for an upscale boutique to study the merchandise. I watched her scan each mannequin from head to toe, her fingers itching by her sides. Meanwhile, I held my breath, desperate to continue on my favorite subject—Brad.

"I didn't imagine you would start shopping for wedding dresses after six weeks, Gabriella. This may be difficult for you, but you need to relax and let this run its course for a while. Shit, it's not a relationship yet. Before you hire the caterer and florist, someone needs to propose."

Rachel walked away from the window and me without waiting to gauge the impact of her statement. Typical. Not that she didn't care, it was simply that she always assumed she was right. Most of the time, she was.

I expected ridicule for bringing it up, and—not one to mince words—my girl, Rachel, had gone straight for the jugular. Drawing even with her when she stopped at another window, I vibrated with annoyance when she pulled out a tiny sketch pad. My future happiness was hanging in the balance, and she was sketching a chartreuse romper no woman would be caught dead in.

"Rachel." I stepped between her and the display, demanding her attention. She put away the notebook and focused on me with a sigh. Even after twenty years of friendship, her remarkable green eyes distracted me. You couldn't help noticing them, huge in her face, the color of new leaves after a heavy rain.

At that moment, they were staring at me above a mouth twisted with annoyance. "Is it the sex? Because you don't marry a stranger to get laid."

"You should know." I grumbled the words, hopefully quietly enough. Not that Rachel would balk. She knew who she was.

"Of course, you're right," I said. "But it isn't just the sex. I'm obsessed. I understand it's too early to be in love, but Rachel, it feels like the real thing, different from any relationship I've been in before." How could I make her see how Brad tilted my earth to a better axis and how I was a worthier human being with him? He introduced me to fresh ideas, and I was more optimistic. Especially about love. My cynical friend Rachel would laugh me out of D.C.

Melanie waved for us to catch up to the rest of the Crazy Eights. These were my friends since third grade when I had created our clique and named it for a card game. The moniker had stuck for twenty years as had the friendships, even if we touched a raw nerve sometimes. We had scattered for college, moved to different cities, married, had children, explored other careers, still the gang held together.

We emailed and talked often, but what helped keep us a unit was our annual long weekend, four days away from home, husbands, obligations. Trips like this one to D.C. assured us we could reconnect on neutral ground—a way to remember why we loved each other. Here we were on a rare vacation, but I remained preoccupied with

Brad instead of engaging with my friends. I was there in body, not spirit. And believe me, my body wanted to be somewhere else, too. The man was like a drug. I was blissfully addicted.

As we rushed to close the gap, I hurried my words, trying to end the discussion before anybody overheard. "I have been looking at wedding dresses and buying those thick *bridal* magazines. I need you to find out Brad's position. See if he feels the same." I yanked on my friend's elbow a little too hard in my enthusiasm. She stopped and looked me in the eye, rubbing her arm. "Sorry," I apologized for the potential bruise, "but you have to help. You know him better than anyone."

Sometimes, I exaggerate a bit. Okay, I might have a habit of hyperbole, if I'm being honest. But in this case, I was right. Rachel and Brad had been thick as thieves for years. She'd dropped his name casually in conversations long before she suggested fixing us up. My curiosity had been worse than any cat's. I was dying to meet him, but Rachel would say the timing was lousy, or he was seeing someone. This had gone on for years until I was ready to rip her red hair out by the roots.

In fact, I hadn't quite forgiven her for taking so long. Had she introduced us six months sooner, I might already have that ostentatious diamond on my hand. Not that I was greedy, or wanted to bankrupt my future fiancé, but it needed to be eye-popping enough to equal Sofia and Melanie's jaw-dropping rings.

When Rachel at-long-last suggested I meet Brad, she confessed why she'd made the match. "You are complete people on your own. I don't see that very often. Neither of you needs a partner, but you would enrich each other's lives."

"What the hell does that mean, anyway?" I was a bundle of nerves and had trouble following everything she said.

"It means he is worth the wait." So worth it, if only she knew. Nah, better if she didn't.

The night in that dark bar when Rachel warned me her friend was going to call, I tried to pick her brain about Brad. But the man-eater was scanning the perimeter of the room. If someone caught her eye, she would be out the door with them in twenty minutes. I needed to work fast if I wanted info before this date. Luckily, that evening the pickings were too young and unappealing, so she returned her focus to our discussion.

"You aren't one of those women desperate for a man," she explained. "You never have been. It's just one of the many reasons I love about you. Look at your life—you have great friends," she gestured to herself, "a close family, challenging work at which you excel. You travel to cool, exotic locations and even volunteer. You are a complete person, interesting and fun without some guy on your arm." I rolled my eyes. "It's a compliment," Rachel insisted. "Brad is the same. Lots of sports, tight with his buddies and his siblings, involved in local politics, not looking for a wife."

The pep talk was great, but left me suspicious. "Why is such a paragon interested in meeting me? Is he a dog?"

"No, my dear friend, he's a looker."

Gotta love Rachel. Here I was six weeks later, goo-goo eyed. She'd been right about everything, except being worth the wait. She should have introduced us ages ago.

The moment I saw him, Brad's dark good looks and deep dimples appealed to me—and then some—setting the nerves in my belly fluttering. Finally, they settled, replaced by the welcome hum of sexual tension. He was laid back, comfortable and when we were together, time flew. Our first drink became dinner, then more drinks, until the wait staff eyed us with longing—longing to see our backs as we left the restaurant. They bounded to lock the doors after us when Brad walked me to my car.

I remember everything, the velvety purple of the sky, the moon hovering over the trees, the wind lifting the hem of my dress. And that goodnight kiss—I felt the softness of his lips, the restrained power behind it, a zing to my toes and a shock of electricity everywhere in between.

Brad felt it too, I'm sure, because we sucked face and groped each other like two teenagers until we were on the verge of making love pressed against the trunk of my car. Rachel had nailed it. We were perfect for each other. Reluctantly pulling apart, we scheduled a second date before we left the parking lot.

As for enriching my life, if being a stellar kisser and a stud in bed was what she'd implied, Rachel was spot on. If she'd meant that Brad would make me laugh and cherish me, then she got that right, too. Surprising, really, since Rachel ran through men like a hot knife through butter. One-night stands were her specialty, yet Brad and I were the fourth couple she'd introduced who were talking marriage or already married.

Initially, I was curious. Why hadn't Rachel dated him herself. In fact, I'd been wary. Only natural when you mention Rachel and a man in the same sentence. Settling for her leftovers just didn't sit well. Both Brad and Rachel insisted they were just friends. Then I wondered why she wasn't interested. Was something wrong with the man? Eventually, I got past all my suspicions and embraced the relationship.

Once that was resolved, nothing stood in my way. I clicked with Brad, and knowing he reciprocated, I saw no reason to keep my emotions in check. I was almost thirty. So was Brad. Briefly engaged before, "when he was young and foolish," showed to me that Brad he was willing to commit. We discussed vacations and his office Christmas party. He might not be proposing, but he was long-term planning. Wasn't that the same thing?

"Don't tell," I begged Rachel, as we caught up to the rest of the women. The Crazies had halted outside an Ethiopian restaurant. I was out of breath but wheezed out my opinion. "I'll eat anything but Ethiopian.

"That's what you said about Indian," Harper said, crossing her arms and jutting out one hip in defiance. "This town is famous for ethnic food, and you're rejecting everything. You rejected the Thai place, too."

"And that southwestern restaurant," Avery added.

"You could tell us what it is you want and save us this incessant debate." Harper's scowling face was flushed, and her exasperation palpable. Did I say we got together to remember how we adored each other? Not so much when hungry.

The Crazies were like family. We loved each other, but we didn't always like each other. At that moment, Harper wanted to bitch-slap me. It had been over twenty minutes since she proclaimed herself 'starving', and I had nixed four potential lunch spots. I wasn't trying to be contrary, in fact I was famous for trying alternative places, but today I needed less fuss.

"We are eating at the next place." Harper gestured her arm to include everyone but me. "Majority rules," she stated with authority. She turned until she was facing me directly. "You can do what you want."

Subject closed as far as she was concerned, Harper spun on her heels and marched down the sidewalk with that enviable athletic stride. I would kill for those long legs, I thought, without resentment. I couldn't be angry with her. After all, the woman was hangry.

I felt a little remorse. Harper was one of my favorite people, and I had brought out the worst in her. These were my peeps, the girls I turned to for advice, for a shoulder, for a laugh. They were the women I most admired and respected.

I'd often wished I could compose one ideal female from the best of each of us. She'd include Avery's logic and compassion, Harper's athleticism and inexhaustible energy, Melanie's faith and sweetness, Willow's sense of adventure. If I could sprinkle in Sofia's poise and unconscious beauty, Sydney's flair for the dramatic, and Rachel's fearlessness, I would be perfect. With Harper's legs, of course. But they would make me taller than Brad. I wasn't sure I would like that.

I halted before a crepe restaurant as sharply as if someone had yanked me by the collar. I vowed to think about food, not my sexy boyfriend, and spoke up. "How about this place?"

Harper scanned the menu posted in the window, calling over her shoulder when something caught her eye. "Ooh, the desserts look amazing. Oh, Willow, they have loads of vegetarian options. Okay, there are tons of choices," she conceded. "This looks great."

"So, we've decided?" Avery asked in her quiet voice.

Before anyone could argue, Harper was through the door, demanding a table. We were seated quickly, and Harper reverted to her usual sweet self, commenting on our good fortune. Getting a spot at a Georgetown restaurant between eleven and two was a miracle.

We emptied the breadbasket in less than sixty seconds. With food in her stomach, Harper's face relaxed and her tone softened. "So, Gabs, you've been quiet about your latest conquest." Harper lifted an eyebrow, offering me a sly glance. "Rachel says you've been inseparable."

I threw a look of trepidation in Rachel's direction, but her bland expression assured me she wouldn't share my secrets. Great. I could decide what to share.

"I like him," I admitted in the ultimate understatement. I waited a beat, rearranging my neatly arranged cutlery. "A lot.

"Yeah, we figured." Sydney tossed her head at the dry remark, then pushed a gorgeous mane of curls that fell into her face, securing them with an accessory that resembled a claw. If I envied Harper her legs, it was nothing compared to my longing for Sydney's hair. Total strangers stopped to complement it. "You've been too quiet about him, so Melanie and I guessed you have something to hide."

A pregnant Melanie blushed as she blew a kiss toward Rachel whose matches have a tendency to stick. She could make a living at it." The pretty blonde would know. Years ago, Rachel introduced her to a serious, somewhat nerdy, speech writer. We attended their perfectly planned wedding last year.

I was selfishly concerned that Melanie would be too busy with the new baby to 'do' my party when the time came. She was a high-pow-ered attorney, but her real passion was everything HGTV and Food Network. Her creativity was endless, and I dreamed of an event as beautiful as hers. "We can sit as long as you want," I said, too little too late.

"You've made it through winter," Avery acknowledged to me. I swear I say one hundred sentences for each of Avery's, but I love her - shy, lovely, smart as a whip. She doesn't say much, but when she does, everyone listens. Sadly, I have to keep her at arm's length, or I will sneeze my brains out. A pet-rescuer, Avery is never wholly free of cat dander.

"What does winter have to do with anything?" Willow asked, or-dering buckwheat crepes filled with spinach and other disgusting things. How did I end up with such a healthy friend? She was our back to nature girl, no bra, no makeup. She was also a hell of a baker. Someday she would run a very successful bakery, and I would grow fat from patronizing it.

"Remember," Sofia answered, "when Gabriella created that rule. No serious commitments until you've been with a man through four seasons. She's made it through winter, so she has three to go."

Sofia was married to Nico, a handsome devil she'd known her entire life. They were a stunning couple, dark, tall, and fit. Once they got pregnant, and she was trying her best, they would have gorgeous children.

One thing I loved about Ellie? She underestimated her staggering beauty. In fact, she always overdressed to compensate for her insecurities. Sitting beside Willow, she was wearing false eyelashes and make-up more appropriate for a Saturday night. She was an exotic peacock to Willow's brown wren.

Speaking of peacocks, I caught Rachel glaring at me from her seat at the end of the table, but she said nothing. We were so different. I was "the vault." Rachel couldn't keep her mouth shut, but I loved her. Her imagination was endless while I was logical, her behavior wild to my straight laced. She was even pale skinned to my Mediterranean coloring. Rachel had flamboyant red hair and those eyes. She embraced her freedom and single state, while I wanted a husband and a family. The budding designer was the closest thing to a sister I would ever have. She was tthe first girl to commit to the Crazies and had been in my life ever since.

Rachel couldn't stay silent any longer. "Yeah, Gabriella, what about four seasons?"

"Maybe I wasn't clear." I looked around the table at seven sets of glaring eyes. I had no one to blame but myself for their derision. I was breaking my own rules. "To wed you should be together a full year, but you can get engaged as soon as you want."

"You're engaged?"

Avery's words acted like throwing a bucket of ice water on the Crazies. Harper stopped chewing bread, Rachel halted doodling on her napkin, Willow nearly choked on the organic juice she had swallowed. Melanie's beautiful blue eyes grew wide as saucers; as did Sofia's gorgeous brown orbs. The clatter of the fork Sydney dropped to the floor brought everyone back to life.

"No, ladies, I'm not engaged."

"But she wants to be," Rachel blurted. I knew I shouldn't have said anything to her. She never could keep a secret, especially not from the Crazies.

The food arrived, offering me a temporary reprieve while the server distributed our orders and took our requests for drink refills and more bread. Everyone was settled too soon, and Rachel picked up where she'd left off. "Gabriella is in love, you guys. She wants to marry Brad."

"Waiting four-seasons was Gabriella's rule." Melanie used her courtroom voice, getting everyone's attention, including two older women at a nearby table. "She made it, so she gets to break it." Also, you will recall Prom, when Rachel didn't have money for a dress, and we all pitched in to buy fabric?" Heads nodded. "Gabriella stipulated that when one of us wants something, we combine forces to make sure she receives it."

"I said that, didn't I?" my pride clear in the lift of my chin. If we operated as a team to win Brad, the poor man wouldn't stand a chance.

A cunning smile curved up the corners of my mouth. "Okay, ladies, what's our plan of attack?"

Get to know the Crazy Eights. Find the novels at www .madisonmichael.net/books

Books by Madison Michael

The Beguiling Bachelor Series

Bewildered: A Beguiling Bachelor Prequel

Bedazzled

Beholden

Bedeviled

Besottted

All's Crazy in Love Series

Crazy to Wed - Gabriella

Crazy to Believe - Sofia

Way Past Crazy - Avery

Artfully Crazy – Leah

Crazy to Dream – Willow

Crazy Loves Crazy Lies – Veronika

Crazy Lessons in Love – Jules *(coming soon)*

Crazy to Score – Melinda *(coming soon)*

Acting Crazy – Sydney *(coming soon)*

and more...

The B&B Billionaire Series

Desire & Dessert

Moonlight & Moet

Standalone Stories

Broken Time–A Time Travel Romance

Studmuffin

About Madison Michael

Meet Maddy. She loves romance: reading it, writing it, watching it. Romance is Maddy's go-to for entertainment and escape. So it came as no surprise when she left her stodgy career in Software Management for a world where rich, sexy men and smart, sassy women fall in love.

Returning to her roots in Chicago after traversing the U.S., Madison embraced old friendships, family, pizza and hot dogs. Then she started writing the steamy love stories of her dreams. Her books embrace deep, abiding friendships, flawed characters and the journeys people take on the road to love.

Set against luxurious and elite Chicago, follow Maddy's stories of billionaire heroes—or heroines—as they learn money can't buy love. Join her Insiders for regular updates and bonus content at ww w.madisonmichael.net.